LEGACY GIRL

ELAYNA MILLER, BOOK THREE

JILL M BEENE

Legacy Girl/Jill M Beene. -- 1st ed.

ISBN 978-1-7347993-1-6

ACKNOWLEDGMENTS

Thank you to Jesus, for saving my soul. Thanks for the imagination and all the wonderful people you've put in my life who make this all possible.

Thanks to my husband, Adam, for eating endless peanut butter and jelly sandwiches without complaint while I'm drafting a book. Thanks for all the encouragement, and for believing in my work. I couldn't do this without you, on so many levels.

Thank you to my amazing, incredible, beautiful beta readers! Kari, Babs, Jamie, Jenny, and Heidi--my books would be far less awesome if I didn't have you guys. Thanks for catching the typos, questioning characters' motivations, and telling me when you laughed. I appreciate you beyond words. I have the best beta reader team in the world!

Thanks to Kari, my amazing sister, for the incredible covers for the Elayna Miller series. They are so fun, and you are so talented. Thanks for sharing your time and gifts with my small business!

And thanks to you, the reader. Without you, this would all be for nothing. Thanks for reading my books, for reviewing them, and for telling your friends about them. Thanks for letting me have my dream job.

To the readers who waited.
This book probably wouldn't have been finished without your
prompting.
Thank you.

Chapter 1

We'd rented out the presidential suite at the most expensive hotel just outside Miami. This wasn't one of the new, boutique luxury hotels full of kitsch that seemed to spring up and die off every other season along the coast. No--this place felt like old money--a grand old lady draped in diamonds who was too proud to acknowledge all the thong bathing suits along her coastline.

The hotel staff was courteous and professional--the bellhops didn't even blink when my mastiff Bruno fogged us all out in the elevator, or when Howard's cat, Sir Darcy, hissed and spit at everyone and everything from his crate. They sorted our luggage into the different bedrooms once we got to the suite. It was everything a hotel should be-- elegant marble-clad bathrooms, expansive finely- furnished living spaces that connected the four bedrooms, and floor to ceiling french doors that opened onto the private balcony and let in the sweeping cerulean ocean views.

It didn't matter. We barely noticed it. We were all so tired. I hoped that a week in this paradise would do something to loosen the knot at the base of my neck that felt permanent now. It wasn't just me who was feeling it. Camilla's smile hadn't reached her eyes in days. Her tan skin lacked its usual rosy glow. Frankie looked wan--her shoulders slumped, her eyes darting all-too-often to Howard's face, which was set in rigid, stubborn lines of nurtured anger.

And Hyde? Hyde had disappeared to 'take care of a couple of things'. I wasn't sure what those things were--he wouldn't come clean even when I pestered him about it-- but I knew him well enough to trust him, albeit begrudgingly. In his absence, the rest of us were trying to come back together as a team. It was a stilted, awkward process.

Our team wasn't broken, but it felt close.

The last case had done a number on morale. Howard and Frankie were being exquisitely polite to each other when they were in the same room, but that wasn't all that often, as Howard was still avoiding Frankie as much as possible. Camilla was distracted, which was understandable, given the circumstances. After all, it was her family we were going to deal with--her past, her demons. The rest of us had the luxury of having no personal history or connection to the Almeida cartel. She'd grown up in it.

When her father Thiago died, it was her cousin who hunted her down to tell her that there was a will, and only she had the safe code to access it. So we were going to Brazil, to deal with Camilla's uncle, Caio, and her brother, Alex. Both had been Thiago's lieutenants--now they were poised against each other--two prizefighters in their respective corners, waiting for the ding of a bell. They both wanted full control, full power. And Camilla was in the middle.

CAMILLA FOUND Bruno and I down by the pool on the second day in Florida. It was still before noon, so the sunshine was hot but manageable. It would edge closer towards brutal as the day went on, but I'd found us a spot in a cabana. The shade, the fan overhead, and a frosty beverage were helping to stave off our inevitable retreat into the air conditioning. Bruno was sprawled out on one chaise lounge snoring gently, his massive fawn-colored head between two huge paws, and I was on another. Camilla chuckled when she found us.

"Want something?" I asked her, when she tucked herself onto the chaise next to me.

Her brown curly hair was slicked back against her head; her tan skin was dappled with droplets from the pool. She was short-- a curvy, compact figure filled with motherly love and Brazilian sass--quick with a smile or a snappy retort, depending on the situation. Our relation-ship was far deeper than employer-employee. She was family. The thought of something happening to her sent a wave of anxiety through me whenever I considered it, so I tried not to. I just pushed the thoughts from my mind, stuffed the queasiness deeper into my stomach.

"I want a lot of things--the first of which would be to have been born into any other family than my own."

"I meant like a bellini or a sangria," I said, wrinkling my nose.

She laughed. "Whatever's in that pitcher."

I sat up, straddling the chaise lounge. "I think the waiter is afraid of Bruno. Or maybe he was downwind the last time he farted."

Bruno stretched and as if on cue, a faint whistling came from his posterior.

Camilla laughed. "Why do you say that?"

"I didn't ask for the pitcher; he just brought it."

"Maybe he just remembers how much you drank yesterday and thought he'd take a preemptive approach."

I raised my eyebrows. "Can you blame me? Howard and Frankie are doing their little dance. Hyde is off doing something 'very important'." I made quotations with my fingers. "But he won't say what."

"Any word from him?"

"He checked in last night. Sounded exhausted, but he still won't tell me what he's doing. Says it's a surprise."

"Yikes."

"You're telling me," I said. "You know how much I like surprises."

"I get the feeling that the trip ahead will hold many for both of us," she said with a frown.

"Why you?" I asked Camilla after a moment of silence.

"Why do you think Thiago made it so that you are the only one with access to his will?"

"My father loved drama. He loved pomp. He loved to be the center of attention. Thiago would have known that I would not come back for his funeral. This was the only way he could think to rope me back into this. This was the only way for him to get my attention on him... by forcing me."

"Alex and Caio both think that your father left something of value to you. Caio especially seems uneasy."

"I'm sure he left me something. Probably more money. Thiago never understood that he couldn't buy me. He never believed that I didn't care about money, no matter how many times I told him, no matter how much proof he had to the contrary."

"If you inherit too much..." I trailed off, not knowing how to phrase it gently. I realized that this was no time for diplomacy and asked, "If you die, where does your money go?"

Camilla smiled, but the smile had barely touched her eyes before it receded again, like a wave slipping off the sand and back into the ocean.

"Worried that someone will off me for the inheritance?" she asked in a light tone.

"Yes," I replied, seriously. "I'm wondering how many people Caio or Alex would have to kill to get your inheritance. And I'm wondering if I'm one of the people standing between them and what they want."

Camilla chuckled. "How gauche of you to ask where my money's going when I die."

"Just honest."

"It's going to charities. All of it. Even if I hadn't already set up my will that way, I would have changed it before setting foot in my home country. I'm no fool."

I frowned. "It won't come to that. We'll get in; we'll get out. You'll open that safe, read the will, we'll fly home. Wham, bam, done."

"I like your optimism, but we don't always get what we want."

Chapter 2

I took a shower and a nap in my room with the thick shades drawn; the air conditioning mingled with Bruno's snoring made a low, comforting hum in the background. When I woke up, I threw on a flowing sundress--more muumuu than anything, but loose silhouettes were easily forgiven when in a designer label's print. I slid on some flip flops and threw my hair in a high ponytail, adding a huge pair of sunglasses to cover my complete lack of makeup.

I hunted down Frankie--she wasn't in her room, so I wandered back down to the pool. I found her on a chaise lounge in the same cabana Camilla and I had inhabited that morning. But now the sun was fully beating down. It was miserable and sticky if you weren't in the shade of a cabana with a fan going overhead.

Frankie had a spread of fruit and a selection of sparkling waters next to her--no nachos or margaritas in sight. She and I had drastically different opinions on the definition of good poolside refreshments.

"How are the financials coming, Frankie?" I said, popping an apple slice in my mouth.

I had been stress eating way too much lately; maybe I would clean up my diet. At least for today. I couldn't help think that the apple would have been ten times more delicious slathered in peanut butter, but oh well.

Frankie ran a hand through her hair and sighed, her focus on the computer screen. Even now, in the low light of the cabana, with her long hair undone in the Florida humidity, not a care in the world, it looked like she was photoshoot ready. It wasn't just her impeccable fashion sense, flawless olive skin, or amazing bone structure, although they certainly helped.

Today, she wore Ray-bans, a white bikini with high-waisted bottoms and a bandeau sweetheart top with a large bow that covered her chest. She topped it off with a huge floppy black straw hat and a pair of high black straw wedges--it was fifties chic with a modern twist.

I half-expected a photographer with slicked back hair to pop out of the bushes and start cooing at her--'yes, that angle's peeerfect, darling,' 'Just a little more to the left with your hand--gorgeous'. But of course that didn't happen.

Frankie was just Frankie--her beauty was epic and seemingly effortless. But it was also the least interesting thing about her, which was even more intimidating. She was a genius with computers, a Stanford graduate, a great friend, and she had a fierce sense of justice. Her family was loaded, too. It was no wonder that Howard loved her, even if he wasn't willing to admit it at the moment.

If I could have, I probably would have hated her. In contrast to her high style, my hair was pulled back in an artless ponytail to ward off the frizz that descended upon me every time I stepped outside of climate control. I wasn't like Frankie--I didn't get dewy and glisten when I sweated--I dripped, my face turned red, and people shot me concerned looks and asked if I was ok.

Frankie looked up, and her eyebrows drew together. "Why are you looking at me like that?"

"Like what?"

"You're frowning at me."

"Oh," I said. "It's not you. I was just thinking how you've been unfairly blessed--those brains in that body, and you have a personality and a sense of humor, too. It's absolutely not right. I'm jealous."

"Shut up," she said, rolling her eyes. "Stop fishing for compliments--it's beneath you."

"Is it?" I asked, smiling. "Are you sure?"

"The financials are terrible," she said, ignoring me. She waved her hand at her screen impatiently. "I can't follow them. I think there's enough information that I *should* be able to figure it out, but my Portuguese isn't good enough, or maybe my accounting isn't good enough."

I chewed my lip. "Do you think you'll be able to get it, if you have more time?"

She winced. "I wish I could tell you that, but I think

that I might need help. I've been throwing tons of hours at it, and I'm not sure that what I have done is even right."

I nodded. "Don't worry about it. You're not a forensic accountant, and I don't expect you to be. Move on to one of the other million things on your list and forget the financials for now. Who knows? Maybe we'll get lucky and we won't even need them."

Frankie rolled her eyes. "We are rarely that lucky."

I shrugged. "Still, your time is better spent elsewhere. I'll let Camilla decide if we need to bring in someone else."

"Is that weird for you? Having someone else be the lead on a case?"

"Yes and no. I mean, it's her family. She knows the situation better than anyone else. It would be stupid for me to not take her advice. Besides--this affects her life, her entire future. I can't control that, even if I know what *I* want. I'm not going to defer to her when it comes to tactical decisions, but when it comes to making decisions about where we fit in with all of this--that's on her."

"Are you worried about what's going to happen when we get down there?"

I could have lied, but dismissed it as soon as the thought entered my head. Frankie was my teammate and my friend, and she deserved the truth.

"Very."

It had been a wild year, both good and bad. About a year ago, our team had a different makeup--Hyde hadn't joined yet, and Wu, our electronics expert, had still been here. Howard and Frankie had started dating, and things had looked very solid. Until.

A case in Oakland had nearly torn our team apart. A group of Russians, an offshoot of organized crime, had started a real-estate speculation scheme. Their methods had been brilliantly simple--buy up inexpensive properties in gang-ridden areas, then methodically eliminate the gangs using professionally trained tactical teams. It was a long play, but they'd thought of every conceivable element. They had bankers, politicians, and the planning board in their pocket, because of an elegant, underground gambling club.

But they hadn't planned for Frankie on their tail. When an eight year old girl was caught in the crossfire, it reminded her of the cousin she'd lost in India. She'd doggedly pursued the case, and when she didn't think that our team was doing enough to avenge the girl, she'd gone behind our backs and given sensitive information to the press that could have put us all in danger.

The aftermath of the case was severe: Hyde had been shot in the shoulder. I'd fired Frankie for two weeks. Howard and Frankie had broken up and still weren't really talking.

Our mutual faith, the very team structure, had been shaken.

And we were all headed down to Brazil to solve Camilla's family crisis, which wasn't the normal kind.

Turns out my fifty year old housekeeper, she of short, curvy Brazilian sass, attitude, impeccable cooking, and motherly nature, was one of the heirs to the gargantuan Almeida drug cartel. Her father had died and left a will locked in a safe that only Camilla could open. Now, her brother and her uncle were waiting for her to come read it, to see which one of them would inherit the colossal family dynasty.

Unlike other cases we did, we were going into this one sorely underprepared. We didn't know who we could trust-- her brother, Alexander or her uncle, Caio-- and we didn't know what we were aiming for.

We'd had missions go bad in the past. I mean, my house was still being rebuilt from when it had been leveled by an explosion. This very morning, I got an email with pictures of the Carrara marble kitchen counters that had just been installed. I couldn't wait to throw myself across them and whisper sweet, sweet nothings to the beautiful surfaces when I got home.

That case had been the beginning of Hyde's and my relationship. A lot had happened since then. We'd lost a team member, Wu, when the CIA had forcibly recruited him. I still thought about him a lot, wondered if he was happy. We'd traveled Europe, been hunted by a man who turned out to be Camilla's cousin, and had rid the world of a bunch of human detritus along the way.

Even now, relaxing in a hotel for a week, I felt itchy, like I needed to get back to work. It had been months since I'd taken a paid case, but I'd done a bunch pro bono. I pursed my lips, drummed my fingers lightly along my leg. I wondered if there was someone in Miami I could take out, if there was some violence that could be prevented if there was one less loser on the chessboard of life. It wouldn't take that long to find a target, not in a city this size...

"Oh no, you don't," Frankie said, snapping her fingers. "Don't even *think* about it."

"What?" My eyebrows raised.

"You forget how long we've worked together," she said, her eyes narrowed. "But I do not have time to cover your ass along with..."

"Hyde?" I said, crossing my arms over my chest.

"I wasn't going to say that," she said, her eyes unconvincingly wide in a show of innocence.

"I knew it. You're in on it, whatever he's doing."

"I told him not to put me in this position," she said, her chin jutting. "I told him that it was too soon after what happened, that I couldn't lie to you."

"It's ok, Frankie..." I began.

"And I won't!" she said, not seeming to hear me. "I won't lie to you again. I told you I'd learned my lesson, and I have. If you want, I will tell you everything I know about what he's doing. I won't risk my position on this team or my friendship with you ever again. I'll pull up all the files. Here."

Her fingers flew across the keyboard.

"Frankie!" I pushed her laptop closed on her hands. "Stop. It's ok. I don't blame you, and I need to hear it from him. Keep the files, and if I need to see them, I will let you know. But as of now, I want to see how this plays out."

"You've known me longer than you've known Hyde, you know," Frankie said, pushing her computer back open.

"What's your point?"

"Doesn't it bother you, not knowing what he's up to?"

I shrugged. "I'm curious. But I know that Hyde would never hurt me or our team. I trust him."

"You trust him more than you trust me," she said, her voice flat.

"Yes," I said, lightly. "But don't be offended. I trust him more than I trust anyone."

"When did that happen?" she asked, tilting her head.

"I don't know. But it did."

"I hope he's worthy of it." She sounded wistful.

"Why? You don't think he is?" That possibility surprised me. I thought that Frankie liked Hyde.

"It's not that. Hyde's great. And he loves you." She bit her full lower lip. "I guess I just... I mean... there were a couple of hours where you didn't know where I was, and you freaked out. But Hyde goes off on some secret mission for a week, and you're cool as a cucumber."

"With you, it felt different. Sneaky. With Hyde--he told me he had something important to do, and I believe him. And, no offense, but he's been in the field. He has that kind of mental framework, to know what might come back and bite us, and what won't. You don't have that. I'm not trying to offend you, but can you say that you're eager to go undercover again?"

"Nah," she said, pushing her sunglasses up her nose

and reclining in her lounge chair. "I have no desire to do anything of the sort, ever again. And I'm not offended."

"Good. Because you weren't exactly great at it."

She pursed her lips. "I could be, if I wanted to, but I don't. I've realized I'm more Bond girl than undercover agent."

I laughed. "Bond girl, really? You know those chicks were usually working for the other side, right? And some of them died?"

"Ok, maybe not Bond girl. But I'm like the hot, stylish computer genius that always gets people out of trouble."

I laughed. "That's exactly what you are. And I'm glad you're still on the team."

"Yeah, at least one person is glad," she said darkly.

"Oh, Howard will come around. You hurt me on a professional level. You hurt Howard's heart. There's a big difference."

"How have you gotten over this so fast?" she murmured.

I grimaced. "I'm not over it, over it. I just--the *why* of things matters a lot to me. And you went against the team because you thought that you were doing the right thing. If you had done it for money, or to make a career advancement, or something, that would be different."

"Career advancement," she scoffed. "We make a very lucrative living while making the world a safer place. Who would want to 'advance' from that?"

"Not me."

"There you guys are," Camilla said, appearing at the

edge of the cabana. "I'm hungry, was going to try the swanky restaurant in the lobby. Anyone interested?"

"Yes, please," I said, chomping another apple slice. "All this one has is rabbit food. There's room in this muumuu for a cheeseburger and fries."

Camilla wrinkled her nose. "I think it might be a seafood restaurant."

"I'm an equal-opportunity eater. Bring on the crab cakes and the fried calamari," I said. "Frankie, you coming?"

"Yeah, just let me pack up real quick."

We ate at a table with an ocean view. Not many tables were taken--it was between the lunch and dinner rush. We ate crab cakes, fried calamari, fresh oysters, and seafood cobb salad, sharing two bottles of good champagne during the meal. It was the first time we'd laughed, the first time we'd truly relaxed.

It was the first time in weeks that I genuinely believed that things might turn out ok.

Chapter 3

I found Howard in his room in the hotel suite. I suspected that he was avoiding all of us--Frankie, for obvious reasons, and the rest of us because we were frustrated with his response to the situation. But I hunted him down to try and engage again. He was sprawled out on his bed, a sullen pout to his features. Sir Darcy hissed at me and darted to hide beneath the bed when I entered.

Sir Darcy Langston McWigglesbottom the Third was a rescue. Well, kind of. He was a rescue cat in the sense that Howard had taken him from a house before we blew it up. His previous owner was a creep who was killing prostitutes down in L.A. I'm not sure that Sir Darcy was grateful for the new home--he seemed to hate all of us with equal fervor, except for Frankie, who was allergic. To me, that was just more proof that the fluffy white monster was far more intelligent and diabolical than Howard was willing to admit.

Howard was taller than me, his frame a balance somewhere between lanky and muscular. His reddish-blonde hair curled at his neck--another victim of the humidity. His goatee had gone a little free-range the past couple of weeks; I wasn't sure if Frankie had been prompting him to keep it trimmed, or if he'd done it reflexively because they were together. It had slid from groomed respectability to wild and woolly in a surprisingly short amount of time.

I'd gone in with the intent of being gentle, but one glance at Howard's resentful glare had me taking a more direct approach.

"How long are you going to hide out from us in here?" I said, looking at the two room-service trays stacked in the corner.

He shrugged. "I'm not hiding."

"Liar."

His eyes flashed, but he said nothing.

"Frankie had her reasons for doing what she did."

"I know," he said, his voice low. His fingers plucked at the throw pillow. "That little girl reminded her of her dead cousin."

"She told you about Nalini, and you still are *this* angry at her?" I said.

"Yes. Why didn't she tell me what she was doing? She could have told me." There was a stubborn set to his chin, even as his lower lip quivered very slightly.

"Maybe she was afraid of how you'd react," I argued. "Maybe she didn't want to make you chose between her and the team. I don't know. *You* won't know until you guys have some hard conversations."

"She could have told me. She was dishonest. She broke my trust."

"Yeah, she made a mistake. A huge, fucking, *explosive* mistake," I said, rolling my eyes in exasperation. "She's not the only one here who's done that. She's human. And maybe that's the real problem here... you saw behind the curtain and didn't find the perfection that you had built up in your mind."

"Excuse me?"

"There is nothing in life that is one hundred percent good. I know that we are all looking for it, and people in our line of business probably crave that more than anyone. We all want something that isn't a grey area, 'cause that's easier. You need to take Frankie off that unreasonable pedestal you've put her on, and forgive her already."

"I thought you weren't getting involved in our relationship," he spat.

"Oh, I don't give a shit if you get back together with her or not. That's not my business. But you not talking to her, you giving her the cold shoulder... that *is* my business. In terms of your personal life, though, I will say this: if you can't face Frankie's emotional ugliness, if you can't handle the fact that she isn't some perfect, walking doll, then you aren't strong enough to deserve her."

I didn't leave time for him to respond, just shut the door quietly behind me on the way out. As much as I wanted things between them to be better, I couldn't control it. It was out of my hands. Like what would happen in Brazil. Like what Hyde was doing now.

I sighed. I liked control a little bit more than I wanted to admit. That was a very useful thing, in some ways-- it would be stupid to blunder into our kind of operations without precise planning. But every character trait had two sides to it, and needing control could ruin my relationships fast if I wasn't careful.

The rest of the week was more of the same. Howard hunkered in his room with Sir Darcy until their room was ripe with man-stink, and his resentment sunk into the woodwork. Frankie slogged her way through her mountainous to-do list, covering the large dining table in the suite with piles of paperwork that threatened to landslide onto the floor if someone slammed a door too hard.

Camilla was uncharacteristically quiet, but she had been since her cousin had shown up to tell her about the family mess weeks ago. I missed her warm, motherly wake-up calls, the way she kept the team together, her gentle laughter and not-so-gentle verbal kicks in the butt when we needed it. I didn't like the feeling of the group without Camilla, without Hyde.

By the time Friday rolled around, I was almost excited to fly out to Brazil and maybe get my head blown off. I was *definitely* excited to see Hyde. I was better when I was with him, and so was our team. Of course, the rest of the team didn't love Hyde the way I did. *I* hadn't even known that I loved Hyde until it was almost too late to tell him. I was still a little ashamed that it had taken me seeing Hyde in a pool of his own blood to realize that I couldn't live without him.

But we were on the same page now, and I was determined to never let him go--not if I could help it.

Chapter 4

Hyde was late.

He was supposed to meet us on the tarmac to catch our flight to Rio de Janeiro at six pm. It was now quarter after, and he wasn't answering my calls.

The rest of us were settled into the plush beige leather seats of the private jet. The politely bland stewardess had offered us a selection of beverages. Frankie was sipping champagne across from me; Camilla had opted for tea. I wondered if the flight crew was used to people being late-- wondered if they built extra time into their flight plan. They didn't seem perturbed that we were running behind--probably used to entitled, rich assholes wasting their time. But it wasn't normal for my team...wasn't normal for Hyde. I checked my watch again, then checked my phone.

"Still nothing?" Frankie asked, wincing.

"He'll be here," I said with more confidence than I felt. "Probably went to the wrong airport or something."

"There could be traffic."

"Maybe."

The truth was, I was nervous. Hyde and I told each other everything...usually. This jaunt of his, these five days of not knowing...I didn't like it. I certainly didn't like that he was late. He'd checked in last night and confirmed he would be here, so where the heck was he?

Finally, at twenty after, a dark SUV came careening up to the security gate. A man got out, slung a duffel bag over one shoulder, and approached the plane. I let out the breath I'd been trying not to hold. Even from this distance, I recognized Hyde's form, his walk.

"There he is," Camilla said.

"Thank goodness he's safe," Frankie said.

"Thank goodness we won't have to refile our flight plan," Howard grumbled.

Hyde's chocolate eyes met mine as his large frame filled the doorway. He had the smattering of a beard on his jawline and there were dark blue hollows beneath his eyes. But he smiled at me and I had to smile back. I was grateful that he was here, and safe, and mine.

"Hey, babe," he said, crossing the cabin and kissing me.

He smelled of sweat and dried blood and...*maple syrup*?

I frowned at him. "Did you roll around in a waffle house, or what?"

He wrinkled his nose. "Something like that. This plane have a shower? I hope?"

I jerked my head toward the back. "Go for it, Stinky. But hurry up. We need to do a briefing."

. . .

"LET'S USE OUR TIME," I said, once Hyde was out of the shower.

I tried to ignore how good he smelled, how handsome he looked freshly shaven, his hair still damp.

He winked at me like he could tell what I was thinking, and I frowned. "Stop distracting me. Frankie, do you have the briefs ready?"

I'd asked Frankie to do a background on the cartel, the principal players, the finances, and holdings. The result was that each of us had been given enough paperwork to choke a herd of ravenous goats. I was counting on Frankie to give a synopsis.

"Ok--Almeida cartel. Got its start in the early fifties with Aberto Almeida, but really took off under Thiago Almeida, now deceased. Page five is the timeline. Major streams of revenue include narcotics and weapons, but those industries have funded new, legal ventures in steel, beef, manufacturing, and petroleum. The cartel also wields great political power, as they have contributed to the campaigns of many political leaders. Now that Thiago is gone, the two major leaders are Caio, Thiago's brother, and Alex, Thiago's son."

Frankie paused and looked at Camilla.

"Whatever you have to say, Frankie, don't soften it on my account," she said. "There's nothing you could tell me that would shock or offend me. Really."

Frankie took a deep breath, nodded, and continued.

"Caio has the men behind him. He is the more overtly violent of the two leaders. But I don't think that's the full story. Yes, Caio is more prone to making an object lesson out of a traitor or competitor, but there are just as many disappearances around Alex. He just handles things quietly. I don't know that either is trustworthy."

Camilla snorted. "They're not. No one there is."

"My best information actually came from hacking some private files in Brazilian law enforcement. There have been a few investigations over the years, although the originating officers always seem to be called off the case, or..." Frankie flopped her hand in the air.

"They are killed." Camilla finished for her.

"Yes." Frankie nodded. "Starting on page twenty-seven, you'll find profiles on the identified players in the cartel. There are a list of the big players and some associated individuals. Camilla has confirmed several of them for us and added information, but there are people who've come into the picture after she left, and we don't have all the info we'd like. Any questions?"

"Let's go over our goals for this project," I said. "Camilla?"

"I'm not sure," she said. "With any luck, I can open the safe, and my father's last will and testament will be inside. And then we can all go home. I'd like to be out of there as soon as humanly possible."

"Alright," I said. "Primary goal is to not die. These are dangerous people. We're on their turf and we don't really know what we're stepping into."

"Ah, winging it," Howard said. "The plan of all idiots since the dawn of time…"

I rolled my eyes. "We aren't going to wing it. We're going to get in, figure out what the heck Thiago's will says, and what it means for Camilla, and then we are going to come up with a plan. But right now we just have to--"

"Wing it," Hyde interrupted with a wink.

Chapter 5

We didn't know the end game of this trip, and that uncertainty gnawed at all of us. Camilla became more and more withdrawn as we got closer to Rio. Her jaw tightened, the furrow in her brow became so fixed it appeared permanent, and her knuckles whitened against the dappled brown leather of her new handbag. When the wheels of the airplane bumped against Brazil for the first time, she released a sigh that had the sound of finality.

By coming to Brazil, the five of us had each gripped the dangling tail end of a convoluted knot. We couldn't see how this problem would be sorted; we were groping in the dark in the hopes of unraveling the mess we were now committed to fixing. I was in the unfamiliar position of following the lead of one of my team members. Camilla knew the two factions in this contest; she would be the one

we looked to for a nod or a head shake that would commu-
nicate trust or command death.

Camilla and I weren't the only ones tense with uncertainty. Howard had kept Hyde by his side on the airplane,
using Hyde's formidable flesh as a makeshift wall between
him and Frankie. They hadn't spoken much since our
whirling departure from the office a week ago, but it had
been a game of social chess since then, with Frankie
pushing forward in strategic, subtle attempts to get
Howard alone, and Howard ducking and dodging those
attempts with the studied practice of a boxer dodging
blows.

The instant we stepped off the plane, the barrier that
we had erected between us and discomfort came tumbling
down. The city was as warm and humid as a bum's shoe
and smelled like one, too.

The airport was busy and overfull of people who didn't
have the same sense of personal space as I did. They
spilled and flowed and jostled in different directions, like a
bucket of human marbles had been poured out over the
worn linoleum. We stayed close together, Camilla and
Frankie in front, Howard, his cat, Bruno and I behind
them, Hyde bringing up the rear guard. The cacophony of
human activity grated on me and made it nearly impossible for Hyde and I to pick out possible scouts or any
enemies lurking.

As we exited the plane and felt the danger of our situation press down on us and fill our nostrils like the thick
haze of the pollution that shrouded the city, I saw

Howard's eyes seek out Frankie more and more. He watched her, watched those who got too close, watched any obstacles in her path. When a man carrying a huge green and yellow duffel bag stepped into Frankie's path, Howard actually reached out his hand toward her elbow as if to guide her. In the last second, he dropped his hand stiffly by his side. Frankie never saw, but I did, and I knew Hyde was even more observant. I wondered how long Howard would play the silent sentinel.

Camilla had arranged for a large passenger van to meet us at the curb. We loaded up, Camilla in the front seat next to the driver, Frankie, Bruno, and I in the back seat, and Hyde and Howard on the center bench. We had glimpsed Guanabara Bay from the plane as we came in for landing. It had looked much like any other body of water from the air. However, now that we were much closer, it appeared that Guanabara Bay was like a modern abstract painting… best viewed from far away, as a close study would prevent any enjoyment.

The causeway that brought us into the city gave an unobstructed view of the filth in the water. An oily sheen of scum coated the surface and many unidentifiable objects bobbed up in the water and then disappeared again like eager goldfish at feeding time. The bridge spewed traffic into the edge of the city. We traveled south, our van just one in the ceaseless flow headed towards the most tourist-infested beaches.

It had been Camilla's idea to book a penthouse at the top of one of the beachfront resorts. We were hoping to get in touch with some contacts in the area without Camilla's uncle, Caio, or her brother, Alex, finding out. It was a far-flung hope, indeed. They were both powerful, well-connected men in their own rights.

Caio Almeida was in control of the illegal aspects of the cartel--drugs, weapons, counterfeiting, etc. He held sway over most of the manpower in the cartel. They were loyal to him, even though numerous reports indicated that Caio had an explosive temper and violent tendencies. If it came down to a ground war, Caio had the numbers. He would win.

Alex Almeida dealt in the legal side of the Almeida cartel. He filtered the organization's money through various businesses until it came out crisp and clean on the other side. Camilla used to know all of the Almeida holdings in Rio de Janeiro, but she had been out of contact for many years.

Frankie had done her best trying to track the various threads of the enormous spiderweb that was the Almeida cartels' financial holdings, but they dealt in cash often, and there were numerous connections that Frankie couldn't trace. We were going in without knowing whether the hotel was under Alex's control, whether the van we had rented would take us to the correct address, whether we would make it to our destination or be taken into a back alley and promptly shot.

While I kept alert for possible trouble, I took in our surroundings. Everything in Brazil was done in excess. There was too much of everything here. The flowers weren't pink and yellow, they were *neon*. Houses weren't built next to each other, they were piled up and on top of each other, like some leaning, teetering layer cake baked by a manic chef. Traffic was madness; you either careened down potholed lanes at a teeth-rattling, bone-jarring pace that made you contemplate your own fragile mortality, or you were stuck in traffic so thick that it inspired claustrophobia, where you wouldn't be able to open your car door wide enough to escape.

It took far too long for my comfort, but we arrived at the hotel. It looked like wealthy tourist central--the kind of place you went when you wanted to tell your friends you had been to a country without actually having to experience any of the differences of that country--wealthy American resort 2.0. The facade was a cream stucco, and valets in full uniform stood at attention in the shade of the palm trees that ringed the circular cobblestone drive. Even though it was morning, they looked uncomfortably hot--I hoped the guests tipped well.

We unfolded from the pleather bench seats. I was sticky and looking forward to a change in scenery. The air conditioning in the van had been blowing full blast, but it couldn't keep up with the heat and humidity outside combined with the body heat and breath humidity of the six adults and two animals inside. But the valets surrounded us like concerned aid workers to a boat full of refugees--they were handing out cold waters, taking our luggage, ushering us inside.

The hotel felt crisp and cool, and I subtly peeled my

sundress away from my body. The lobby was three stories tall, ringed in glass. I could see the rolling waves of the beach from where I stood--this part of the coast was beautiful, but that wasn't why we were here. Large arrangements of orchids sat on carved tables next to clusters of sofas and chairs. Howard sunk into one, pointedly placing Sir Darcy's crate on the seat next to him as Frankie moved in his direction. She frowned and chose a different spot to sit.

Camilla was already at the front desk. She had made the reservations; she would check us in. That was part of the very loose strategy that we had, coming into Brazil. Here, Camilla was seen as the boss. Yes, the men in her family knew that she worked for me, but we were trying to downplay that dynamic. Perhaps, if we were lucky, they would all be like Fernando, her cousin, who hadn't understood that the entire team was a threat. I don't think he took us seriously, and that could be an advantage if we played it right.

Hyde sidled up to me. With his olive skin, dark hair, and chocolate brown eyes, he looked like he might belong in Brazil. He was six foot two and his muscles had been built and hardened by years of dedication in the kitchen and gym. Even with his shoulders rolled forward, his posture slouched--a deliberate attempt to look smaller, weaker--he was an imposing figure. Only a blithering idiot would look at him and not see power.

He bumped my elbow gently with his own. "You forgiven me, yet?"

"I'm not mad at you. Just curious."

"All will be revealed in due time," he said in a mystical-sounding voice, waving his hands as if over a crystal ball. "I see a great revelation in your future, dearie."

I elbowed him in the ribs. Knowing his reflexes, he let me do it. He grinned, showing off a lady-killer smile.

"Knock it off. You'd be curious too, if I disappeared for a week and wouldn't tell you what I was doing."

"I would be. Believe me, hiding stuff from you isn't easy. But it's a surprise. What fun would it be if we couldn't surprise each other now and then?" he said, smiling.

His melted chocolate eyes had crinkles at the corner. He looked so happy, so proud of himself, like a little kid who'd finally beat his dad at checkers. I couldn't take that smile away from him. On the heels of that thought came the question of what I would deny this man if it made him happy. I wasn't losing my good sense, was I? I wasn't exchanging--as so many women do--my own solid reasoning abilities for the thrill and comfort of a hand-some smile aimed in my direction?

"I'm not lying to you," he said. "I promise that you'll know what I was up to within two weeks."

"Stop reading my mind," I grumbled.

He chuckled, that low sound that I had learned to love. He slung an arm around my waist and pulled me close, giving me a soft, quick kiss on the lips.

Of course that's when the armed gunmen came through the front door.

It was a struggle to stay loose in Hyde's arms. I felt him

tense, then relax--he was doing his best to stick with the plan, too. After all, the guns weren't raised or pointed at us--yet. We had known that they would find out that we were here, eventually. But we had hoped for a few days to poke around, see if we could connect with any of the sources that our friend Luis had in the area without being watched. That hope was now well and dead.

There were six of them, all dressed in black suits, all flanking the two men in the center. Those men were dressed in casual-chic--button-down linen shirts rolled to the sleeves, expensive leather driving mocassins, designer jeans. One of the men in front I recognized immediately--it was Fernando. He was looking far too smug for my taste, his eyes making a derisive sweep over Hyde and I, before ignoring us completely. I suddenly wished that I had just shot him in Hyde's hospital room when I'd had the chance.

"Easy," Hyde said.

"Like I said...stop reading my mind," I hissed, under my breath.

He chuckled once more.

The other man in front was older. Although he shared the same tan skin and brown eyes that Fernando and Camilla had, he had salt and pepper hair and a goatee to match. His face was creased from the sun, and his eyes, although hard, softened a bit when he saw Camilla.

"Hello, my gorgeous Camilla," he said, approaching with arms outstretched. When he got in range, he enfolded her into a hug and rocked her side to side. "My beautiful girl. Why did you not tell me you were coming?

You will come and stay with me. It isn't safe here, in this city. It isn't safe here for you and your friends. I have a place where you will be safe from your brother."

"Thank you, Uncle. I didn't want to be a bother. I brought guests and didn't want to impose," Camilla said.

"This is my country," Caio said, spreading his arms wide again. He fake chuckled and looked around. "And I can certainly put you up in better style than this. Besides, you've been gone a long time, little niece. We wouldn't want you to get hurt. Your brother is a madman. We need to resolve this situation before someone dies."

He said this last sentence with obvious relish, like the thought of someone dying was actually not that bad of an idea. This was not a man skilled in subtlety. These were not the silk-sheathed words of one trained in the high art of manipulation. He was threatening Camilla. He was threatening us.

A large man standing just to the right of Caio shifted subtly at his words. The man looked vaguely uncomfortable at what Caio had said. I guessed the man was only slightly younger than Camilla. He was a tall man, several inches taller than Hyde and powerfully built through the shoulders and chest. He had thick brown hair the color of the richest coffee, gold-tanned skin, and a scruff of beard that was struck through with silver. His eyes were a clear, intelligent hazel with set crow's feet at the corners.

His reaction to Caio's thinly-veiled threat was nothing more than a tightening at the corners of his mouth and a slight lowering of his eyebrows, but it was there. It was shame, at being present for this, for being involved in Caio's bullying of Camilla. Whether his chagrin had to do with Thiago's daughter being treated in such a manner, or if the emotion was about Camilla specifically, I didn't know and it didn't matter.

A potential ally, I thought. *A potential weakness to exploit.*

Hyde gently squeezed my upper arm with calloused fingers. He had seen it, too.

"Very well," Camilla said lightly, her head held high with a nearly regal bearing. "We would be happy to accept your hospitality."

There was no hint of sarcasm in her words, no hint of fear or anger. She pulled her suitcase along behind her, but Caio held up a hand.

"My men will be happy to get your luggage." Caio smirked.

Camilla's movements stuttered, but she relinquished the handle to her bag. I dropped my suitcase unceremoniously and heard the others follow suit. I forced my face into a look of subtle concern, but sent a silent prayer of gratitude that we had armed ourselves before we got off the plane. Alex's men would find numerous guns hidden in Hyde's luggage. Those were the decoys.

I had a .22 caliber pistol hidden in the heel of each of my hollowed-out wedge sandals, two .40 calibers at the small of my back that were hidden beneath my flowing sundress, and a rack of deadly throwing knives strapped to each thigh. Every card in Howard's wallet was C-4 pressed carefully into different colored plastic molds, and the wallet itself was woven from fuse cord. His boots weren't as innocuous as they seemed, either.

Frankie had a set of jeweled lockpicks shoved into her hair, and a 9 millimeter pistol taped on the back of each thigh directly below the shelter of each buttock. It was the only place we could find where the lines of her short jersey cotton dress didn't give anything away. And Hyde? Well, Hyde didn't usually wear baggy jeans and oversized button-down Hawaiian shirts. If Hyde were to walk through a metal detector right now, it would shriek like a banshee. The guards would pee a little if they saw what was strapped to his muscular form.

We allowed the men to pick up our suitcases and we followed them outside. I had to tug Bruno's leash a bit--he wasn't too sure about the new additions to our group. There were four black SUVs blocking the driveway. Camilla was escorted to one and joined by Caio and Fernando. Frankie, Howard, Hyde, Bruno, and I piled into the back of another. Two men sat up front. I wanted to smile so I frowned instead--they shouldn't have let us all in one car--the men in the front seats would be vastly outgunned if something were to happen.

As the cars began to fight their way through traffic, I just prayed we'd all end up at the same destination. I thought we probably would--Caio would try and court Camilla's cooperation at first, was my guess. If she didn't go along with his plans, that's when the real trouble would start. But for now, I thought we were probably safe. Ish.

It took hours. I played the part of a spoiled socialite. I

sighed, fiddled with the air vents, complained about the traffic, wondered out loud when we would get there, and informed the driver that my dog was going to need a bathroom break if the ride was longer than forty-five minutes. That last part was a lie--Bruno had taken a massive dump at the airport and he could hold his pee longer than a camel. It was a real problem to get him motivated to go outside sometimes--he thought he was a precious, furry flower, and he didn't like the rain or cold or extreme heat.

The reason I was complaining wasn't to annoy the heck out of my fellow passengers, although, by the scathing looks I was receiving in the rear-view mirror, I was succeeding. I was trying to paint a picture, trying to sell the narrative that the four of us weren't a threat.

I was a rich businesswoman who had hired Camilla as a housekeeper, that Hyde was my pretty gym-rat boy-toy and security guard, and Frankie and Howard were my sycophantic entourage. After all, I didn't know if my cover had held up under their scrutiny. If it had, if they believed that I was a wealthy antiques dealer who traveled a lot to source things for celebrity clients, that would work to our benefit. And if they knew the truth about all of us--that together we were deadly and formidable--well then, annoying them was enough.

The drive took too long for my nerves. We wound out and away from the city to a well-guarded airstrip. While we were at the gate, Bruno farted. It was silent, but it was deadly. I pulled a magazine out of the back of the seat in front of me and did my best to waft the thick odor to the front seats. The driver cursed under his breath, and both the men rolled down their windows.

"I warned you," I said, gasping. "If he doesn't get a bathroom break soon, it's gonna be all over the seats. Flying gives him runny tummy. He doesn't like to change time zones. It's going to come out like pressurized pudding. And I'm not cleaning it up! This was supposed to be a vacation. I was supposed to get a tan, do some shopping. Not clean up diarrhea because the driver wouldn't pull over when I asked him to."

The guy in the front passenger seat leaned over and said something to the driver, shooting a concerned look at Bruno. Bruno was seated very politely between Hyde and me, his tongue lolling out. He didn't look in duress at all, but the guard must not have liked what he saw, cause he frowned.

"It'll be a shitpocalypse!" I said. "Sometimes, when he gets like this, it's like the family-sized frozen yogurt. *That* size. Do you want to be responsible for cleaning that up? Look at him! He's very uncomfortable! He's giving me *the look*."

Bruno was exceedingly comfortable, and proved it by farting again. Hyde started coughing. I knew it was to cover up a laugh, but it sounded like he might be gagging. Actually, maybe he really *was* gagging. Bruno had put some effort behind it. I held my nose.

"We are getting out here, ma'am," the front guard said. "Your dog can use the grass, over there."

The man pointed at a scraggly brown patch at the

corner of the helipads. Two large helicopters waited for us on the helipads. I frowned.

"He doesn't like to get his paws dirty. Really. Camilla's uncle says that he'd give her hospitality, and you guys didn't even think to accommodate one of your *guests*?"

I gestured grandly at Bruno, who gave a doggy grin and laid down, his slobbery head and massive front paws in my lap.

"I know, baby," I crooned, petting his head and trying not to laugh. "How thoughtless. But this is a third-world country, and these men are just doing their best. I won't let anything get your poor little feet dirty."

From beneath my lowered lashes, I saw the front passenger roll his eyes. Perfect. People could rarely be annoyed and on guard at the same time. They passed through the gates without speaking to the guard station and stopped just short of the asphalt. We all got out, and I led Bruno over to the brown grass in the corner. Frankie followed me while Hyde and Howard stayed close to the men.

"What do you think they're going to do with us?" she asked.

"I'm not sure. As long as they don't push us out of the helicopter, we'll be fine," I said, shrugging.

"Is this normal? The helicopters?" Frankie looked over at them and shuddered. "I don't like helicopters."

"If you're a wealthy Brazilian, it's a regular mode of transport. Apparently, it's too dangerous for some people to ride around in cars next to civilians. Too much crime, too many kidnappings and ransom demands."

"That doesn't make me feel better."

"It is what it is. We need to play along for a while until we figure out what's going on here. We need to keep Camilla safe." I shook Bruno's leash. "Come on, buddy. I told them you had to poop. I promised a poo-pacolypse."

Bruno gave me the side-eye and sat down.

"Actually, if I remember correctly, you said it would be a shitpocalypse," Frankie said, sarcastically.

"Whatever. I guess we'd better get over there before someone comes to retrieve us. I hope Camilla's doing ok--I wouldn't want to have been in that car."

"Yeah, I don't think I'm fond of either of those guys." Frankie looked over her shoulder.

"Come on, buddy," I said to Bruno.

We rejoined the group and watched as our luggage was loaded into the back of the helicopters. Once again, it was Camilla, Fernando, Caio and a bunch of armed men in one helicopter, and the four of us with guards in another. Camilla met my eyes and nodded her head before getting in her helicopter. Frankie and Howard got in the back row of ours, and Hyde hopped in the middle seat. As I was about to load Bruno, he popped a squat in the center of the heliport symbol and dropped a massive turd.

"See?" I said, turning to the horrified guard behind me. "He won't go in dead grass!"

I helped Bruno load up, affixed headgear to his head and mine, and strapped in. The guard was still staring at the remains of Bruno's lunch. Even I had to admit it was an impressive pile. Not Bruno's record, though--not by a long shot. The rotors began turning, and the guard shook himself out of his trance. He hopped into the seat furthest from Bruno and closed the door.

The flight out of Rio wasn't long. We lifted off the ground and the buildings became smaller, the cars diminutive, the people specks. The city was swathed in one side by ocean--from this height it was beautiful again--and a huge expanse of trees on the other. There were small cuts in the growth indicating roads, some small villages designated by a grouping of buildings. The headgear dispelled the deafening rotors well, but the cords that would have allowed us to hear the conversation from the pilots or to speak to each other were disconnected.

I played the part of the dumb American tourist once more, pointing out everything of interest that we saw. There wasn't much to see, just miles and miles of green, several rivers, and then, finally, a city. Even from this elevation, it was clear that this was far different than Rio. It was cleaner, for one thing, and better organized. There were sections of the city where the buildings were smaller and closer together, but the streets were clear and well-paved, and everything looked like someone had just given it all a fresh coat of paint.

Just outside the city, the properties were extensive and gated, the homes mammoth in size. This was where some of the truly wealthy in Brazil lived. We flew over houses grand enough to make the White House look like a homeless camp, and the helicopters aimed for the largest one at the end of a long road. The house, if it could even be called that, was settled on a large rise, with three hundred sixty degree views. It was made of light gray stone, with huge, symmetrical windows everywhere.

I counted four separate pools, if one included the long reflecting fountain. Acres of lawn surrounded the house. The stone wall that ringed the property was exceedingly tall, and tipped with what, at first glance, appeared to be decorative finials. On closer inspection, however, the finials looked less decorative and more like clusters of razor wire. There was a huge helipad in the back, where two other helicopters were parked. One was smaller, the other was identical to the ones we were in. We were definitely in a different league, here, but I tried not to show it.

We landed and exited the helicopters.

"Plenty of room for Bruno to run, which is nice." I patted Bruno's head. "How many square feet is it?" I asked the guard next to me.

"I've never asked."

"Hmm," I said, wrinkling my nose as if disappointed in his tour guide skills. "I hope they have Chardonnay. Do they?"

"What?" He was leaning back from me, his eyes wide.

"Char-duh-nay," I said. "Do they have it? It's a kind of wine. Oh my gosh." I put a hand to my chest and gasped theatrically. "Please tell me you have wine here."

"South America is known for its wine production,

sweet lady," Caio said, from behind me. "And we are honored that you are our guest."

I took the arm he offered. "Thank you. What a lovely house."

We began walking towards the double doors that would lead us into the monstrosity.

"I am glad it meets with your approval," he said, smiling.

"Oh, now that I know there's wine, I'm sure I'll have a great time. I'm surprised we left Rio, though. I was hoping to do some shopping while I'm here." I leaned in and whispered conspiratorially. "I buy inexpensive antiques in other countries and sell it to rich idiots back home for twenty times what I paid for it."

Caio laughed, and I glimpsed Fernando behind us, frowning.

"It sounds like you have a wonderful business model," Caio said.

"Obviously not the *best* one, though," I said, whistling as we entered the house.

The room we were in was large and round. The walls were mostly full-length glass doors struck through with wood mullions. It was furnished richly, in burgundy and gold tones. Carved tables sat between cushioned leather armchairs. A huge, marble-topped sideboard anchored the far side of the room. On either side of it were archways that led into the rest of the house.

Something about the decor struck me as odd, though-- while most of the design was impeccable, the rug was far too small for the space, and there were several patches on the wall that looked like a different paint color. I pursed my lips and pretended not to notice.

"What has Camilla told you about her family?"

"Her father was in oil and politics. Or politics and oil?" I flapped my hand. "She mostly told me about the great antiquing in Rio. I hope I'll get the chance to shop? But if it's dangerous, maybe I should have an escort. Maybe he can take me?"

I pointed at the guard I'd been chatting at earlier. He froze, his eyes wide.

"I'm sure we can arrange something," Caio said, patting my hand.

I caught Fernando's eyes narrow into suspicious slits at the motion. He didn't seem to be buying my act. Who knew if Caio was, either. But at least I might be able to throw some doubt in the mix. The last time I'd seen Fernando, I'd been holding a gun. I'd yelled at him. He'd seen the real me, but he'd still underestimated me. Let's face it--seeing someone holding a gun was much different than seeing them use one. I was hoping that my new act might soften those memories, make him question his first impression of me. After all, for a few weeks, he'd followed me around on vacation. Nobody seems badass when they're passed out at noon on a lawn chair after too many mimosas.

"Camilla, you and your guests will be staying in the family wing," Caio said. "My men and I are in the guest wing."

She nodded and headed through the doorway. I didn't know what it must be like to be back here. This was her father's house, I knew that much from the dossier. Caio didn't live here; neither did Alex. This should have been neutral territory, now that Thiago was dead. I didn't know if Caio offering Camilla the family wing was a gesture of goodwill or of manipulation.

We followed Camilla as she led us all past giant sitting rooms, a kitchen complete with working staff, and large hallways that led off to who-knows-where. The place reminded me of a castle-meets-high-class-Vegas-casino--huge scale, easy to get lost in, and expensive, overwrought decor. Up the stairs we went. All of it was impeccably decorated--not my taste, but then, I wouldn't expect a Brazilian cartel leader to choose 'New England WASP' as his decorating muse. Camilla finally paused at a set of double glass doors. I thought it was odd that there were doors in the middle of the hallway. I wondered if they'd always been there.

"The code is still the same," Caio said.

Camilla nodded and entered it. When she opened the door, I could see that it wasn't normal french doors, as I had originally thought. The doors were three inches thick, reinforced metal with bulletproof glass.

Caio caught me looking. "The entire family wing can be placed on lockdown, making the entire wing a panic room."

My eyes went wide. "Is it safe here? Camilla, I thought you said we'd be going somewhere safe."

"My father installed it in case of... political insurgencies," she said. "It won't be an issue."

"Oh, thank goodness." I breezed in, Bruno on my heels. "Camilla, which room should Hyde and I take?"

"Third door on the right," she said. "I'll be right next door to you then."

"Wonderful," I said.

The room was enormous, with a large gold-veined marble fireplace, a seating area with tufted leather chairs and a red velvet sofa, and a king-sized, four-poster mahogany bed. Oil paintings hung under painting lights, and lush ferns in ornate porcelain pots dotted the room. It was a grand, masculine space. I wondered who the room had been designed for, if this room had belonged to Thiago, or Alex. Or maybe it was just an extra. A house this size was bound to have plenty of those.

Through another set of double doors was the marble-clad bathroom that had a tub nearly wide and deep enough to do laps in. The shower was one of those technology-infused monstrosities that I could never figure out. Call me old-fashioned, but I preferred water to come from *above* in my shower, not from every angle known to man. Sprayers in the wall made turning around or bending over a high-risk move.

I knew that Camilla would have given me and Hyde the room with the best exit points. Sure enough, the room had a balcony overlooking one of the swimming pools. Worse come to worse, we could jump and *probably* make the deep end. Maybe. If we weren't under lockdown, that is. The doors and windows in this room were just as thick as the double doors we'd needed a code for. Bullet-proof and lockdown ready. I just hoped that no one would lock us *in*.

"I'll let you rest and refresh yourself for dinner," Caio said, kissing Camilla on both cheeks. "Then we can talk about the safe and the will."

A hungry gleam entered his eye. He went from thoughtful host to predatory wolf in a half-second flat. I committed that to memory. Caio could turn on a dime, and he was wearing a mask, too. Our luggage was delivered, and the staff retreated past the double doors. I held my breath, waiting for the tell-tale whoosh and click that would have signaled a lock-down. But it never came.

"Apparently, we've been sufficiently polite so far," Camilla said with a sigh.

She sounded tired and her shoulders were slumped. Howard bent over to let Sir Darcy out of his crate. The cat disappeared down the hallway with a yowling shriek. Bruno trotted after him with his tongue lolling out like it was a fun game.

I made a face as I watched them go. I wasn't a huge cat fan. Or, more accurately, I was neutral. I felt the same way about Sir Darcy as I did with other random wildlife--you leave me alone and we'll get along just fine. I preferred dogs, mainly because they don't crap inside, and they stay off the kitchen counters--that, and they actually seem to care about you.

Sir Darcy was the antithesis of any pet I would have

chosen for myself. He was prone to leaving nuggets in your shoes if you left them unattended, he hacked up hairballs on couches, vomited smack in the center of hallways, jumped out of unexpected hiding places, and took a swipe at your ankles if you got too close. To say I was sick of this cat was the understatement of the century.

"Whatever," I said. "Frankie, do you have a tampon?"

It was our code, a signal to have Frankie do a sweep for bugs. Frankie nodded and went to her bag. A half an hour later, we were all sitting on the bed in Hyde's and my room.

"No surveillance, then?" I asked.

Frankie shook her head. "I scanned everything. They obviously searched my bag, but left the computers, the mobile routers, and the bug scanner. Hilarious."

"Just check everything. Make sure they didn't like...stick a tracker in your computer?" I finished, lamely. Computers were not my thing.

Frankie pressed her lips together to keep from laughing. "I'll be sure and check for...trackers."

I stuck my tongue out at her.

"Yeah," Howard said. "They didn't catch the stuff in the bottom compartment of my luggage. We're really well set up, considering."

"Same here," Hyde said. "Got the obvious guns, but everything in the sides and bottom was safe."

"Those don't show up, even on x-ray. But now that we've got everything in, we need to make sure that it isn't found," Camilla said. "Put stuff back and keep things hidden. I used to have a couple spots that I could count on the maids not looking, but I don't know if that's still the case."

"I've already stashed some guns around the apartment," I said, thinking of the loaded revolver in the bottom of the oatmeal container in the kitchen and the 9 millimeter taped to the back side of one of the sinks in our bathroom. "But I'll keep the rest hidden with my things. How are you doing? I hated that we weren't with you on the trip over."

She shrugged. "I'm fine. It was fine. I think they're trying to feel me out, figure out my motives. Fernando kept asking if I had missed Brazil. I can't tell if they want me to stay or want me to go away. I just don't know." She ran a hand through her hair.

"We will figure it out," I said, putting a hand on her knee. "We are all here for you. Whatever you need."

"Thank you."

"By any chance, do you think Caio bought my idiot tourist act?"

Camilla tilted her head. "Maybe. But I think you definitely have a couple of the men convinced."

Hyde chuckled. "She has a couple of them running scared, you mean."

"Scared I'll make them go shopping with me," I said. "Or scared that I'll make them clean up after Bruno."

"I had a window view of that deuce Bruno left on the helipad," Howard said. "You don't want to know what happened when the rotors got going. I'm not going to be able to get that sight out of my head for a long time."

Camilla rang for hors d'oeuvres and wine, and we all showered, dressed for dinner, and met up in the huge living room down the hall from our bedrooms.

"You know," I said, taking the glass of wine that Hyde extended out to me. "As far as panic rooms go, this is a really nice one."

The sunset was putting on a vibrant watercolor show outside the floor-to-ceiling windows. A chandelier sparkled overhead and my feet sunk into the expensive Persian carpet.

Camilla chuckled.

"I can think of worse places to ride out the zombie apocalypse," Howard said.

"Yeah," Hyde said. "All we'd have to do is clear out everyone on the property, and it would be pretty safe."

We were all thinking that we might have to do that, anyway.

Chapter 6

Dinner was served downstairs, in a massive, mahogany-paneled dining room that looked straight out of a castle brochure. Antique swords and axes hung on the walls, interspersed with tapestries that depicted scenes from feudal life. The table had legs carved in the shape of roaring lions and could seat fifty. It felt like that's how many people were there, too. But really, there were the five of us, plus Caio, Fernando, the man who might be convinced to be an ally, and two of the guards from earlier in the day. There was also the unexpected addition of the three men in military uniforms who were seated with us at the table, and the four in military uniforms standing with stiff posture around the perimeter of the room. So seventeen, plus the army of staff who bustled in and out.

Camilla and I looked like we were on the same page-- we both just wanted to go to bed. A full day of traveling, of looking forward to *this*--it had taken its toll on our energy levels. I sipped my wine and tried to pay close enough attention to the conversation so I didn't look like an idiot. My main goal was to people watch--to start figuring out who were the main players, and who, if anyone, we could count on if things went to shit. This used to be Camilla's home; was there anyone here who might still feel some loyalty? Or were bloodlines of little value here--did these people value Caio's power more than Camilla? Or maybe they didn't care at all. Maybe they were all new.

Judging by the warm smiles on some of the older staff's faces, that didn't seem to be the case. The pastry chef, an elderly man with a grey handlebar mustache and a thick French accent, came out to kiss both of Camilla's cheeks.

"My little dove!" he said. "I will bake your special treat tomorrow, yes? You still love the *pain au raisin*? You shall have it! I will start the dough tonight! Enjoy your dinner! Eat, eat!"

I noticed that Fernando looked completely relaxed through that exchange, but that Caio seemed stiff, his lips pursed for a moment, then he schooled his face into pleasant lines once more. I looked away before he caught my glance--I had learned a little more of what I wanted to know. He was jealous on some level--didn't want Camilla to have attention, resented that this had been her house once, and it had never been his.

The man to Caio's left was the real mystery to me. He was the one who had frowned when Caio had spoken to Camilla the first time. Through introductions, I learned that his name was Tristao dos Santos. Tristao said he'd been in 'politics and oil' for all his life. But what I found most interesting was how often he looked at Camilla...and how the corners of his eyes creased almost every time he did. He wasn't smiling when he did it--but there was a softening of his features when he looked at her that belied a deeper emotion. It wasn't hatred--that was for damn sure. The man had feelings, and they were of the warm and fuzzy sort. I wondered if those sentiments ran deep enough to help us.

On Caio's right was General Gilberto Horta. He'd been mentioned briefly in Frankie's information packet, only as one of the country's leaders, not as a real player in the Almeida melodrama. But his presence at this dinner proved that we needed to take a closer look at the man. He was tall and broad, with one of those physiques that made me think of a football player who'd long given up playing the sport, and now settled for drinking beer and talking about it.

My stomach growled as the food was laid before us. There were grilled meats--lemon garlic chicken, skewers of beef drizzled with chimichurri, and garlicky pork medallions with bright parsley. There were little rounds of fried cheesy dough, a steaming clay pot of *moqueca*--shrimp in a tomato coriander sauce, grilled corn, beans with sausage, and a cucumber tomato salad. I was so hungry, so focused on the gorgeous meal being laid before us, that I almost missed the other show that was taking place.

Almost, but not quite.

One of the maids bringing out the food seemed to be more interested in ogling the men at the table than in doing her job. The name on her tag was 'Lynsee'. She was beautiful, in that way that made me think of too-tight jeans and lower back tattoos. She would look out of place in a high-society function--there was something in her mannerisms that would always seem cheap, no matter how many carats of diamonds or yards of couture she was draped in.

Heavily lined eyes and fake, fluttering eyelashes competed for attention with garish pink lipgloss slicked on overfilled lips. Even though she was wearing the same uniform as every other female servant in the place, her hemline seemed higher, her neckline lower. Maybe it was just her movements--she didn't walk, she *sashayed*. She didn't look, she *simpered*. Everything about her was sinuous, feline. She knew how to get and keep male attention.

I internally rolled my eyes. Women like this were exhausting to be around. This wasn't someone confident in who she was--this was someone cultivating men's reactions to boost her small reserves of self-confidence. This was learned behavior, though.

My mother might drive me nuts most of the time, but something she had done well was to teach me that I had inherent value, whether or not a man recognized it. My father had reinforced this belief, too, starting well before the first time I'd come home crying because some boy had pushed me down and called me fat on the playground. My father had dusted off my dirty knees, given me a hug, and taught me how to throw a punch. Then he'd shown up to the parent-Principal meeting and looked imperiously down his nose at the Principal until he reduced my punishment for giving Bobby F. a black eye.

I was betting this girl had a very different home life experience growing up, one in which she was taught, overtly or through subtle reinforcements, that the only power women had was that given to them by men, and the best way to get that power was to wear a short skirt and bounce when you walked. For some reason, these kinds of women were the same ones who looked at all other women as competition--if another woman was beautiful or had a handsome man, they were competition. The only ones completely exempt were the morbidly obese single ones.

Her gaze slid around the occupants of the table. She was a lioness on the prowl, sizing up the gazelles. Her eyes landed on Hyde and widened oh so slightly, but then kept sliding to me. I narrowed mine. She might be a lioness, but I was a fucking big game hunter with a bipod, scope, and heat-seeking bullets where Hyde was concerned.

I gave her my very best 'please fuck off at your earliest convenience' look, and she gave an expression like she'd smelled something foul, and her eyes moved on, and that was that. The next time I caught Hyde's eye, he was smiling.

"What?" I murmured, leaning closer.

"You're sweet," he said in a low voice. "I think it's cute when you get territorial."

"Well, she-tiger can find another target..." I trailed off as I saw the maid's eyes settle on Howard, and a sly smile turned her lips. "Shit."

The lioness had found her wounded gazelle.

As the dinner progressed, I got the impression that it was more about getting a reaction from Frankie and me than it was about securing Howard's attention. He seemed oblivious. I mean, sure he saw her, in the same way every man sees a beautiful woman in his periphery. But he wasn't *looking*--he wasn't doing that lingering, top to bottom perusal that some men do, nor was he looking to see if she was noticing him. He didn't seem to notice that she stepped a little too close when she set a dish on the table in front of him, or that she fluttered her eyelashes and pushed up her bosom when she was in his line of sight. But I noticed.

And Frankie *certainly* did.

I saw Frankie's eyes track the coy movements, saw her take a deep breath when Lynsee oh-so-casually brushed Howard's shoulder when she set a platter down. I knew what this woman was doing. Frankie knew what this woman was doing. Even Camilla raised her eyebrows at one point. It was only Howard that seemed oblivious. Thank goodness for that.

I thought Frankie's head might pop off if she held any more tension in her neck. If Howard had been flirting back, Frankie might have sprung a violent nosebleed or thrown a plate at the woman's head. We didn't need an added layer to this already painful dinner, but here it was, anyway. The dinner was the gift that kept on giving, like some sort of horrid, re-wrapped fruitcake.

"So you buy trinkets," General Horta said, leaning forward to make eye contact with me. "How amusing."

If that really had been my profession, I would have been much more offended by his tone. As it was, I was glad that he'd dismissed me as beneath any real notice. He talked to me like I was a little girl with a lemonade stand.

"I like it," I said. "It keeps me busy."

"Ah, busy is good for a woman," he said, then nodded and leaned back, as if that was all the attention the topic deserved.

"Yup," I said, then took another slug off my wine.

I couldn't wait to ask Camilla what she knew about this guy, couldn't wait until Frankie's nimble fingers could pluck his entire history from the ether of the internet. What was his connection to the Almeidas? And why was he here? It was perplexing. It was as if Caio was flexing his social clout or sending us a message, but I couldn't figure out what it was. I hoped that Camilla would have more insight.

"So when is the election, General?" Camilla asked. "Forgive me, I am not up to date on the politics in Brazil."

"The election is not for another eight months," the General replied, with a smile that one usually reserves for precocious children. "But I hope that I can count on your vote when the time comes."

Camilla laughed. "I doubt I will still be here in eight months, General. But I wish you luck all the same."

Caio raised his eyebrow at that comment. I couldn't tell if Camilla's statement had pleased him or not. Did he want her to stay, or to go? More questions and no answers. Along with the General and Camilla's uncle, I watched Tristao as he tried not to stare at Camilla.

I couldn't wait to hear *that* story as soon as I got Camilla alone. But as it was, I was tired and irritated. I wanted a shower and clean sheets to slip into. Our hosts didn't seem to feel the same. The dinner stretched on, long past the point of my patience. Each course, I loaded up my plate and dug in, not caring if I was supposed to look or act a certain way. Caio smirked at my enthusiasm, but I shrugged internally. It was only my affection for Camilla that kept the smile on my face.

"Where is my brother?" Camilla said. "I thought he would have come to greet me by now."

Under the expensive fabric of his shirt, Caio's shoulders stiffened.

"I've told you that things are... tense between me and Alex at the moment," he said, his mouth pulling down at the corners. "Why? Have you been speaking with him?"

Something ugly flashed in his expression. This was a forbidden subject--he was irritated that Camilla had brought it up, even though it was a natural thing for her to ask. Caio's violent streak was under a thin but convincing veneer--until now, until someone displeased him. Then that violence shot to the surface, simmered right behind his eyes.

His 'invitation' to the house now made more sense. It

wasn't just about control, wasn't just about keeping an eye on Camilla in general. It was specific to Alex--he didn't want Camilla and Alex having contact. After all, Caio didn't know what Camilla's feelings were. What if Camilla and Alex were plotting against him?

"No." Camilla shook her head. I was sure she'd seen his displeasure, but she was pretending that she hadn't. "And you said things were tense, but I don't really understand why. You've always worked well together in the past."

"The matter of Thiago's will, may he rest in peace, is of concern to both of us. Neither of us understands why Thiago would have left the care of it to you, a daughter whom he hadn't seen or spoken to in years."

Dangerous waters--an accusation, but not.

Camilla sighed and shook her head. "You knew my father well, Uncle. You know that he would not have been pleased if I never came home to pay my respects. You know that he loved to exert control. He wanted to ensure that I would be forced to come back, if only to open the safe."

Caio nodded. "I had thought of that. But you don't miss your home? You don't miss your beautiful country?"

"I miss my childhood," she said with a sad smile. "I miss watching Alex run through the yard in bare feet. I miss Mama. I even miss the father of my youth--but that man died long before Thiago drew his last breath."

"May he rest in peace," Caio prompted.

"But no--I don't miss this house. I don't miss the politics or the power struggles. And as for my country...this will always feel like home, in some ways. But I have found a new place that feels like home, a new life."

Caio pursed his lips in clear disapproval.

Camilla shook her head. "Regardless of whether you understand or approve of it, it is my new home. And all I want is to get that safe open, have the will read, and go back to the home and life that I chose."

Caio nodded, seemed pleased by her answer. "I understand."

"But I had hoped to tell my brother the same thing. I had hoped that you both could put aside your differences while I was here, that we could act as family."

Caio frowned, the creases around his mouth prominent. "A few weeks ago, I heard that he was here. We had both agreed that this was your father's house, and that we would wait for you to open the safe. But I got a call that he was here. He... hurt one of the staff, Rosalia. And he tried to open the safe. It was only after drastic measures that we convinced him to leave."

I thought of the patches I'd seen in the plaster, of the rug that seemed new and poorly sized in the rotunda. Drastic measures, indeed. I wondered how they disposed of their bodies, if there was a local pig farm that handled such things. Or maybe there was enough wildlife activity in the jungle-esque greenery behind the house. Maybe they just tipped the bodies over the barbed-wire fence and let nature take its course.

I realized I'd been lost in thought and staring at Tristao, who was studying me openly. I returned my gaze to my plate and took another bite of the grilled corn dish. Delicious. Everything was incredible. They might have to roll me away from the table at the end of the meal. Finally, *finally*, plates were cleared--a comforting clatter of compliments given to the chef and dishes efficiently whisked away by the staff. Coffee and tea were offered and brought, and an array of desserts were laid in place of the savory dishes we'd decimated.

I sampled the desserts that I wasn't familiar with--balls rolled in toasted coconut, and chocolate truffles with a dusting of chili powder on top. There was also something that looked like flan, and an assortment of cookies. Everything was decadent and rich. I would have to run four miles to make up for it tomorrow, but it was still worth it.

Just when I thought that the meal *had* to be finished, Caio stood.

"These are dangerous times," he said. His smile was a little too controlled to be convincing--it felt as if he was baring his teeth at us. "I'm so glad that you've come home, that you are here to say a final goodbye to your father, may he rest in peace. And I am glad that myself and my men are here to keep you and your guests safe."

He left the table quickly, in what I now realized was a show of power--*he* decided when dinner was over, no one else. Tealight candles in crystal holders glowed and flickered as we pushed back from the table, the light dancing off the abundance of dishes and crystal spread across the red damask tablecloth that suddenly reminded me of blood.

Chapter 7

I wasn't sure what woke me. Everything was the same--the AC piped in fresh, cool air, there was no movement in the hall. But still, I slipped out of the high thread count sheets and pulled a robe over my silk pajamas.

"What is it?" Hyde whispered.

"Nothing," I said. "I want to look around."

"Want me to come with you?" he wiped the sleep from his eyes and pulled back the sheets.

"No," I said. "If I need you, you'll hear it. Nothing's wrong. I just want to look."

"Alright," he said, begrudgingly. "I'm here if you need me."

I slipped out into the hall. Bruno huffed as he stood and ambled out after me. He was a smart dog and knew that sometimes I liked a midnight snack if I couldn't sleep.

And then there were the other times, more numerous, when I only *thought* I wanted a midnight snack, so he was the one who got to eat it.

Across the hall, Camilla's door was ajar. I stuck my head in. She wasn't in bed, but her sheets were mussed. Down the hall was the great room we'd had drinks in. When I didn't turn into the kitchen, Bruno dutifully followed me anyway, my hand brushing the top of his back as we went. I took the staircase up, my feet soundless on the plush carpeting. The stairs brought me to the corner of a hallway--to the left was darkness, but a light was on in a room down to the right.

As I turned that direction, a spitting, white flash of fluff darted across my path, pausing only to take a swipe at my ankles before disappearing down the dark hallway with a parting hiss.

"Fucking cat," I said, pressing a hand to my chest to calm my racing heart.

Bruno gave a solemn, low 'boof', as if to chastise Sir Darcy or agree with my assessment.

"You know you're the best doggo that ever lived, right?" I said, pausing to scruggle his velvet ears. "You're just the bestest, most cutest sweetie pie that ever was."

Bruno exhaled a whuff of air, as if to say 'duh', and we continued on our way.

I found Camilla in the study, sitting on a leather Chesterfield sofa, staring at the painting of a man on the wall. I recognized the man in the painting as her father, Thiago.

"He wasn't that tall," she said. "But he made it clear that he would like to appear tall. He told the painter that, without actually having to say the words."

"Some people are good at that. I've always been a fan of the clear and direct route, myself." I settled onto the couch next to her and stared at the painting, too. "There's something off about his face."

"My father made the man fix his scar, and harden his jaw. It never looked quite human, after that. But the scar was from something he'd never talk about--I think it was probably a takeover attempt that came a little too close, something of that nature."

"Huh." I turned toward her. "What are you doing up?"

"I opened the safe." Her voice was toneless. She jerked her head toward the desk without looking away from the painting.

"How did you know the code?" I asked, my eyes round.

I stood and rounded the desk. The paper on top read *'Last Will and Testament of Thiago Alexander Almeida'*.

"The prompt was that it was six digits of the one I loved above all others."

"Who's that?"

"My nanny, Maria. My father and I fought about it when I left. I told him that I never should have come back after college. He asked why I had, and I admitted that at first, it had only been to attend the funeral of Maria. In my grief, I decided to stay, decided to try and make a familial connection with my actual family. It was his final mockery of me. He knew that I wouldn't come back for his funeral."

"But you came back for hers," I breathed.

"Yes."

I let that sink in for a moment, that a nanny had been more dear to Camilla than her own father. I skimmed the document in my hand, and my heart sank.

"That's not the only interesting thing," Camilla continued. "When I opened the safe, it had a record of the first attempt to open it. The combination that Alex tried was your birthday."

"Shit." I frowned.

If Alex thought that I was the person that Camilla loved above all others, then he might try and use me as leverage against her. My presence here was supposed to help protect her, not make her more vulnerable.

"Yes," she said. "Keep Hyde close."

I smirked. "That's not really an issue. Apparently, him getting shot has made him more paranoid about *my* safety, not his."

Camilla smiled gently. "That's not why he is more paranoid about you. I think it has more to do with the declarations that came out because he was shot."

"Part of me wonders if he let himself get shot, just so I'd say it back to him."

She chuckled. "I was shocked that you told him you loved him, even when he might be dying. "

"Really, Camilla? All the four-letter words in my repertoire, and 'love' is the word that shocks you?"

"Coming from you, yes."

I grinned. "I wasn't going to let myself be pressured into it. But it's true."

"I think you were the last one to know."

"Maybe," I said with a shrug. "What are you going to do about this?" I waved the paper. We had both been ignoring the billion-dollar elephant in the room until now.

"Part of me wants to burn the will. Go home and pretend I never got the safe open."

"That's a valid option." I was serious.

The words on the paper I held were dangerous... dangerous to Camilla, dangerous to me, dangerous to the relatively comfortable life we'd carved out with the team.

"Why do you think he did it?" I asked, scanning the document again.

"Left it all to me?" Camilla said with a resigned smirk. "He always hated that I wasn't more involved. Even when I was second to Alex and then to Caio, it wasn't enough. Plus, this was in the safe, too."

She tossed me a little figurine. It was the bust of Abraham Lincoln done in cheap brass. I glanced up, the question as plain on my face as if I had spoken it aloud.

"I wrote my thesis on Lincoln's influence on the American Civil War. I found his leadership style inspiring. My father, however, got a copy and sent it to me with red pen marks all over it. He had some choice words regarding my assessment that the people would not have followed Lincoln half so well if he would have been a tyrant."

"But what does it have to do with this situation?" I

turned the brass figurine over in my fingers. It was already warm from Camilla's hands.

"Look at the inscription on the bottom."

I flipped the small Lincoln bust, and etched on the bottom were the words, *A house divided against itself cannot stand.*

"Oh," I said, seeing the situation more clearly, like someone had just lifted smudged glasses from my eyes. "That's way worse than I originally thought."

"Yes. And leave it to Thiago to get the source of his quote incorrect. That's a verse from the Bible; it didn't originate from Abraham Lincoln."

"He wants you to lead." The hair on my arms stood and I felt chilled.

"I believe so," Camilla said, quietly. "He has backed me into a corner in a very tidy manner."

"Ok," I said, slowly. "What are you thinking?"

"Thiago left me all the accounts. He left me all the businesses. He left me a list of men who were loyal enough to him that they would abide by his wishes and follow me. My father left me a very clear blueprint for a nearly bloodless transition of power."

"*Nearly* bloodless?" I asked.

"He also made a list of people within the organization who should be eliminated prior to my claim." Camilla rubbed her temples.

"Ah," I said. "Well. How long is *that* list?"

"Fewer than ten, actually. Considering my father's

nature, it's a short list. The real problem is the last two people on it."

She handed over a sheaf of paper. I skimmed the list, only recognizing three of the names until I got to the bottom two. In clear handwriting, Thiago Almeida had written, *Caio Almeida* followed by *Alex Almeida.*

"He can't be serious!" My head jerked up and I met Camilla's eyes.

"My father wasn't in the practice of making jokes." The corners of her mouth dipped into a slight frown. "If I were to take up the leadership, they might band together and kill me, take things back over."

My mind reeled.

Camilla handed me another piece of paper. "He left me a letter, too."

I snatched it and began to read.

Camilla,

I am dying. As a young man, I would hear stories of men on their death beds. They regretted things. Sometimes, they regretted the very things that had brought them fame and fortune. In my youth, I thought these men fools. I wondered how anyone could ever regret having power, no matter how they had obtained it. I think it is ironic that I am now dying and, for the first time, I have regrets.

I have created two monsters. You think that you know Caio, and maybe you do. But you do not know Alex. The Alex of your youth is dead and gone. He had some principles when he got out of college. I took it as a sign of weakness, of American softness that had seeped into his bones while he got his education. Maybe things would have been different if I would have listened to his ideas, but I didn't. Instead, I beat them out of him. He turned colder than I could have imagined. A younger me might have been proud, but truthfully, I became frightened of him, of his ambition. I might have been able to change him, once. I fear what will happen if Alex gets his way.

But my brother, crafty as he is, is not fit to lead, either. He is a blunt hammer--prone to succumbing to flattery and always choosing the wrong people to surround himself with. He would see this country burn to the ground if it turned against him.

These last few years have been a delicate dance, Camilla. A ravenous jackal on my right, a poisonous adder on my left. I am sorry--this is the legacy I leave to you. I cannot find a way out. It is my prayer that you will succeed where I have failed. I know what position this will put you in. I pray that in time, you will be able to forgive me.

-THIAGO

"WHAT IS it with dead guys and their letters?" I said, thinking of a recent case. "Nevermind. What are you going to do?"

"This doesn't change my plans. I want to figure out

who's the best person to lead, then hand control to them and get back to life."

"So who are these other people on the list?" I said, sinking back down next to Camilla on the couch.

Bruno took that as his cue, and he clambered up into the empty space next to me and laid his huge head in my lap.

"Is this ok?" I asked Camilla, gesturing to the massive animal on her leather couch. "I swear, he has no manners."

Camilla waved her hand dismissively. "It's fine. He can lay on anything. I don't care."

"Glad to hear it, 'cause you know how he is."

I studied the list once more.

Camilla said, "I recognize a lot of the names on the list. I even agree with my father's assessment, for some of those names. But I don't know who a couple of the people are." She rubbed her face. "It is so weird being back here. I mean, I thought I would never see this place again. I never *planned* on seeing it again. But yet, here we are."

"What's the weirdest part?"

"Probably the fact that nothing has changed, but it all looks so different to me. And so many of the same people are still here! I can't imagine that. I thought that some of these people would have gotten out somehow, but they didn't..."

She trailed off.

"What's the deal with Tristao?" I asked. "Don't think I didn't notice *that* undercurrent."

Camilla sighed. "We were very close. Lovers."

I swatted at Camilla's arm, delighted. "I knew it!"

"But when I left, he would not come with me. I wanted to start over, start fresh. But this land, this life? It's all he's ever known, all he ever wanted."

I could hear the sorrow in her voice over something that had happened years and years ago. I remembered another conversation, much like this one, that Camilla and I had after a bottle of exceptional Pinot Noir. I had teased her about trying online dating, told her to download an app. She'd mentioned that she had already met the love of her life, but it wasn't meant to be.

"Wait," I said, sitting up straighter. "Is he your one great love?"

Camilla smiled, but it was sad. "Yes, he was."

"Oh, Camilla, I'm so sorry. And seeing him like that--without any warning--that must have been hard."

She nodded. "It is alright. We have both moved on. He had another life, after I left. So did I, even though mine didn't include marriage or children."

"Still. It couldn't have been easy."

"No," she said. "Not easy. But I still wouldn't change how things worked out for us. I know that his late wife made him happy while she was alive, and he has children. If we couldn't be together, then that is one thing, but I still wished him happiness. It seems he found it. I am glad."

She didn't sound glad, but I didn't point that out. I knew what it was like to have been in a relationship where you thought that person was The One. When it didn't turn out to be true, the initial pain was breathtaking, and it echoed for a long time.

"What are you going to do about this?" I asked flapping the list in her direction.

"I don't know," she said.

Even after we talked deep into the night, I didn't know the right thing to do, either.

Chapter 8

The next morning was clear and bright. I woke up early enough to feel the lingering crisp of morning, which was quickly engulfed by the rising tide of humidity and heat. I brushed my teeth, splashed some water on my face, and got ready quickly, throwing my hair up in a bun on top of my head and pulling a sundress on.

It was one that Frankie had ordered for me during our short stay in Miami. It was crossed in front, tied around the waist, and flowed down to just graze the tops of my feet, which were encased in strappy flat sandals. It was expensive and beautiful, but more importantly, it was loose enough to hide the holster and pistol I had strapped to my thigh.

We had breakfast on the deck that was off the great room of the family wing. There were no stairs to the deck on the outside--I guessed that was considered too much of a security risk for the family wing. The height allowed views of the vast gardens--green lawn and exuberant profusions of flowers that were neatly contained within strictly edged planters.

I sipped my coffee and watched as a teenage boy in pressed khaki pants and a white polo shirt wound the cranks on the row of umbrellas over the chaise lounges at the edge of the pool. It looked like a row of white flowers slowly opening one by one. He then placed a rolled white towel on the foot of every chaise. I wondered if this was a special effort for our benefit, or if this was part of his regular, daily routine. How many actions like this were habit, unnecessary and wasted effort? Would those towels be stored and laid out again tomorrow? Or would some poor maid in the bowels of the house wash, dry, and refold them before they were set out again?

I waited until the maid had ducked inside the house for a moment and said, "Frankie, I need a full workup on everyone on this list."

I slid a copy of Thiago's list over to her.

She picked it up and frowned at it. "I recognize several of the names as people within the organization, but there are some I don't know. What is this?"

I looked to Camilla. However much we told everyone else was up to her.

"The list my father gave me. In his opinion, these are the people I need to kill in order to assure my seamless transition as leader of the Almeida cartel."

There was a beat of silence, then Hyde said, "Is that what you want?"

"No." Camilla's voice was grave. "But I do need to know why my father thought these people were threats."

"Right." I nodded. "These people may end up being useful, or they may need to be taken out. That's where Frankie's research comes in."

She was studying the list. "I obviously have dossiers on Alex and Caio," she said. "But there are a few people on here I'm not familiar with."

"So that goes to the top of your to-do's," I said. "I know that you're swamped and the financials are a mess, but we're going to make contact with Luis and get some help on that end."

Frankie nodded and started clicking away on her keyboard. The silence lingered, thickened, then curdled.

With the undercurrents of relational demise swirling between Frankie and Howard, and the stress that Camilla was under, our team meetings were becoming awkward, stilted things. I didn't realize how much I missed Howard's uncouth comments or the banter between him and Frankie until it was gone. It felt like a bad family Thanksgiving--where everyone knows what the issue is, but no one is willing to address it head-on, because there isn't any point. It would just end up in a screaming match or icy silence.

Bruno interrupted my train of thought by snuffling my hand. I frowned down at him, then looked at the maid, who was standing like a silent sentry on one side of the double glass doors.

"My dog is hungry. Do you guys have dog food, or is there a place I can buy some for him?"

She nodded and left.

"Do you know most of the staff, Camilla?" Frankie asked.

"For the most part, no." Camilla frowned. "If you see someone under thirty, I probably don't know them. But some of the old standbys, I know."

"What about that guy, the one at dinner last night?" Hyde asked. "Tristao?"

Camilla frowned again. I knew that Hyde had tried to keep the question light, but there were some topics that would never be easy. This seemed like one of those to Camilla. Then again, maybe it was just this place. Camilla hadn't really smiled or laughed since we'd touched down on her native soil.

I knew that the revelation that her father had left all his assets to her wasn't helping. Instead of feeling freed by her father's death, his final actions had made Camilla feel trapped, wound up in a family and political drama that she'd never wanted or asked for. I thought of the documents locked back in that safe, about the ramifications of what Thiago's last wishes were.

"Tristao and I were close, once," Camilla began, then faltered. "Then I moved away, and he married, had children."

The pause that followed this announcement was tense

and heavy. The air felt dense with the words, like a thunderstorm was rolling in. We all knew what 'used to be close' meant. Camilla had just told them more of her past, more of the heartbreak of this place.

"And where do you think he stands, in terms of your uncle's plans for the cartel?" Howard said.

"I don't know. I don't know what Caio's plans are for the cartel. I don't even think *he* knows. He just wants the power. I think that is his sole focus right now." She chewed her pastry, looking thoughtful. "But I bet that Alex has concrete plans that extend past gaining control. I hated playing chess with my brother. He was always playing three steps ahead. He could visualize multiple hypothetical outcomes and plan for them all at once. I'm not going to lie...it bothers me that he hasn't visited yet, that he hasn't contacted me this entire time. If he is waiting in the shadows...there's a reason."

At Camilla's dire words, I felt edgy. I resisted the urge to look over my shoulder, to scan the trees at the edge of the property for the glint of a sniper rifle.

"If we don't know what your uncle and brother are up to, how are you going to choose who gets control?" Howard said, feeding a piece of bacon to Sir Darcy under the table.

"I don't know," Camilla said. "We really need to unravel the finances, see who is doing what, whose fingers are in which pies."

"What..." Frankie started to ask, but stopped when the maid stepped back through the door with a stainless steel bowl of food.

"We didn't have dog food, ma'am, but the cook assembled a meal that I hope meets your approval?" she sounded tentative, as she showed me the contents of the bowl. "There's ground beef, raw eggs, some cooked sweet potato, and a little bit of plain cooked rice."

And there was a lot of it.

"Thanks," I said, taking the dish. "This is perfect." I stood and walked to the edge of the space, setting the bowl down far away from our table, so Bruno's enthusiastic dive into his meal wouldn't send food shrapnel onto anyone. "Would you please grab six towels?"

The maid looked momentarily confused, but she nodded and left.

"What should we do about Alex?" Frankie said, finally getting back to the conversation.

"Nothing, yet," Camilla said. "There's no way to predict what he's thinking. Maybe he is being patient, and waiting to see what my reaction will be. I wouldn't doubt that he has spies here. He probably has people close to Caio, though my uncle wouldn't ever want to believe it. But I don't think Alex is the type to just bide his time, although it would be nice to think that. My gut says he has a plan to try and manipulate me into doing what he wants."

"But how could he know that you have anything to offer him yet?" Hyde asked, carefully.

"My support in this conflict could be the deciding factor," Camilla said. "Family is still the most important thing to many people in this culture. If I am viewed to give my support to either side, that side will most likely have the support of the men on the ground...at least, those whose loyalty can be swayed."

The maid returned with a stack of towels and looked at me.

"Thanks. Please pass them out."

She did. To her credit, she refrained from raising her eyebrows as we each took one and spread it over our laps like it was normal. Which, to us, it was. The maid was left holding one, and lifted it slightly, in question.

"Oh, that one's for you," I said, waving my hand.

She resumed her place near the door, looking a little bewildered.

"So what is the plan for the day?" I asked, a bright smile that I didn't quite feel on my face. "Is there shopping in that town that we passed?"

"Yes," Camilla said. "Not as many antiques, although there is one shop you should check out. But there are many local artisans and lots of delicious food in the market."

As she spoke, Bruno had finished his meal and lumbered over, strings of drool dangling from each of his jowls, a little froth and bits of food on his chin. Bruno laid his massive head in Hyde's lap, and the strings of drool snapped as they were wiped with the towel. I saw the maid's eyes widen, and she unfurled her towel and held it in a defensive position, like a bullfighter with a cape.

"I'd like to see the town, too," Hyde said, slipping a sausage from his plate to Bruno, who instantly began to drool again.

"Sounds good to me," Frankie said. "Let's all go."

As if on cue, Caio and two of his men stepped through the door.

"Where are you going?" he said with a smile that didn't quite crinkle the corners of his eyes.

"Into town," Camilla said, dabbing her mouth with a linen napkin. "My guests want to shop and see the sights."

"Wonderful!" he said. "There is a little church on the hill overlooking the lake. Very quaint, very old. You should take a picnic lunch and eat on the grounds. There are huge jacaranda trees that bloom this time of year. You are very lucky to come during this time. I will send Ignacio and Jorge to accompany you."

Jorge looked neutral at the news, but Ignacio's lip curled. At that moment, Bruno shook his head, slinging a six inch drool missile directly onto Ignacio's face.

"Aack!" he cried, slapping the slime from his cheek and chin. "That fucking dog!" He started forward, towards Bruno, but Caio put a hand to his chest.

"Ignacio," he snapped. "Do not be rude to Camilla's guests."

Ignacio looked as if he wanted to strangle Bruno, then all of us, but he snapped his mouth shut and yanked the towel from the maid to wipe his face when she offered it.

"Excellent," Caio said, clasping his hands. "Camilla, you will stay with me, as we have much to discuss. Family business. You understand. But your guests can have a lovely day of sightseeing, and we will all meet for dinner again this evening. We will have special guests again tonight, so please have them back by early evening, as they will need time to get ready. It will be a formal dinner tonight, so you ladies may want to shop for a new purse or barette, or whatnot. And the dog..." Here, he frowned.

"Oh, I'll take him for a walk before we leave, and then he can just nap inside my room," I said, waving my hand. "He's very lazy during the day. The maids can just clean around him. Although be sure they know he doesn't like the vacuum."

"Excellent," Caio said. He looked at his watch. "Let's plan on the helicopter being in the air in one hour, yes?"

He turned and left, his entourage trailing him, without waiting for an answer.

Less than an hour later, we were in the chopper flying back the way we'd come the day before. It was different that helicopters were the preferred method of transportation, but crime was notorious in Brazil. Muggings and kidnappings for ransom were a part of life here, and the risk became greater the wealthier you appeared to be.

We landed and transferred to a dark SUV, with our security guards taking the two front seats. The helicopter took off before we were out of the parking lot. The car was a black, expensive SUV with a cream leather interior. The air conditioners had been running for some time before we got in, so the heat and humidity were only briefly problematic. It seemed hotter here than at the house, possibly because of the amount of concrete and paving.

The city was a strange juxtaposition. One block would be high-end stores--concrete and glass monuments to excess, with designer stores, some French, some American, some Brazilian. Then, a couple blocks away, potholes decimated the roads and apartment buildings with patched metal roofs and laundry hanging from each cinder block balcony loomed over us. Extreme wealth next to extreme poverty. Even so, the city was beautiful. Bright colors, lush foliage, and a shimmering heat suffused the buildings.

The people were tan and the smiles I saw from behind the bullet-proof, tinted windows seemed genuine. It made sense--the things that inspire happiness are found at every socio-economic level. Love, family, friends, shared meals-- these things aren't reserved for those with gargantuan bank account balances.

"Where are we going?" Frankie asked, leaning forward to speak to Jorge.

"We are headed toward the shopping center. Miss Camilla told me to take you to *Casa Amarela*, which sells antiques, and there are clothing stores nearby that she thought you would enjoy, Miss Frankie. After that, we can head to the open-air markets, and we packed a picnic basket for your lunch at the church."

"Great, thanks," she said.

It didn't escape my notice that while Jorge seemed perfectly happy to be our guide for the day, it seemed to rankle Ignacio. Every time one of us spoke or asked a question, his frown seemed to deepen. He was two clicks away from crossing his arms and stamping his foot like a petulant child.

I didn't care that he didn't like us, didn't want to play

guard and tour guide. He thought it was beneath him, and maybe we could use that. I needed to get a message out to Luis, and I hadn't felt comfortable making the call from the Almeida compound. I had my cell phone in my purse. I hoped I could get fifteen minutes alone to make the call today.

I played my part at the antiques store--buying several large pieces and arranging for their shipment. Frankie and I bought new dresses at an upscale clothing store, too. But in both these instances, there wasn't enough time or cover for me to slip away and make a call to Luis. I had my fingers crossed that our next stop would be the one that gave me the chance.

Chapter 9

The market felt open air, but it was encased within a very tall, concrete building with open archways to the streets beyond. Inside was a clatter of people trying to be heard, booths using every centimeter of space to display and sell their often disjointed wares. A fruit stall was not just a fruit stall--the same vendor that had rows of orderly oranges stacked more masterfully than a Jenga game also had cotton candy and stuffed animals hanging above his head, a strip of cell phone chargers along one wall, and cigarettes, lighters, and condoms along the other. Everyone seemed to have a bit of everything, and the posted price was just a starting point for negotiation.

Some stalls were nothing more than a flimsy easy-up erected over plastic tables, lending a temporary quality to the scene, like we had stepped into some sort of weekly rummage sale that would be torn down by nightfall. Other shops appeared more permanent--shipping containers with roll-up doors here and there, and a section of stalls built from cinder block and sheets of brightly painted plywood in the center.

And the smells--grilled fish from one direction, the heady aroma of fresh-baked bread from another. We passed a man flipping and basting beef on skewers on a barbecue. A woman nearby called out about her hot cheese bread, but she didn't need to bother--the scent of the fried dough around a ball of melted cheese was all the advertisement she could ask for. Breakfast hadn't been that long ago, but my stomach rumbled in appreciation all the same.

It was huge and loud and disorienting, perfect for me to escape Ignacio's seething presence and Jorge's watchful eyes to find some privacy to make a phone call. Howard and Frankie were going to cause some sort of distraction--a sprained ankle for Frankie--and then Hyde and I would slip away while our tour guides were distracted. I would have gone alone, but a foreign woman who looked relatively wealthy probably shouldn't be wandering around unguarded.

Fifteen minutes in, I could see the determined jut of Frankie's chin, and I knew she was about to do something. It was her tell, one of the reasons she probably shouldn't play poker for money.

"Howard," she demanded. "We need to talk."

Uh oh. She had gone off-script.

He looked wary, his eyes like a hunted deer. "What about?"

"Us," Frankie said, clenching her fist. "I'm sorry that I hurt you, but you can't go on ignoring me like this."

Hyde grabbed my hand and gave a gentle tug. I knew that this was the distraction we'd been waiting for, but heaven help me, I wanted to listen, too.

"I'm not," he said. The color had already risen in his face.

"You are. And I understand that you don't want to be with me anymore...like that." Frankie swallowed. "But we need to get along. You can't keep hiding."

Howard's face was pink now, the color of an under-cooked hamburger. "I haven't been hiding."

Frankie's expression was resolved. "Yeah, you have. Hiding like a little kid behind mommy and daddy. Hiding like a little *bitch*."

"Whoa!" I whispered to Hyde as he led me away. "Shots fired!"

"I am *not* a bitch!" Howard yelled. Cords stood out in stark relief on his neck. "If anyone has been a bitch in this situation, it's you!"

"Big mistake, Howard," I said under my breath.

People around us stopped and looked, and the decibels of the market activity in our area dropped by several notches as people looked for the source of the outburst. Ignacio and Jorge looked shocked and stepped towards

Howard and Frankie like they didn't quite know what to do.

"That's our cue," Hyde murmured.

We let the crowd engulf us, then wove the opposite direction like two salmon swimming upstream. It seemed that some of the shoppers wanted to get a look, wanted to see and hear the free tele-novella that was being played out live in the market. I could hear Frankie and Howard's raised voices, but I couldn't hear their words any longer. Hyde and I ducked around the back of a shipping container, and I wrestled my phone from my purse.

I squatted down and dialed the numbers I'd dialed a hundred times before.

"Daisy Cleaning Service, how can I help you?" A cheery, female voice answered.

"I need to place an order."

"I can certainly help you with that. Anytime you're ready, go ahead."

"Please tell him that Elayna Miller is calling and that I need a forensic accountant, preferably on-site near Sao Paulo within the next few days."

I rattled off the GPS coordinates.

"Would you like a receipt emailed to the address on file?"

"Yes."

"Have a great day, and thank you for choosing Daisy Cleaning Service."

There was a click, and I smiled up at Hyde. "Ok, we can..."

My words cut off when Hyde whirled around and grunted.

I sprang to my feet, but before I could move, two men rushed me, one from behind, one in front of me. My hands were incapacitated before I could strike out, but I got a couple of solid kicks in before a hood was jammed over my face. I kicked out again, but someone caught it, yanking me off my feet.

"Careful!" the man behind me hissed. He caught my shoulders before I hit the ground.

I kicked out again and made contact, heard a grunt and a curse. Then I heard the plastic whir of zip ties and felt them bite into my ankles. Just that quickly, I was useless, my hands behind my back, my ankles together.

The man grunted as he lifted me, and I heard the soft noise of an engine, the creak of a car door. A van? A truck? I could see light variations through the hood over my head, but not much else. I was lifted and placed on scratchy carpeting. My sundress rode up to my thighs, and I flinched as I felt a hand there, a brief touch, and then my sundress hem was back to my ankles.

I felt Hyde when they lifted him and laid him out next to me. The cadence of his breathing, deep and slow, made me think that he was unconscious, whether from a sleeper hold or drugs, I didn't know. My guess was drugs. It's what I would have done.

Think. Think.

This wasn't an average mugging, obviously. So...what?

A kidnapping for ransom? Possibly. Although I thought it was more than that.

Why do you think that? I asked myself.

They would have left Hyde behind. They only needed one target. Also, they didn't have accents. The words I had heard were spoken in clean, perfect, unaccented English.

My nose wrinkled under the scratchy fabric of the hood. *Foreigners?* Why on earth would a group of well-organized foreigners single me out for an abduction? Who even knew I was in Brazil?

When I figured it out, I sat up. "Oh, come on, guys," I said. "How far are we going?"

I heard one of them snort incredulously. "They did say she was smart."

"Shut up, Sanders."

"Yeah," I said. "Shut up, Sanders. Where's your boss? And if you hurt my friend or ruined my dress, I'm submitting a claim for damages."

One of them chuckled. "We'll be there soon, Miss Miller."

"Can we lose the hood, please? It's hot as hell in this thing."

"Sorry. Orders."

I rolled my eyes, even though they couldn't see me. "You think that you guys could have sprung for a van with air conditioning, at least."

I heard the whir of air through vents. Someone had turned the AC up. I sighed, indignant.

They hadn't lied. It wasn't far. Maybe about five

minutes, and one of them cut the ties at my ankle and helped me out of the back of the van by my elbows.

And then we entered a building, where the sudden lack of sun made it completely black within the hood. But it was cooler, even if it did smell vaguely of mildew, like someone hadn't cleaned the evaporative cooler filters in ten years. I was gently pushed into a chair, and the hood was pulled from my head.

"Really?" I said, blinking in the sudden light. "You couldn't have just *called*?"

The room was dark but cool. There was a single light overhead, and I couldn't see past the small ring of light. But I could hear how the sound moved, and I could tell we were in a big, echoing space. The floor was concrete, and my guess is we were in some sort of large garage or warehouse.

I was sitting in front of a plastic white folding table, the same kind my mother would dress up with a tablecloth and flowers for her garden parties. For a long while, there was a tense silence, enhanced only by the shifting of bodies I could not see.

Finally, a figure detached from the darkness. It was only through my training that I was able to keep the reaction from my face.

He looked different now. Gone was the softness of his smile, the almost self-conscious way he'd push his hair out of his eyes. That hair had now been trimmed and gelled back into the latest style, and it made me sad to see it.

"You're doing fieldwork now?" I asked him.

Wu slid into the seat across the table from me, but it felt like we were a lot further apart than six feet. Time and experiences we hadn't shared stretched between us. I knew how someone could change in the hands of the CIA, how quickly that could happen. I wondered who he was now.

"No. But they thought you might listen better if you saw a familiar face."

He smiled, but it didn't reach his eyes. He was tense, his back straight, and as I shifted forward, his eyes narrowed ever so slightly and he leaned back in his chair.

"You're angry with me." It was a revelation.

All this time, I'd mourned his absence in my team. Wu, the genius, the diamond amidst the slew of cubic zirconiums that were tech workers in California. He'd built things for me, inventions that we still used, minions. I hadn't brought any to Brazil, afraid they'd be confiscated by the Almeidas if they found us, which they had.

Wu's goodbye message to our team had been sad, but not angry. He'd ignored several invitations from the CIA, and they didn't take kindly to that. So they'd sent a team to retrieve Wu, and members of my team were hurt in the process. It had never occurred to me that he'd be angry at me, but he was.

"You're angry," I repeated. "Why?"

He shook his head and smirked. It was a mean smile, and I felt a pang in my heart for it. I don't think I'd ever seen that expression on his face before--bitterness, that's what that was. Bitterness that had festered into anger, maybe even hate. I cringed internally.

"Have they been that bad to you, then?" I said. "Your message--it seemed hopeful."

He shook his head again, and his lip curled. "You didn't even try," he said. "Anyone else, and you would have moved heaven and earth to get them back. But me? You traded me for a pardon."

"Is *that* what they told you?" I said, jerking forward. My eyes were wide. "That's a lie, Wu. I tried to get you back. I asked the Committee, asked Senator Mathers, even though I knew they probably wouldn't pardon me if I kept pressing. I came to the CIA, met with Nathaniel Spanos. Then that asshole tried to kill me. It was a whole thing."

He frowned, his eyebrows drawn together.

"And they never told you that, did they?" My lips pressed together. I shook my head. "Probably easier to get you to comply and assimilate if you thought your team had turned their backs on you."

He leaned forward, studied my expression as I spoke.

I continued, "Did they ever show you the tape, from the Senate Committee meeting? The one where I asked for you to be released, yet again, and was told no, yet again?"

He shook his head.

"Of course they didn't. Well, Frankie recorded the feed. I can send it to you if you don't believe me."

Wu's expression had become more and more open, more and more like the man I'd known, the gentle guy who wanted to help amputees regain use of their damaged bodies, the guy who chose thoughtful, beautiful Christmas gifts for his team members, the guy who used to catch and release bugs from the office.

I thought of all the times I'd walked in on Wu murmuring to a belly-up Bruno as he scratched his belly. Wu didn't care that Bruno had slobbered on his impeccable outfit; he just loved him. And Wu had been with the CIA for almost a year. The CIA was a terrible place for someone so sensitive, someone who felt injustice so keenly.

"We've gotten off track," a male to my left said. He stepped into the light.

I didn't recognize the agent. He was only a little bit older than me, the crow's feet just starting to settle in around his eyes. His nose was prominent, one of those beaks that proclaimed a European heritage. He peered down the length at me and didn't smile. It made him look like a great bird of prey--a hawk, or a vulture.

"This meeting isn't about your past relationship," he said. "Miss Miller, I am Agent Darby, from the CIA." He sat at another chair across from me.

"Oh, thanks," I said, sarcastically. "Thanks so much for redirecting. Heaven forbid we deviate from what the CIA wants. Unlock my fucking hands before I get really pissed."

He looked a little surprised at my vitriol, but he waved at someone out of my sight. A young, fresh-faced kid with a smattering of freckles across his nose came forward with a set of wire cutters.

"Good heavens," I said, as he snipped my ties off. "Does your mother know you're an agent?"

He chuckled and winked. "Of course not, ma'am. That's against the rules."

I laughed. Agent Darby frowned and waved the guy away. He took his time spreading some papers across the desk. I got the impression that this guy liked the pomp and circumstance of being part of the agency that was, to a lot of people, the boogeyman. I bet he was used to people being impressed by his title, by the purposeful way he organized his official-looking paperwork, at the gravitas that he communicated through tense silence.

I wasn't most people.

I snapped my fingers. "Ok, I'm here. Get to the point."

Someone tried to turn a laugh into a cough, somewhere in the shadows. But Agent Darby and I both heard it. His eyes narrowed.

"I'm sure that even someone with your background can understand the agency's interest in the Almeida cartel," he said.

"Insulting me isn't the best way to start this interaction, buddy."

He sat there, waiting.

"It doesn't surprise me that the agency is interested in the cartel," I said. "What I want to know is why I am here talking to you. What do you want? What is it that you think I can help you with?"

He frowned, but said nothing, just shuffled some paperwork around. I felt like I had ruined his wind up, like I wasn't playing the part that he wanted me to play. Now, he was either being petulant, or he was trying to figure out where to go from here.

"Hey," I said, looking into the darkness. I flicked my hand back and forth between Agent Darby, Wu, and I. "This interaction isn't going well. Anyone else want to jump in and help?"

A sigh, to my right, and then a younger agent, a woman with creamy skin and thick red hair pulled back into a low ponytail, stepped up. She plunked a folding chair down next to Darby.

"I'm Agent Wignow," she said. "We know that Camilla Almeida is the late Thiago Almeida's daughter. We also know that there is a huge power struggle going on between her brother and her uncle. Word is that Camilla Almeida is the key to deciding who gets the power."

"And you want her to choose the side that *you* want," I guessed.

Agent Wignow nodded. "Yes. If the wrong side comes to power, we think it will lead to economic and social instability within Brazil, and may also affect..."

Here, Agent Darby turned his head to glare at Agent Wignow.

"Well," she continued. "Let's just say that we have a vested interest in making sure that whoever the next leader is, that they are open to playing nice with the US Government."

"Fair enough," I said. "But why not call me? Why not email? This is a little dramatic." I spread my hands to encompass the dark room, the single lightbulb, the hood on the table. "I mean, it's downright cliché."

Again, a laugh-turned-cough from the cheap seats. Darby glared out at someone, though I was pretty sure he couldn't see them anymore than I could.

"There were those who thought a more intimidating approach might serve us better," she said, choosing her words carefully.

I rolled my eyes at Agent Darby. "You don't do a lot of field work, do you?"

He sniffed.

"Alright," I said, focusing my attention on Wignow. "What do you need from me? And what support are you willing to give me?"

"We have three full teams in Sao Paulo," she said. "We have, ever since Thiago died."

I frowned. They'd been here for months.

"So we can offer pretty extensive mission support, if needed," she continued. "But obviously, we need to keep our involvement under wraps. We have reason to believe that Camilla is being monitored very closely, but we thought that we might be able to speak to you without anyone noticing. The Brazilian government also has a vested interest in who takes control. Have you seen this man?"

She flipped through a folder and pulled out an 8x10 glossy of a man in a military uniform--a man I'd eaten dinner with just last night.

"No," I lied.

"This is General Gilberto Horta," she said. "Leader of Brazil's armies. Close ties to the Almeidas. The uncle, Caio Almeida, has promised him that if he gets into power, he will support Horta's bid for the Presidency. The United States is not in support of this plan."

"Alright," I said, slowly. "So you'd like..."

"Alexander Almeida to be the leader, yes," she said. She seemed to steady herself, and met my eyes. "Or Camilla Almeida."

Chapter 10

I barely heard the rest of the pitch, that Camilla had spent time in the United States, so she was more likely to be sympathetic to their point of view, that she might be more open to the Brazilian people having freedoms that General Horta would do his best to quash. I sat and listened to it all, but didn't react. I wondered if they knew that was the outcome Camilla and I wanted least. If Agent Wignow knew that, she soldiered on anyway. I was given instructions on how to reach them--hanging a towel over the railing of the family deck would signal someone to contact me.

I was anxious. I knew that our absence would have been noted by now--we'd been gone for at least fifteen minutes, but I wanted to ask a hundred questions. I wanted more time with Wu, time to talk and explain. But I didn't get to do anything more than make meaningful eye contact with him before I was loading back up into the van next to a just-coming-to Hyde.

"What," he said, starting to sit up. Then he thought better of it and slumped back down.

"What did you give him?" I asked Agent Wignow.

"A mild sedative. He'll be groggy for an hour or so, but he'll be fine."

"Next time, don't let that idiot Darby have a say in how you contact me." I pointed at Hyde, who was drooling ever-so-gently. "*This* does not make me want to cooperate with you. Do you get that?"

She nodded.

"And how are we going to explain this to the men watching us?"

Hyde giggled and mumbled something too low for me to hear.

"*That* we do have a plan for," she said.

A FURIOUS IGNACIO found us at one of the bars in the market not five minutes after we'd been dropped off. They'd poured a little cachaça liquor down Hyde's front, ordered me three rounds and watched me take them as shots, and disappeared with a promise to be in touch soon.

"Halloooo," Hyde said to Igancio. "Join us. Have a drink. May I push in your stool?"

Hyde gave a little wave, nothing more than the fluttering of his fingers. It was a decidedly feminine wave, and it made me giggle, the nervous energy finding an unlikely release valve in my laughter, until soon I was nearly doubled over, tears pinching the corners of my eyes.

"It's not that kind of bar, Hyde," I said, hiccuping with laughter.

"You know," Hyde slurred, ignoring Ignacio's enraged presence, and pointing a finger at me. It wavered in the air between us in a slightly circular motion. "I never wanted to own a gay bar, but I think it would be a hoot to name one."

"Yeah?" I said, sipping my drink. It was fruity, but all the sugar in the world couldn't disguise the amount of liquor in it. I grimaced. "What would you name this hypothetical bar?"

"What about 'The Long Shaft' with a mining theme, or a surfing bar called 'Woodie's'? Come on, that's pretty good. I've got loads more."

"I'm sure the gay community is mourning your lack of input on their bar scene," I said sarcastically.

"Hey!" Iganico yelled, his face about a foot away from mine.

I jerked, sloshed my drink a bit down my front. I had completely forgotten he was there. Hyde laughed again, another silent shaking of his shoulders.

"You made me shpill my drink," I said, patting the dampness on my front with a paper towel.

I tried to pull the fabric away from my skin, tried to duck my head to see the damage, but I ended up reeling in a circular motion on my barstool. I felt like my head was a plumb-bob on a string that was waiting to stop at level.

"We have to go," Ignacio hissed, grabbing my upper arm.

"That's one," Hyde said, all mirth gone from his voice. It had taken on an edge, a deepness, and although he spoke more quietly than he had moments ago, it was the kind of tone that everyone nearby heard, the same reason a quiet rattlesnake rattle still stops everyone nearby.

Danger, the tone clearly said.

"Touch her again, and you're going to have problems."

Ignacio snarled, but immediately released me. I noticed that Hyde hadn't mentioned where the problem would come from, me or him. I smirked.

"Oh, come on," I said, acting like he was joking. "We're all friends here. Reynaldo, can't we buy you a drink?"

"It's Igancio," he hissed. "And we've been looking for you for an hour."

I squinted down at my wrist, even though I wasn't wearing a watch. "No. We just stopped for a drunk. Ha! I meant, a *drink*."

"Everyone is waiting for you." The hands on his hips and the tension in his posture told me that he wasn't used to waiting for anyone.

"Well, shoot," I said. "Hyde, pay the bartender. We'd better go."

I slid off the bar stool and leaned against it until I found my center of gravity. Hyde threw a few bills on the counter. I didn't see what denominations they were in, but the kid's eyes went wide, and he whisked them out of sight and into his pocket so fast it looked like one of those slight of hand magic tricks. *Now you see it, now it's mine.*

I wrapped my arm around Hyde's middle when he slid from his barstool, and he wrapped his arm around my shoulder. I knew that whatever I was feeling, he had it ten times worse. After all, I'd had three shots. He'd been drugged.

We staggered together, each of us pressing toward the other like we were in a demented game of three-legged race. A very slow, crooked race. It took us a while to get back to the others. Ignacio kept sighing dramatically and muttering under his breath in Portuguese. It wasn't hard to guess what he was saying. His attitude towards us since we'd first met him was that he thought that our presence was a nuisance, and it was beneath him to guard or even be around us.

That was fine. I could work with negative attitudes like that. I could mold that in my favor. Hell, I already had. I giggled at the thought, and Hyde patted my head too hard, like he was Lennie and I was a rabbit. I snorted at the thought.

"How drunk *are* you?" Hyde asked, poking me in the ribs until I squirmed away.

"You shut it, or I'll leave and let you fall over."

"You wouldn't."

"Be nice or I might."

"You know why you wouldn't?" he said. "Cause you looooove me."

He laughed like it was hilarious, and I punched him in the side.

"Ugh, too hard," he said. "Go easy on me. I've been drugged."

"It was just alcohol, Hyde," I said, a little too loudly. "Why are you so cranky, Reynaldo?"

Ignacio didn't answer me--just kept plodding doggedly forward.

"It's cause his name isn't Reynaldo, honey. It's Nas. Like the artist currently known as Nas."

I snorted.

Unsurprisingly, we didn't end up picnicking at the quaint little church. Hyde and I were wrecked. Howard and Frankie were back to awkwardness--although it was Howard who kept sneaking looks at Frankie now, not the other way around. I was dying to know what had been said, but I couldn't ask until I got Frankie alone.

IGNACIO AND JORGE seemed relieved to drop us off at the doors to the family wing. They didn't talk to us much, and Jorge thrust the picnic basket into Frankie's arms before they turned and strode quickly away.

"What happened?" Frankie hissed, when we were alone in the family wing's dining room.

This one wasn't nearly as grand as the formal dining room in the main part of the house. The table here only sat twelve, and the wood paneling was lighter, the carpet blue. It felt cozier-- less like a display of wealth and more like a room a family might actually eat in.

I shook my head. "The short version is that we got the message out to Luis. Frankie, keep an eye out for his email and let me know when we should expect someone to arrive."

Luis' emails were written in code. They looked just like a receipt from a cleaning service, but had an embedded file in the logo image that held all the pertinent, encrypted information.

"Fine, fine," she said, waving her hand dismissively. "But then they couldn't find you. *We* couldn't find you. What happened?"

My eyes cut to Hyde, but he was no help. He'd taken a chair, and was sleeping with his head on one large arm on the table.

"We got waylaid. Lost. Ended up at a bar."

I didn't want to tell them the truth--that once again, the CIA was involved in one of our cases, that they wanted Camilla in charge of the Almeida cartel. Sure, Agent Wignow had presented another option--Alex. But I was guessing that Alex was one of the last people who should be given lots of power and sway over the direction of anything, let alone a country.

No, the CIA wanted Camilla in control. I was going to hold that information back from my team until I could see a way around it. I didn't need them worrying about the possibility, not when there was so much else to deal with. And selfishly, I didn't want Camilla to know. I didn't want her to feel pressured to stay--didn't even want the possibility of staying on her radar.

Deep down I knew that I was acting like a child--pretending that if I didn't look at the problem, it didn't exist. I just wanted more time... time to think about it, time to run it past Hyde when he wasn't literally drugged to the point of drooling. There were already too many actors in this play--I was going to ignore this new diva as long as possible.

I could tell that Frankie wasn't buying what I was selling. Hyde never got lost--the man had a nearly infallible brain compass. And Hyde and I would never just slip off to a bar, not when the rest of the team was waiting, worrying about us. But Frankie also knew me--knew that if I didn't feel like sharing the details, there was a reason.

"Fine," she said, her eyes narrowed.

"And what about you?" I said, crossing my arms. It hadn't escaped my notice that Howard had fled to his room the moment we were back. "What happened after we left? I saw the start of the fight, but we had to leave."

Frankie pursed her lips. "It's not worth repeating."

"Alright. Did you guys at least apologize for calling each other bitches?" I teased.

"We did, actually. I think...I think it might have been good for us to yell. I mean...I would rather *not* yell, obviously. But at least we communicated. At least we got some things out there."

I nodded. "Yeah. Kind of hard to resolve things when he won't even talk to you."

"Exactly." She bit her bottom lip. "We might never go back to how things were. But I still want us to be friends. I've never felt that way about an ex before."

I shrugged. "It doesn't feel like it's quite over, yet. Not to me."

"It might be." Her face was sad. "It really might. But now the ball is in his court. He knows that I want to work it out. That I want to get back together. If he chooses to be an idiot and not take that chance, that's on him. I've done all I can for now."

"Fair enough. I'm going to get some food and get this guy into bed," I said, nodding at Hyde. "We both need a nap, but let's plan on a meeting later today. Can you let Camilla know, if you see her?"

Frankie nodded.

"Oh, and send Wu the footage from the Senate Committee hearing," I added.

Her eyes narrowed again. "Why? That was months ago."

"I was thinking about him today. I want him to know that we tried to get him back."

Chapter 11

I set an alarm before I slipped into the cool, clean sheets. Hyde hadn't bothered--he'd just kicked off his shoes and sprawled on his side of the bed. I hoped that he'd feel normal again once he woke. But I couldn't sleep--I just laid there and stared at the ceiling, wondering what Camilla was dealing with today, thinking about what the CIA had told me. Really, they hadn't told me anything, just that General Horta wasn't the man they wanted to lead the country. But they hadn't said why, and when Wignow had started, Darby shut her down.

I tossed and turned, listening to Hyde's deep breathing until my alarm sounded. We made our way to the dining room where the others were already waiting. Frankie had her travel projector and screen assembled, so I figured she had something to tell us. Camilla had pastries and strong coffee waiting. She poured a cup for me and one for a bleary-looking Hyde. I wondered if they'd accidentally overdosed him--it had been far longer than an hour and he still looked exhausted.

I shoved a flaky apple turnover into my mouth and mumbled, "Let's get started."

"Ok, I have an update on that list," Frankie said, waving a file at us. I would have printed you all a copy, except that we are keeping this on the down-low, so I only printed one." She raised her eyebrows at Camilla, who nodded in confirmation.

"Ok," Frankie continued. "We all know Alex and Caio, why they were on the list. So let's start with Manuel Cazacas, 43." She pressed a remote, and her mini projector clicked on. A candid shot of a man on a cell phone appeared on the screen. "He is the leader of the gang known as the Cobras."

Howard snorted a laugh, interrupting her. "Someone's been watching every after-school special from the eighties."

"In Portuguese, they are called As Cobras."

"Ass Cobras?" Howard shrieked, his voice a full octave higher. "How could they have any street cred with a name like that?"

Frankie raised her eyebrow and coolly replied, "Despite the problems with their moniker, they are quite formidable. Like the Almeida group, they have both legitimate and illegal operations, mainly based in the smaller cities south of Sao Paulo, although in the last few years, they have been trying to make inroads into Almeida territory. As of yet, they've had limited success, but that could change if the Almeidas became even slightly destabilized. Unlike the Almeidas, whose power has become more centralized in the last twenty years, As Cobras have lots of support in the small communities."

"A grass-roots gang," I said. "How quaint."

"Sarcasm noted," Frankie said. "But that's how a lot of these gangs start."

Camilla nodded. "That's how my grandfather started. He and his friends could not find honest work. So they created dishonest work."

"But the Cobras don't have near the resources that the Almeidas do," Frankie continued. "Their businesses are mostly small markets, bars, and brothels. They are pimps, small-time gun runners, and drug dealers. Until recently, their leadership was somewhat divided between Manuel and his brother Pedro. But Pedro died in a car accident that some claim was not an accident at all. Since then, Manuel has been consolidating power, making bigger moves. He seems like the brains in the operation, where his brother was a bit more reckless and scattered."

"Alright," Camilla said. "So Father thought he was a threat. Who else?"

"Heitor Pereira. Alex's second in command."

Another click and the picture changed to a handsome man in a suit. He appeared to be smiling for the picture. I tried to ignore the pretty woman and the cute kids who flanked him-- I didn't want to think of him as a husband, a father.

"He manages Alexander's legal businesses. I'm not sure

exactly why he is on this list, other than that Alex depends on him. But I will keep looking."

Another click. Another picture, this time of a middle-aged man with a paunch. "Delmo Souza. Another leader in Alex's crew. He's a bit lower level, so I'm not sure why he's on here, either."

"I know why my father included him," Camilla said. "He's a complete male chauvinist. He would never accept a female in charge--we clashed when I was working with Alex. In my father's eyes, he would be a threat to me and my leadership."

"Alright," Frankie said, making some notes on her paper. "Next up is Inacio Silva. He is one of Alex's men, the head of his fighting force, for lack of a better term."

He was younger, but had a mean, angular face and beady eyes.

"I completely agree with this one." Camilla's lip peeled back in disgust. "If I'd have stuck around longer, I would have shot him and thrown him in a roadside ditch long ago."

"Geez," Howard said, sarcastically. "Don't hold back. Tell us how you feel."

"He and I butted heads, but that's not why I would have killed him. He, too, is a chauvinist. Likes to hit women. Makes him feel like a big man, apparently."

"Seems like Alex is willing to overlook a lot of problems with his associates," Hyde said.

Camilla shrugged. "It is hard to trust people. Once you build that trust, it is easy to overlook other issues. Alex...he doesn't see things the way other people do. He is more black and white. There is a line in his mind, a line between him and his people and anyone against him. If you're on the right side of that line, he won't question too much."

Hyde frowned, nodded.

"Who else?" Howard said.

"Lucio Oliveira and Fabian Iberia are both Caio's men."

Frankie flipped back and forth between the photos. I recognized one of the men from the first dinner we'd eaten in this house. He'd been quiet, observant.

"But obviously, this list changes, depending on who will be put into power," Frankie said. "I mean, if you want to wipe out Alex's camp and leave Caio's, or vice-versa, then our list is cut almost in half."

Camilla nodded. "There was one more on the list, Frankie."

Frankie winced but clicked the last picture into place. "Tristao dos Santos. Another of Caio's men. We've all met him."

"Yes, but what about him makes my father think he needs to be eliminated?"

"I think it is the dogged loyalty. I haven't found anything else in audio files, phone calls, no police record on the guy. I think he's just supremely faithful, and that's why he's on the list."

Camilla nodded. "I agree with that assessment. Once Tristao gives his loyalty, he will hold true to that, no matter what."

"Yeah," Frankie said, flipping through her paperwork

once again. "I can't even find evidence that the guy had so much as a girlfriend when he was married..." She trailed off, then wrinkled her nose. "Sorry, Camilla."

Camilla waved her hand. "No apology needed. The past is the past."

"Well," I said, polishing off the last of my pastry and wiping my hands. "At least this gives us a starting point. Frankie, dig into these guys, see if you can get us anything else. Until Luis sends a forensic accountant, we won't be able to make a determination on which of these guys we have to move on."

"If any," Howard said. "Once Camilla chooses who inherits the cartel, we can just give the info to the other side."

"That is an option." Hyde tilted his head.

Bruno heaved himself from the floor and meandered out of the room, crop dusting us as he went.

"Bruno, you stink," Frankie said, wrinkling her nose.

"Don't mock him for his smell," I said. "It's just his natural musk."

"That sounds like the name of a terrible perfume," Camilla said.

"Dog musk," Howard said, in an announcer's voice. "For when you want to attract the bitches."

Hyde grinned. "Mastiff Musk. For when you want to feel like the biggest dog in the yard."

"You guys are seriously twisted," I said.

"Bruno's insides are seriously twisted," Howard said with a gasp.

"Not his fault," I said. "A long trip and we've completely changed his diet like three times in a month. Poor guy's got a rumbly tumbly."

"To change the subject," Frankie said, pointedly, "Wu emailed me back."

I sat forward. "He did?"

"Wait," Howard said, wrinkling his forehead. "When did you email Wu?"

"This afternoon, when we got back," Frankie said. "Elayna asked me to."

"What did he say?" I asked.

"Nothing. Just sent us an address in our old song lyrics code. Very strange."

"What's the address?"

"I pulled satellite imagery," Frankie said, clicking the projector button again. Another grainy image appeared-- an aerial shot of a building with a dirt parking lot. "Looks like a restaurant or a bar or something. Way out in the middle of nowhere--about two hours from here."

"I wonder why he sent us that," Camilla said.

"I don't know," I said.

I felt guilty not telling them that I'd had contact with the CIA, contact with Wu, earlier that day. But I needed to figure things out before I added another wrinkle to this mess.

"It must be important if he risked sending it," Camilla said. "We should go check it out."

"Well, we would need a car. And a way to get out from under all this attention," I said. "I don't really see your Uncle letting you out of his sight. He's too paranoid."

"He's leaving tonight," Camilla said, studying the image and tapping her chin thoughtfully. "He's throwing a party for the General and some of his other cronies, and he will leave when they do. He's got business in the South, he said."

"Who is he leaving behind?" Hyde said.

His voice sounded rough, gravelly. I shot him a concerned look. If he wasn't completely himself by morning, I was going to hunt down Agent Darby and force-feed him copious amounts of aggressive laxatives.

"Several men, but I think Tristao will be in charge," she said, lightly.

"We might be able to use that," I said.

"Yeah, the guy can barely hide it," Howard said. "He looks at you like I look at a nice steak."

"What a strange thing to say," Camilla said.

"I just mean that he looks at you like you're delicious," Howard said, earnestly. "Like he can't wait to get you alone and smear some herb butter or steak sauce..."

"Getting weirder, Howard!" I said.

"No, I just mean..." Howard started.

"We get it," Hyde said, chuckling. "Tristao likes Camilla."

"What a perfectly reasonable way of putting that," I said sarcastically.

Camilla took a deep breath and pressed her lips together. "I will see what I can do."

Chapter 12

Camilla woke me early the next morning, which was rough, because the previous night's dinner had dragged even more than the first one.

"Get up and get ready without any lights," she whispered. "My uncle left late last night, and I think we can sneak away."

I slid out from the bed, surprised that she'd been able to wake me without Hyde waking up. He was still breathing heavily on the other side of the bed--I hoped that he'd be his normal self when he finally woke. I used the bathroom, brushed my teeth, threw on some jeans and a t-shirt, and met Camilla in the kitchen.

"I got us a car," she whispered. "And I'm leaving a note for everyone else. They should just pretend that we're sleeping in, if anyone asks. With any luck, we'll be back before anyone notices we're gone. But we have to hurry; the guy at the gate will be back in thirty minutes."

"How did you... never mind. I'll leave Hyde a note, too. It's just a restaurant, and I'll bring a gun."

THE ROADS to the restaurant became rutted the further out of town we went until finally, the sedan was bucking over the ruts in the lane, albeit slowly. I didn't know what we'd find at the end of this hellacious ride, but if the beer wasn't the frostiest, most delicious on the planet, I'd wonder why anyone would make this trek. We'd been driving for hours.

Then again, little villages kept surprising me along the way. We'd drive for a stretch of miles where there would appear to be endless nothing--huge swaths of clear-cut land for farming, or dense thickets of beautiful trees, then out of nowhere, a cluster of houses--shanties, really--stuck against the roadside like an afterthought.

"This is it?" I said, once we'd arrived.

I didn't understand how this bar was still standing, both figuratively, because it was in the middle of nowhere, and literally, because it looked like it had been cobbled together over the years from whatever leftover building materials were around. It was painted a bright, pinkish plum color, which I found odd, considering that the clientele seemed exclusively male. We sat in the parking lot for several minutes, just looking. A small painted sign over the door was the only thing that alerted us that we were in the right place. We sat there, watching the heat of midday shimmer off the dirt in the parking lot.

"Why would Wu send us here? I feel like I'm getting punked."

"I couldn't begin to tell you."

I shifted in my seat. "It was a butt-blistering ride in. Could be that's all he wanted us to find--chafe and new bruises."

We watched the front of the bar.

"Doesn't it feel off to you, though?" I finally said. "It's a million degrees out here, and the building's not open-air, like every other restaurant we've passed."

"It's bigger, too," she said, sounding thoughtful. "Why would they need such a big place all the way out here?"

I let that sink in, tried to let the silence help our thought processes.

"I don't know," I finally said. "You want me to go in and check it out, see if it's safe?"

"Psh," she said, opening the center console and pulling out two pistols. "What good would I be sitting in the car if something went wrong?"

"Did you tell Tristao where we were going?" I said, checking my firearm and wiggling forward in the seat so I could shove it down the back of my pants where my shirt would cover it.

"Not where," she said, frowning at my tone. "Just that we needed the car."

"I thought maybe you stole it or borrowed it without people knowing."

Camilla chuckled. "There's no getting anything done at

that house without help, Elayna. You'd do well to remember that."

"Fine," I grumbled.

I didn't want to examine my mild dislike of Tristao too closely. I knew that it wasn't *him*--it was the fact that Tristao was another tie to Brazil. I wanted to get this case resolved before Camilla put down roots in her home country. It was an intensely selfish desire, and I didn't like myself for it.

"I'm sorry, Camilla," I said. "Tristao is... fine. I'm just... I feel weird about this whole thing."

"Me too," Camilla murmured.

"Well, we will get through it together," I said, opening the car door.

Or at least, I hoped we would.

We went through the doors and it was like a bad movie cliché--everyone stopped what they were doing to stare. All conversation, all activity--stopped. It was a solid three seconds before even the pretense of a murmur kicked up again.

The interior was dim. A worn tile floor, dark blue walls, and overly loud music for midday dominated the space. A bar was shoved against one wall, with two young women in jean shorts and bikini tops working it. And we were wrong--there *were* women inside. Several of them, all scantily clad.

"Shit," I murmured, to Camilla.

I knew what this was. Exclusively male patrons and a lot of demoralized-looking young women? This was a brothel. And it was really difficult for two outside women to blend into this scenario. Luckily, Camilla was a quick thinker.

"Excuse me," she said to the nearest barmaid, loud enough for the room to hear. "We are lost. Can you please tell me how to get to Velho?"

I recognized the name of a village we'd passed about two miles back.

"You need to turn around. You passed it," she said, her eyes darting anywhere but at us.

I decided to play the part of the oblivious foreigner.

"Do you guys have food?" I asked, putting a hand to my stomach. "I'm *starving*. And if we have to turn around and go back over that horrible road just to see where your Grandfather was born without lunch, I'm going to *die*."

"Fine," Camilla said, rolling her eyes. "We'll eat here, then go."

She turned and placed an order with the waitress, who scurried off surprisingly fast in five-inch heels. We chose a plastic table near the wall, where I had a good view of the room. Our food arrived within five minutes. They wanted us out of there, fast.

There were about half a dozen men scattered around the room at different tables, and about ten women milled around. Some were at tables, one was on the lap of a man, others served drinks or leaned against the walls at the fringes of the room. They all looked zoned out. Even when they smiled or twirled their hair, their eyes looked faded, washed out, like twenty-year-old jeans. But there was one woman who was the exception.

She was a little older than the rest of the women, although she still appeared young. She was dressed like the rest, in jean shorts so small her butt was in danger of falling out, and a tank top that showed a bit of modest cleavage. But even though her hair was slightly mussed and her makeup looked sloppy, I didn't buy it. She didn't belong.

She was thin, like the others, but where their bodies looked malnourished and bruised, her body looked toned and strong. Her eyes were too sharp, as well. A deep brown that matched her hair, her eyes had the honed intelligence of a jungle cat. That's why I thought she stood out to me...she wasn't prey like these other young women--she was a *predator*.

As the thought entered my mind and coalesced into certainty, her eyes lifted and met mine. A flash of anger, there and then gone, moved across her face, fast as a flinch--an infinitesimal narrowing of the eyes, tightening of the lips, but it was so intense that I could almost feel it on my skin, like I had just walked in front of a roaring furnace.

I turned to Camilla, to direct her attention to the strange woman, but found her head ducked, her shoulders nearly hunched.

"We need to go," she murmured, and inclined her head ever so slightly toward the door, where a group of four men had just entered.

They weren't the regular clientele. Their clothes were too nice, for one thing. Not fancy, but their jeans were dark wash and clean, and their leather boots had a sheen. Their shirts had pearl snap buttons and looked pressed, in stark contrast to the faded, stretched-out t-shirts many of the other men in the room wore. The mood in the room shifted again, different this time, from when we had entered. The men in the room all sat up and straightened; the women all lowered their eyes and tried to blend into the background.

I tossed a bill on the table and slowly slid from my seat. The group of men had meandered to the bar, and their backs were to us. Camilla followed my lead, and we moved to the door. I didn't realize I had been holding my breath until we were outside, the sun causing my eyes to squint even through the sunglasses I quickly pulled down over my eyes. Camilla's fast walk toward our car let me know we weren't safe, yet.

"Who are they?" I asked in a low voice as I kept pace beside her.

"I don't know." Her voice was tight. "But they all were armed, and with the way the people reacted, I thought we should get out before they really noticed us. They could have been part of As Cobras or one of the other gangs."

"The Cobras?" I hissed.

Is this what Wu wanted us to find? A brothel that As Cobras owned? Why?

"I don't know what any of the rival gangs would do if they caught me on their property. I don't really want to stick around and chance it. I'd hoped that people forgot about me, forgot my face, but it's hard to know after all this time."

She was speaking so low and walking so quickly that I had been leaning forward to catch her words. I wasn't watching our backs the way I should have been, which is why what happened next was my fault.

A cloth-covered hand clamped over my nose and mouth, and I instinctively held my breath and rolled my hips, nearly displacing the man who held me. He was on my side, and I caught a glimpse of a pearl buttoned shirt.

Camilla was being wrestled to the ground by two other men, but she was putting up a fight. I kicked out at his knee and connected, but it was ineffectual. My vision was starting to blur a bit; whatever was on the rag was potent and fast-acting. The man holding me grunted as I landed a sharp elbow hard to his gut, but his grip tightened.

And then I was falling into blackness--whether real or just in my mind, I couldn't tell.

Chapter 13

I woke up to Camilla shaking my shoulder roughly, murmuring in my ear.

"Elayna, wake up," she was repeating.

I grunted and tried to open my eyes. They felt swollen and grainy. When I lifted a hand to wipe them, I ended up smacking myself in the lip, instead.

"Ow," I said. My voice was guttural, as if I was waking up too soon from a drunk night's sleep.

"Shhh," Camilla hissed, in my ear. "We're in a trunk. I think there might be someone in the car, guarding us. I'm not sure."

I grunted again and focused on taking deep breaths. After a few more moments, I was able to blink my eyes until my vision cleared. I regained use of my limbs enough to wipe the copious amounts of snot and drool from my face.

"Yuck," I said. "What did they drug us with?"

"They didn't drug me," she said. "Just you."

"Lucky me," I groaned.

My throat burned and my body ached, but I kept wiggling my toes and breathing deeply, trying to help my body clear the drugs enough to function. Whatever came next, I needed to be ready. The trunk was spacious; we were obviously in an older car. It smelled familiar--oil and gasoline baked with heat into the fragrance of a thousand repair garages. There was no carpeting or lining. I was laying on my side, and the metal of the trunk floor was digging in. I would definitely have bruises the next day. I hoped I made it long enough to see them.

"Did they say anything?" I said. "How long have I been out?"

"They didn't say a word. I think it's been about fifteen minutes, but I can't be sure. My sense of time gets a little skewed when I'm locked in a hot trunk."

"No kidding," I said. Sweat had nearly soaked my shirt, and my hair was plastered against my forehead. "I suppose it's too much to hope they didn't take the guns."

"No. They're gone." She jostled my shoulder, as if I still wasn't awake. "We need to get out of here. If they are the Cobras, I don't want to know what they'll do. If they aren't with an organized crime group, we will be held for ransom."

Her voice was tense, and for the first time, I realized how frightened she was. Which should have been obvious, since we were locked in a trunk in a foreign country and no one knew where we were. I giggled, and it came out like a nervous exhale. I think I was still under the effects of whatever they'd knocked me out with. I kept breathing deep, trying to clear my head completely.

"Ok," I said, after a few more seconds. "There's no trunk release, obviously. Not in a car this age. Can we kick out a tail-light?"

"I thought about that," she said. "But what good would it do? We could maybe do it once we get on the road, hope that someone sees it and then cares enough to call the police. But in this country? People are self-preserving. They know that if they get involved, they very well will be hunted down for it. The gangsters own the police. If someone calls them, the police will tell the cartels who called."

It didn't escape my sense of irony that this was an Almeida explaining this to me, as if the situation was disgusting. But she was explaining how her family had affected the makeup of the entire country. I took a deep breath and tried to focus. I was still a little off. I knew that, because I wasn't as scared as I should have been. My heart wasn't pounding.

"Anything else in the trunk? Tools? A crowbar?" I asked.

I heard rustling, felt her moving around, felt the car shift. I resisted the urge to close my eyes and rest. I knew that a fight was coming--I just hoped it would be well after the effects of this drug wore off. I felt like I could sleep for a week, but there wasn't time for that, and this was certainly not the place to indulge in a nap.

"A screwdriver!" Camilla whispered, sounding delighted.

She transferred it into my hand, and I gripped the handle. It was maybe five inches long, total.

"Awesome," I mumbled. "The tables have turned."

If she heard the sarcasm in my voice, she ignored it. For good reason, because a shot rang out. It was close, too close, to the car we were in. It seemed to reverberate in the confined space, like someone had slapped a couple sheets of metal together right above our heads.

As if that had been the cue that everyone had been waiting for, shots began blasting back and forth, like two lines of competing fireworks. These shots didn't seem as close as the first, and so were muffled a bit by the trunk. But that was of little comfort. There is nothing quite as terrible as being trapped in the middle of a gun battle without being able to hide.

The glass was shot out of a nearby car, and the crashing noise made me jolt. Both Camilla and I had made ourselves as small as possible, curling ourselves into balls. It did little to comfort me. My breath was coming in sharp pants. The only positive in this scenario was that my adrenaline seemed to have kicked back up, clearing most of the fog I'd been feeling. I finally felt that I could run well, or put up a half-assed fight, if necessary.

It seemed to last forever. My heart pounded at a slower rate than the bursts of gunfire. Distant groans of the wounded, female screams, and masculine shouting filtered through the rushing of blood in my ears. I had counted the gunshots, on instinct, but lost count at seventy-two. It was fascinating how time seemed to stretch when in a life or death situation. Logically, it had only been about three minutes since the gunfire started. But it felt like we'd been listening to the metallic pops for far longer than that.

My thoughts seemed to rise and explode in my head along with the gunfire--what if everyone who knew we were in the trunk died? Who was shooting? Why? Was this a prostitute purchase gone wrong, or something more organized? What if one of us were shot? Could I break us out of the trunk before we bled out? Before we baked to death in this sweltering heat, breathing in our own exhalations and the smell of stress sweat?

After a minute or two of silence that felt taut and expectant, like blowing one of those massive bubbles you know has to burst at *some* point, I shifted.

"Are you hit?" I whispered.

"No." Camilla's voice sounded strained, small.

"Alright. You're closer to the backseat than I am. Feel around for screws that we can undo to get out of here."

I heard Camilla shift, heard the sound of her running her hands over the metal. For my part, I began feeling the underside of the trunk lid. It seemed to be a metal 'x' shape on the interior, but I could reach my hand through and touch the smooth metal that made up the exterior of the trunk. I wasn't sure that my screwdriver would be able to penetrate the exterior metal.

This car was built before the time when engineers decided that fuel efficiency trumped the safety of the occupants. Taking something apart would be our best option, but I wasn't sure what we would do if the screws required a flathead instead of a Philips'. I didn't even want to think about what we would do if the whole thing was held together with welds.

Before I could panic too much, I heard the crunch of footsteps in the hard dirt coming towards us, then a jingling of keys and scrabbling at the trunk. The lid opened with alacrity, throwing us into stark white sunlight, a huge contrast to the impenetrable gloom of the closed trunk from a moment before.

Though I was blinded, I half-launched, half-rolled from the trunk, the screwdriver held aloft as a weapon, my eyes squinted to help them adjust. I'd fought blind before, but there was more than one individual. I could see several large shapes in front of me, but no identifying features as of yet. I crouched into a defensive position in front of the open trunk, and I could hear Camilla trying to scramble ungraciously out behind me.

Coarse laughter greeted me--it was hostile, and surprisingly, *female*.

"We aren't here to hurt *you*," she said.

A few more blinks and I was able to see that it was the woman from inside, the one who looked like she hadn't belonged. Flanking her were two men, one built like a concrete block wall, the other slender, with a pinched face like a ferret and the flat eyes of a snake.

I couldn't decide who I'd rather fight if I had to choose. In my state, I didn't like my odds. Based on how my body ached, I was pretty sure whoever had put me in the trunk had let me fall to the ground after they drugged me.

The woman who spoke was sneering at us now. Her eyes flashed, her teeth bared, and her posture suggested that she was three seconds away from trying to choke me with her bare hands. This woman *hated* me, and I had no clue as to why. Now that she was speaking, I could tell that she was a bit older than I had originally thought.

"We'll let you walk away from this," she said, her furious eyes meeting mine. "But *she* isn't leaving here without answering for her crimes." She extended a finger at Camilla's chest.

I tilted my head in Camilla's direction but didn't let my eyes leave the trio in front of us.

"You know this bitch?" I asked Camilla.

"No, I don't." She sounded genuinely confused, like the woman in front of her was some sort of puzzle that she couldn't work out.

"I kind of feel like you should, 'cause she seems awful mad at you." I raised my eyebrows.

"Nope." I saw her shrug in my peripheral vision.

"That's awkward."

The three people facing us had heard every word, of course. The slender, ferret-like man hadn't changed his neutral expression. The WWE-wannabee looked faintly amused, and the woman in front looked *livid*.

"Humor me for a moment," I said, holding my hands out in a placating gesture. "She doesn't know you, so why do you think she has committed crimes?"

"I *know* she has," the woman hissed. "She deserves to be put to death for the lives she has destroyed."

"What are you talking about?" Camilla said, perplexion clear in her voice. "Who are you?"

"You are part of the Almeida family!" she said. "You must be held accountable for the crimes against the women who were held here against their will! The crimes against the people of Brazil! Against the women and girls of South America. You have been buying and selling slaves at places like this for years! Transporting them away from their friends and family, kidnapping them off the streets and sending them too far away for them to get back home without help." She clasped a fist to her chest in obvious passion. "*We* are the ones who steal them back from you. *We* are the ones who return them to their families. And if their families do not want them back, they become part of our family. We will never stop. And you must die for your sins."

"They are trafficking these women?" I said, my brow drawn together in confusion. "They weren't just prostitutes?"

"Of course not!" the woman said, then jabbed her finger at Camilla again. "But *she* already knew that."

"No," Camilla said, her voice grave. "I didn't know."

"Liar," she hissed.

"Just calm down a second," I said. "Neither of us knew about this place until someone gave us the address and told us to look into it. Camilla didn't know about *any* human trafficking, I can guarantee you of that."

The woman scowled. "Who cares what you say? You're her employee; you're paid to agree with her and keep her out of trouble."

I smiled at the irony, which only seemed to enrage the woman further.

"Look," I said, trying to use my most soothing voice. "I don't know who you are. You don't know who I am. But I am telling the truth--Camilla would be the absolute last person who would ever be involved with human trafficking."

"My name is Iris Vanessa Montes. And I am here to make Camilla Almeida pay for what she has done to our country."

I had an irrational flashback to Mandy Patinkin saying, 'I am Inigo Montoya. You killed my father; prepare to die,' like in *The Princess Bride*, but my amusement rapidly faded when Iris took a swing at Camilla's face.

I swiped her fist away with my forearm, and kicked her in the knee, hearing a satisfying crunch. It wasn't enough to take her down, though, so I threw a follow-up punch into her gut. She let out a low grunt. The thin man made a move toward Camilla, but Iris' full attention was on me now, and I couldn't take on two at once. I had to trust that Camilla could hold her own until I could get this bitch down.

That was easier said than done. Iris had a wicked right hook and she was fast. I took an ear-ringing punch to the left temple and managed to block a couple more, but I quickly decided that I couldn't beat her with speed of striking or length of limbs. I lunged forward, tackling her around the waist and taking her down.

Hyde and I had been working on my grappling a lot more in our training sessions, and what had once been a mediocre skill of mine was quickly becoming one of my greatest strengths. It took about thirty seconds of scrabbling in the dirt with her before I had her in a sleeper hold, but as soon as I took the dominant position and it was clear that I was winning, the large man, who had been helping the thin one wrangle Camilla, turned to come to Iris' rescue.

Which was when the shot rang out.

Chapter 14

The bullet hit the ground between the large man and where Iris and I lay.

I was on my back on the bottom, with my feet acting as hooks into her knees. She was lying with her back on my chest. Even as I saw the plume of dust puff between us, Iris went limp in my arms. I held the sleeper hold for a couple more seconds in case it was a ploy, then released her, rolling her to the side. The large man took another step forward, and another shot rang out, this time landing directly in front of his foot. I reached down and snagged Iris' gun from the back of her jean shorts, and pointed it at the thin man, who held Camilla.

"Let her go," I said.

He stared at me and didn't comply, so I shot a bullet right past his head. He showed no reaction other than a slight widening of his eyes, but he released her, and she hurried to my side. We took cover behind the fender of the car.

"Do we know who is shooting?" I asked the big man, who had wisely put his hands up.

"Not one of ours," he said, his eyes not leaving Iris' prone form.

"I didn't kill her," I said. "We wouldn't hurt anyone trying to free innocent victims."

His eyes finally flickered to mine. "You were telling the truth about not knowing."

"We were, but we should discuss this later, once we figure out who's shooting at us," I said, annoyed.

At that moment, two figures emerged from the thick stand of trees at the edge of the parking lot. I wasn't sure I'd ever seen a stranger pair, except maybe for that time in San Francisco when I'd seen a guy in a Darth Vader mask and a kilt, riding a unicycle. He had been followed by someone in a Wookie costume on a low-rider bicycle. The Wookie had been wearing a top hat.

I felt like I was seeing the same once-in-a-lifetime phenomena now. The first guy was in full black tactical gear, including a balaclava that covered his entire face except for his eyes. He was holding a state-of-the-art sniper rifle that was pointed in our direction. He was tall with wide shoulders and an athletic physique.

The man walking directly behind him was short and thin, with narrow shoulders and hair that had been dyed stark black. He was wearing a crisp black suit complete with a bow tie, except instead of pants, he wore cuffed shorts. He had completed the ensemble with black horn-rimmed glasses, and hot pink socks that peeked from the top of his lace-up black combat boots. He was clasping a large leather attache case to his chest.

While the man in front had a confident stride, the man in the shorts suit was picking his way through the under-brush nervously.

"What fresh hell is this?" I mumbled as I got to my feet and pointed the gun in their direction.

"Elayna Miller?" The guy in front called out, when they got a little closer.

"Who's asking?"

He dropped the business end of his gun toward the ground and pulled off his balaclava, revealing a straight-teethed grin and a mop of curly dark brown hair that I recognized from our last job file.

"Marcos Borges, is that you?" I said.

I was confused. Why was Luis' nephew out in the middle of a Brazilian jungle? He seemed to read my expression.

"You ordered a forensic accountant, and I came along to deliver this guy," he said, jerking his thumb at the skittish man behind him.

"This guy has a name, you know," the guy in the suit said, sarcasm thick in his voice.

I swung my eyes back to the other members of the group. The thin man was eyeing Marcos with barely-guarded hostility, while the big man only had eyes for Iris' prone form, still lying in the dirt.

Marcos and the other man were secondary. They were on our side, so they weren't threats. Camilla looked heartbroken, her face folded into creases of devastation. I ignored her expression so as not to draw attention to it. First things first, and all.

"What are you going to do with the girls?" I asked the big guy.

"Transport should be here any minute." He frowned. "You guys getting kidnapped in the parking lot messed up our plan."

"Sorry about that," I said, dryly. I jerked my chin in Iris' direction. "If she hates Camilla so much, why didn't you just let us get taken?"

"Iris wanted to question her." He glanced at Camilla. "Thought she might have some information we need."

"Anything I know, I would tell you," Camilla said. Her voice and face were once again strong. "But I'm afraid I probably can't be much help. We didn't know this place existed before today, and I certainly did not know that the Almeida family had any involvement in human trafficking. It's...it's disgusting. I will do anything I can to help shut it down."

He looked thoughtful. "You might be able to help us." He looked down at Iris. "She lost someone close to her, years ago. That's how we started this. She thinks you might know...but that's her story to tell, not mine."

"Great," I said, checking my nose for blood. "Glad we're all one big happy family."

Iris groaned a little, and her feet shifted in the dirt. I

looked at the big guy. "I'm counting on you to communi-
cate that we're on the same side now, before she gives me
another black eye, or I'll have to put her out again."

He chuckled. "She's going to be so pissed that you got
the upper hand." He shook his head, ruefully. "Name is
Ruben, by the way."

He held out a hand to shake, but I ignored it. I could
have pretended that it was because my hand had a bunch
of snot on it, or that I didn't trust the guy not to grab me,
but the truth was far pettier--I was pissed. Not just because
in the past hour I'd been knocked out, stuffed in a hot
trunk, and then beat up.

The real reason I was mad was because of the depth of
feeling Camilla had shown when she learned about her
family's involvement in this brothel. It was more than the
natural disgust and anger that anyone would feel faced
with the real, live horror of human trafficking.

It was personal. She felt personally responsible for this,
and personally responsible when it came to stopping it. I
could understand that, but it didn't mean that I liked it.
This case wasn't going at all how I wanted. We were
supposed to get into Brazil, choose a successor for Thiago,
and get back home. It seemed like every day we were here,
things got messier.

It was like one of those nightmares where you try to
run, but you are stuck in quicksand. It felt like everything
was against us, like Camilla was getting drawn back into
her father's web. I could see it coming from a million miles
away, but there was nothing I could do to stop it.

Three beat-up SUVs trundled into the far end of the parking lot, and the thin man went to talk to the drivers. He gestured at us, at the bar, then went inside. The doors to the brothel opened moments later, and sixteen young women came out. Their movements were furtive and they squinted at the sun like they hadn't been outside in ages. My lips pressed together.

Ruben had helped Iris into a sitting position, and he was murmuring to her in a low voice. I couldn't hear what he was saying, but judging by the venomous looks she kept directing at me and Camilla, I was pretty sure he was trying to convince her that violence wasn't the answer. I watched as the young women piled into the SUVs, and they left.

I frowned. "Where will they go?"

"We'll help them get back home if that's what they want," Ruben said. "But sometimes, home was worse. We have a couple donors that help them get job training." He shrugged, like he didn't really have a good answer for my question.

The thin guy sauntered back up to our group. He jerked his head at the building. "What should we do with it?"

He had directed the question to Iris, but it was Camilla who answered.

"Burn it," she said, her lip curled, fury etched into every line of her face. "The bodies and the cars, too. Let the families of *these* men wonder what happened to *their* loved ones."

Iris narrowed her eyes like she thought Camilla's statement had been some kind of trick, but she nodded at the thin guy, and he went to the back of one of the SUVs and grabbed a couple of massive gas cans, which made me think that fire had been the plan all along.

"We should go," I said to Camilla and Marcos. "Even in this part of the country, the police will probably be involved. There's got to be a dozen bodies inside."

"Ten," said Ruben from behind me. "But you're right; we should all clear out."

"She's not going anywhere until I get some answers," Iris hissed, pointing a claw-like finger at Camilla.

"Oh, shut up already," I said. "Give us your number. We need time to look into this. We'll meet you in town in Bastillo in a few days. You know the little cafe there?"

Ruben nodded.

"And how do we know you'll call, that you'll show up?" Iris said.

"You don't," I snapped. I was sick of her attitude. I could understand her anger, but she was directing it at the wrong person. "You'll have to wait and find out."

It looked like she was about to snap back at me, but Ruben put his hand on her shoulder and led her away.

The four of us piled into our vehicle. I drove.

"Ours is around the corner," Marcos said with a good-natured smile. "Right up there on the left, the dirt turnout. You guys look like you had a rough go of it. We only got there after the shooting started. Why were you in the trunk?"

"Long story," I muttered, right as Camilla said, "A bunch of guys rushed us in the parking lot and threw us in the trunk."

"So I guess it wasn't *that* long of a story," I said, giving a side-eye to Camilla. "And how did you guys end up out here today?"

It wasn't that I wasn't grateful--I just didn't trust coincidences. They hardly ever worked out in my favor, and I was doubly suspicious when they did.

Marcos shrugged. His sniper rifle was awkwardly leaning on the floorboard between his legs. He was holding the barrel of it to his chest. Even so, it barely fit in the sedan.

"My uncle told us to come down here and find you. We called that guy--Hyde? And he gave us the address; told me to hurry up and keep an eye on you."

I smirked. It was just like Hyde to try and protect me, even when he wasn't there.

"Guess it worked out ok, though, huh?" Marcos said.

He was smiling, and I couldn't find an ounce of sarcasm in it. I think he was genuinely happy to have been in the right place at the right time. There was no judgment in it. He just seemed glad to have been of help.

I pursed my lips. I wasn't sure what to think about that--usually, people I dealt with had strong opinions about the situation they found themselves in. Not this guy, apparently. Howard would have been giving me a metric ton of shit over getting thrown in a trunk.

Frankie would want revenge. If the guys who had

thrown us in the trunk had still been alive, she would have tried to get all the information possible, in order to ruin their lives as thoroughly as possible via keystrokes. If there was one person in the team I didn't want truly, deeply angry with me, it was Frankie.

Hyde? Hyde would be concerned. He'd want to run through the scenario and show me different ways to avoid the same outcome in the future. He'd feel even *more* protective of me, if possible. The shitty part was, I had been smacked in the head a few times by Iris--there was no way to avoid that conversation with Hyde. He was going to feel guilty that he hadn't been there. Nothing I could do to stop it--it was inevitable.

I sighed at the thought.

"We got a hotel room in town," Marcos said. "Our contact info is in the email my uncle sent."

"I'm sorry." I glanced in the rearview at the slight man sitting next to Marcos--the forensic accountant. "I didn't catch your name."

"Elio Ricci," he said, barely meeting my eyes.

"Nice to meet you," I said, hoping that he caught my meaning.

Because it wasn't the first time I'd met Elio. Not by a long shot. But if he wanted to pretend it was, I was more than fine with that.

Camilla and I dropped them off at their car with promises to be in touch soon. There was silence for a mile or two. Both of us were lost in our thoughts. Then--

"Does your nose hurt?" Camilla said, the ghost of a smile on her lips. "It looks like it hurts."

"Thanks," I said sarcastically.

"I can't wait to tell Howard that you got beat up by a girl," she said with a giggle.

"Hey," I said, smacking her shoulder. "*I'm* a girl. There's no shame in it. Besides, you were no help at all."

"I was fighting off two men!" she said, batting her too-wide eyes. "I expected you to be able to handle one little girl."

I rolled my eyes. "She was a badass, and you know it." I laughed. "And she does *not* like you."

"She detests my family," she said. Her brows drew together and she looked out into the distance. "She hates what my family has done. And right now, I agree with her on both points."

I reached over, put my hand on her shoulder, and squeezed gently. I couldn't give her my full attention--the road was rutted and twisty, and we could not afford any delay--but I needed her to know that I heard her, and I knew how much she was hurting.

Camilla had a past--everyone who had grown up in the family she had would--but she had kept that part of her, that warmth, that so many people with her history lose. She was the glue that kept our team together. At the end of a terrible day, we could come back to the house, weary and battle-worn with our tails between our legs, and Camilla would be waiting with her warmth and a hot meal that had been cooked with love.

She would listen and console and support us however she could. I was terrified to lose that. I was also worried that this experience down here would drag her down, would steal the smile from her face and the joy from her heart. Whatever the outcome, the tables had most definitely flipped--she was the one who needed the hot meal and the comfort.

Chapter 15

That thought stuck in my head when we returned to the house. After a shower and some ibuprofen, I requested some ingredients, kicked everyone else out of the family wing kitchen, and got to work. An hour and a half later, my hair had reached the height of it's frizz capability, my black eye had really set in, there were sweat rings in my armpits, the kitchen was a cataclysmic mess, but dinner was on the table. I watched proudly as everyone took their seats.

"So, I wanted to cook dinner to express my appreciation of all the care that Camilla has done for us over the years. I figured it was time that she had a night off," I said.

I took my seat and spread my napkin over my lap, my smile wide.

"Nice shiner." Howard grinned. "I can't believe you got beat up by a girl."

"Would *you* like to get beat up by a girl?" I asked, eyes narrowed.

"Nah, I'm good."

I frowned when I realized no one had made a move toward the dishes, I nodded encouragingly. "Eat up."

Howard reached for the bowl in front of him and frowned down into it. "Um..."

"Oh, those green beans were in the oven a little too long, but they should be fine," I said, putting a piece of chicken on my plate and passing the platter down.

Howard nodded and spooned some of the crispy beans onto his plate and passed the bowl without meeting Camilla's eyes.

"And these?" Frankie asked, a strained smile on her face.

I frowned. "Carrots."

We passed around the dishes in marked silence, until my plate was full.

"So, it's not as good as Camilla's cooking..." I trailed off as I really, truly looked at what was on my plate.

I twisted my fingers together and clenched my molars. I had tried...honestly tried. And the result was absolutely *nothing* like Camilla's meals. How did she make it look so easy? My onions weren't caramelized--they were burnt. They looked like the ashes that had fallen when Mt. Vesuvius had erupted. The mushrooms were shriveled, reminding me of photos I'd seen of mummies in caskets. The mashed potatoes were so runny I had to serve them in ramekins. My carrots were burnt twigs--the remnants of a campfire. There were no high points on this plate.

"This just makes me so sad," Frankie said, her eyes downcast.

She kept picking up a spoonful of mashed potatoes, then letting it slide back into the ramekin with a 'plop'. *Plop. Plop. Plop.* It was a depressing soundtrack--the shitty crescendo of a trainwreck aria of a cooking opera.

"I don't know how you managed it," Hyde said. His expression was serious, but I knew him well enough to see the twinkle in his eyes. "My chicken is both burnt and undercooked."

"Oh, shut it, Hyde," I snapped.

Camilla's eyes were steadfast on her plate, her head ducked. It took me a moment to realize her shoulders were shaking.

"Are you *laughing* at me?" I said, aghast.

She raised her head, and there were tears in her eyes from trying so hard not to laugh.

"Yes," she finally managed to squeak.

It was as if her one word was a bomb that brought down the dam. Hyde started laughing, great big guffaws that would maybe have hurt my feelings, had his eyes not been so warm and full of love for me. Frankie laughed, too--one of those elegant, movie-star kind of laughs. Even Howard began to laugh, which was something I hadn't seen in weeks.

I propped my fist on my hip. "You guys have no loyalty!

It's not *that* bad." I paused and looked down at the plate. "Is it?"

The laughter just increased. Camilla was openly crying now.

"Oh, you guys didn't even try it!" I said, stopping just short of stomping my foot. "I'm sure it doesn't taste as bad as it looks." I frowned down at the plate. "I mean, it can't, right?"

Hyde stood and manhandled me into a quick hug, laughing the whole time. Bruno huffed his way to his feet and plodded over to lean against my legs.

"Thank you, Bruno," I said, rubbing his ear. "At least *someone* here loves me."

"If we didn't love you," Howard said, "We never would have sat down at the table. I mean, *look* at this." He gestured to his plate like Bruno had made a mess on it.

"You're being rude," I said, offended. "I really did try."

Hyde kissed my temple, but he was still chuckling.

"Well," I said, raising my eyebrows. "I'm not cleaning, because I cooked."

This statement brought another round of laughter, but I was finally able to join in.

Frankie stood and began clearing. To my surprise, Howard joined her.

"I'll call the kitchen and see if they can whip us up something simple," Camilla said.

I felt like I should help clear the dishes, since I had made them all, but when I made to stand, Hyde snagged my elbow gently, keeping me in place. I still was a bit miffed at him for how *much* he had laughed, because I really had poured my heart into trying to cook. I frowned at him. He gave a subtle nod to where Frankie and Howard were making the first trip through the family dining room to the little kitchenette beyond.

"Howard hasn't been voluntarily alone with Frankie in weeks," he said. "Let them have it."

I nodded and studied the mess on the plate in front of me.

After a few moments of silence, I asked, "Was it really that bad?"

He smiled, the corners of his eyes crinkling. It washed over me again, in that moment, how good-looking he was, how kind, how smart, and the fact that he loved *me.*

"Elayna, I would eat this whole plate of food if it would make you feel better. That's how much I love you."

I cocked my head to the side. "Would you?"

"Yes, but please don't make me."

I pointed at the mashed potatoes in the ramekin. "How about just a bite of that? I want to know where I went wrong."

He grimaced but took a watery bite. His mouth puckered.

"Is there raw flour in there?" he asked after he swallowed thickly.

"What do you mean *raw* flour?" I said. "Flour is flour. But yeah, I put a little in there after I saw how runny they were. I was trying to thicken them up."

I didn't tell him the truth--that I had put at least a cup in.

"Why were they runny?"

I tried not to be offended that he was taking huge drinks of his water, trying to rinse the taste of my potatoes out of his mouth.

"Well, I read the directions on how to make mashed potatoes, but there was a lot going on, so I must have missed the part where you're supposed to drain the water out after they're done boiling."

He was laughing again.

"In my defense, I went back and read the directions, and there was just a picture. It's like they assume you're supposed to know to drain them."

He grinned at me. "You didn't know, though."

"I've never really cooked before. Nothing past mac and cheese, at least. And *those* directions are very clear."

"Well, you're lucky that you have so many other wonderful qualities that make up for your lack of basic kitchen skills."

"You mean *you're* lucky," I said.

"I am," he said, his expression serious. "And I got you a little present to show you my appreciation."

He pulled an envelope from his back jeans pocket and handed it over. I shot him a suspicious look as I opened it.

"I'm not sure I'm going to like a gift that's still warm from your butt," I said.

Hyde chuckled and I unfolded the photo within.

And gasped. Hyde had found him--the one I'd been looking for, for years.

Alonso was old now, past seventy. The lines on his face were so deep, they reminded me of splits that you sometimes saw in great boulders that had been weathered by ice and time. I didn't blame his neighbors for not knowing a monster was in their midst. I wouldn't have seen it, if I didn't know.

He was stooped and his hands were starting to gnarl, the knuckles too large for the fingers they held together-- an effect of hard manual labor and age. Of course, there was part of me that thought maybe his body was revolting against its owner, that maybe his hands were rebelling at the hundreds of lives they had destroyed. And it *was* hundreds.

When he'd been arrested for trying to kidnap a little girl in the marketplace thirty years ago, the vendors had held him down until the police arrived to take him away. Alonso had confessed to hundreds of child rapes and murders. The police thought they had a lunatic on their hands. They didn't think that the five foot seven, slightly built man with a crooked, sheepish smile was capable of such a thing. They threw him in a cell until they decided what to do with him.

That night, it poured.

Flash floods sent hundreds to higher ground, and mudslides blocked roads. When they were clearing one road of mud and debris, horror was uncovered: six young girls in a shallow, roadside grave. All had been raped and strangled. Digging unearthed seven more, and the police remembered the lunatic in the holding cell who'd claimed a lifetime victim count of three hundred.

He led them to more bodies. All children. All girls. All abused and killed. They tried and convicted him, and sentenced him to sixteen years. He got out early for good behavior, but not before neighboring countries unearthed more bodies. He was extradited, charged, convicted, and placed in a mental institution for several more murders.

And then they released him on fifty dollars' bail and acted surprised when he absconded and was never seen again.

His mother reported that after he was released, he came to her home and demanded an inheritance, even though she hadn't seen him since he was ten years old. She told him that she was poor, with barely enough money to feed herself, so he stole her one bed and one chair, sold them on the street, and was never heard from again.

Until something interesting happened. It turns out that sometime after this, he changed his name to Paulo, briefly shacked up with a schoolteacher, and sired a son. Who had recently taken one of those fun DNA tests that you can get, that will tell you where your ancestors came from. It was for school, as he was in his second year at university and had to do a genetics presentation.

The college student, Tomas, said that his father was a groundskeeper for a small beach-side resort a few towns over, that catered to European yoga enthusiasts. It was a four-hour drive to Canacas.

"You found him," I breathed, after reading the case file.

My eyes filled with tears. I wasn't sure that anyone had ever given me a better gift.

"And he's still alive?" I said. "We can..."

"We have a hotel reservation there next week Tuesday. We will be Justine Clappinger, and Harrison Child, yoga tourists from California."

I flung my arms around Hyde's neck and kissed his cheek. "Thank you."

Chapter 16

Over the next few days, Hyde and I made a lot of noise about needing some relaxing couple time. Why anyone would buy that was beyond me--we were staying at an enormous resort-like house, where the staff carved our breakfast fruit into flowers and plied us with delicious, booze-laden drinks day and night.

But relaxing couple time it was, then. I don't think that Caio cared. As long as he had Camilla under his watchful eye, he felt the illusion of control and was content. He didn't seem to care that Frankie had taken up a work-like schedule of going into town. The first few days, she'd been tailed persistently, but she never moved from her spot at the upscale cafe.

Frankie's favorite table was in the shade of a fringed umbrella, and she only paused her ceaseless tapping at her keyboard to use the restroom. It quickly bored her guard, who took to napping with his feet up on a nearby table.

They didn't notice that Frankie was in view of the resort hotel across the street, and that within the first hour of her arrival, either Marcos or Elio would exit the hotel, saunter across the street, order a coffee, and drop off a keyfob in the ladies' restroom with connectivity codes.

Once Frankie synced up with Elio's computer, she spent hours hunting down leads that he had deciphered the night before. Despite their hard work, we didn't seem any closer to having the answers we needed. Elio was very good, but the sheer amount of information he had to go through was daunting.

"Tomorrow," he would type to Frankie via instant messaging, before severing their computers' connection. "Tomorrow I will find what we are looking for."

He had typed that for a week now. Elio was looking more and more haggard every time Frankie saw him. She was getting concerned that he wasn't eating or sleeping well. But we still didn't know who was behind the human trafficking.

HYDE and I borrowed a minivan from the compound, with Caio's blessing. It wasn't anything to look at, with its faded paint job and worn seats. But it had bulletproof windows, and Camilla assured me that it would run. It was supposed to look unimposing, she said, but it was serviced regularly. I certainly hoped so. Where we were going, we might need to get away fast.

It was a four-hour drive to Caracas. We got terrible

reception on the radio, and I shut it off out of frustration a half an hour in. Someone had failed to mention that in *this* particular minivan, the AC didn't work. Our windows were rolled down, but if we slowed below forty, the humidity and heat overtook us. We got stuck in traffic on the way out of town. I hit hot and sweaty in five minutes flat and coasted into cranky shortly after. After turning off the radio, it only took two sighs before Hyde turned to me with a little smile on his lips.

"What's wrong?" he said.

"Nothing." I was being petulant, and I knew it, but I couldn't seem to stop myself anyway.

"Your crossed arms and sighing say otherwise." He chuckled. "We can stop in the next village and pick up cold drinks if you'd like. I doubt open container laws are highly enforced here, so we could even get you a beer."

"No, that's fine." I looked out the window.

"A margarita? An entire bottle of chilled champagne and a straw? What's it going to take?" He poked my shoulder a few times, teasing.

"Where were you, anyway?" I said, turning my head to look at him.

Gone was my determination to not ask him what he had done the week he was missing in Miami. I had done so well, too... made it a long time without asking. But I was irritable and tense and needed an outlet, and my big fat mouth had decided this was the bear I was going to poke.

If I had expected chagrin or a stuttering defense, I was to be sorely disappointed.

Hyde just laughed at me and checked his watch. "I'm impressed! You made it 242 hours, fourteen minutes without asking."

I wrinkled my nose. He laughed again. With one arm resting on the open window of the car, the breeze ruffling his hair, his deep tan set against the white of his straight teeth, and his sunglasses on, he looked like a Ray-ban advertisement, one that you might see in the pages of *Vogue* or *Architectural Digest*.

Meanwhile, I'd jammed all my adorably curled hair into a messy topknot the second we decided to roll down the windows, and I'm pretty sure the makeup I'd carefully applied was sliding off my face like a melted Halloween mask. I had pit stains and ass-crack sweat, and my all-too-handsome boyfriend was laughing at me.

I took the high road and flipped him the bird. He laughed again, and I sunk lower into my seat, pouting.

"I have a plan to tell you," he said, sliding his hand to the back of my neck. He rubbed there, in a soothing pattern, in the way he knew I liked. "If you want, I can tell you right now. I'd rather wait, but it's up to you."

"How long?" I all but grunted.

"Huh?"

"How long do I have to wait?" I liked there to be a time limit to suffering, which is why I set a distance goal on the treadmill and ran flat out until it was done.

He chuckled. "If all goes well, less than thirty-six hours."

"You know, I could die on this case we're doing," I said. "And then I'll never know."

"You won't really care if you're dead."

He was teasing and fully rational, and I wasn't in the mood for either.

"Well, if *you* die, I'm going to have Frankie tell me everything," I retorted.

"Frankie can tell you the what, but she can't tell you the why." He chuckled. "But it's good to know that you can joke about me dying again." He checked his watch once again. "That only took 967 hours, and seventeen minutes."

I rolled my eyes and punched him lightly in the shoulder.

"Ow," he deadpanned.

I laughed.

We stopped in the next village and bought one of those styrofoam ice chests, filled it with ice and Brazilian orange sodas. I didn't care how many grams of sugar they had; they were delicious. With my feet on the dash and our new tape of Journey's Greatest Hits playing loudly, my mood improved dramatically. If someone had graphed it, it would have looked like the beginning part of a roller coaster, where it goes clickety-clack, straight up.

We talked about the case, about what Frankie and Elio would find.

"And what about that slutty maid setting her sights on Howard?" I asked. "What is *that* about?"

The maid, Lynsee, had gone out of her way the past week

to be around our group as much as possible. She served drinks by the pool, sashayed around the dinner table, and made enough fluttering eyes at Howard that he'd finally noticed. He seemed a bit bewildered by the attention, but I was concerned he might do something he--or Frankie--would regret.

Hyde rolled his eyes. "I don't know, but he better not flirt back. He might be tempted to, in order to make Frankie jealous, but if he takes it too far, there will be no coming back from that."

"They're not together, anymore, though," I said, uncertainly.

"Yeah, but they still love each other. Everyone who knows them is looking like this is some sort of weird intermission. But if he goes and sleeps with someone else..." He shook his head. "Frankie doesn't suffer from low self-esteem."

I shrugged and nodded. "True."

"It would hurt her, but I really think she would be done with him. She's not the kind of woman who wants to play tug of war with a man. She knows she's worth more than that."

"Damn straight," I said, sloshing some orange soda onto my skirt with the force of my agreement.

I was glad the skirt was a busy print--the orange stain kind of blended in with the coral parrot next to it. Trina Turk knew what she was doing when she designed this thing. Vacation wear, indeed.

"I just hope that he doesn't lose sight of what he really wants, just because he is angry," Hyde said.

I was silent for a few moments, thinking. Hyde's words made me nervous. In a perfect world, with perfect people, Howard would realize that his pride and fear of rejection weren't great enough to keep him from Frankie's love. He would forgive her, and they would grow up a little bit, and never repeat the same mistakes. All would be well, and this would be something hardly worth remembering, a blip.

But life wasn't perfect, and neither were people. The part of me that itched to control things wanted to try and fix it. I could talk to Frankie or Howard. As soon as the impulse arose, I tried to drown it with logic and self-control.

The fact is, I'd talked to Howard already, and it hadn't gone well. I had already spoken to him as a boss. I couldn't go back and try to have the same conversation as a friend. That was one of the shitty things about being the boss. You had to choose one lane on an issue and stick to it. I gave Hyde the side-eye. Maybe he could...

"Yeah, I know," he said. "I should try and talk to him."

"How do you do that?" I said. "It's like you're in my brain sometimes."

"I'm pretty good at reading body language, Elayna." He smiled. "But I will admit that I might be extra attuned to yours."

"Good answer."

"We haven't talked about what the real problem is, though," he said.

I raised my eyebrow in question.

"Camilla." He glanced away from the road to take in my expression. "What do you think she's thinking?"

"She's hard to read right now." I squinted through the windshield as if I could focus hard enough to have a clear answer. "She's worried, I think. Worried about the situation, but also about what decision she's going to make."

Hyde shook his head. "I get it. It's a huge choice. Not just for her, but for everyone. I mean...the whole country is riding on her decision, in some ways."

My foot bounced up and down with nerves at the statement. Hyde was right. I wanted to keep tunnel vision on this, but the reality kept busting through my mental walls like the damn Kool-aid man.

I wanted to think it was about me, about our team, about us. It wasn't. That was just a small cog in the working machine that was this clusterfuck. It made me regret leaving Camilla behind, unprotected. And yet, the man we were hunting called to me like a siren song across the water. In some ways, this might be my most important mission. I couldn't help but feeling like I needed to be in two places at once.

"Do you think it will be ok until we get back?" I said.

"Yes. Camilla is safe there. Her uncle wants her alive, thinks he is getting her cooperation. I have no idea what her brother wants or thinks, but Caio will protect her until we can figure things out."

"You sure?" I said, wincing.

"Yes," he said, grabbing my hand and giving it a squeeze. "I wouldn't have been alright with us leaving if I thought anyone left behind would be in danger. Besides, we need to look this guy up. He's gotten away with it for too long."

I started paying attention when Hyde slowed the car. To our right was a break in the greenery--two half stucco walls holding back the undergrowth. A small carved wooden sign said, *Vila do Mar*. This was our stop. Our tires rolled over the rounded cobblestones of the driveway, setting a low percussion to our progress. Fresh sea air wafted through our open windows.

About a half a mile down, the foliage gave way to an opening where you could see the pale blue ocean and the resort. There was a large main building, done in the same stucco style as other buildings in the area. It was painted a deep mushroom color with cream trim and shutters. Dotted along the beach were about fifteen small bungalows. Some were tucked halfway into the jungle, giving the appearance of an amoeba taking over a cell.

We hadn't even stopped the car before a valet was approaching Hyde with a bright smile on his tan face. I went to check us in while Hyde unloaded our bags. We were booked for five nights, but I sincerely hoped that we had this finished before we saw the next dawn. Our plan was to leave because of a family emergency.

For the next however many hours, I was Justine Clappinger, and Hyde was Harrison Child, a long-term dating couple from Los Angeles, who had heard about Vila do Mar from our friends in Switzerland. The interior was air-conditioned with large overhead fans with blades in the shape of feathers swirling. The terra-cotta tile floors and the cushioned furniture were welcoming, and I paused for a moment, getting my bearings and enjoying the feel of cool air against my sticky skin.

The young woman behind the receptionist counter was smiling at me so hard I wondered if it hurt, or if she was one of those enviable people who genuinely felt happy all the time. I smiled back, and tried to act like I was carefree and looking forward to a week of yoga and five-star pescatarian food. No wonder this place wasn't popular with the locals. In a country that prided itself on high-quality beef, who wanted to come and not try any of it?

Apparently, yoga people didn't like really good food. But maybe it was a precautionary measure. I wouldn't want to tuck into a thick porterhouse the size of my head if I were going to have to do sunrise group yoga the next morning. No one likes the farter in yoga class.

"Hello, and welcome," she said in English. "Reservation?"

"Under Clappinger."

I tried to amp up the wattage of my smile so it would compare to hers, but the effort was too great and I slowly let it fade back to what I thought was reasonable. I wasn't one of those people who could show all my front teeth without looking like I was a manic mental patient on the loose, or desperately holding back a questionable fart.

"Very good," she said. "We have you in the Shell Cottage. It has an excellent view of the ocean."

I almost rolled my eyes. They *all* had an excellent view

of the ocean. That's what comes with the territory when all the bungalows were built on the beach. But I thanked her and produced the requested ID and credit card, and signed the statement with my fake name when I was asked to do so. I was wondering what the bathroom situation was like when she interrupted my thoughts.

"And you are very lucky," she said, her grin getting larger, a feat that should have been impossible. "Our vinyasa guru has been held over from India due to a flight cancellation, and he has agreed to lead a sunset flow on the beach. I've taken the liberty of signing you and Mr. Child up for the class."

"Oh, how exciting," I said, leaning close.

I hoped that she wouldn't read the shock in my expression. Hyde had decided to make our reservation for when there were no teachers in residence, so we wouldn't get roped into things like this. This vinyasa guy was supposed to have been gone this morning, and the ashtanga lady from Bali wasn't supposed to arrive until tomorrow.

But here we were, two supposed yoga enthusiasts, getting a *treat*. I tried to act like it was an unexpected chocolate mint on my pillow instead of the dead rat I felt it was. Me and Hyde, doing yoga? We stretched, and I had taken yoga classes. But those were the kind that you could find at any gym across the country. I knew the basic moves, and that was it. I hoped there was a lot of child's pose and corpse, otherwise I might blow our cover.

"Honey," I trilled, as Hyde came in with our bags. My eyes were wide and my teeth were a bit clenched, but my back was to the receptionist and I kept my tone light. "Guess what? We get to do yoga on the beach tonight. A sunset *flow*."

I could tell that he was trying not to laugh at my expression--I could see the little tell-tale tremor of his lips--but he managed to smile widely.

"Wonderful," he said, sounding like he really did think it was wonderful.

The receptionist was still smiling. "Our restaurant is remaining vegan for one more evening, in honor of the guru. Enjoy your stay."

I smiled and nodded.

We got directions to our cottage, and as soon as we were out the back door of the place, heading down the cobblestone path, I hissed, "I'm not really good at yoga."

Hyde chuckled. "You never cease to amaze me. We're literally about to try and kill a man who murdered *hundreds*, and you're more scared about the yoga?"

"I'm good at killing people. I'm inexperienced when it comes to yoga."

"You'll be fine," he said. "Just do what everyone else is doing, and it will be ok."

"Ah, public sweating and conforming to a group. Two of my favorite things." I knew I was being unreasonable, but I really didn't like group workouts, and I *hated* not knowing what to do.

Hyde shook his head and chuckled.

We didn't see anyone else on the way to our cottage, which turned out to be darling. It was just two rooms, a living room bedroom combination, and a bathroom, but it was sparkling clean and done in soft yellow and cream. The tile floor was cool under my feet once I'd kicked off my sandals, and there were three huge, floor to ceiling windows that faced the ocean.

I flopped onto the bed, which was surprisingly soft, and rolled to my stomach. "Can we go on a real vacation one of these days?"

He raised an eyebrow. "Have you forgotten our time in Italy already?"

"Doesn't count," I said. "Camilla's cousin kept chasing us. It's not a real vacation if you think you're being hunted."

"True," he said. He sat down on the bed next to me and began walking his fingers up the back of my leg where my skirt had hitched up. "Then again, every day feels like vacation when I'm with you."

I rolled my eyes at the cheesy line, but promptly forgot my sarcasm when he leaned down to kiss me.

Chapter 17

There were about twelve people already assembled in front of the instructor by the time we made it to yoga that evening. That made me happy--we'd be able to get a spot in the back. The beach was stunning. It was the perfect beach to drink a margarita and read a good, mindless book, and we were about to ruin it by doing yoga.

The sun was low in the sky, but it was still bright. There was a breeze, and I was glad I'd wound my hair into a messy bun low on my neck. I knew that much about yoga--hair placement was very important. Your ponytail or bun had to be very high or very low, otherwise you wouldn't be able to do all the moves.

To the side of the group was a pile of foam blocks and some rope. Everyone who was already there had one of each, so Hyde set up our mats in the back and I went to grab the supplies. When I handed Hyde a foam block and a length of soft rope, he raised his eyebrows in question. I shrugged lightly, letting him know that I had no idea what they were for, either.

We waited about five more minutes. Other people were stretching, so I sat on my mat and gave a half-hearted run-through of some basics while I scoped out the group. Most of the people were of European descent--there were some straight-up pasty white people in the mix. I wondered if they were from Scandinavian countries, or maybe Ireland.

The teacher was the main exception. He was a tall, thin man with beautiful dark skin and expressive brown eyes. He was relatively plain-looking but carried himself like a dancer--light and precise movements, all grace. I wondered if I studied yoga long enough, whether some of that elegance would rub off on me. I wasn't light on my feet--not in that enviable way that ballet dancers are. I contemplated the possible benefits of yoga with a slight frown.

"Welcome," the teacher said, in melodiously-accented English, after checking his fitness watch one last time. Along with the watch, he wore numerous bangles with different crystals. He lifted his arm, and I heard a faint jingle.

The class came to their feet at his words, so Hyde and I did, too.

"I am Rahul Laghari. Welcome to our sunset yoga class. It has been a wonderful week here. I couldn't pass up the opportunity to enjoy another flow with you, after my travel plans were delayed until tomorrow. Welcome to the newcomers in our midst. Namaste. Class, namaste to the newcomers."

As one, the class turned to me and Hyde, put their hands in prayer position over their hearts, bowed slightly, and said, "Namaste."

Hyde and I repeated the motions and words, and I hoped that I didn't look as freaked out as I felt. There was something about entire groups doing things at exactly the same time that reminded me of Children of the Corn, or Bodysnatchers, or that one episode of Buffy the Vampire Slayer where Willow was controlled by her science project egg.

We went through a series that the instructor called a 'heart-opening', which conveyed very different imagery for me than it did for others, I'm sure. It was slow and methodical and easy to follow, so when he said that he was moving into a rhythm flow, I had built up a certain level of confidence...which turned out to be a mistake.

Up and down we went, holding poses, feeling our breath, talking about opening our chest to the sky (again, different imagery), and feeling grounded to the earth. Every pose had a name, which everyone else seemed to already know. All I knew was child's pose and some of the warriors, and even those I got mixed up.

But now there were a slew of different animals, one after another, as if in a mad dash to make it onto Noah's ark. Camel! Frog! Cow! Lion! Monkey! I stopped trying to remember which was which, and just followed the petite woman in front of me. She was probably early sixties, but the muscles under her skin were solid and thin--she looked like the bystander to an accident that would be able to lift the car off a trapped child from adrenaline.

Sweat dripped from my temples, made damp half-moons under my armpits, settled in my crotch and butt. This was not a relaxing 'flow' by any means. I huffed and puffed and tried to hold my breath and exhale when the teacher told me to, but I felt like Lucy and Ethel in the chocolate factory--the poses and instructions kept coming, and I couldn't quite seem to keep my chest high, abs in, back straight, breath held lightly in my center (whatever the heck *that* meant), while holding poses that would have made a contortionist proud.

I looked over at Hyde at one point and almost hissed at him when I realized he had achieved a perfect swan pose, while my attempt looked like deranged body origami. But I kept on, keeping my thoughts off my face, even when the instructor deigned to leave his throne-like mat and walk around the group to instruct and critique form.

Cool hands appeared on my back while I was doing downward-facing dog, and I had to resist the natural urge to throw an elbow at whoever was at my unguarded back. But it was just the instructor.

"Flat back, high bottom," he said in a soothing tone. "Release the tension. You're doing great."

But I wasn't, and we both knew he was lying. Still, it was kindness, and I couldn't get mad at him for it.

After what seemed like hours, he finally stopped calling out animal names in rapid succession and moved us into a remarkably slower flow. A cooldown, he called it. I was grateful. The hair at my temples was plastered against my skin, and my face felt like it was on fire. I was going to need another shower before dinner.

At the thought of dinner, my stomach sounded a long, low lament. It sounded like the mating call of a frustrated lion, maybe, or perhaps a crane. Hyde gave me the side-eye and a smirk, and I very casually flipped him the bird. He smiled the kind of smile that said he would have been laughing if we weren't in public.

"And from Child's pose, we are moving into Corpse. Lie on your back, and we will go through the relaxation process. Now, deep breath in, find your center, and wiggle then relax your toes. Wiggle, wiggle, wiggle...relax. Now your ankles. Imagine they are at rest. Let your healing breath move in and out at your own pace, and send your breath down to your ankles to let them relax."

I wanted to educate this guy on how the human circulatory system worked. We couldn't send our breath anywhere, unless he meant via oxygen-rich red blood cells, in which case, our breath was being sent everywhere in our bodies, all the time.

"Now your fingers. Wiggle, wiggle, wiggle, and...relaaaax. Send your breath to your hands and wrists, feel them become heavy and grounded to the earth. You are a corpse, becoming one with the earth."

I was going to *make* a corpse soon, and send it to become one with the earth. Or ocean. We didn't have a firm disposal plan yet.

"Visualize what you want..."

I pictured Alonso Lopez dead, pictured his victims' families getting resolution.

"Now send your breath into your visualization."

I knew *that* shit wasn't possible, even accounting for red blood cells.

"Now focus on your forearms. Let them become heavy and one with the earth."

I followed the instructions, and let my eyes close against the sunset rays that were painting a vivid water-color in the sky and against the ocean. A coolish breeze wafted in my hair.

"Now your calves. Let your feet fall to the sides as you relax your ankles and calves."

What was I so worried about, anyway? This guy was old. He would be a cinch to eliminate. And the situation with Camilla? We would figure that out, too. In a few weeks, we would wrap things up here, and head back to California together. We'd been together for many years. Nothing could change that.

"And your knees...relax your knees..."

I WOKE up to Hyde nudging me in the leg with his foot. I scowled over at him, but he was barely containing his laughter. I could see it dancing in his eyes, his lips pressed together against the sound that wanted to erupt. And there was quiet snickering among some of the yoga class.

"What?" I silently mouthed to Hyde.

"You were snoring," he mouthed back.

My eyes went wide, and I could feel the intense blush heat my face.

"Oh shit," I mouthed back.

He turned his face back to the sky, clamped his eyes shut and clenched his fists, but his whole body was shaking with suppressed laughter. The sight of his laughter made me giggle, and I slapped a hand over my mouth, my eyes wide.

"All of our bodies need different things after an intense session." The pleasant tenor of the instructor's voice said, from the front of the class. "It is up to each of us to honor what our own body requires. There is no shame in any reaction to a flow, whether that be laughter, sleep, pain, or tears."

We'd come full circle to tampon commercials, again.

I barely stifled renewed laughter by biting my lip. But a tear did leak from my eyes. Despite my inappropriate hilarity, I was grateful for the instructor's words. He was kind, and the other snickers in the class had abruptly stopped with his commentary. Kindness was so under-rated. Our world needed more kindness.

The class ended, and I dusted the sand from my mat as I rolled it up. I looked up to find the teacher at my elbow. His eyes were full of mirth.

"I take it as a personal compliment whenever someone falls asleep in corpse pose," he said, low enough for just me to hear. "So I thank you for boosting my ego."

I grinned. "Glad I could help, and thank you for the great class."

I was surprised to find I meant every word. I hadn't been looking forward to doing yoga with a bunch of strangers on the beach, but now that I was finished, I was glad that I had done it. If nothing else, I wouldn't need to warm up and stretch before our mission tonight.

He nodded in acknowledgment and went to greet the class members who were waiting to speak with him.

"At least you didn't drool," Hyde whispered, his rolled yoga mat beneath his arm. "It really could have been worse."

"I don't drool in my sleep!"

"Are you sure about that?" He waggled his eyebrows.

I elbowed him in the side. "Shut it, mister. I am a *lady*."

He laughed and took the lead on the trail.

I moment later I said, "Do I really drool?"

He just laughed.

Chapter 18

The restaurant was beautiful, even if it wasn't my style. It was hippy-chic--textured, woven wall hangings adorned dark taupe walls. The tables and chairs were teak with tufted cushions, and there was a floating candle in a glass bowl in the center of every table. On the far side of the room, a wall of glass let people look out onto the ocean. The lighting was low, and most of the patrons seemed to be trying to make a romantic dinner out of the ambiance.

Our table was off to the side, but still had a great view of the ocean. I frowned down at the menu that the waiter offered. I really wanted a juicy steak or some grilled chicken. I didn't understand how people only ate plants. I mean, if it was for medical or religious reasons, sure, but I was a carnivore through and through. A meal without meat was like a romance novel without a happily ever after, or sex without orgasm to me. I didn't understand anyone who would willingly choose such a thing.

I put the menu facedown with a sigh. "Will you order for me, Hyde?"

He chuckled. "You really aren't feeling like yourself, are you?"

"I know. I'm sorry. I'll try to be good dinner company."

"You're fine. Just get your mind in the game, Elayna. We've got a long night ahead of us."

He was right. I'd glimpsed where we needed to go tonight when I was contorted upside-down and backward during yoga. It was one of six buildings tucked into the jungle on the other side of the main building. A path leading up to the cluster of houses was plainly marked, 'Employees Only' in several different languages. If we got caught over there, it would be hard to come up with a justifiable reason.

Also, we didn't know which house was his, and some of them had appeared to be split into two or three, which meant we had a lot of recon to do before we even located our target. Add to that the fact that we hadn't so much as seen him, and we were working off a grainy picture, and things got a little messy.

The only bright spot was that Frankie had gotten us a list of current employees. Even including the employees that lived in nearby towns, most were females. There were only ten or so men that worked on the property, and most of those were young. Only Alonso and the chef were in the same age bracket, but the kitchen was open until midnight, so the chef would be out of play until then.

We were hoping to make an appearance at dinner, be visible on the way back to our room, and then sneak back over to the employee huts without being seen, all in the time the kitchen was open. We had a lot to do, and not a large window to do it. My fingers drummed carelessly against the polished wood tabletop.

When the waiter returned, Hyde ordered us drinks and the roasted cauliflower as a starter. I wasn't hopeful, but when it arrived, my eyebrows rose.

The cauliflower had been chopped into bite-sizes, then roasted and covered in toppings. Several different sauces had been drizzled over the cauliflower bites, and minced green onions were sprinkled over the top. It looked like nachos, but with cauliflower instead of chips. I shrugged and popped one in my mouth.

"Oh my gosh," I mumbled around the bite. "This is so good."

Hyde laughed. "I was hoping it would surprise you. I've had a version of this dish before. Granted, I had a steak afterward, but still, this is a sleeper vegan dish."

I couldn't reply, cause I had another piece of cauliflower in my mouth, but I nodded.

When I finally swallowed, I said, "This gives me hope for the rest of the meal. You're hired as an orderer. Don't let me down."

"Oh, no pressure. Thanks," he said with a smile.

The next course was salad, which hardly inspired

enthusiasm, but it was also surprisingly good. It was arugula and roasted beets with toasted squash seeds and maple syrup and dijon vinaigrette. For the main, Hyde had ordered us ravioli, which were filled with cashew cream and spinach, in a leek and butternut sauce.

"Very good," I said after I took my first bite. "Surprisingly good. It would be better with a grilled chicken breast on top, but..." I shrugged. "Still, it's very good. Good job, orderer. If you ever can't make it as a hitman, there's always food recommendation."

"Yeah, I don't think that's a thing," he said with a raised eyebrow.

"Well, you could start a food blog or something. Or maybe be a food critic."

"They wouldn't want me as a food critic. I like food too much. Have you noticed that most food critics are thin? They spend too much time picking apart the plate in front of them to actually have time to eat."

"You're right," I said, pointing my fork at him. "But we could be the world's first fat food critics."

"Oh, you're in on this now, are you?" He laughed.

"We'll roll in on our Little Rascals, cause we'll be too fat to walk. They'll feed us; we'll enjoy it all immensely, and then we will leave good reviews. All the restaurants will be clamoring for us to visit."

Hyde laughed. "I'm pretty sure that the newspaper is the one that has to hire us. Or a magazine."

"Nah." I waved my hand. "We're going to change the whole food critic model. We'll just start our own website and offer our critiquing skills on there. I'm thinking Fat and Happy dot com. Or maybe Chubby Food Chasers dot com. Or Fats and Carbie do Dinner. Something like that."

"I like it," he said. "But I'm only going along with this plan if I can do a custom paint job on my scooter."

"Deal. But the paint job has to be in line with our branding strategy."

"Oh, does it, now?" He smiled and raised his eyebrows.

"Of course," I said. "It's in the contract you signed, duh."

Hyde laughed.

Dessert was delicious--coconut sorbet with fresh fruit-- but by the time it was served, my mind was fully on the mission. Hyde had always been good at reading my moods--he remained mostly silent as I sunk into the reality of what had to be done, the reasons behind it. I wish I could say that I enjoyed killing, but I didn't. Oh, don't get me wrong, I loved my job and I was damn good at it. But the killing was always a necessity, not a thrumming desire. It was the means to a needed end.

I certainly hoped that the day I started looking forward to the gush of blood or the struggle with my hands around a neck, I would have enough self left to retire and leave the game. My thought process had always been focused on justice for the victims and preventing future ones, not the adrenaline rush or the control of ending a life.

With this man, regardless of whether he would ever strike again, he had hurt so many--not only the girls them- selves, although the horror of what he had done to them could not be overstated. But that's not where victimization ended. There were the families of the girls, the society that would not benefit from their lives well-lived. All those bright sparks that were snuffed out at the hands of a greedy, selfish man.

There were the police, the detectives, the crime scene technicians. What Alonso had done to those girls was imprinted in shadow on a hundred other souls. Then there was the fact that he had escaped justice. How much anger and fear had that reality sown in the minds of the citizens of this country? Alonso was the proverbial boogeyman and proof that the justice system couldn't protect its citizens, all in one.

By the time the check was paid and we were heading toward the door, my body was alert and ready. I had shifted into battle mode somewhere between butternut squash pasta and coconut sorbet. If Alonso lived to see the morning, something had gone terribly wrong with our plan.

The waiter was standing near the door. "How was everything?"

"Wonderful," Hyde said with an easy smile.

"That is good to hear. Our chef is out with an illness, so we are sorry if things were a bit slow this evening."

"Tomas Tovaras?" I asked. "He is sick?"

"You know him?" the waiter asked with a broad smile.

"We have heard of him," Hyde said, smoothly. "From our friends who recommended the resort."

"Ah, yes." He nodded, gravely. "Chef Tovaras is recovering from an illness, but he should be well enough to rejoin us tomorrow. The recipes served tonight are still his, however," he added, looking concerned that we wouldn't be pleased.

"Everything was delicious," I said, mustering a smile. "And we will be here for a few days, so we will get to enjoy more of his cooking."

"Very good," the waiter said. "Enjoy the rest of your evening."

Hyde thanked the man and opened the door, and we were out in the night air.

"That complicates things a bit," he murmured when the door shut behind us.

"Yes, and no. I'm just so glad that we found out."

I shuddered to think of killing the wrong person. It was one of my very greatest fears. I had swaths of blood on my hands, but none of it was innocent. At least, I hoped not. I'd killed bad guys for good reasons, and bad guys for bad reasons, but I never wanted to kill a good guy.

"We will just have to confirm the target, and we were going to do that, anyway," I said. "Now, let's get going. Our time requirement has changed, now that the chef is in play, but we still have a lot to do."

Chapter 19

"Second window," Hyde whispered, nodding to the building before us.

After dinner, we'd gone to our cabin, dimmed the lights, got dressed, and returned to the night. We'd separated for the recon, using night-vision to spy on the occupants of the employee cottages before we approached. But now, Hyde thought he'd found our target.

I crept forward, Hyde beside me. I felt better working this together. I knew that I could focus on looking in the window and he would make sure no one was coming.

The man was sitting at the table, eating something, soup maybe. He was old and grey, his back was hunched and the skin on his face had leathered and wrinkled, like a worn jacket. But I thought it was him. I watched him as he ate.

It was always strange to come across something so dangerous doing something so mundane. A mass murderer eating soup for dinner. It was like seeing a cobra doing the laundry or a cheetah brushing its teeth. It didn't compute. I pulled away from the window and we retreated into the thick overgrowth once more.

"I think that's him," I murmured. "No other single males on your side?"

Hyde shook his head.

"There was one on mine," I said. "But he looked sick; I think it was the chef."

"How do you want to make entry?" Hyde said.

"I think we keep an eye on him until he goes to bed. Then go in through the back window. We can use the fire ladder."

Hyde nodded.

"Unless you saw a better way to do it?" I said.

"Nah. I think the window's the best bet. Front door is too well-lit, too exposed. If we go through the back, the only way people would see us is if they are staring out their back windows."

"Let's hope that doesn't happen," I said. "I would really like to get this done cleanly. We have enough tangles in this country; we don't need another."

"Agreed."

We stood in the trees for two more hours. Every once in a while, one of us would check on our target. He went to the bathroom, watched TV. Finally, he clicked off the light in the kitchen and walked to a small back room, and went vertical in bed.

"It's kind of strange to see the person but not what

they're interacting with," I said. "It looks like he's levitating."

Hyde chuckled and rummaged through his backpack, coming up with the fire ladder. It was a very handy device that I had used on several cases. Designed for people to exit upper story windows in case of a fire, it had two hooks for the bottom of the window, and a collapsible string of footholds that dropped into place when you pulled a tab. It was essentially a fancy rope ladder. They usually were red and white or silver for good visibility. I had spray-painted this one black.

We were lucky that the back window was already open to coax a breeze. All we needed to do was remove the screen, hook the ladder onto the windowsill, and climb in. The ladder helped make things quieter. It was easier to control the thumps and bumps when you weren't hoisting yourself up and kicking against the house.

We waited another half an hour or so. I watched him the whole time, and he hadn't so much as turned over. I could imagine that, for an old man, groundskeeping would be a physically demanding job. He would probably sleep soundly until the morning.

"Ok. So we go in, confirm identity, complete the mission, and ex-filtrate," I said.

"Yup. Let's go."

We had worked together long enough that we knew how to help each other without getting in the way. I kept my thermal imager on our target while Hyde carefully pried the screen from the frame and leaned it against the outside of the house. Then he hooked the ladder onto the windowsill and gently let down the steps. The sleeping man didn't stir the entire time. Still, I would feel better once we were in the same room and he was incapacitated.

"I'll go first," I said, slipping my imager into my backpack and zipping up.

Hyde nodded and held the bottom of the ladder stable as I climbed up and in. I worked my head and shoulders inside the bathroom. It was a small room, with chipped yellow tile on the floor and walls. A stall shower, a toilet in the corner, and the faint mustiness of mildew were all I noticed before it happened.

Something crumbled and gave way beneath me, and I felt Hyde's hand on my rear trying to hold me up.

"Shit," he gasped.

Then the window frame holding the ladder up crumbled away, and I went face-first through the window onto the bathroom floor.

WHAM.

My entrance was so loud, it felt like it shook the entire triplex. Behind me, I could just hear Hyde whisper-cursing outside in the dark. I made it to my hands and knees on the bathroom tile and a figure appeared in the doorway before me. I didn't think--there wasn't time. I launched myself at him, but it was clumsy.

I lurched forward, my arms around his knees, and tackled him into the small hallway. He gave a small cry of alarm, then took a deep breath--to yell for help. In one awkward move, I jerk-scooted myself up the length of his body and slapped my hands over his mouth. His teeth closed hard on the flesh of the palm that was in his half-open mouth, and I grunted. It was a bad injury, I could tell. People forgot how painful a bite could be. I briefly saw stars, but I held on.

Behind me, I heard Hyde scrabbling into the newly-enlarged window hole, but I couldn't change my focus. The man took a swing at my face, but I leaned back, still jamming his head against the floor, up against the wall. He couldn't reach my head, so he settled for punching me in the boob instead. I think the softness he felt there shocked him--his eyes went wide. For the first time, I think it registered to him that I was a woman.

The knowledge seemed to calm him. I shrugged internally. If he wanted to think he was safe because I had ovaries, I'd take that advantage. But then the large figure of Hyde loomed behind us, and he began struggling anew.

"You got him?" Hyde said.

"For the moment," I grunted. "Go turn on the TV?"

In case anyone came to the door to ask about the thump, we could use a little cover noise. Hyde was back within seconds, which was good because I'd taken another few shots to the boob while he was gone.

"Stick him, would you?" I said.

Hyde nodded, unzipped his pack, and came up with a syringe. Alonso's eyes widened, but Hyde already had the business end jammed into his neck, the plunger depressed. Within seconds, he went slack.

I pulled my hand from his face and inspected the

damage. Not as bad as I'd first thought--there wasn't a chunk of flesh missing, but there was a large gash.

"I'm really sick of getting bit."

"Maybe we should have worn gloves," Hyde said, rummaging through his pack once more.

"Hindsight is twenty-twenty." I let Hyde bandage my wound, then flexed my hand.

It was throbbing, but I could still use it. I wasn't sure if it needed stitches, but that was a problem for future Elayna to deal with. I had enough on my plate right now.

"I bled in his mouth," I said. "This is a mistake I've made twice, now."

"Stop letting people bite you, maybe," Hyde suggested lightly.

I snorted. "Thanks for that helpful tip."

But Hyde was already one room over, rummaging through the kitchen cabinets. He came back with a bottle of whiskey. He uncapped the bottle, rolled the limp body to the side, and rinsed out his mouth.

"That's one way of dealing with the DNA, I guess." I shrugged. "Let's check identity and get this done."

We separated. The sedative that Hyde had injected Alonso with should last a good hour. We had time to find something to establish his identity--his real one or his fake one, I didn't much care. I just needed to know it was him.

Hyde waved an envelope at me. "Here we go. Paulo Chavez," he read. "He's our guy."

"Good," I said.

I was tired. I wanted a shower and a bunch of antibacterial solution for my hand. Human mouths were nasty in the best of cases, and who knows where that mouth had been? I looked down at my hand, at the stark white bandage. Mine wasn't the first human flesh his mouth had tasted. My stomach turned.

"Are you alright?" Hyde was studying my face.

"Physically, I'm fine. I was just thinking of all his victims. All those poor girls." There were tears in my eyes. I swiped them away, embarrassed. "I'm sorry."

"Do not *ever* apologize for that," Hyde said, fiercely. "That's one of the reasons I love you, Elayna. You still have a soft heart. You care about the victims. That's a heavy load to carry in this line of work, but that's what makes you so special."

I sniffled, still embarrassed, but his words had helped. I did care. That's why I hunted monsters in the dark.

"Ok," I said, taking a deep breath. "How are we doing this?"

"Think he's suicidal?" Hyde suggested.

"He's too self-centered to do that," I said. "The people around him might not know that he's a monster, but they probably know him well enough to find a suicide suspicious. Besides, we kind of ruined the wall on the way in. Stupid dry-rot."

"Indeed," he said, dryly. "But you're right. How about a burglary gone wrong?"

"Fine," I said. "I'll take care of him. You find something worth taking."

Hyde nodded and moved into the bedroom. I heard

drawers opening and closing, stuff being tossed quietly to the ground.

"Alright," I said, to no one in general.

I clicked the timer on my watch on, then put my foot on Alonso's throat and shifted my weight there. It took about four minutes to strangle someone, so I watched my watch as the seconds ticked by. I tried very hard not to think about what I was doing, where my foot was placed.

It took two minutes before Hyde emerged from the bedroom. He held up a watch and a ring and shrugged, then moved to the living room. At three minutes, Hyde was loading up liquor bottles into his backpack, then slid a manila envelope full of newspaper clippings and a lock of hair into a desk drawer. He was standing by as my watch clicked up to four, then hit five. I stepped down from my awkward perch, and Hyde checked his pulse.

"No pulse, not breathing," he said.

We stood by for another two minutes just to be sure, then we dropped out the same hole we'd gone in. It was larger now, a section of the wood surrounding the window frame had been torn away. The upper section of the window was still in place, but the bottom was a jagged hole.

"Let's go," Hyde said, packing the ladder into his backpack and scanning the area to make sure we hadn't left anything behind.

We retreated into the treeline once more and moved parallel to the employee path until we could go no further.

"Moment of truth," I said.

There was no way for us to see if anyone was coming up the path. If someone caught us up here, our presence would be remembered and reported once Alonso's body was found. This would be a nerve-wracking thirty seconds. I stepped out first and began to jog down the path, acting as if I'd been trail-running with a backpack. My heart pounded, and sweat collected at my temples.

I heard Hyde coming behind me, doing the same thing. Hopefully, we would look casual, not at all like the killers we were. I counted the seconds as I ran along the trail, my heart pounding a whooshing pattern in my ears. I pushed hard--not so hard it would look like we were fleeing, but just hard enough that it looked like we were running.

It seemed to last an eternity, but we finally hit the guest trail. From there, we melted into the shadows and made our way back to our cottage. It wasn't until we were safely in our room with the door locked behind us that I could start to breathe normally again. I shucked off my backpack and let it fall to the floor. Hyde did the same, bottles clanking together as his bag hit the ground.

"What are we going to do with those?" I asked, still a little out of breath.

"I'm going to dump the booze down the drain, bust them up inside a garbage bag and dump them in the ocean," he said.

I nodded, impressed. "Good plan."

"There wasn't anything else there worth taking," he said. "I figured with the alcohol missing, they might think a drug addict or some teenagers did it."

"Here's hoping. Think the newspaper clippings will be enough to tip them off?"

He shrugged. "I hope so. It would be interesting to me if I were police investigating a murder. Plus--his picture is in some of them. He looks the same--just older."

It was all we could do, for now. If worse came to worst, we could always call in an anonymous tip. I wanted the victims' families to know that the nightmare was over. It probably wouldn't help their pain, but it would be some kind of closure.

We took turns showering. There hadn't been any blood splatter, but I wanted the feel of that house, the sweat of what I had done, off my skin. It was weird--I believed in what I did, but there was a part of me that abhorred it. It took a certain amount of conviction to stand on another human's throat for five minutes, to feel the life and breath of another person leave at your hand--or foot, as it were.

I needed the hot shower to move on. When I finally emerged from the bathroom, a towel wrapped over my wet hair and a billow of steam in my wake, Hyde was sitting at the small dinette table, working over a charcuterie board. I stopped and gaped at it.

"You mean you had this packed the whole time, and you didn't tell me?" I said, accusingly.

He smiled as he sliced salami. "We had to go to dinner for our cover, so I figured this would be a nice surprise when we got back. Besides, I can't take all the credit. Camilla helped me put this together."

"Wow," I said, surveying the bounty.

There were mounds of salami, soppressata, and prosciutto, several different cheeses, glistening stuffed olives, a baguette, crackers and some kind of dip, and one lone stalk of celery on the side.

"What's with the celery?" I said, cocking my head to the side.

"Camilla says you need something green on every char-cuterie board." He shrugged. "She packed it, so I put it on there."

"She does have very specific guidelines about meat platters." I ticked off my fingers as I recited, "At least three different kinds of meat, lots of cheese, pickled or brined items for salt, minimum two kinds of carbs, and if she's really feeling fancy, she'll pair brie and a little pot of rasp-berry jam."

My words trailed off as I slipped into worry once more.

Hyde kissed my temple. "That frown is for tomorrow." He opened a bottle of sparkling wine with a crisp 'pop' and poured two glasses. They were the plastic-wrapped glasses from the side of the sink--not quite champagne flutes, but I didn't care. "Tonight, we are celebrating a successful mission, and another target down."

I accepted the glass he handed me and dutifully clinked my glass against his, then took a sip.

"I don't know if I would call it a *true* success," I said. "We kind of broke the building on the way in."

"We did management a favor," Hyde said, lightly. "We rid them of one kind of pest and alerted them to the presence of another. Now they can get rid of the termites or the rot and move on."

"True." I loaded up a cracker, popped it in my mouth, and slumped into one of the dining chairs. "So when we get back tomorrow, we need to check in with Frankie first thing and see if Elio has made any decent progress on the numbers. We need to see the flow of money in this organization."

"We're not going back tomorrow," Hyde said. "I've got you for two more days."

I frowned. "I don't want to stay here for two more days. There's a cooling corpse with our name on it just up the hill."

"That part of the plan is still in place. We'll go do the sunrise yoga and have Frankie call in a family emergency to the front desk, and then we'll leave."

"Where are we going?"

"It's a surprise," Hyde said, doing jazz hands to complete the statement.

"You know how much I love those." I tried to sound put out, but Hyde had just pulled one of my feet into his lap and started rubbing it, so I couldn't even pretend well.

"I promise it's a good surprise," he said. "It includes an ocean view at a hotel where we won't be killing anyone, and a day of spa pampering, because you deserve it."

Hyde knew he had me, I could tell by his smug smile. He knew how much I loved a day at the spa.

"Fine," I said. "But what are you going to be doing while I get buffed and scrubbed?"

His eyebrows rose. "Oh, I'm going to be right there with you. I've never passed up a massage a day in my life." He frowned and wiggled his toes. "I am a little scared for the pedicurist, though. Not sure when was the last time I had callus' remover."

I snickered. "You'll just have to tip well." I thought for a moment. "Alright. I'll go along with your surprise."

He grinned. "How magnanimous of you. But just so we're clear--you didn't really have a choice in the matter."

I snorted.

Chapter 20

Morning yoga wasn't as intense as sunset yoga. This was what I had in mind yesterday-- gentle stretching, and no talking from the instructor so that you could really hear the ocean and the sounds of the jungle waking up. I was glad--I was sore from the shots Alonso had got in last night. My hand throbbed, too. I prayed that the glue we'd applied to the wound held up under the strategically placed bandaid.

I was in the middle of cobra pose, my eyes blissfully closed, as close to achieving zen as someone like me ever can be, when I felt a gentle tap on my shoulder. I looked up, alarmed by the possibility that I had somehow fallen asleep and started snoring while holding myself up in a stretch. It was one of the ladies from the front desk. She had come down onto the beach in her pantyhose and heels, and there was sand all over her feet.

"Ms. Clappinger?" she said in a low voice, her eyes full of concern.

"Yes."

"There is an emergency phone call holding for you in the lobby."

Her eyes were wide, and I wondered what Frankie had said to her to put such a fearful expression on her face. I played the part--I leaped off my mat and left it and my sandals, hustling along barefoot with the poor woman who was struggling in her heels in the sand.

When we finally got inside, the lady fairly trotted to an office to the side of the front desk, ushering me inside like I was gravely wounded, and seating me in one of the chairs in front of the desk. She plucked the phone from the receiver, and thrust it at me, then pushed a button and retreated, shutting the frosted glass door behind her.

"What on earth did you say?" I said.

Frankie's laugh tinkled like delicate wind chimes on the other end of the line. "I told her that your mother had died unexpectedly, and that your stepfather had been arrested for her murder, and that you needed to come home immediately because your stepsisters are trying to take over your mother's property."

"What?" I exclaimed. Then a little more quietly added, "Shit, Frankie. You know I'm not good at crying on command."

"Just pluck one of your eyelashes. Or nose hairs. That's what the actors do."

"I don't have nose hair long enough to pluck. Or at

least, I hope I don't." I tried to make my tone frantic, but keep my voice low enough that my words wouldn't be distinguishable. I would bet fifty bucks that the desk clerk was still hovering near the door. "When did this happen?" I asked, louder.

"Bruno says hello," Frankie said. "He's snuffling my lap right now, and drooling all over. But it's my fault--I ate a bagel at my desk and I think he's looking for crumbs."

It was hard not to smile at the image. Finding invisible nibbles was one of Bruno's favorite past-times.

"What happened?" I shrieked.

"Wow," Frankie said. "That was piercing. You're really trying to sell this, aren't you?"

"We kind of need to," I murmured. "Plus, Hyde has promised me a spa day if we can get out of here on time."

"Oh, lucky." Frankie sounded wistful. "He's such a great boyfriend. I want a spa day."

"Just tell Camilla," I said, my voice strong. "She will take care of everything."

"You're right," Frankie said, sounding thoughtful. "I bet she has a masseuse who could come out to the villa."

"I have to go! We'll be home tomorrow! I need the first flight out." I slammed the phone down.

I was right about the desk clerk listening, because she'd opened the door before I even got there.

"Is everything alright?" she asked, her face etched with worry.

"No." I hadn't managed tears, so I just kept my eyes wide and my lips pressed tightly together. "I'm so sorry, but we will be checking out immediately. We need to get back home as quickly as possible."

"I am so sorry for your loss, Ms. Clappinger," the woman said. "Is there anything at all that we can do?"

For a moment, I felt a pang of regret. She really seemed to mean it.

I took a deep breath and tangled my fingers together. "Can someone go tell my boyfriend to meet me back at our cottage? I need to start packing. Oh, and I left my shoes." I gestured lamely at my bare feet.

"Of course, of course," she said.

"Thank you." I hung my head and nearly jogged out of the lobby.

I felt bad lying to these people. I felt bad that someone would discover Alonso's body today. I hadn't seen any police or heard a disruption, so I didn't think it had happened yet. But with as hot as it got here? It wouldn't be twenty-four hours.

They would be fearful that there was danger here, and it would be painful for the people who found him to hold those memories. And yet...I thought back to that pair of little pink shoes in front of the next-door neighbor's door. That little girl would never be his victim, and that was worth the peripheral discomfort. They would move on, and eventually everyone would forget him, and nothing like that would ever happen again, here.

My feet carried me down the smooth path and I retrieved the key from the zippered pocket along my thigh. Once inside, I rinsed my feet and changed my clothes, and tossed things haphazardly into our suitcases. I planned on leaving a sandal, a sports bra, and our toothpaste behind, to complete the appearance that we had left in a rush.

Hyde came rushing in moments later. "What on earth did you and Frankie do to that woman?"

I told him the story in a hysterical-sounding tone, and he grinned.

"No one's listening, but that was an excellent performance. I asked the lady to have our car brought around."

"Well, as soon as you get changed, we can leave." I scanned the room. "Does it look like I panicked?"

"Yep," he said. "But then, hotel rooms always look like this when you leave them."

I swatted at him, but missed. "Go get dressed. I was promised spa treatments."

He grinned and we were out the door minutes later.

HYDE WOULDN'T TELL me where we were going. He knew it was driving me nuts, but I refused to ask and he refused to tell me. We both knew this dynamic was playing out. It made me suspicious but made him all too cheery for my liking. All I knew was that we were heading the opposite direction from how we'd arrived. This didn't make sense to me, but Hyde had an almost infallible sense of direction, so I knew we probably weren't lost.

I chewed my lip and tried to guess where we might be going. From what I remembered of the map, there wasn't much up here. Canacas was the only real town for miles, and even that was a little blip, nothing more than a small market, a gas station, a few scattered buildings, and the resort. But we were headed North? East? I couldn't tell.

I tapped my fingers against my leg, impatient and curious.

"You're just going to have to get used to not knowing," Hyde said. "It's a forty-eight hour surprise. Can you handle that? Forty-eight hours of not knowing everything?"

"I guess so."

"I promise you--I have it all planned. Can you trust me?" He turned his big brown eyes on me and looked like he really cared about my answer.

"Of course I trust you, Hyde." I grabbed his leg and squeezed. "I'm just not used to not knowing. I'm sorry. I'm excited about whatever you have planned. Really."

He grinned like I had just given him a great gift, and I resolved to try to relax and enjoy myself.

"Good," he said. "Cause the first surprise is behind your chair."

I raised my eyebrows and turned around to find a small ice chest tucked there. I opened it and found two mini bottles of champagne, and a package of plastic whirly straws on top.

"Whirly straws!" I said, my eyes bright. "I love those things. So underrated. So fun!"

He chuckled at my reaction. "One for each of us, now. Don't bogart the champagne."

I retrieved the bottles and unwrapped the straws,

giving Hyde a bottle with the yellow straw. I took the electric green for myself--it had an extra loop.

"Ah," I said, taking my first sip. "So refreshing."

He chuckled. "Cheers."

It wasn't a long drive--just about an hour--and we were pulling off the main road. But I was really confused when he pulled into a small fishing village. There was what looked like a dilapidated bait shop to one side, one small wooden dock, and about a hundred half-deteriorated boats sitting around on land in a dirt lot. The smell of brine and too-far-gone fish assaulted my nostrils.

"Swanky," I said with a grin. "So tell me, is that guy going to give me my pedicure? Or is it *that* guy?"

I pointed first at an obvious wino who had fallen asleep curled on his side. It was a wonder that the breeze against his half-bare arse didn't wake him. The second guy was wearing nothing but overalls that had been cut into shorts. He smiled and waved at us, but the effect was somewhat ruined by the fact that he was missing three of his front teeth.

Hyde smiled. "Now, now. Don't be judgmental. Things aren't always as they appear."

We parked next to the bait shop, and two men exited. These guys were dressed in clean clothes and had all their teeth. They were very tan, but the kind of tan that comes from hours upon hours in the sun, not from genetics.

"Elayna, meet Harry and George," Hyde said.

"Harry," the older one said, sticking out a roughened

hand, which I shook. He jerked a thumb at the younger guy. "This is my son, George."

"Hello," I said, shaking George's hand, too. It was like gripping a block wrapped in sandpaper.

"Well, let's go," Hyde said, getting our bags from the back of the van and locking it up.

I gripped my champagne bottle and followed them down the dock, where they loaded our bags into one of those large, inflatable boats. I accepted George's help stepping down and settled myself up front.

"So, George," I said, once they'd pushed us away from the dock. "How long have you been doing nails?"

Hyde just laughed and shook his head.

"Private joke," he said.

Despite my confusion, it *was* beautiful. The green hills dropped right into the ocean, and from here, I could see that we were in a little cove. Harry started the motor and soon we were whipping out over the mostly-still water.

"A good day for it," Harry commented.

"A good day for what?" I asked with a smile.

He just winked and laughed.

Five minutes later, we had cleared the bay, and I saw her. Sitting in the waves, at least ninety feet long was a beautiful yacht. I sat up straight, my eyes wide.

"We're going on *that*?" I said.

"Yep," Hyde said. "That is the *Francine*, George and Harry's boat."

"I've only been on one that big for work," I said, thinking back to a job in Cannes. "Never for fun."

"What kind of work do you do?" Harry yelled, above the roar of the motor and sea spray.

"Antique sales and installations," I called back.

He nodded. It wasn't a career that inspired a lot of questions, at least not from most men. That's why I'd chosen it as a cover. It was a little mysterious and explained all the travel. Apparently, I was very good at my fake job because I was rolling in the dough.

"Thanks, Hyde," I said, smiling up at him. "This is awesome."

He grinned and landed a kiss on top of my head.

The ship was even more beautiful up close. When we boarded, there was a staff of six lined up and waiting to greet us. They all wore the same uniform--navy shorts, white polo shirts, and deck shoes. There were four men, all in their forties or beyond, and two young ladies, probably early twenties.

The thing that struck me the most was how kind everyone's eyes were. They were all smiling like they were genuinely happy to see us. Even the women. I was used to women ogling Hyde and then turning sullen eyes on me like I was an obstacle or a hindrance to their goal where he was concerned. Not these girls. They greeted us warmly and introductions went back and forth, though I was grateful that their names were embroidered clearly on their crisp collars.

"The chef has prepared brunch," the blonde girl, Amy, said. "I'll show you to your cabin. You can get freshened up and then join us on the aft deck if that works."

"That sounds wonderful," I said.

We followed her down some stairs, through a surprisingly spacious sitting and bar area, then down a long hallway. Amy kept up a running explanation of every area in the ship that we passed. There were more rooms or areas than I could keep track of, so I didn't really try. It was luxurious. Everywhere I looked was polished wood, tasteful decor in navy, white, and gold, and expansive windows.

I was seriously considering whether I could afford one of my own by the time we reached the cabin. It was at the front of the boat, so the room was triangular in shape, with huge windows on two sides of the triangle. It felt like we had been cantilevered over the ocean itself, because that's all I could see. I sunk into the plush carpeting as I crossed to the sitting area before turning back to Hyde.

"I want one," I said.

Hyde laughed. "I'm sure you do."

"I'll leave you two to get settled," Amy said, then shut the doors behind her.

"This is seriously amazing," I said, turning back to the incredible view. "Thank you."

"I'm glad you like it," Hyde said, putting his arms around me. "And you're welcome."

I kissed him lightly on the lips. "Best surprise ever."

"Let's go have brunch," he said. "I'm hungry."

The deck where we were seated for brunch had just as beautiful a vista as the one from our cabin. I felt the ship's engines churning gently beneath us as the ship moved through the water.

I spread my cloth napkin over my lap. "Where are we going?"

Hyde shrugged. "I guess you'll have to wait and see."

I laughed. "Well, as long as we are on this boat, I don't really care where we go.

I took a sip of the mimosa that the other woman, Jenny, had set before me. It was frosty and the perfect ratio of champagne to juice. Delicious. I smacked my lips.

I turned to Hyde. "Think we can train Bruno to use a toilet?"

"Huh?"

"Well, if we are going to buy one of these and live on it full time, Bruno is going to need somewhere to do his business."

Hyde laughed. "We can carpet the lower deck in astroturf."

"Perfect. Problem solved."

"I hate to tell you this, but I'm not sure buying a ship like this is a sound investment. You know what 'boat' stands for, right?"

I shook my head.

"It means 'bust out another thousand'. And this isn't just a boat--it's a ship."

"I *love* it," I crooned, sliding my arms back along the buttery upholstery. "If we aren't going to buy one, then we are at least going to vacation on one once a year."

"That we can definitely manage."

Our conversation was interrupted by the arrival of many dishes. There were waffles with fresh fruit, mini quiches, perfectly crisp bacon and browned sausages, and an entire tray of bagels and lox.

"Oh, mercy," I said, pulling the tray of bagels closer to my plate. "I'm so excited."

"You really are easy to please," Hyde said.

"Oh, yes," I demurred, fluttering my lashes. "Just ply me with mimosas and four-course meals on the deck of a million-dollar yacht, and I'm happy as a clam."

"You really know nothing about boats if you think this cost a million."

I paused in loading up my bagel. A couple capers dropped off the cream cheese and rolled across my plate.

"Two million?" I guessed, piling shaved red onions and draping thinly sliced sheets of lox over my bagel. "Three?"

Hyde shook his head. "I don't think you can touch this thing for less than double-digit millions."

"Mercy," I took a bite and the flavors exploded across my tongue. "Oh my gosh, this is so good," I mumbled behind my hand.

"Which is why renting is so much better than buying when it comes to aquatic vehicles of any kind," Hyde said.

I shrugged. "Fine by me. But maybe the Captain can take us home instead of flying back."

"I like that idea," Hyde said. "When we know our schedule, I'll check with him."

Chapter 21

Hyde hadn't been lying about the spa day. It turned out that everyone on the ship performed multiple duties. Mikeal, a thirty-something French man who loved to chat in an accent I couldn't quite understand, was a masseuse. He'd set up his folding massage table in the shade on one of the decks and rubbed my back for an hour and a half while I stared at the ocean and relaxed until I felt boneless. Amy was a licensed manicurist, and gave me a detailed manicure and pedicure in the small beauty room on board. Jenny was an esthetician, so I had a facial as well.

Dinner that night was more formal than expected. When I saw Hyde putting on a suit, I frowned down at my casual sundress and swapped it out for a full-length silk number that billowed when I walked. I paired it with jeweled sandals I'd bought in Italy and dangly chandelier earrings and pinned my hair into a low bun. I slicked on nude gloss and added eyeliner, then shrugged at my reflection. I thought I looked nice, but I was pretty relaxed about such things.

"You look beautiful," Hyde said, slipping an envelope into his interior jacket pocket.

"Thank you." I kissed his cheek, then wiped away the residual gloss. "You look good, too."

A table for two was set up on one of the higher decks, giving us complete privacy. There were several squat glass oil lamps lit on the table and a low bouquet of riotous flowers in the center. The table was set with china, glass, and silver, and the whole thing sparkled in the moonlight.

"How lovely," I said, as Hyde pulled out my chair and I sat. "Thank you."

A light salad was served with some fruity vinaigrette and scallops. Then crab cakes. Then there was pasta in a delicate butter garlic sauce, with mussels, white fish, and shrimp. It was so delicious that I was focused on my food and I almost missed the first sign that something was slightly amiss.

Hyde was *fidgeting*. My eyes sliced to his face. He was biting his lip, looking out over the water, like he was deep in thought. I thought back over the day. What could be wrong? We hadn't fought. Everything was going really well. But there had been signs that he was a little distracted. I eyed his glass. He was on his second glass of white wine, and that wasn't even his favorite. He preferred red.

My fork clattered to my plate. "What's wrong?"

He gave me a smile that I couldn't quite read. "I'm nervous."

I glanced around, looking for a possible threat. "About what?"

"I'm going to tell you where I was, when you were in Miami."

I sat up straight. If he was nervous about telling me, what had he done? Heaven help me, if he had cheated on me, I was going to stab him with a fork and pitch him over the side of the ship. I took in his frame, and my eyes narrowed. Well, I would *try* at least.

He laughed at my expression. "Nothing like that, Elayna. This is information, not a confession."

"Alright." I relaxed and took another bite of my pasta.

He pulled out the envelope from his inside coat pocket and slid it across the table to me. I looked at him questioning, but he just nodded.

"Open it."

Inside were several newspaper clippings, all dated from the time that Hyde had been missing. They were folded, and I smoothed them against the tablecloth and began to read.

William Peterson, prominent local global financier, was found dead in his Port Ramsmeth home Monday. Peterson, 32, owned a financial firm in Miami, and was considered one of the city's most eligible bachelors. Police state that cause of death will be released once an autopsy is performed.

I read the rest of the article, which was fairly short, just detailing Peterson's involvement in the local chamber of commerce. A picture of the man was on top. I frowned, turned that one facedown, and picked up the next.

Suspected Gang Hit, the title read. *Jusef Hamal was shot while dining with his family yesterday. Hamal, a resident of the Little Havana neighborhood in Miami was under investigation for racketeering and attempted murder at the time of his death, though he had not been formally charged. No arrests have been made, although an inside source states that it appears to be consistent with a gang hit.*

No picture on that one. I flipped it over and went to the next. This one was short, not even an inch by inch of small script below the title.

Inmate at Arcagolee Correctional Facility Murdered, the title read. *Inmate Mark Anderson was found strangled to death on Wednesday morning, Captain Sheryl Mathews states. No suspects have been charged, and the investigation is still ongoing. This is the fourth murder that has taken place at Arcagolee Correctional Facility this year.*

I frowned and moved to the next.

Local Businessman and Philanthropist Dead, proclaimed the title. *Renowned local businessman Eustace "E." Philip Edwards, 43, was found dead by apparent suicide at his office on Thursday. Although the investigation is still ongoing, sources within the police department confirm that Mr. Edwards was found by a business associate, dead by hanging.*

This article was much longer, complete with pictures, detailing Edward's numerous contributions to local charities, his involvement coaching Little League and providing internships to local community college students. Edwards was shown smiling widely in every photo. He had been a handsome man.

I glanced up at Hyde, but couldn't read anything in his expression. I moved to the last one, which was a long one again. *Mysterious Tip Leads to House of Horror: Butcher of Biscayne's Wife Found Dead, Innocent Girl Tied in Basement.*

My head jerked at the title. I knew the story of the Butcher of Biscayne and his wife. Together, they had kidnapped, raped, and killed several teenage women. The husband had been convicted and sentenced to death, but the wife had gotten a much lighter sentence, since she had cooperated and testified against her husband. I gripped the article and continued to read.

Melissa Lysell Harper, better known as the Butcher of Biscayne's wife, was found murdered on Friday morning. A mysterious phone call, first thought to be a prank, led officers to the house. There, they discovered Ms. Harper, 52, dead in the upstairs hallway. The cause of death has not been released. In the basement was a teenage girl, whose identity has not been released. Investigators held a press conference late Friday, stating that the teenage girl had been an apparent victim of Ms. Harper, but was rescued when police arrived. No further information is available at this time.

The article then proceeded to outline the facts of the previous case that Harper had been involved in, including her family history, the facts of the previous case and victims, and the fact that the Butcher of Biscayne had released no comment through his attorney at the news.

When I finished, I looked up at Hyde with confusion. "These were all you?"

He nodded.

"I assume they were all deserving targets?"

"Of course."

I frowned and shuffled through the articles again. "But why keep it a secret? Why wouldn't we do something like this together?"

He gently took the articles from me, and pulled out a highlighter, which he clicked open. He made several notations on the articles, then handed them back to me. I flipped through them. He had highlighted the first portion of the names. 'Will' 'Ju' 'Mar' 'E' and 'Me'. It took me a second to get it.

I gasped. "Will you marry me?" I read.

"Yes," he said, laughing. "I will."

It seemed to happen in slow motion. Hyde got down on one knee and pulled an oddly-shaped jewelry box from his pocket.

"Elayna Blythe Miller, you are my best friend, and I love you. I love your strength and your passion. I love your sense of justice and your strong will. I want to spend the rest of my life by your side, working, laughing, playing, and loving together. Will you please be my wife?"

He cracked open the jewelry case, which turned out to have two rings in it, side by side. But I could only see a blur of sparkle through the tears in my eyes.

I flung my arms around his neck. "Yes, of course I will!"

He laughed and slid both rings onto my left ring finger,

then stood and swung me around. I was dizzy with all of it--that Hyde wanted to marry me, that he wanted forever with *me*. I felt like the luckiest woman on earth. I got to have and hold Hyde forever. I laughed as I swiped tears from my face.

"And you were knocking people off for this proposal while I was getting a tan?" I said, laughing. "How long have you been planning this?"

"I've wanted to marry you as soon as I got to know you, Elayna. You're my forever."

He kissed me soundly, then. I swear I saw fireworks behind my eyelids, but when I heard a boom, I realized they were in the sky.

"Aw, crap," I said, swiping new tears from my face. "Knock it off. Apparently I'm as sappy as the next chick when I get a proposal from the man I love."

I looked down at my hand and gasped. There was a massive, cushion-cut solitaire set in platinum, next to a truly impressive diamond band. It was a half-eternity, so the diamonds didn't extend all the way around my finger.

"Do you like them?" he asked, sounding a little uncertain.

"Are you kidding? You could land an airplane with the light this thing is putting off. It's insane! Thank you, Hyde."

He grinned. "Good. I figure that you can wear them both when you're not working, but just the band when you are."

I inspected them again. "Yeah, cause the band won't interfere with me working a slide."

"Exactly." He smiled.

I held my arm out straight and examined my hand again. "They're beautiful. Not to be gauche, but that's got to be what... like eight carats?"

"Twelve, actually."

I fanned my face. "You really know the way to my heart. A bunch of bad people dead, and a huge rock?"

He held out my chair for me again and we sat to watch the fireworks.

"This is amazing, Hyde. Thank you. I love you so much."

"I love you, too." He kissed my hair.

"Good. Now tell me all about the missions. How did they go? Were they clean?" Even I could hear the eagerness in my voice.

He laughed. "No, I wouldn't say they were clean."

Chapter 22

I woke up late the next morning to a dim bedroom. The blackout shades in the bedroom were incredible; I could barely see until I clicked on a lamp. Hyde was already up and gone--that didn't surprise me. He was a creature of habit and he liked to get his workout in early.

I brushed my teeth, used a face wipe, threw my hair into a high bun, and pulled on another loose sundress. I loved the kaftan look--much fancier than a bathrobe, but the same forgiving shape. I slipped on flip-flops and went in search of coffee. I found Amy first, and she invited me to sit on the mid-deck to wait.

Outside it was bright, and I was grateful for good sunscreen and big sunglasses. A cool breeze off the ocean kept things from getting too hot. When my latte arrived, I sipped it slowly, trying not to disturb the foam heart that someone had put on top. I admired my rings again. They looked even bigger and more beautiful in daylight.

I was a total magpie--I loved glittery things. I already had the big diamond studs, but that was the extent of the jewelry I'd spent my own money on. Now, I would have a husband to buy me baubles. *Husband.* The thought used to terrify me, but it felt right with Hyde. Before I'd met him, I thought of marriage as some kind of compromise at best, an ever-narrowing hallway at worst. Depending on who I applied the thought to, I felt absolutely nothing or a sense of claustrophobic terror at the same level as the thought of being buried alive.

Not with Hyde, though. He was my best friend. He loved me. I loved him. Sure, we had arguments sometimes. It wasn't all daisies and tulips. But that was true of everyone. He made me better, and that's what I wanted--an equal that would challenge me to be the best person I could be. I had a strong personality. I needed an equal to match well, and I had found him. Not to mention the fact that we worked well together, and I never had to hide who I was or what I did from him. My huge rock of an engagement ring twinkled merrily up at me, and I smiled.

"Well, that's a nice thing to see," Hyde said, kissing my cheek and taking the seat next to me. "I'm glad you like them."

He was freshly showered; his hair was still damp and he smelled of cedar.

"Love," I corrected. "I love them."

"Well, I love you, so I'm glad."

I looked out over the ocean. "Where are we? I can't see any land."

"We're headed back toward Rio," he said. "Camilla had a guy who will pick up the van. We'll just go straight back to the house."

"More like the compound," I grumbled. "Can't we just stay on this boat forever? Roam around from port to port the rest of our lives?"

I was *not* looking forward to the mess that waited for us back on land. Camilla's family, the CIA, the Brazilian government, and an anti-trafficking group? There was no way to please them all. This usually wouldn't have bothered me, but several of those entities were dangerous enough to seek revenge if we pissed them off *too* badly. I wasn't keen on having the CIA for an enemy, for one. I'd done that last year for about a month, and it was a serious shit-show.

"If you want," Hyde said lightly. "But I know you don't really mean that. Your trigger finger would get itchy after a week."

I shrugged. He wasn't wrong.

"Alright," I said. "But I want our honeymoon to be on this ship. You and me, port-hopping for a full month. Maybe on French Riviera? Something like that? Or down the coast of California into Mexico? Somewhere sunny and warm with good food and lots of wine."

"Sounds like paradise to me. You won't have to ask me twice."

"It's settled then," I said.

Amy and Mikael appeared with trays of food and coffee and set them before us.

"Oh, look," I said. "We're eating again. What an amazing proposal. Lots of good food and drinks, the ocean... not to mention these *gorgeous* rings. How could I say no?"

"I'm no dummy," he said with a grin. "I know how to stack the odds in my favor."

I selected a newspaper from the three fanned out on the silver tray. *The Monster is Dead*, read the headline, with a picture of Alonso when he was younger. There was also a small, inset photo from the crime scene, with an investigator posing in front of the body with only slightly more tact than that of a big game hunter with a kill.

I read the first few lines of the article and chuckled. "I guess the packet of information we 'hid' in his apartment did the trick. But the article reads like the police are the ones who tracked him down and killed him."

"That works for me." Hyde shrugged.

"As long as the families and investigators can have some closure, I don't care what they say."

Chapter 23

When we stepped off the helipad back at the house, I noticed a small crowd of people gathered near the front door.

"What's going on?" I said.

Hyde grabbed my hand. "Elayna, that's..."

A small figure in shorts and a t-shirt detached itself from the group and came barreling at me. I gasped.

"Aunt Elayna!" Jake said, throwing his arms around my knees with wild abandon. "You're here!"

I swayed on my feet for a moment, and not from the force of the hug. Hyde gripped my elbow and kept me grounded to reality. For a moment there, I thought I was floating away. Then reality settled like a burning rock in my stomach.

"How did you get here, Mr. Magoo?" I said, tousling his hair.

"A plane. A great big one. Grandpa napped, but

Grandma played with me on my tablet. I drew you a picture; want to see?"

"Of course, I do. Run and go get it."

He was off like a dervish. Now that we were closer, I could see my mother and father, my brother and sister-in-law in the group, all waiting for us. My mother was wearing wide linen pants and a big floppy hat. She was waving. I turned to Hyde. I didn't know what my expression was, but horror clawed at my gut.

"Why are they here, Hyde? How did they get here, and why?" I sounded frantic.

"Breathe, Elayna." His face was grim, but his voice was steady. "Just breathe, and we will figure this out."

I slipped my engagement rings off, and stuck them in my clutch. I couldn't deal with my mother's reaction to that, not on top of everything else.

"You understand, right?" I said to Hyde. "You're not mad? I just can't..."

"I get it. We're good. Just breathe and try and smile and we will figure this out."

"Ok," I said, taking a deep breath and pasting on a smile. "How's this?"

"A little manic. Tone it down a notch."

"Ok."

My mother hollered something from the front porch. She was waving us over more emphatically now. We walked over. My steps were slow, and the entire time, my mind was working on overdrive. There were six men standing around my family. Most of them wore the classic bodyguard outfit--nice jeans, button-down shirt. But there was one man, tall and slender, with wavy brown hair that was observing us closely. He was wearing nice pants and a button-down shirt rolled to his elbows. His dark eyes were sharp on my face. He was watching me, particularly.

"See him?" I muttered to Hyde through smiling lips.

"Oh yeah, I got him."

"Honey, get up here!" my mother called, when we were finally within hearing distance. "There's some sort of problem. They won't let us in the house."

"I'm sure it's a mistake," I yelled back. "Let me make a quick phone call!"

I pulled out my cell phone and dialed Camilla. She answered on the second ring.

"Where the hell are you?" I muttered.

"I just heard," she said, sounding out of breath. "I'm coming up from the back of the property. I'll be there in two minutes."

"They aren't letting them in?" I said. "But why are they even here?"

"They aren't letting them in because my brother and his men are with them," she said.

I turned and looked back at the strange group at the front portico. The man with the cold eyes was still watching me. So that was Camilla's brother. He looked different than his picture. It was his eyes. In the picture, he had been smiling, and his eyes had seemed warm. That picture must have been taken a long time ago.

"Well, it would be great if we could get them inside and

deal with this," I said. "And tell the men no guns. If my cover's not already blown, I would really like to keep suspicion down. Who knows if that's even possible at this point? What the hell did he say to get them here?"

"I don't know, Elayna. I'm so sorry."

"I got to go," I said, feeling numb. "They're waiting for me."

I took a deep breath and went to greet my family.

"Hello, everyone!" I said, giving the biggest smile I could muster. "I'm sorry we weren't here to greet you!"

"It's very hot out here," my mother said, holding her hat in place as I gave her a hug. "We've been waiting twenty minutes!"

"Very sorry," I said, hugging my dad and then my brother. "The security is very tight here. I called Camilla and she's fixing it as we speak. When did you guys get in?"

I gave a half-hearted hug to my sister-in-law Sybil and smooched my niece Isabella's cheek with a big smacking sound.

"We landed this morning, had lunch on the coast, then just flew in by helicopter," my mother said. "It's a lovely country, Elayna, but the poverty! And the potholes! They should really do something about the roads."

Ah, my mother. Faced with poverty and potholes, she'd fix the latter first.

"Well, that doesn't matter, because there's helicopters," I said, trying to sound bright and airy.

In reality, my worlds were colliding. *Why was my family here?* They didn't seem to be under duress. My father was off to the side, surveying the group with mild distaste, but that was probably just acid reflux or something. How on earth had they gotten here?

"It was so thoughtful of you to send Alex to meet us at the airport, darling," my mother said, smoothing a wisp of my hair back into place. I resisted the urge to shake her off. "But it would have been a lot nicer if you had made the time to come get us yourself."

"Very sorry that didn't work," I said. "I was finalizing a deal on some artwork up North. Hyde and I are just getting back now."

At that statement, I saw Alex narrow his eyes ever so slightly.

"But I'm so glad we're all together now," I added. I turned to Alex. "Thank you so much for getting them here safely. I'll have to owe you one."

He inclined his head graciously, but by the small flash in his eyes, I knew he'd received my message. This was his doing, and I would pay him back.

"Family is everything," he said. "I know that I would do anything for mine."

Ah, so that was his angle. My family was to be hostage unless I swayed Camilla toward his agenda. I smiled.

The front door swung open, revealing a sweaty Camilla, who looked like she had just run five miles.

"Come in, come in," she said, swiping sweat from her brow. "I'm so sorry; I completely forgot you were arriving at this time, and I was in the back of the property."

"Goodness," my mother said, putting a manicured hand to her throat. "How big is the property?"

"About three hundred acres," Camilla said, ushering us inside. "So it takes awhile to get anywhere. That's why we have our own little fleet of golf carts."

There were six of Caio's men in the entry rotunda. None of them had guns visible, but I could see them bristle when Alex and his men followed my family through the door.

"Alex, darling," Camilla said, kissing his cheek. "So lovely to see you. I was wondering when you'd show up."

"I have been very busy, sister," he said, his voice smooth as poured honey. "I have been very eager to see you."

"Wonderful," Camilla said. She turned to my family. "Are you hungry? Or would you just like to rest? Your rooms are all ready."

"I thought they would be staying in the guest house, with me," Alex said, smoothly.

"No," I said. The word came out a little too sharp, and I tried to amend it with a smile. "We have them in the family quarters, with us."

"But Mr. Alex said the guest house is right by the pool," Jake said, tugging at my dress.

"There are *three* pools here, honey. And the very best, biggest one is right next to the family apartments. I bet you can see it from your bedroom window!"

"Is there room enough for all of us?" Sybil said. "Jake and Isabella are getting a little older. I was going to put them in a separate room..."

"There's plenty of room for that," I said. "Plenty. Let me show you."

My family started to gather up their luggage.

"Leave it," I said, nearly manic in my desire to get them away from Alex. "Someone will bring it."

Alex made to follow us, but Camilla stepped into his path.

"Brother, let us speak in here," she said, touching his elbow to guide him into the nearby sitting room.

There was a tense moment when I wasn't sure if he would argue. His eyes followed us as we trailed away. Me stealing his hostages, Hyde bringing up the rear.

Then Alex nodded and said, "Very well."

And the moment defused as if someone had snuffed the spark at the end of a stick of dynamite.

I walked quickly, not caring that my mother and Sybil were giving step by step critique of everything they saw. I had Jake's hand in mine, and I couldn't wait to get them into the fancy panic room that was the family apartments. My father kept pace beside me, and he was watching my face, so I made an effort to smile up at him.

"How was the flight?" I said.

He shrugged. "Not bad, since it was first class. But it was still a flight."

I nearly snorted. Alex may be trying to manipulate and threaten Camilla and me with the presence of my family, but at least he wasn't cheap. When we reached the double-glass doors of the family suite, I punched in the code.

"Such tight security," my mother said. "Should we be

concerned? Is it dangerous here?"

I forced myself to laugh. "No. It's an abundance of caution. Camilla's family is very wealthy and her father was a stickler for security. If you're on the estate, you should be perfectly safe. But as a foreigner, there is a danger if you are off the estate, but that is why we have plenty of security personnel here to help us."

"Yes," Sybil said. "That's the case in many third-world countries. You can't go anywhere without bodyguards. You'll get kidnapped."

You've already been kidnapped! I thought. I fought back the inappropriate, hysterical laughter that threatened to bubble up in my throat. My stress meter was pegged, but nobody seemed to read it.

"Here we are," I said, pushing open the double doors. "Your bedrooms are all upstairs. I hope that's ok. Let me show you., and I'll let you pick who sleeps where."

I escorted them up the stairs, pointing out the sitting room, dining room, and the veranda as we passed.

"And upstairs is an office, another sitting room, and six bedrooms, so you should be very comfortable," I said, feeling as if my face was going to crack if I smiled any harder.

I remembered Hyde's warning about me looking manic, and tried to tone it down.

"Mom, I want this one," Jake said. "Aunt Elayna's right-- you can see the pool!"

"Then I guess we'll take the one next door," Peter said.

"Peter, wait," Sybil hissed. "Does it have an attached

bathroom? We need an attached bathroom."

"They all have attached bathrooms," I said.

"This room is huge!" Peter said from behind the next bedroom's door. "Sybil, come look!"

"We'll just make it easy and take one of the ones across the hall," my mother said, ducking into another room. "That way the kids can find us if they get up too early."

"Wait, what?" my father said, following her in.

They all were gone for a moment. I inhaled sharply. Oh, shit. I was going to cry.

I turned to Hyde. "I need a minute. Keep them in the apartment, no matter what. Do you understand?" My eyes were wide like a crazy person, and I didn't care. "I mean, physically restrain them if it comes down to it. We cannot leave until Camilla says it's safe."

I didn't wait for his nod, my eyes were already spilling over. I ran down the stairs, half blind by my traitorous, leaking eyes. I fumbled with the doorknob to our bedroom when I reached it, then slammed and locked the door behind me.

My parents. My brother and sister-in-law. *My niece and nephew.* My breaths came ragged, one right after another. I knew I had to calm down, to stop and think, but for a couple of minutes, I just *couldn't.* I had gone from the highest of highs--Hyde's proposal--to the lowest of lows-- the terror of seeing my family in danger. And I wasn't in charge, here. I couldn't protect them. This situation was completely out of my control, and I just couldn't *breathe.*

I finally slumped down on the foot of my bed and put

my head between my knees. *Breathe, Elayna,* I said to myself, over and over. *Just breathe.*

It took me nearly five minutes to get my breathing back to normal and my eyes to stop leaking, but I did it. I was in the bathroom splashing my face with cool water when I heard a knock at the door.

"Elayna," Hyde's muffled voice said. "It's me."

I dried my face with a towel and let him in.

"You ok?" he said, shutting the door behind him.

I shook my head. "Not really, but I have to be. Are they getting settled?"

He nodded. "Your dad's planning on taking a nap. I called down to the kitchen for lunch and set Jake up with a cartoon in the media room. The bags were delivered outside the apartment door, but I shoved them all in Frankie's room so she can debug them if needed before we hand them out."

I took another deep breath. "Thank you."

"It's going to be alright, Elayna," he said, hugging me to him. "It really is."

"I hope so," I said, muffled against his chest. "But right now, I can't see how."

"I know. We will get there."

I lifted my head to search his face. "You really aren't mad about the ring thing? You understand?"

He smiled. "As long as you aren't changing your mind, we're engaged. That's all that matters to me. Tell people at your own pace."

"I'm not changing my mind," I said, pecking a kiss on

his chin. "I just couldn't handle my mother's inevitable epic freak-out at that exact moment."

He chuckled, a deep rumbling against my ear. "I get it."

I texted Frankie and Howard, who were both in town, to let them know what was going on, then reapplied my makeup. Hyde took the delivery of lunch at the door. If that confused the maids, they were polite enough not to let on. I rummaged through Frankie's things, found the debugger and triple-checked my family's luggage for bugs, explosives, ninja stars, or anything else I could think of. They were completely clean, so I made trips up the stairs myself, dropping them off. Then we sat down and ate lunch together, except for my dad, who was still sleeping.

"This is very good," my mother said, poking at her salad with her fork. "I wasn't sure how the food would be, but this is excellent."

"I think they have three chefs on staff," I said. "So the food is always excellent. There's even a food ordering device in the apartment kitchen, so if you're craving something specific, you can have it delivered. But I usually just let them serve whatever they want."

"Do they have pizza?" Jake said, his eyes wide. "And hot dogs?"

"They have that *and* the best cheeseburger you've ever had in your life," I said. "And maybe we could have a movie night while you're here, and eat junk food while we watch it."

"That would be so cool!" he said. "Can we have nachos?"

"They make the best chips here, so we totally can have

nachos."

"But only if you eat your vegetables first, Jake," Sybil said, her lips pursed. "Everything green on your plate."

"We're on vacation, Sybil," my brother drawled. "The kid can eat whatever he wants."

"Woo-hoo!" Jake said, throwing his hands in the air in victory.

"I wish you wouldn't undermine my authority like that, Peter," she said.

I don't know how she did it--when she got mad, her mouth just got tighter and tighter. Right now, I bet I couldn't fit a pencil in there.

"Heaven's sakes, Sybil," Peter said. "Have a margarita or something."

Hyde slid back from the table. "That's a great idea. Who wants margaritas?"

All the adults said yes, except for Sybil, who wanted a vodka soda instead. Pleasant conversation resumed, with my mother at the helm. I could barely hear Hyde on the house line in the other room ordering drinks. I was pretty sure I heard him tell the staff to make Sybil's drink a triple, and my suspicions were confirmed when he slid back into his chair and gave me a conspiratorial wink.

Camilla was wearing her usual smile when she met up with us about an hour later, but I could read the fatigue around her eyes. Still, she greeted everyone warmly.

"So glad you all could make it," she said. "Sorry again about the mix-up with security. I've let them know that you can go most anywhere on the estate."

I'm sure that Camilla had given the security team *extensive* instructions regarding my family.

"*Most* anywhere?" Sybil said, her eyebrows raised.

"There are some parts of the estate that are private," Camilla said, nodding. "The employee housing, for example. And a house this size has many mechanical rooms that are only safe for technicians or repairmen. I'm sure you understand. Everything else is open to you."

"Miss Camilla," Jake said. "Aunt Elayna says there is a computer where we can order nachos to eat, and we are doing a movie night tonight in the room with the big screen. Do you want to come?"

I exhaled a laugh. Of course Jake thought that I'd meant we could have nachos and watch movies *tonight*.

"That sounds wonderful," Camilla said. "What a great idea. I will make sure that we have all the movie snacks on hand, too."

From the corner of my eye, I could see Sybil's mouth tighten. Three shots of vodka hadn't done much to soften her up.

"Awesome!"

"But for now," Camilla continued, "the pools are open, and we have plenty of chaise lounges and towels. I think we have pool toys and floating rafts somewhere, but if not we will get some. We have a tennis court, a basketball court, bocce ball, and a sand volleyball court. I have a traditional cooking class lined up for later in the week, and tomorrow,sometime I thought it might be nice to use the salon room, which is just down the hall. I can have several technicians come in and do massages, mud wraps, nails, facials...whatever you'd like."

"That sounds great," I said, hiding my hands beneath the table. "I could really use a mani-pedi. And I haven't had a massage in *forever*."

Hyde quirked his eyebrow at me, as if to say, *really?*

But I was determined to support Camilla's plans. It hadn't escaped my notice that Camilla had not once suggested an activity that would take us off the estate.

"A spa day does sound lovely," my mother said.

Sybil nodded, too. Free spa treatments? It was hard to say no to that, no matter how much you wanted to find something wrong with it.

"Can I go swimming? Mom, Dad, please?" Jake said. "Pleeeaase?"

"Alright, bud," Peter said, tousling his hair. "I'll take you guys."

"Don't forget the sunscreen!" Sybil called after them as they raced up the stairs to change. Then she got up and followed them. "Someone should watch Jake and Isabella," she muttered.

I didn't point out that Peter had literally just said he would do that. The more people out in the pool, the better.

"What about you, Mom?" I said. "There's huge umbrellas out there if you don't want to get too much sun."

"Yeah, that sounds nice," she said. "I can read my book. I should probably wake up your father, too," she said, checking her watch. "I don't want him to get the jet lag."

When they were all gone, I sunk back into my chair and turned to Camilla.

"What the fuck is going on, here?" I said in a low voice. "Why are they here?"

"You know what my brother is trying to do. He is trying to show us that no one we care about is safe."

"Not a great way to get me on Team Alex," I said. "But what I mean is...how did he get them here?"

"Your mom told me that she got an email from you," Hyde said. "I was just waiting for a chance to tell you."

"From *me*?" I looked back and forth between them. "Have I been hacked?"

"That's a question for Frankie, not me," Hyde said.

"How are you?" I said, reaching out to clasp Camilla's arm. "How was it, seeing him?"

"It was hard, and then again, it was easy." She gave a sad smile. "You know how it is with siblings. No matter how much they hurt you, there is so much history there."

I nodded. I did know. No matter how much I disliked Sybil on a personal level, she made my brother happy. And I wanted to see my brother happy. Plus, she was family.

"Did he say anything about them?" I said, jerking my head in the direction of the stairs.

"Not really. Made a few veiled statements." She sighed. "My brother is an intelligent man. He knows that at a minimum this will be a distraction for you. At most, it might make you pressure me to give him what he wants, so that your family will be safe."

"So he doesn't buy my cover," I said.

"I don't think so. I'm treating it as if he knows what we really do. Caio is perhaps stupid enough to believe that we are just friends that work together. But my brother knows me. He knows I work for you and that you must do something a bit more than antiques. Does he know the whole truth? I don't know."

I nodded. "Makes sense." I paused for a few moments. "So what now?"

"I really don't know. I guess just wait and see? We need those numbers so we can figure out who is best to lead, so we can get out of here."

I nodded.

The doorbell chime to the apartment sounded, and Camilla went to get the door. When she returned, Frankie and Howard were with her.

"So you were serious?" Frankie said, looking at a pair of Jake's flip-flops that were strewn on the floor. "They're really here?"

"Yes," I said. "And my mother told Hyde that they came here because they received an email from *me*. Have I been hacked?"

"Impossible," Frankie said, swiping her hand through the air. "I have so many safeguards and circular trips on your stuff, I would have known immediately. The only stuff that has ever attacked your database has been first-level, juvenile shit. I would get an alert if anyone ever got to the second level of protection."

"That means nothing to me, Frankie. No offense. It sounds cool. But you're saying no?"

"No," she said, shaking her head. "No way."

"But it didn't need to *actually* come from your account, did it?" Howard said, slowly.

"What?" I said.

"Like, I can go online and open up an email account that says I'm Peter Pan," he said, his eyebrows raised. "That doesn't actually *make* me Peter Pan."

We all thought about that for a second.

"Frankie, get into my mother's email. Actually, everyone's. I want to know what these emails said."

"On it," she said, her dress billowing behind her as she went to retrieve her laptop.

"What did you do today?" I asked Howard.

He opened his mouth to say something, but there was a thundering down the stairs. My brother and Jake appeared in bathing suits and t-shirts, lathered so heavily in sunscreen that their faces had a white tint.

"Here's your flip-flops, buddy," Peter said, pointing out the shoes.

"Towels are outside on the chairs," I said, waving them out the french doors. "Have fun!"

"I drank coffee," Howard said, belatedly answering my question.

I contemplated that, decided not to comment. Howard was going out of his way to be near Frankie again. I wondered if this trend would last.

"How was your trip?" Camilla asked, a sly smile on her face.

"Fine, fine," I said, waving my hand. I was thinking of

my family, of Alex, of Caio.

"Just fine?" Hyde asked with a raised eyebrow.

"Oh," I said, blinking stupidly. "Hyde and I got engaged. But we're not telling my family right now."

Camilla grinned. Frankie's mouth dropped open. Howard's eyes went wide.

"Congratulations!" Frankie whisper-screamed. "That's wonderful!"

Howard clapped Hyde on the back and congratulated us. It didn't escape my notice that he kept glancing at Frankie, who was wiping little tears from her eyes. Camilla engulfed me in a hug.

"I'm so happy for you," she said, squeezing me tight. "He's a good one."

"Thank you," I said.

It felt surprisingly good to share the news with my team. But even through the joy of sharing such happy news with the people I loved the most, I couldn't help feel a constant thrill of anxiety along my back.

What were we going to do about my family? How were we going to keep them safe?

Within an hour, my entire family was out at the pool. Peter and Jake were splashing around with some pool toys that someone had scrounged up, while Sybil yelled cautions at them. Isabella huddled at the edge of the umbrella shade under my mother's watchful gaze, and my father slept through the cacophony under the next umbrella over.

Meanwhile, I tried not to chew off my new manicure as

I paced back and forth in front of the windows. Frankie had gotten into all of the email accounts easily enough. My mother had been the main correspondent with Alex. Just as Howard suspected, Alex had used a fake email account easily opened through Google.

The emails themselves weren't nefarious at all. It was just the intent behind them that had me concerned. It surprised me how readily my mother had believed that I'd invited the entire family to an all-expenses-paid, no-end-date vacation in Brazil. Then again, my mother had always believed what she wanted, and she'd been bugging me to come along on a buying trip for years.

So now here we were. And I did not know what to do about it. Things had been difficult and confusing before my entire family was added to the mix. Now I had six other lives to protect, six other people to worry about. I felt like time was getting short, like this was all going to reach a boiling point, and I wouldn't be able to control what happened. It was hard to believe that this morning I had woken up newly engaged, as happy as I had ever been.

I felt guilty that I hadn't wanted to tell my family we were engaged. What should have been a homecoming full of celebration and joy was now stress-filled and confusing. How quickly a day could change. I wondered if Alex had done this to distract Camilla as much as to threaten me.

Whatever his plan was, I just hoped we would stay ahead of him.

Chapter 24

I didn't want to leave my family at the house for even a minute, but Hyde, Howard, and Frankie promised me that my family would be safe for an hour without me. Camilla and I were off to meet Iris, as promised, but my gut was in knots.

The cafe was bright. With the white, scalloped umbrellas and the intricate cobblestone sidewalk, it felt like we were in Paris or Rome. Camilla and I went inside to order coffees, and Tristao followed us in, standing respectfully at the back.

The coffee shop was cute, done in an airy white tile that covered the floor and walls. Their signage was black, and there were old brass foot rests beneath a wooden bar off to the side. An elaborate silver espresso machine hissed and whirred as young baristas deftly made complicated drinks. It looked like a chic coffee shop you'd find in New York.

"Him, huh?" I murmured to Camilla. It was the first time Tristao had been out of earshot since we'd left. "When did that happen?"

"My uncle assigned him to my security detail. I think Caio thought it would please me. I think he is trying to butter me up."

"Is it working?" I asked, my eyebrows raised.

"I like Tristao. What we had was years ago. A lifetime. But I still like him."

I kept my thoughts to myself. I wasn't so sure that the feelings were as deeply buried as Camilla claimed. Her eyes landed on him with frequency. She always seemed aware of where he was in a room. That wasn't behavior one acted out with a friend.

Still, love was as much a choice as it was a feeling, if not more. It didn't sound like Camilla was choosing to have feelings for Tristao at the moment, so I would have to take her at her word. But I was keeping an eye on her, and on him, too. Nothing I could do about that, though. I sighed and tried to relax. I ordered a vanilla latte and Camilla ordered a hot chocolate over ice, which made me frown.

"What's that look for?" Camilla asked, nudging my side.

"I'm jealous of your order," I said. "I think you need to order for me from now on. I wish I had thought of iced hot chocolate."

"If you're nice, I'll let you have a sip," she said, teasing.

I wrinkled my nose at her and she laughed.

The door chimed behind us, and I saw Iris and Ruben

in my peripheral. Iris was much more casual today. She was wearing jeans that were artfully torn at the knees, a loose floral top, and brown strappy sandals. She looked young, like she could be a graduate student or a starving artist. Heck, for all I knew, maybe she was.

We chose a table outside, far away from where anyone else was sitting. Tristao immediately took the next closest table, and Ruben took the one next to that. The two men sized each other up and frowned.

I laughed. "Sheesh. This isn't awkward or obvious at all."

Iris' eyes narrowed at me and Camilla. It felt like we were sitting across the table from a snake who was ready to strike at any provocation.

"Let's set some ground rules," I said. "First of all, there will be no violence today. This time, I'm not going to fight you. I'm just going to have that guy over there shoot you." I jerked my head in Tristao's direction. "Not that we want that to happen." I held up my hands in a placating gesture. "We are all on the same side, even if you don't believe that, yet. I'm just letting you know where I stand."

"Fair enough," Iris hissed. "But if I get shot, it will be the last thing either of you ever does."

I kept myself from rolling my eyes, but barely. "Sure, sure," I said. "I've never heard that threat before. Thank you for your originality."

Iris stiffened even further, and opened her mouth to retort, but Camilla stopped her.

"This isn't how I wanted this to go," Camilla said. "So

both of you stop it." She turned to Iris. "Why did you think that I was involved in what was going on at that brothel?"

"Brothel?" she hissed. "That was a slave market. Men who own brothels come there to try out the merchandise before they buy them."

My nose wrinkled at the thought.

"But why did you think I was involved?" Camilla pressed.

"Because it is your family who owns that place, who runs the girls," Iris said.

"Since when?" Camilla said. "How long has this been going on?"

"Five, maybe six years. Well, that is how long I've known of it." Iris swept her hair back, and I was surprised to see the glimmer of tears in her eyes. "My sister was taken five years ago. I haven't seen her since the day she was taken from me."

"What was her name?" I asked.

"Her name is Marriena. She is still alive. I know. I can feel it." She clasped a fist to her chest.

I didn't bother telling her that statistically, her sister was probably long gone. I understood the need to believe until you had irrefutable proof otherwise.

"And your family took her from me," she said, pointing a finger at Camilla. "I have been searching for her ever since."

"How?" I asked. "What has been done to find her? Did you go to the police?"

She laughed--a dry, humorless sound that reminded me of a bleak desert.

"The police are paid to look the other way whenever the name Almeida is involved." She spit Camilla's last name from her mouth like it was a detestable thing.

"It's true," Camilla said, nodding at me. "The police are paid off. Most of them, actually. The good ones have been intimidated into compliance as well. There is no going to the police when you are trying to bring any part of the Almeida cartel to justice."

It was as if Camilla agreeing with her took some of the fire from Iris' speech.

"My sister was beautiful," she said. "Too beautiful. It was why she was taken, I think. She is two years older than I am. And so smart. She wanted to become a doctor."

"What happened?" I said.

"We come from a wealthy family in Curitiba. Marienna and I were walking home from school one day when a car pulled up next to us. We had never had any problems with kidnappings in Curitiba, not like they do in Rio and Sao Paulo, but still, my parents had warned us not to fight. Marienna went with them, told them she wouldn't fight if they left me alone. I ran home and told my parents. They called the police and we waited for the ransom call, but it never came. We waited and waited."

Iris seemed to collect herself. "It was a week later that my father hired the private detective. He was a good one, very expensive. He had a report within a week. I remember so clearly. He came to the house, and his face was grim,

and my father and he went into my father's office and shut
the door. The man left about an hour later, but my father
did not come out until it was time for dinner. He had been
crying. That terrified me, because my father never cried.
That was when he told my mother and my brother and me
that Marienna was lost to us."

Camilla reached over as if to reach for Iris' hand but
Iris jerked her arm back. It was an awkward moment, but
Iris continued.

"My mother and brother both thought that meant that
she was dead. But my father didn't say *dead*, and he
wouldn't tell us what had happened. He just kept saying
that she was lost. Lost to us. Gone. He never said dead. So
that night, I picked the lock on his office door. He didn't
know that I knew where he kept his desk key, but I did. I
found the report from the private investigator. It said that
Marienna was most likely still alive, but that she had been
sold by the Almeidas to a brothel in Rio. I knew that to my
father, she was worse than dead. His daughter? A whore?
What would happen to his reputation if the story got out?
What would happen to his business, his other children? I
think that is why that investigator stayed for so long. I
think he was trying to reason with him. So I stole all the
money from my father's safe, took the report, and found
the investigator. I asked him if it was enough to purchase
my sister back. He said it was, and took the money. But I
never saw or heard from him again. I still do not know if
he was killed by the Almeidas, or if he took the money and

ran. What could I do to him, after all? I was just a teenager."

Iris paused, looked out into space as if reliving her helplessness.

"What happened then?" I said.

"I went back home. I confronted my father, and told my mother. The next day, I was told that I was being sent to boarding school." Iris' eyes narrowed. "As if they could have made me go. I ran out to the country, to the house of a friend, the boy who took care of the horses. He hid me." She jerked her head toward Ruben. "We have been working together ever since, finding out what we could and taking down the brothels. Freeing the girls. But by the time we had enough resources, and we went to the brothel in Rio, Marienna was gone. No one there even knew her name."

"I'm so sorry," Camilla said. "I didn't know."

"Wait a minute," I said. "These resources. What do you mean by that?"

"My grandmother was a famous woman," she said. "She left me money that I was able to access at eighteen."

"Ah," I said.

It had been bothering me, wondering how they were getting their intel and carrying out missions. Now it made sense. They were paying for information.

"How do you know it is the Almeidas doing this?" Camilla asked, leaning forward.

Iris scoffed and flippantly gestured to encompass everything in sight. "Everybody knows."

"Everyone might *think* that," I said. "But that doesn't mean it's actually true."

"Are you calling me a liar?" she hissed, jutting her chin forward.

"No. But we need proof," I said. "We don't know you. We can't just believe that it's the Almeida's business because you say it's so."

Iris pulled her backpack onto her lap. It was a worn navy Jansport. I was pretty sure that I'd had the same one in Junior High. She pulled out a manila envelope that was tight around whatever it held.

"There. That's how I know," she said. "Now, will you help me find my sister?"

"If I can, yes," Camilla said, staring down at the envelope like it was a ticking bomb. "But I will need time to look into this, to make sure that the right people are held accountable."

"I don't know if I can trust you," Iris said, getting to her feet. "But it is a chance I have to take. If there is any human feeling left within you, try and help me find my sister."

Camilla nodded, her face grave.

Iris slung her backpack over her shoulder and slipped into the crowd, Ruben following in her wake.

"I think she's telling the truth," I said, frowning after her.

"That's what terrifies me. I think she is, too."

Chapter 25

When we got back to the house, we were greeted first by my mother.

"Where have you been?" she said, flapping her hands. "We met Camilla's uncle. What a dashing man. He says there is a cocktail party in the *ballroom* tonight. I didn't know this house had a *ballroom*. How exciting! But I don't know what to wear. It sounds fancy."

I wanted to sigh, but I smiled instead. Caio seemed to love throwing expensive parties last minute. For all his assertions that this wasn't his house, he did seem to love showing it off. Camilla ducked out, presumably to hear the news from Caio himself. I hoped she'd have more information for me when she returned.

"Sounds wonderful!" I said, my tone chirpy enough to almost make me wince. "I'm sure whatever you have to wear will be lovely. Parties like that are a dime a dozen in Brazil."

But when Camilla found me a half an hour later, she shook her head.

"He's invited over a hundred people," she said. "A bunch of government officials, high-powered business-men. I think he's trying to prove that he can hobnob like Alex and my father could. I think this is part of his strategy, to show me and these people that he can fulfill all the demands of a cartel leader. That's all I can figure. And this party had been planned for over a week, Tristao just told me. I don't know if Caio didn't tell me because he was afraid that I'd invite Alex, or some other reason." She chewed her lip.

"That doesn't make sense," I said. "You're not in contact with Alex."

"*We* know that. But I'm starting to wonder if Caio believes that."

"Who knows what's going on in his head. He's paranoid."

"In this business, you kind of have to be, or you don't survive long. Caio knows that his position is precarious. Alex is the son. I'm the daughter. If we banded together, he'd be screwed."

Our conversation was interrupted by my parents, my brother, and Jake coming in from the pool.

"I was instructed to shower and get ready," Peter said with a smile. "And you're having a nanny come in to watch the kids tonight, right?"

Camilla smiled. "Two of them, actually. I've known both of them for years. Jake and Isabella will be in excellent hands."

"Great."

"Do they know how to use the food ordering thing in the kitchen?" Jake asked. "Do they know how to use the big TV in the movie room?"

"Yep," Camilla said, smiling.

"Awesome! We're gonna watch Swiss Family Robinson!" he hollered, running up the stairs like a dervish. "And eat cupcakes!"

"Don't let your mom hear you say that," Peter said, following him up.

They left the room, Sir Darcy prancing after them.

I raised my eyebrows in alarm. "Has that cat been hanging around the kids?"

My mom nodded. "They love him. He's been sleeping in Isabella's room at night."

"That cat's a sociopath; you better watch it."

"Don't be melodramatic, dear," my mother said, smoothing her perfectly-coiffed hair. "The cat is fine."

"I'm just saying--I'll still love the kids, even if they have to wear an eyepatch, but I'm definitely not going to spare them the pirate jokes."

"Really, Elayna. The things you come up with."

I put on my best pirate voice and swung my cocked arm a couple of times in front of my chest. "Avast, ye' land-lubber, I give ye' fair warning. That cat be nothing but a dirty bilge-sucker, and if he harms my niece or nephew, I'll cleave him to the brisket!"

My mother raised an eyebrow. "Are you quite finished?"

"You're no fun," I mumbled, taking another sip of my coffee.

Chapter 26

I was in a pissy mood, and I was running late. Sybil had asked to borrow a dress since she hadn't packed for a cocktail party, then complained in front of everyone when the dress was too big and begged one off Frankie, instead. Somehow, everyone had managed to get ready and leave in time, except me. Frankie had laid out my outfit--a stark white jumpsuit with an artistic bow on one shoulder, paired with high-heeled sandals with clear jewels and pearls on the straps.

I slipped out of the family apartments into the exterior hallway hoping that I was alone, and frowned when I saw Ignacio up ahead. His back was to me--he was walking in the same direction--so with any luck he wouldn't hear me and turn with his trademark sneer. Bruno was heading towards me down the hall. He saw me and increased his pace. I couldn't help but smile at him. I reached out my hand so he could snuffle it when he made it to me.

It happened fast, for no reason.

"Fucking dog," Ignacio growled.

He crossed the hallway and kicked Bruno hard in the hindquarters. Bruno yelped.

I ran forward, reached up, grasped Ignacio's chin with one hand, the back of his head with another. When he started to turn his head toward me in shock, I used the momentum and added as much force as I could muster. *Snap.* A clean break.

He slumped to the ground, lifeless.

My eyes went wide. *Shit.*

It had been instinct--it was the same reaction I would've had if someone had hit Frankie or decked Camilla. Bruno was under my protection. He was my baby; I loved him fiercely.

But now I had a dead body in a hallway. Shitballs. At least no one had seen it, yet. I checked Bruno quickly. He seemed to be ok, more confused and indignant than hurt. He was putting good weight on the leg that Ignacio had kicked, so the injury wasn't too serious, at least.

I needed to get rid of this body. My heart was pounding with the shot of adrenaline I'd felt when he'd kicked Bruno.

"Well," I said to the corpse. "Even a dumb ass knows not to kick a cub when the mama bear is around."

Footsteps, at the other end of the hall. I scurried to the corner and crouched low. In for a penny, in for a pound, I guess. I had no time to hide the body, so I'd just have to knock this person out before they saw it. As they came around the corner, I leaped from my hiding position with a hiss.

"Shit and hellfire, Elayna!" Howard said. "You trying to give me a heart attack? What the hell are you doing?"

"Shh," I said. "I need you to help me hide a body."

"Well, why didn't you just say that in the first place?" Howard said, confused. "I nearly shit myself. And I've been eating a lot of beef, Elayna. Like--a *lot*. I swear, these days I could shit through a screen and not leave a mess on it. We are solidly in 'don't trust a fart' mode."

"Well, thank you for all of that information," I said. "Now hurry up."

I was feeling a bit frantic. I was already late to the party. Someone was bound to notice and come looking soon.

"What did he do?" Howard said when he caught sight of the corpse.

"Kicked Bruno."

Howard whistled. "I'm impressed at your restraint. I'd expect this hallway to look like a Jackson Pollock painting if I'd known."

"You know who Jackson Pollock is?" I said, momentarily distracted.

"I am a redneck of many layers, Elayna," he said, seriously.

"Help me get this body into the closet. I'll figure out how to dump him later."

I leaned down to grab Ignacio' shoulders, and felt something give, right as a sharp *riiip* sounded in the air.

Howard dropped the legs he had been lifting and

pressed a hand to his stomach. "Please tell me that was you. Otherwise, my asshole has gone numb from overuse."

"Shit," I said.

"Exactly," Howard quipped.

"No, I ripped my pantsuit. Get his legs! We don't have time."

I lifted my end of the body, and Howard and I struggled our way down the hall, Ignacio's corpse spread between us. I could feel air on my bare cheeks, cause I had worn one of those flat-lying thongs so my underwear wouldn't show through the white pantsuit. Now my butt was hanging out for anyone to see, though it was the corpse that was my biggest problem.

I was walking backward and had turned my head to look where we were headed.

"Watch out, Elayna," Howard said, his tone droll. "Someone's getting a little fresh."

I jerked my head back around and looked down to find Ignacio's head flopped back, his mouth and chin bumping against my crotch.

"Ack!" I dropped the body, the head bouncing on the marble.

Howard started to laugh.

"Not funny!" I hissed, picking my end back up.

But it was, a little. By the time we made it to the closet with our awkward burden, I was laughing too. I dropped one arm to open the door and turn on the light switch in the closet. Then I backed us in, and Howard closed the door after us. I was grateful it was a bigger than average linen closet, but it was still crowded with me, Howard, and a corpse.

"Sheets!" I said, pulling a sheet off the shelf. "Help me cover him."

"Nighty-night," Howard said in a sing-song voice, as we tucked the sheet over Ignacio.

I couldn't help it; I started giggling again. Then we both bent down at the same time and knocked heads, which just intensified the laughter. We were fumbling and bumping into each other and the shelves, and we could not stop laughing.

"Can you take off your shirt?" I asked. "I need it. My ass is out."

"You are really lucky that I'm the male, and you're the female in this situation, cause otherwise, that would be grounds for a sexual harassment claim," Howard said, unbuttoning his shirt.

"In your dreams."

"Hey!" he said, laughing. "We're in a closet, you're my boss, your ass is out, and you just asked me to take off my shirt. These are irrefutable facts."

"Oh just give it here. We need to get going before anyone finds us in here."

I took his offered shirt and wrapped it around my waist, tying it. Then I opened the door, tripped over the corpse, and tumbled out into the hall, splaying on the tile floor in an undignified manner.

Where I found Hyde, leaning up against the wall. Howard began cracking up anew behind me.

"Whatcha doin'?" Hyde asked in a conversational tone, an amused smile on his face.

"This is not what this looks like at all," Howard said, stepping out of the closet bare-chested with his hands up. "I was just helping her hide a corpse, I swear."

Hyde tipped back his head and laughed. Then he looked at the body. "Who's that?"

"Ignacio kicked Bruno," Howard stage-whispered.

Hyde's eyebrows raised, and he lifted the sheet to take a peek. "And he only got his neck snapped? Wow."

"That's what *I* said," Howard said. "I think the old girl's losing her fire."

"I better not be the old girl in this scenario," I said, getting to my feet and dusting off my pantsuit. "Otherwise I'll be willing to show you just how much fire I have left."

Hyde chuckled. "I came to find you. Your mother is looking for you."

"Ugh," I said. "I have to go change. I split my pantsuit and my butt is hanging out."

Hyde lifted Howard's shirt before I could slap his hand away. "Sure is. You're lucky I'm a very self-assured person. Cause when I walked up to this closet, there was a lot of banging around and giggling."

"Howard was talking about poop," I said primly. "It was funny."

"Why is poop only funny when Howard talks about it, but not when I do?" Hyde said. "Such a double standard."

"I don't want to hear about that from my boyfriend!" I said, throwing my hands in the air.

"Fiancé," he corrected, mildly.

"And I certainly don't need you sending me all those emojis when you're on the toilet, letting me know how it's going!" I said.

"You know," Howard said, thoughtfully. "That's an excellent idea. Although lately, mine would be like bomb, fire, poop emoji, shocked face, ocean wave."

"We're going to share everything when we're married," Hyde said, ignoring Howard. "Maybe we'll even be that couple that has those side-by-side toilets. We can hold hands while we drop our deuces."

"Gross, Hyde!" I said, pushing past him to go change. "That is foul."

"Dude, if you need to talk to someone about your poop, I'm always free," Howard said.

"I sure hope you're joking!" I yelled back at them.

They just laughed.

I CHANGED INTO A VOLUMINOUS SUNDRESS. It wasn't nearly as uptight or dressy as my pantsuit had been, but I compensated by adding lots of jewelry and a bold lip. I knew that Frankie wouldn't be pleased, but it just would be evidence that she was buying my clothes too tight. Or maybe my butt was getting bigger? I turned and checked it out in the mirror, but couldn't see any change under the sundress. Which made me promptly decide that flowy sundresses were my new uniform and I was never wearing anything else again.

Hyde was waiting for me by the door, smiling.

"What's got you cheery?" I said.

"Just you. I love you."

"Excellent answer. Ten points to Griffyndor!" I said.

He laughed. "Is that our new points system?"

"Today it is. How's my mother? Is she in fine form? Has anyone in my family figured out that they're hostages, yet?" I tried to keep my tone light and airy, but failed toward the end.

"We'll get them out safe, Elayna. We will figure it out."

"Without outing my secret?" I said.

"Yes," he said, kissing the tip of my nose. "It will all work out. We just have to figure out how."

Chapter 27

The party was more than I had expected. Grossly oversized floral arrangements sat atop tables covered in burgundy cloth. Candles glimmered everywhere. Waiters passed hors d'oeuvres and champagne. It looked like a mobster's daughter's wedding. I instantly felt under-dressed.

Frankie rolled her eyes when she saw my outfit. "What happened to the pantsuit?"

"It was too tight."

"No, it wasn't. It looked amazing on you."

"I split it when I had to hide a body in a closet," I murmured, accepting a glass of champagne from a passing waiter.

"From anyone else, I'd think that was a joke."

"Wish it was," I said, pasting a smile on my face.

"Who?"

"Ignacio."

"Oh," Frankie said, waving her hand, airily. "He was a jerk. No one will miss him."

"Except for his boss, the megalomaniac cartel kingpin," I said, my stomach clenching.

"Yes, except for him."

I saw my mother and father over by the canapes. Hyde was with them, so I had a few more minutes before I needed to make an appearance there. Sybil and Peter were across the room talking to a lovely woman in an expensive-looking dress. Sybil was nodding emphatically, like the woman had just said something very profound.

From the corner of my eye, I saw a redhead in a green dress sidle up to me.

"Frankie, go check the punchbowl or something," I said.

She looked at the woman curiously, but nodded and found somewhere else to be.

"What are you doing here?" I asked Agent Wignow.

"I'm here to see if you've made any progress with that issue we spoke about. Things are in motion, and we need to know where you stand."

"What *things* are in motion?"

"The election is only eight months away," she said. "We need to act now."

"Why does the agency even care who gets elected?" I said, keeping my face pleasant, as if she were asking me about where I got my dress, or who had designed my shoes.

Just a couple normal gals, talking normal gal party stuff.

"This party isn't long enough to give you all the details, but here are the broad strokes--the U.S. has recently invested more money into Brazil and has shared technology with them, in exchange for allowing certain aspects of our government access of certain sites along certain borders."

I raised my eyebrow and pursed my lips. "You're going to have to give me more than that."

She sighed. "Fine. You've heard of Venezuela, I presume?"

"No need for sarcasm," I said lightly.

"The U.S. has repeatedly sanctioned Venezuela because of drugs and human trafficking issues. There's a huge pipeline in South America, and we think Venezuela is the key player."

"Fine, except that the CIA doesn't care about human trafficking or the drug trade, not unless it ties into something more important in their eyes."

"You're right," she said, sipping her drink. "They don't. But about a year ago, an analyst tracked some suspicious transfers from Iran to Venezuela."

"Ah," I said, things clicking into place. "That's why they're interested."

"That's what got them looking in the first place, but there's much more to it than that. The new Presidency in Venezuela is tentative at best. There are some in power who aren't even pretending to care about the welfare of the people, or anything else, for that matter. So when the agency started digging into the history of the transfers, they found drugs and trafficking, but they also found guns and terrorism. Some powers that be are making connections with very dangerous enemies of the US in order to keep their power. They're scrambling, desperate. It doesn't help that the United States and Brazil have closer ties than ever before. The U.S. has agreements to share defense data, they're partnering on satellite launches...the list goes on."

"So this is about Venezuela more than Brazil."

She frowned. "Sort of. Like I said, it's complicated. It's really about terrorism, the stability of South America as it pertains to the United States, and avoiding war. General Horta has some radical ideas about the direction he would like to take Brazil in. He sees Venezuela as a kind of flawed model of what Brazil could be."

"Venezuela's people are starving. The economy is in shambles. What could General Horta possibly see there worth repeating?"

"He sees that the president took control of all major private companies, that he has unmitigated control over the government. These kinds of men don't care about the plight of the average citizen. Or they have deluded themselves into thinking that the people will one day be grateful for the changes they have made."

"So...what? General Horta wants to be a despot? Is that what you're telling me?"

"He envisions a new dynamic in South America. If he

can succeed where Chavez and Maduro have failed, he would not only be the wealthiest man in the hemisphere, but he would also control many of the military installations that officially do not exist within his country, that the U.S. may or may not have placed there. In addition, he would be well-positioned to partner with Venezuela against the United States. With Venezuela's new friends in the Middle East, this could be extremely problematic for the security of the U.S."

"I'm tracking," I said, trying to keep my expression and my tone light.

"Not to mention the satellite and air defense issues," she said. "Or the fact that Brazil and the U.S. have enjoyed long-standing, stable trade. There are many implications here, not just on a Homeland Security level. But that is the biggest one. General Horta has several very powerful supporters, in South America and beyond. In fact, we have a team trying to follow financials to see if we can prove that his campaign might be funded by overseas investors."

I was still unclear as to why they were so focused on the Almeidas. "How does the Almeida cartel fit in?"

She shrugged. "They've picked the last few leaders of the country with surprising accuracy. They have ties to numerous politicians. I know you might not see it that way, but the Almeida family is powerful and dangerous. You're kind of in the eye of the storm right now."

"Let's hope the wind doesn't shift." Then I added, "But the U.S. has dealt with issues like this before."

"It's true. But if you've been paying attention to the

world stage, you know that things like this are popping up all over the world. You know that song, "The Farmer in the Dale"?"

"Yes."

"The United States doesn't want to end up being the cheese standing alone against all these threats. So we deal with them, one threat at a time."

"Then the agency wants to see Prosecutor General Patricia Bradley elected."

She was the other candidate for President, the current underdog, but only by a margin.

Wignow shrugged. "That would be best. She is a true believer, wants to fix this country from the inside out. She's willing to keep trade between our countries open. She might demand better terms, but we can take that hit. The difference between Horta and Bradley is that Horta sees absolute control as the goal, whereas Bradley wants to reshape the country to be more democratic, more capitalist."

"And we all know that the U.S. loves that," I said, dryly.

Wignow shrugged. "It's not a perfect system, but it is the best one that the world has come up with."

"I agree."

"Then you'll help us? I should warn you that the agency reached out to you first as a courtesy. If you don't act as a liaison between the agency and the Almeidas, we'll have to go above your head in this matter."

"You mean you'll threaten Camilla."

"Not threaten. Just explain."

The thing was, I believed her. Wignow seemed rational and honest, without that slimy veneer or bluster that so many of the agents acquired.

"So we understand each other, I want to know how far the CIA is willing to go to get what they want."

Wignow shook her head. "You already know the answer to that."

"Fine. So that also means you should be willing to expend resources in order to help us achieve your goal."

She raised an eyebrow. "If we can give you something, within reason, we will. But you know what the parameters are--we can't be seen as interfering. We were never here. This conversation never happened."

"Yeah, yeah, I know. But if I needed an emergency exfiltration, no questions asked, could you provide that?"

"Yes." Her eyes scanned the room. "We know the dynamic that is playing out here, better than you might think. This is a campaign--both in military terms and election terms. Whoever is going to take charge of the cartel has to win the hearts and minds of the other members. She is the one best poised to do that." She nodded at Camilla, who was talking with Tristao and Caio across the room.

I tried not to audibly grind my teeth together.

Wignow continued. "But whoever is going to take over better do it quickly. The jackals are circling the wounded deer."

My gaze whipped to her face. "What does *that* mean?"

"You think that this, what's going on here, is a secret?"

She shook her head. "The second that Thiago died, other groups in Brazil have been testing the Almeidas. They need to consolidate power, resolve this internal struggle. The CIA *wants* the Almeidas to succeed. They are part of the stability of this country, part of the foundation, like it or not. But they are an organization, just like any other, and this is a critical time. If the leadership falters, if there's too much infighting... well, they'll all go down--probably in a bloody fashion."

She sipped her cocktail like she hadn't just predicted the demise of one of the people closest to me. I tried to keep my expression neutral, when my emotions were anything but.

"I'll pass along the message," I said, tersely.

"Just remember that we have information and assets that could make this process easier," she said. "You know, once everyone is on the same page as to what the plan is."

My lips tightened. "I'll remember that."

"Well, I should get out before anyone realizes they don't know me. I'll make contact soon. Don't take too long in deciding. This situation is balancing on the edge of a knife. One move in the wrong direction, and it will get ugly, fast."

I thought of the body I'd hid in the closet earlier, and winced. "I know."

I watched her red hair as she wove her way casually to the exit.

"What was that all about?" Frankie asked, at my elbow.

I sighed. "We should have a team meeting tonight. Can

you sweep the rooms for bugs again, and let everyone know not to drink too much? I need all the brainpower I can get on this."

Frankie nodded and disappeared into the crowd. Across the room, the strains of a string orchestra warming up could be heard.

"You've got to be kidding me," I grumbled under my breath.

I'd hoped this would be an hour-long thing, tops. Appetizers, cocktails, wham, bam, done. But I hadn't noticed the dance floor or the musicians. We weren't going to be out of here in an hour--we might not be out of here until the wee morning hours.

"Isn't it beautiful?" My mother gushed, appearing at my elbow. Her eyes scanned the party. "I haven't been to a party in *ages*. So nice to get out, socialize. Did you know there's a General here? And he might be the next President of Brazil? I never knew Camilla's family was so well connected." She gave a slight frown. "Kind of makes you wonder what she was doing working as your housekeeper."

I turned to her and raised my eyebrow.

"Not that there's anything wrong with being a house-keeper," she hurriedly added. "Just...you know, someone with a lot of options and family money...you'd think she would have found something else to do. Oh, there's your father over by the food table again. I better go remind him of his cholesterol."

She bustled off into the crowd, probably to slap a

canape out of my father's hand. I took a deep breath in through my nose and released it slowly through my mouth.

"I recognize that breathing technique," Hyde said with a twinkle in his eye. "I've used it before, myself."

I smiled. "I find that it helps keep the screams internal."

"This is quite the crowd." Hyde gestured to the couples starting to fill the dance floor with his half-full tumbler of scotch. "Caio is really trying to prove something."

"Wignow was here," I said, frowning.

"I noticed that."

"She mentioned that there's a lot of attention on this power struggle. That there are 'interested parties' who are hoping to see the Almeida group collapse. That there's a bunch of people willing to help that process along. She says that this situation needs to be resolved soon, or the Almeidas might lose control."

"Makes sense. In their business, if you show weakness, you're halfway dead."

"So maybe these parties aren't just about Caio trying to prove himself to his own people. Maybe he's trying to send a signal that everything is business as usual, that things are fine."

"I think that's right." He set his drink on a nearby table. "We should probably help him out with that. May I have this dance?"

I smiled. "Sure, but I'm not a great dancer."

"Unfortunately, my mother made me take lessons until

I was big enough to put my foot down and make them stop."

I laughed. "Well, let's go see if her money was wasted or not. But I'm warning you that you've got your work cut out for you."

"Challenge accepted," he said, and pulled me towards the dance floor.

DANCING WITH HYDE was surprisingly enjoyable, once I stopped fighting him for control. I had to keep telling myself to stay loose, to not try and predict which steps or direction were coming next. By his occasional deep laughter and teasing, I knew he could tell it was a challenge for me.

The music was beautiful, as were many of the people around us. Hyde's arm was strong around my waist, my hand secure in his. My other hand gripped his solid shoulder. He grinned down at me, and I felt that familiar swooping sensation in my gut. *Mine,* I thought.

"What are you smiling about?" I said.

"Just thinking how much fun it's going to be to try and lead you in our first dance. At the wedding."

"Ah, that. Maybe we'll elope. Just you, me, and Elvis in Las Vegas."

"If that's what you want."

His voice was light, but I knew him well enough to hear the slight hesitation.

"Wait," I said, my tone teasing. "Don't tell me you're

one of those guys who has a dream wedding binder under your bed."

He grinned. "And what if I was?"

"Then you'd get to plan the whole thing, cause I don't have a binder."

He laughed, then his eyes focused on something beyond my shoulder. "*That's* interesting."

Before I could ask, he swung us around so I could see what he was talking about. It was Camilla and Tristao, dancing. His movements were sure and strong--a natural dancer. Her floral dress eddied like silk water as he twirled her around the dance floor.

There was a tension in the way that they held onto each other--it was the same tension found right when someone leaned in for the first kiss--the tension of whether or not something was about to change. And the way they looked at each other...her eyes were soft, while his seemed to blaze. It seemed almost scandalous to be in the same room with them. Despite what Camilla said, they so obviously weren't just friends.

"Well, shit," I murmured.

"Yeah."

Chapter 28

Hours later, we piled into the dining room in the family apartments. Hyde and Howard had shucked their jackets and lost their ties, but Frankie, Camilla, and I were still in our dresses. My family was long asleep, but I had an electronic tripwire up to notify us if someone came our way.

"So...I don't know where to start," I said.

"Rip off the band-aid," Hyde said, his voice grim.

Camilla nodded in agreement.

"Alright...the CIA has been contacting me regarding this situation," I said, rushing to get the words out, get the confession over with. "And tonight I killed Ignacio and hid him in the hall linen closet. Hopefully, he's still there."

"He is," Howard said. "I checked."

"What?" Camilla said, leaning forward, her eyes wide. "How long has the CIA been in contact with you? What do they want?"

"See?" Frankie said, blithely. "No one cares that Ignacio is dead."

Camilla made a shushing motion with her hands. "What does the CIA want?"

"The short of it is that they strongly oppose General Horta coming into any sort of power. In fact, I really get the impression that they would like him gone altogether."

"Why?" Camilla's voice was stern, her face grave.

"Because he's a leftist, power-hungry whacko," I said, taking the pins out of my bun and tossing them on the table. "He looks at what Chavez and Maduro did to Venezuela, and he thinks that the principles were sound, but the execution left a little to be desired."

"When are people going to figure out that socialism doesn't work?" Howard said. "How many times are people going to run that same experiment? It's like throwing a Mentos into a liter of Diet Coke and being *surprised* when you get blasted in the face. It's insanity!"

"When did they first contact you?" Camilla said, her eyes flashing.

I sighed. "When we all first went to the market."

Her eyebrows jumped. "That was well over a week ago!"

"I know. I'm sorry. I should have told you. I was trying to figure out a way to fix things without worrying you."

"This is my family, Elayna. As messed up as this situation is, it is still my family. I know things that you don't. I need all of the information to make this decision!"

"I know." I shook my head. It was hard for me to admit I was wrong, even harder when it was Camilla I had wronged. "It won't happen again. I was just trying to..."

"Oh, I know what you're trying to do here," Camilla said. She was furious, and I couldn't blame her. "But please don't pretend that you were withholding information for *my* benefit. You are trying to control the outcome, just like everyone else."

"Can you blame me?" I retorted. "You've spent the last twenty-some years trying to get as far as possible from these people, from this situation. But Thiago managed to rope you back in. You've had the safe open since the night we got here. Why haven't you made a choice yet?"

"It is not that easy."

"It is!" I threw up my hands. "Just give them each half and let them tear each other to shreds. We can be back home within twelve hours if we leave right now."

"There are people here that would get hurt! Innocent people would be killed if there was an internal struggle. You know that!" Camilla's face was incredulous, pain-filled.

"I do know that," I said, trying to calm down. "And I understand why you haven't done that. But can you understand that I don't want to encourage any more emotional ties for you here? You are *not* responsible for the mess that your father created. Just because you have the same last name doesn't mean you have to inherit this burden."

She shook her head. "I thought of all people, you would be most likely to understand. I *am* responsible, because I have the power to change things. I can make a difference."

I shook my head, pressed my lips together against the tears that threatened to build in my eyes. If she was thinking like this, the battle was half over. I was going to lose her, and there was nothing I could do about it.

"I still want to come back home," Camilla said, her voice gentle. "I just need time to figure out how to extricate myself. I need to know where the money is going, so I can see who is behind the human trafficking. I cannot let that stand, Elayna."

"I know." I nodded.

Despite how I felt, what I wanted, I knew Camilla was right. How could she walk away, knowing that she could change things? Even I couldn't leave, without trying to fix the human trafficking issue. I thought of Iris, and my heart hurt. She was a bitch, but circumstances had forged her into one.

And Camilla felt that way about so many people here. Every day she looked people in the face, people she had known nearly all her life, and talked to them. And she was the one in charge of choosing whether they lived or died, won or lost. Add to that the fact that the Almeida cartel was a huge part of the country, and that numerous inno-cent lives would be lost or ruined if there was a gang war or a power vacuum?

I shook my head again. "I really do understand. I just don't like it."

Camilla grabbed my hand and squeezed. "I know. Me, neither. But I can't do this without you. And I can't do this without having all the information. You can't hide things from me, just because you think it's better for what you want if I don't know."

I nodded. "You're right. I'm sorry."

"So start from the top. Tell me everything."

I told her everything about the CIA, starting with the kidnapping at the marketplace, the fact that I'd seen Wu in person, to what Agent Wignow had told me tonight. By the time I was finished, she was rubbing her face like she was exhausted.

"And why is there a corpse in a linen closet?" she asked, her voice strained.

"Well, that's not Elayna's fault," Howard said. "Ignacio kicked Bruno. Right in front of her. And Bruno *yelped*."

Camilla sat up, her eyes wide. "Was there blood? Do we need to bleach anything?"

"Why does everyone think I'm some sort of maniacal slasher?" I held my hands out, confused. "I'm not a psycho. I just snapped his neck."

"A perfectly reasonable reaction," Hyde said.

I narrowed my eyes at him, but couldn't sense any sarcasm.

"Knowing how Elayna feels about that dog, it was downright polite," Frankie said, folding her arms and grinning.

I looked over at Bruno. He was sleeping half-on, half-off his bed. Who knew how he found that position comfortable, but he was snoring away.

"He's a sweetheart. Why would anyone kick him?" I said.

Bruno farted.

"Show off," Howard said, then turned back to the group. "Is anyone else having severe gastrointestinal upset?"

"Stop eating so much damn meat!" Frankie said, exasperated.

"But they put it on the table!" Howard said, using his hands to measure. "Great, big platters of perfectly done steaks! And you expect me just to *not eat it*?"

Camilla and Hyde laughed.

"If it makes your poo runny, then yes!" Frankie said. "Show some self-control!"

Howard made a face like he thought Frankie was insane. "It's *steak*. Really good *steak*."

"And it's giving you diarrhea!" Frankie nearly yelled.

"Oh, it's bad, too," Howard said. "Like, next stop Sphincter Malfunction, bad."

"Alright," I said, pushing back from the table. "I'm going to take that as the signal that this meeting has concluded. I've already been treated to the minutiae of Howard's bathroom problems, so I don't need to hear it again. Let's talk again in the morning, yeah?"

The meeting dispersed. I lingered behind. Hyde brushed a kiss across my cheek and left. Frankie and Howard argued their way out the door and down the hall.

"That's something, I guess," Camilla said, nodding her head in their direction.

"A start. Seems like they're almost back to where they were, before they got together as a couple," I agreed.

"But there's no going back to just friends," she said. "Not really."

I thought of the dance she had shared with Tristao, then remembered why I had hung back.

"I really am sorry for not telling you sooner, Camilla," I said. "I just want things to stay the same, with us. I don't want things to change."

"I know. I don't want that, either. But if I have learned anything in my life, it is that we often don't get to choose where life takes us--we only get to choose how we react. That, and change is constant."

"Ugh, stop sharing your wisdom," I said. "I want to live in my own little imaginary world where I think I can control and fix everything, and things don't change unless I want them to."

She laughed. "Is there room in that imaginary land for me?"

I hugged her. "Always."

Chapter 29

Hyde, Camilla, and I stayed up late to dispose of Ignacio. There were guards still up, but less than usual. The party had been heavily guarded, with every man on duty, so those still left on shift were sleepy. Some were drunk. At least, that's what Camilla had said would happen. I hoped she was right. My first idea had been to dismember Ignacio in the bathtub, put him in a couple of duffel bags, and then drop him in the nearest body of water. Camilla had chuckled.

"Why so much work, when we can just take him to the basement?" she said.

My head whipped toward her. "What's in the basement?"

She wiggled her eyebrows. "You will have to wait and see. As long as the codes my father gave me still work, we just have to get him down the hallway to that door."

When I opened the closet, a wall of foul odor, thick and cloying, hit me in the face.

"Ugh," I said. "He shit himself."

"They usually do," Hyde said pragmatically. "Let's wrap him up."

We found a few more sets of sheets and wound them around the body, which was now stiff and graying. I tried not to blanch at the pallor of the skin, or the way it felt firm, like cool plastic with hard gel underneath. There was a reason I did the vast majority of my body disposals immediately. Everyone understood the feel of a fresh corpse, because it was similar to a sleeping person. Floppy, still warm, minimal body control. I could handle that, even if most of them did make a mess as they died. It was the stiff ones or the bloated ones that grossed me out. It wasn't normal; it wasn't natural. I didn't like it.

"Man, for someone who offs people on the regular, you sure can be picky," Hyde said when I made a face.

"I prefer them fresh," I said, winding another sheet around the stiff legs.

"You sound like a woman at the deli counter-- 'Is it fresh? I only want it if it's fresh'."

I swatted him with a towel, then put it beneath the corpse's butt. "Hey, I have a certain way I prefer to do things. That doesn't mean I'm picky or that I can't handle a stiff one."

"Oh, you can handle a stiff one, all right," Hyde said, waggling his eyebrows.

"Grow up!" I chucked another towel at his face. "We're

dealing with a dead body here. No sex jokes near dead bodies. It's a rule."

"Oh, there's rules now?" he said, a sparkle in his eye.

"Yes, and that's one of them."

"Fair enough. Now, help me pick this up. It's so big and stiff, I can't lift it alone."

"Gross, Hyde."

"What?" he blinked at me, an all-too innocent expression on his face. "It's not my fault if you have a dirty mind. Help me pick up Ignacio."

We wrestled the body out into the hall. It was awkward--Howard and I had not planned well when we left him sprawled in the closet. Ignacio had apparently landed with one arm up above his head, and his knees bent. It was difficult to get a grip, and I swear the guy had gained fifty pounds in the hours I had left him.

Camilla met us at the end of the hall, her nose wrinkling at the sight of our awkward bundle. "He stinks."

"You don't have to tell me that," I said, huffing with exertion but trying not to breathe through my nose. "It's worse the closer you get."

"I got the basement open. There shouldn't be any problem, but I'll go wait around the corner, make sure nobody comes."

"Ok," I grunted. "We'll be there when we get there."

It took us several minutes to get to the end of the hall. I kept losing my grip and having to adjust. Sweat was pouring down my temples. It was like moving the world's most awkwardly-shaped piece of furniture, which smelled like every bodily fluid that existed. As we neared the corner, I heard voices. I set down my end of Ignacio and went to listen.

"I was going to the kitchen, to see if there were any of those canapes left over," Camilla said. "I had so much fun, I couldn't sleep. Did you enjoy yourself?"

I heard the low rumble of a male voice. I thought it might have belonged to Tristao, but I couldn't be sure.

"Let's go together, then," she said. "Maybe you can pour me a glass of wine and tell me all about your life since I last was in Brazil."

The voice must have answered in the affirmative, because I heard them walk off together towards the main kitchen, talking as they went.

I hustled back over and picked up my end of the corpse. "Camilla bought us some time, but who knows when they'll be back."

"Who was it?" Hyde said.

The cords in his neck stood out a bit from the strain of lifting a grown, dead man, but he wasn't sweating nearly as profusely as I was.

"I think it was Tristao," I said. "But I can't be sure."

"If it was him, we have all the time in the world. Did you see that dance they shared? Muy caliente."

I wrinkled my nose. "Gross. I don't think of Camilla that way."

"Well, I'd be a little offended if you did, considering. But I think Tristao *definitely* thinks about her that way."

"Oh, good, she left it cracked," I said, spying the door down the hallway. "Hurry up."

There was no more spare effort left for conversation. We got the body down the hallway and through the door as quickly as possible. I didn't shut it all the way behind us, because what if it required a code to get out? We set down our burden on the threshold on the other side.

"Stay here," Hyde said. "I'll make sure it's clear."

IT SEEMED like twenty minutes had passed. I was starting to get worried and debated going after him. I had just decided to count down five more minutes and then I'd go look for him, when he came jogging back around the corner.

"This place is *huge*," he said, swiping sweat from his brow, then picking up his end of Ignacio. "Some gnarly shit down here, too, but I know where we need to go. Let's hurry up and get this done."

Under Hyde's direction, we ended up in the third door on the right in an endless-looking hallway. The room was built of concrete block, and the floor and halfway up the walls were sheathed in stainless steel. It had a chemical smell that made my nose itch. There were large plastic tubs of varying sizes along one wall--there was one big enough for one body, one big enough for four, and one large enough that I hoped it had never been used. The other side had huge racks of various chemicals. If nothing else I'd learned about the Almeida cartel had convinced me that they weren't to be trifled with, this room alone would have.

We lifted Ignacio into the first plastic tub. His arm still hung out, standing straight up like a cry for help or some demented salute, but once the chemicals got to him, that would change.

"Better suit up," Hyde said, nodding toward a row of hooks that held rubber-looking bodysuits. "This stuff is going to be strong."

I followed his lead. He flipped the switch for a massive exhaust fan in the ceiling, and selected several chemicals from the shelves. I was grateful for the thick walls and the evidence of extensive sound-proofing in the ceiling. We didn't want to be caught down here.

I mainly watched him work. Chemical disposals weren't my specialty; they were Hyde's. I preferred to let nature or the police clean up after me, but I was grateful he knew what he was doing. It didn't take long. Within twenty minutes of bubbling and a smell that made my eyes sting, Ignacio' arm began to lower into the sludge like the mast of a sinking ship. Soon, it was under. Hyde waited another twenty minutes.

"Check this out," he said, flipping another switch on the wall.

I heard a distinctive noise, one I'd heard a thousand times before, just more amplified this time.

"Is that...are those *garbage disposals*?" I said, half-aghast, half-impressed at the idea.

"Yep," he said, watching the slimy mixture lower. "They have them built in to every tub."

I went and looked at the next size bigger. Hyde was right--there were four built into the bottom. They were bigger than what I had seen in normal kitchens, industrial.

"Wow," I said.

"Yeah." He unrolled a garden hose from a holder on the wall and turned on the spigot. "I don't want to end up down here during this trip again."

I shivered at the implication. This whole time, I had known that we were in danger. Somehow, standing on this floor with drains spaced evenly below my feet made it real. This room was used for people just like me--people who thought that they could deal with the Almeida cartel and make it out alive. But this mission wasn't just skirting the edges of danger like we usually did. We were in the belly of the beast. Heck, right now, Hyde and I were standing in the bowels.

"We need those numbers," I said, my voice serious. "We need them as soon as possible so we can get out of here."

"I know," Hyde said. "I don't trust anyone here. There seems to be a few bright spots, but even those people..."

I knew what he meant. I wanted to be able to trust someone, anyone, in this mess. Besides Camilla, there was no one. I didn't know if Tristao really was interested in Camilla, or if he had been instructed by his boss to butter her up. I didn't know if Iris was really a good guy, or if she were playing us. She could work for another cartel for all we knew. I resolved to have Frankie run a background check on her first thing in the morning.

And Agent Wignow? I wanted to trust her. My gut told me she was telling the truth. But I had been trained to lie well by the CIA, too. I didn't think it was an accident that they had sent her to talk to me tonight. They'd seen that I'd reacted best to her during our prior meeting. She could be lying through her teeth. There were too many threads in this knot. It was too complicated. There was no clear right answer. Caio or Alex? We were trying to choose the lesser of two evils.

"We'll find our way through," Hyde said, shutting down the disposals.

The tub was sparkling clean again. There was no evidence that we'd made corpse soup. Ignacio was no more than a memory and a thick sludge down the drain.

"So far, we always have," I said.

But I wasn't so sure about it, this time.

We shucked off our suits, hung them up again, and surveyed the room to make sure there was no evidence of us being there. Except for a slight dampness in the first tub, there wasn't, and that would be dry by morning. We shut off the lights and the fan and made our way back up the stairs. The hallway was clear when we got to it, so we shut the basement door behind us this time.

"I'm going to go shower," Hyde said, dusting a kiss on my temple. "It's been a weird night."

"Yeah. I'm going to check on Camilla, let her know everything worked out."

He nodded and ducked into our bedroom. I knocked quietly on Camilla's door. When I didn't get an answer, I pushed it open. She wasn't there. Her bed was still made. A shiver of worry trailed up my spine. What if something had happened? She had been gone for at least an hour, now. What if something had gone wrong?

Just then, her door swung open behind me and Camilla rushed in.

"Oh!" she said, when she saw me. Her hand went to her throat. "You scared me."

"I'm sorry. I just came to tell you..." I faltered. "Is that a *hickey*?"

"No," Camilla said, her eyes wide, her hand covering a spot low on her neck. "It's not."

I stepped closer. "It is! You got a hickey!"

Camilla's cheeks turned pink. "Shut up."

"And your hair's all messed up, too. What did you guys do--find a backseat?" I cackled.

Regardless of how I felt about Camilla making connections down here, the situation was hilarious.

She self-consciously smoothed her shirt. "Oh, like you and Hyde are any better. Don't think I don't know what you guys get up to."

"Oh, we're not talking about me right now, young lady," I said. I tapped my wrist where my watch would be. "Do you have any idea what time it is? It's past your curfew! I was worried sick!"

Camilla laughed. "Hush. We were just talking."

"Oh, yeah," I said, waggling my eyebrows. "I'm sure."

"It was nice to see him. Nice to talk without other people listening. It felt like old times." She looked wistful.

I sat on the edge of her bed. "Tell me all about it." I paused, then frowned. "Well, not *all* about it. Give me the bold headings."

She sat next to me. "I never felt like we got closure. Even when I heard that he'd married, it still didn't feel finished, not to me." She lifted pleading eyes to me. "Not that I ever would have acted on my feelings when he was married. I just mean..."

"He moved on, but you didn't."

"Right. Yes. So I think that tonight was more about me getting to say goodbye than anything. I feel like I have that closure. Like I can move on."

"That does not look like a goodbye to me," I said, gesturing at her distinctly disheveled person. "That looks like a *hello.*"

She smiled. "I think it might have been, for him. But for me, it was closure. The last kiss I never got, before now."

"I don't know, Camilla. He's single now. You're single. And the way he looks at you..." I shrugged. "Do you trust him?" I tilted my head.

"Yes." She smiled. "He is still the same Tristao. Older and wiser, maybe. But I can still tell when he is lying."

"Well, that's something, I guess. I can't tell if anyone here is telling the truth."

There was a long pause.

"Did you guys find the basement alright?"

"Yeah," I said. "He's taken care of."

I yawned so wide my jaw ached a little with the motion.

"You'd better get to bed," she said, making a little shooing motion.

"I just wanted to make sure that you got home safely. Glad you had a good time." I waggled my eyebrows at her once more. "Let me know if he gets too fresh--I'll have a talk with him."

"Oh, get out of here," she said, grinning.

I chuckled all the way into Hyde's and my bedroom, where he was still toweling off his hair.

"What are you smiling about?" he said. "Camilla get back alright?"

"Oh, she's fine. A little bruised, but not too bad." I laughed at my own joke.

"Huh?"

"Tristao gave her a hickey. She's going to be wearing scarves or turtlenecks for a week. And in this heat. Can you imagine?" I laughed again.

"Maybe I ought to give you one, so she can make fun of *you*," he said, advancing forward with a prowling stance.

"Don't you dare," I said, wagging my finger at him and backing up. "I'm serious."

He picked me up around the waist and threw me onto the bed. I squealed--a very undignified sound that I cut off abruptly. Hyde pinned my arms and lowered his head to my neck.

"Hyde!" I said. "I'm serious! I don't need to worry about wardrobe choices on top of everything else!"

He put his lips to the crook of my neck--and blew a loud raspberry into my skin. Then he leaned back and grinned, letting my arms go.

"I just wanted to show you I *could*," he said, looking very satisfied with himself.

"Oh, is that right?"

I hooked my legs around his torso, and flipped myself up and on top of him.

"Ha! Now who's king of the mountain?" I said, tickling his side.

"I never should have taught you how to grapple," he said. "But just so we're clear, I *let* you do that."

I raised my eyebrows and shrugged, climbing down from the bed. "So *you* say."

He snapped my butt with his towel as I walked away. "Hurry up and shower and get to bed. I can't sleep without the soundtrack of your snoring anymore."

I blew a raspberry at him, and he laughed.

Chapter 30

The next morning dawned cloudy and humid, so the team ate breakfast in the family dining room while my family slept in. Camilla came to the table wearing white capri pants, a navy and white striped short-sleeve blouse, and a navy scarf tied in a jaunty bow.

"Well, what a *darling* outfit, Camilla," I said, around a mouthful of almond pastry. "You look cute as an undone button."

She narrowed her eyes at me and poured herself a cup of coffee. "Thank you."

"Yeah, I just don't think I could pull that off," I said, a serene smile on my face. "It's very retro and innocent. You look like you're about to go to a drive-in movie theater."

"Huh," she said, noncommittally, filling her plate with fruit and pastries.

"If I wore that, I'd be rumpled in less than an hour. I'd look like I'd rolled in the hay in no time."

Camilla glared, and I gave her a cheery smile in return.

"What on earth are you going on about, Elayna?" Howard said. "Will you be quiet? It's a little early for fashion talk, and I drank too much last night."

"Not my fault you're hung over," I said. "Besides, Hyde, Camilla, and I were up much later than you. We had to take care of our closeted friend."

"Oh yeah?" Frankie asked, her eyebrows raised. "How did it go?"

I shrugged. "Really well, considering. Hyde and I took the body down to the basement, and Camilla was our look-out. She did a *very* thorough job."

Camilla gave me another frown of warning, but I took another bite of my pastry with relish.

Frankie was looking back and forth between us, oddly. "Am I missing something?"

"Nope," Hyde said, giving my thigh a warning squeeze, under the table. "Elayna's just a bit loopy from lack of sleep, that's all."

"Oh, scandalous," Frankie said. "But I don't want to hear any lovebird details over the breakfast table."

"But..." I said, just as Camilla started laughing.

"Let's move on," Hyde said. "Aren't these pastries delicious?"

I gave him the stink-eye, but let him change the subject.

"You are *never* going to guess what I just saw in Peter and Sybil's room," Frankie said, her eyes wide.

I plugged my ears. "La, la, la, la, la! That's my brother. I don't want to hear it."

She pulled my hands down. "Nothing like *that*. I was walking past, and the door was open, and Sybil was lying on the bed..."

My nose wrinkled.

"...petting Sir Darcy," Frankie finished, to my great relief. "He was curled up right next to her, and I thought I heard him *purring*."

"Wow." Camilla frowned. "Didn't see that one coming."

Frankie nodded. "Me, neither. It's so bizarre."

I tilted my head. "Actually, it makes a lot of sense, if you think about it."

"What?"

"His old owner was a sociopath, so it only makes sense that he's attracted to that kind of personality."

Frankie rolled her eyes. "She's not *that* bad."

"Says the person who only has to see her once a year."

After breakfast, I asked Frankie to run a background check on Iris and Ruben. I wanted to see if she could find anything to corroborate her story, or to find anything out about her sister. Maybe there was a morgue record with a Jane Doe, or whatever they called their unknown dead in this country.

"Hey, that's interesting," Frankie said, awhile later. "I found her. And you'll never guess who her grandmother is."

"Who?"

She turned her computer screen around, and I saw a

black and white photo of a beautiful actress. "Ramona Cortez. Apparently, she emigrated to Hollywood after finding success here. Then, you know, she blew up. Huge star. She died in L.A. a few years ago."

"That makes sense," Camilla said. "Iris said that her grandmother had left her money."

Frankie whistled. "Seventy million dollars, all to Iris. Apparently, Ramona took the money she made from acting and invested in real estate. She did very well."

"Seventy million is no joke," I said. "But I don't know if it's enough to dismantle an entire human trafficking network."

Camilla shrugged. "It's enough to start."

"What about this Ruben guy?" I said.

"Nothing too odd or special about him," Frankie said. "No real records after Iris got her inheritance."

"That party was really something," my mother said, coming down the stairs and stifling a yawn. "Is there any coffee left?"

Frankie closed her computer gently and gathered up the few papers sitting next to her.

I nodded. "In the kitchen. There's pastries on the counter, too. Or you can order something from the main kitchen."

"You didn't wait for us to eat?" Sybil said with a frown, appearing at the top of the stairs.

Ears like a bat, that one.

"We've been up for hours." I managed to keep my tone

civil and force a smile to my face, but it was work. "But feel free to order something."

"An eggs benedict *does* sound divine," my mother said, smoothing her hair back. "But of course I'll wait for everyone else to get up."

It was all I could do not to sigh or roll my eyes. It seemed like no matter what I did, there was fault to be found with it, at least in my mother's eyes.

"Excellent." Camilla smiled. "I've set up a wine and cheese tasting in the afternoon for the adults, and there's childcare. At three, I've scheduled an esthetician and a masseuse to come if you'd like a facial and a massage. This evening we are having a sushi chef come to the estate to give a demonstration..."

"Jake and Isabella don't eat sushi," Sybil interrupted, her tone sullen.

"Which is why there will also be a teppanyaki station set up for anyone who wants it," Camilla finished, her smile still intact.

"Thank you, Camilla," my mother said. "That sounds like a lovely day."

"Fine. I'll get Peter and the kids," Sybil said, and ducked from view.

A chime sounded--the doorbell to the family suite. Camilla answered it and came back, her mouth tense.

"It was Tristao. My uncle is requesting our presence."

"Whose?" I said.

"You and me. It might be about Ignacio."

"Shit." The knot that had been in my stomach ever since I'd killed him tightened until I was nauseated. "That's not good. Frankie--you're on family duty. Order some mimosas or something. Keep them here until we get back. Howard, find Bruno and guard him. Hyde, you armed?"

He nodded and stood.

The three of us met Tristao at the door. He was frowning, looking much older than he had when he'd danced with Camilla the night before.

"He knows," Tristao said to us in a low voice as we followed him. "You'd better think quickly. He is very angry."

Camilla nodded.

Caio and his men were waiting for us in the dining room. He was bristling with anger, agitated, pacing back and forth. The men around him all were posturing for maximum intimidation--shoulders back, stern frowns in place, guns visible. My heart pounded and my adrenaline surged--I started walking through the fight to come in my mind. I'd take the guy on my left down, first.

"What is this about, Uncle?" Camilla said.

"Ignacio!" he roared. "This is about Ignacio!"

"Ignacio insulted me by hurting one of my guests, Uncle," Camilla said calmly.

"I have watched the surveillance tapes!" he said, spittle flying from between his bared teeth. He extended a pointed finger at me, the end curved like a claw. "Antiques dealer, my ass! She killed him. Like it was nothing."

I raised my eyebrow. If I remembered correctly, his

neck had provided *some* resistance. It wasn't like it hadn't taken *effort*. But I figured now wasn't the time to argue the point.

"Ignacio attacked her dog," Camilla said, calmly.

It was the same tone of voice one would use with a man standing on the ledge of a fourteen story building, or a mentally unstable person waving a gun.

"A dog!" he screeched, his eyes wide, wild. "Who the fuck cares about a fucking dog?"

"I do," Camilla said. "These are my guests. Ignacio kicked my guest."

"It's a fucking *dog*," Caio screamed. A vein throbbed violently in his forehead. "A fucking *dog!*"

"Not to me," Camilla said, her voice getting lower, colder. "This is my house, and I will not have my guests disrespected."

"*Your* house?" Caio said, his face contorting into a scowl. "*Yours?*"

"Yes, Uncle," she said. "It is my house."

I watched the men around the edge of the room. Tristao shifted ever so slightly closer to Camilla, as if he were fighting the urge to protect her. He looked nervous, his eyes as alert as mine. Good. If this went sideways, we'd need all the help we could get.

Camilla sighed, patted her hair. "I didn't want to tell you this until I had completely figured out the transition of things, Uncle," she said. "But my father has left me everything."

There was a moment where I really thought he was

going to pull out a gun and shoot her, just for uttering those words. That, or have an aneurysm. His face went purple, his eyes wide.

Camilla, however, looked unfazed. "I don't want it, of course," she said.

It took a moment for the words to register.

Caio blinked. "What?"

"I need wine. Can someone get us a bottle, please?" she pulled out a chair and sat.

The move seemed to decrease the tension. Camilla was smart. Sitting showed that she wasn't scared of him, or what his reaction might be. It communicated to him that he wasn't going to hate what she had to say. Caio took the seat across the table from Camilla.

"Get the wine," Caio said, even though someone was already uncorking a bottle at the sideboard.

Camilla waited until she'd sipped her wine, then she leaned forward. "My brother cannot hear of this."

Caio nodded and leaned forward. His eagerness could not have been more obvious. If he'd been a cartoon dog, his tongue would have been hanging out.

"The night that we arrived," Camilla said, "I opened the safe."

Caio leaned back as if pushed back by an invisible hand.

"My father has left me everything," Camilla said, waving her hand to encompass their surroundings.

"Everything?" Caio asked, leaning forward once more.

"Everything. Every company, every property, the estate, the cars, the helicopters, the stock portfolio. Everything."

Caio leaned back. His face had gone a sickly greyish color, his jaw was clenched. He looked like he was about to hurl. I was keeping an eye on the men scattered around the room, watching the reactions that were flickering on faces and in postures, like a bunch of individual flames dancing to a breeze that had just blown through.

"But of course I don't want it all," Camilla said, as if she had no idea that tensions were at a peak within the room.

"You don't," Caio repeated, expressionless.

I wasn't sure if it was a question or a statement--I didn't think that Caio knew how he meant it. It looked like he was in some sort of shock.

"No," Camilla scoffed. "I have no desire to move down here. My life is in the U.S."

A slight tremor, in Tristao's fingers.

"That being said," she continued, "I need more time to decide which assets can be effectively separated from the organization, and which must remain. I don't want certain...*businesses* in my portfolio. I'm sure you can understand."

Caio nodded, but it didn't look as if he *did* understand.

Camilla must have seen the uncertainty there, too, because she said, "Of course you understand. The last thing I need is for the United States' IRS to come after me because of improper accounting practices. And I think it would be best, moving forward, for the businesses that I retain to have no ties to the Almeida organization."

Caio nodded, slowly. "So you just want the legal businesses. You have no desire to lead the organization?"

Camilla laughed, as if she'd never heard a more ridiculous idea. "Of *course* not. You know me, Uncle. I've never had an interest in leading."

Caio relaxed back into his chair once more, and smiled. It was the smile of a cat with a belly full of canary, the smile that the coyote would have grinned if he'd ever caught the roadrunner. The raging bull of a few moments ago was a distant memory.

"But I am still going through the numbers," Camilla said. "I've identified several businesses I intend to keep, and several that cannot be separated from the Almeida organization umbrella. It will take some time. I hope you understand."

"Take all the time you need," Caio said, the relaxed and generous host once more.

I realized how deftly Camilla had done it--Caio no longer cared about Ignacio. He wasn't angry. That situation had been completely defused. In fact, if Camilla had taken out a gun and shot another of Caio's men point-blank in the head, I don't know that Caio would have done anything more than blink.

"I would have told you before," Camilla said, giving a sad smile, "but I wasn't sure if I could trust you yet. I wasn't sure if you were working with Alex."

"Never," Caio said. "He is no longer my family."

Camilla nodded. "I know that now, but I wasn't sure if it was a ruse, at first. I had to be sure."

Caio chuckled. "Well, no more secrets between us." He paused, frowned. "Do you know what you are going to do with this estate?"

"This is the seat of the Almeida organization," Camilla said, smoothly. "It would make no sense for me to retain it. The memories I have here are not the ones I want to focus on. I *am* going to keep the vacation home on the northern coast, however," she teased, wagging her finger. "So you will have to buy your own."

Caio laughed. "Very well."

"And I may take a couple of cars from Father's collection," she said, then waved her hand. "But we will work out the details later. That is why this has been taking so long. The books are a mess. I have an accounting firm going through them. They're very discreet, I assure you. But then there are the paintings, and mother's jewelry. And above it all, I have to decide if I want to leave Alex anything more than the money that has been set aside in trust. It's very complicated."

"What money?" Caio said, bristling once more.

"Just a couple million that his mother set aside," Camilla said, waving her hand as if that amount were inconsequential. "And I do not wish to be cruel," she said with emotion, her eyes wide and sincere. "Despite all that my brother has done, I do not wish to be unfair to him. He built the manufacturing in Sao Paulo from scratch, so that will go to him. His mother's jewelry, to hand down if he ever marries or has children, and the painting of his mother. The small yacht, the one that he loved as a child.

These are things that I believe are due to him, and I cannot be persuaded otherwise."

Her chin jutted, her expression was determined, as if prepared for a fight.

"You are very generous," Caio said. He could barely conceal how delighted he was, but he tried to give the approximation of a solemn nod. "You have always been kind-hearted. If you feel that you need to give him these things, I will not stand in your way."

As if he could. I wanted to roll my eyes, but kept my face blank.

"Thank you," Camilla said, lowering her eyes deferentially. "I was worried as to how you would react."

Caio drummed his fingers on the table. "And what about the ports, the manufacturing in the south, those holdings?"

"Those are inexorably linked to the Almeida organization, as well," Camilla said, dismissively. "I don't want them. They have no value, except for the function they serve to the family."

Caio beamed. I'd never seen him look so happy. This news was Christmas, his birthday and Carnival all wrapped into one. Camilla was giving him all he'd ever wanted--all the illegal holdings of the Almeidas, and was only taking what he didn't care about--the legal businesses. And she wasn't asking for anything in return. Just a little time, to get the paperwork together.

"Well," he said, pushing back from the table. "Please let me know what I can do to help."

Camilla nodded, looked relieved. "Thank you, Uncle. This will be much easier now that you know. There is some information that might be helpful. And, of course, I will need the contact information for your attorney; I'm sure they will want to start reviewing the paperwork that mine have already drafted."

"Excellent," he said, smiling so widely I glimpsed his back teeth. "I will help in any way I can."

"Wonderful," Camilla said. She stood, moving to hug him. "But it is very important that Alex not find out. I have drafted and signed a will that will donate all holdings to charity if something should happen to me, to try and protect myself. But I am scared that would not stop Alex from hurting me if he found out about our plans."

"You will be safe, *minha sobrinha*," Caio said. He sounded sincere, although it could have been the information about her will that fueled his resolve. "I will make sure that you are safe."

"Thank you, Uncle," she said.

When we were back in the family quarters, Camilla said, "Could you please try to not kill anyone else? I don't have any more good news to smooth things over."

I chuckled. "I'll do my best."

My family was at the dining table with an impressive brunch spread before them. Frankie was in the living room with her laptop open, but she was watching them surreptitiously as they ate. She breathed a sigh of relief when she saw us.

"Everything ok?" she said.

"Camilla missed her calling as a hostage negotiator," Hyde said. "She smoothed it over."

"Where's Howard?" I asked with a frown.

Frankie rolled her eyes. "He's in his room with Bruno."

"I'll go get him," I said.

Guard Bruno, I'd said, but I hadn't expected *this.* Howard was pacing back and forth in front of the dog bed, completely tacked out. He was wearing full tactical gear, including a balaclava. He had knives strapped to his thigh and a pistol in a holster on his hip. I could read the tension in his stance in the half-second before he realized it was me.

Bruno, for his part, didn't seem to be reading the room. He had no idea that he was the subject of tension. He was sprawled on his bed, his furry bum on the floor. When I entered, he lifted his head in mild interest, then laid back down with a sigh, probably disappointed that I wasn't Hyde.

"What's going on?" Howard said.

"Things have calmed down for now," I said, sweeping my hair off my forehead. "I still want to keep a close eye on Bruno."

I wouldn't put it past Caio to try and get some sort of revenge on me, even though he'd sworn not to. He wasn't a paragon of rationality, that man.

"While you guys were gone, Elio and Marcos made contact with Frankie. They're requesting that you and Camilla come down to their room for a talk. Sounds like they have information on the numbers, finally."

I nodded. "Thank goodness. It's about time."

In the end, it was decided that Howard, Frankie and Hyde would stay behind and keep an eye on Bruno and my family. Camilla and I would head to town and see what information Elio had found. Tristao would come with us, as a guard. Camilla said he wasn't happy with what had happened the last time he'd helped us sneak out.

Chapter 31

The room was tidy, but it had that un-aired smell that is unique to young men, like a locker or dorm room. But we weren't here for the smell. We were here for information. Camilla and I sat side by side on one of the double beds. Tristao was out in the hall, guarding the door.

"So we were finally able to figure it out," Elio said.

He smoothed his suit jacket as if he was self-conscious about standing in front of us, which was in direct opposition to the confident message his ensemble was giving. Today he was wearing a hot pink and black argyle tweed jacket over black pants and black wingtips with hot pink laces.

"It's not good," he said, his face grim. "But the findings do make me feel better about why we couldn't find all the numbers."

"Alright," Camilla said. "What is it?"

"Human trafficking," he said, his face tightening in anger.

I couldn't help it, my eyes darted to the fourth finger of his right hand, where the tip had been removed. Just as quickly, I forced my eyes away. We were playing a game, he and I, where we both pretended we had never met before. Or maybe I was the only one pretending, and he didn't remember that I was the one who'd answered the hotel door that night in Milan and given him a way out. Regardless of whether or not he remembered me, I knew that human trafficking would be as despicable to him as it was to anyone.

More so.

Camilla's face pinched in confusion. "We already knew about the brothel. It's been destroyed."

Elio shook his head. "That was nothing. Once I knew what I was looking for, it was easy to spot. But I needed to know for sure. So yesterday, Marcos and I took a drive out to the factory in Netalas."

My gaze went to Marcos, who was sitting on the bed, his elbows on his knees, looking at the ground.

"It was the creepiest thing," he said. "The factory was running. We could hear it. But there weren't enough cars in the parking lot for the number of workers that place would take."

"It's Brazil," Camilla said impatiently. "Most factory workers would take the bus."

"We wondered that, too," Marcos said. "So we waited."

I didn't like the sound of Marcos' tone--it was the same

voice of a police officer, hat in hand, at the front door of a parent's house at two am. It was the sound of an oncologist right before he dashes all hope.

"The whistle blew. No one came out, but then the factory started up again," Elio said.

"So I went to take a look," Marcos said, without lifting his head. "Got up onto the roof, looked through the high windows. They have people straight-up chained to the lines in there. I mean...not all of them. Some people were moving freely. But about half were chained to something. It wasn't just adults, either. They had a bunch of kids in there, man."

"They probably only chain the ones who have tried to escape," Elio said, clenching his right hand into a fist. "It's a common tactic--to punish the ones who try to leave, to make an example of them to keep everyone in line."

Camilla was shaking her head. "But..."

We all waited for her to finish, but she didn't, just kept shaking her head.

"I looked at the financials. There have been no payments to a workforce at any of the sixteen manufacturing centers that Alexander Almeida owns," Elio said, breaking the awkward silence.

"Sixteen!" Camilla found her feet, began to pace the short length of the hotel room. "This can't be happening at *all* of them."

"I found no accounting differences between the Netalas factory and the other fifteen manufacturing sites," Elio said. "I'm not sure why they would be different, but I'm always open to the possibility that I've made an error."

Camilla shook her head. "I don't think that you made an error. But I hope you did."

"Let's pretend he didn't," I said. "Tell us what this means."

"Well," Elio started, with a quick look at Camilla, as if to see if it was ok, but she was studying the floor. "It means that there are possibly hundreds of people, if not thousands, who are slaves," he finished, bluntly. He cleared his throat. "It also means that none of Alex's businesses are legal."

Camilla plopped on the bed next to me, and put her head in her hands. "I can't believe this."

I pressed my lips together. I knew Camilla. I knew that she had been hoping that the stories about her brother weren't true--that they were the exaggerations of his enemies. But instead of finding the brother that she had known, the brother who wanted to make the family business legitimate, she'd found a pimp and a slaver.

"Could they be?" Camilla said, after many tense moments. "Could the businesses be profitable if they actually paid their people, instead of using slave labor?"

Elio frowned. "I could do the math, but I wouldn't have precise numbers until I knew exactly how many employees and what the wages..."

"How many people did you see, Marcos?" Camilla demanded, cutting Elio off.

"I don't know... maybe a hundred?" he said.

"Run the numbers with a better than average pay for the area," Camilla said, turning to Elio once more. "Say there are a hundred fifty people on each shift, to be safe. Could it be profitable?"

"I...I don't know," he stammered. "I need to find out what a compensation package looks like around here."

Camilla stood abruptly, and snatched the folder from the desk. "I need the numbers by tomorrow morning. Come on, Elayna."

I stood and followed her out, not daring to speak. We ran into Tristao in the hallway, and it was as if Camilla had forgotten he was there.

"We have something we need to do alone," she said, her words choppy. "We will pick you up on our way back home."

He frowned, his forehead crinkling, but I think he saw that this wasn't the time to argue with her. He nodded.

I was silent until we hit the parking lot. Camilla's movements were agitated, jerky.

She fumbled with the keys at the door to the car, and I held out my hand. "Give 'em here. You aren't driving."

She turned to me, and it was like all the anger and grief she felt over Elio's announcement was aimed at me. I'd never seen that expression on her face before. She was livid. But like a stormcloud that finally broke into rain, her rage crumpled into straight grief. She slapped the keys into my palm and circled to the passenger side, her shoulders hunched.

"What's the first address?" I said, pulling out my phone and bringing up the GPS.

She read it to me. I typed it in, started the car and made a right out of the parking lot, away from the way we came.

WE WERE silent as we drove. She had her thoughts; I had mine. I knew what Camilla wasn't saying--she'd hoped that Alex would be the one to take over. We'd both seen Caio's outbursts. How could she possibly leave so much power in the hands of a megalomaniac?

Camilla and I both had hoped that Alex--Harvard-educated, business-minded Alex, would be the one who'd inherit. But now, who was left? It was just Camilla, and we both knew it. Knew it, but didn't want to accept it. What would that mean for her? The thought boggled my mind.

"We have to get them out," Camilla said.

"Ugh," I grunted, instantly ashamed to my core.

Shame sunk low in my gut like a lead weight. I hadn't been thinking about all those people, all those slaves. I had been thinking about *myself*, how to keep the comfort, the team I had. But Camilla was right. We had to get them out.

"How do we do that?" I said, drumming my fingers on the wheel, thinking through the options. "If we hit one, the other locations will get spooked. They might kill the others."

Camilla nodded, chewed her bottom lip. "The best would be to hit them all at once."

"Yes," I said. "But if we know about the sixteen, which ones *don't* we know about?"

"There can't be more than that, do you think?" she said, her head whipping to look at me.

"Think about it," I said, my voice guttural. It went against all my instincts to hurt Camilla, but I wouldn't lie or put an operation in jeopardy, either. "We didn't know about the brothel until Wu gave us the address. What if there are more?"

I was met with silence, but glanced over to see Camilla nod.

"And how did he get that address?" I said, thinking aloud, voicing a question that had lay dormant for some time. "Does the CIA have more information on Alex than they are letting on?"

Camilla shrugged. "When have they ever laid all their cards on the table?"

She sounded tired.

"We don't have to do this tonight," I said, nodding at the quickly darkening road ahead of us. "It can wait."

"Thanks, but I won't be able to sleep until I know. I may never sleep again, actually."

I exhaled in the approximation of a laugh. I knew the feeling. I'd had some cases where I thought that I would never be able to sleep without waking up with screaming nightmares. But sleep always won, for me. Not that I didn't have nightmares, but I recovered quickly.

We drove through some uninhabited jungle, then the road dumped us into something I could only describe as tightly-packed suburbs. That wasn't our destination, and suburbs soon gave way to an industrial zone--metal clad or cinderblock buildings with smokestacks and parking lots. Once we crossed over the railroad tracks, my GPS started chattering about right turns.

"It's that one," Camilla said, pointing to a two-story concrete structure with a metal roof.

There were windows toward the top of the roof, and we could get a good vantage point there. I saw the ladder that Marcos must have used. It wasn't too high off the ground, and there was a bucket nearby that Camilla could use to help her up. Marcos was right--there weren't enough cars in the parking lot. We parked on the street, and I prayed that the car would still be there when we returned. As a safeguard, I opened the hood and removed the distributor cap, shoving it in my pocket.

I was grateful for the cover of evening as our footsteps crunched across the gravel parking lot. We crossed the lot quickly and huddled low against the building. We had no idea what kind of security was present, but there had to be some. You couldn't keep hundreds of human beings contained against their will without a large show of force. I just hoped that they were all inside. I hoped they were all complacent.

At the base of the building, I overturned the bucket. Camilla climbed the ladder first, with me giving her a foothold with my hands between the bucket and the bottom rung. I waited until she waved at me from the roof and moved the bucket back to where it had been, then took hold of the bottom rung and hoisted myself up. I climbed quickly, grateful that the ladder felt sturdy, but feeling the itch of being exposed and vulnerable the whole time. I did not want to get caught here. I had my .45, but little else. I hadn't thought we would be doing any recon tonight--it was just supposed to be a meeting. I wasn't excited to tell Hyde about it, later.

"Let's make this quick," I said, ducking low and making for a window.

Up here, the whir of the machines churned beneath us, making me feel as if I were walking on a vibrating metal plate. The windows were small, and were too high for us to get a good angle of visibility to what was happening below.

"Over there," I whispered, heading in the direction of an open window down at the end.

The noise was nearly deafening as we approached. I couldn't imagine what it would be like in the building, down among the machines. It was a clatter with several parts, like four drunks going to town on metal garbage cans with hammers. My ears were pounding by the time I leaned into the square of light.

The room below was a large cement rectangle that was well lit. Nothing else positive could be said for it, though. The room was dominated by a wide conveyer belt down the center of the space, with various machines chugging away below. At first glance, it didn't seem as if much was amiss.

There were people moving about, wearing hair nets and, I was relieved to see, ear plugs. The workers appeared well-fed, approximately clean, and were dressed in clothing that looked relatively new. There was a mix of ages--a few teenagers, but mostly people ranging from twenty or so to early fifties--nothing that would make me suspect that things were awry.

But here and there, there were signs that things weren't as they first appeared. There were chains around the ankles of several workers on the line--old school manacles that would have looked at home in a Spanish inquisition dungeon or a slave ship from Africa. Also, only some people were moving around freely. There was no talking, which could have been explained by the deafening clatter, but no one was so much as making eye contact, either.

Then, of course, there were the men with the guns. They were dressed in jeans and button down shirts--some flannel, some cotton, although the ones in flannel made me raise my eyebrows. Flannel, in this heat? A couple of them wandered around, watching the workers, guns in hip holsters, a couple with shotguns or long guns slung across their backs. A few played cards at a table off to the side. They looked relaxed, but the message to the captives was clear. I counted eight men total, but there were probably some in that office on the upper level, and there were a few doors down below that I couldn't see behind, either.

I watched the activity below for a few moments more. Camilla was beside me, doing the same. She soon ducked back from the opening, but I counted entrances and people, tried to memorize the layout and devise a plan. When I pulled back from the opening, Camilla was sitting on the metal roof that was still warm from the day's sun. She was staring off across the parking lot.

"I still didn't believe it," she said, picking at a spot of rust beside her. "I didn't want to believe that my brother could do such a thing."

"I know," I said.

We both let the gravity of the moment suck us down into melancholy for a few moments, like a boot in mud. We'd had a target--the goal had been for us to find which of Camilla's relatives was worthy of leading. The answer, unfortunately, was neither. Where that left us--I didn't want to think about where that left us.

"We better go," I said, coming to my feet and dusting off my butt.

Little flakes of rust scattered and swirled downwards like a red-brown snowfall.

Later, I'd think back and remember the level of noise pounding from the open window at our backs, think about the cover of night, our inattention, and partially forgive myself. But in the instant that the guard came around the corner and caught us there, all I could say to myself was, *Idiot.*

He was fumbling with the long gun on his back by the time I lunged at him. He cried out--but I wasn't worried about that. The machinery down below was too loud. But a gunshot? Gunshots had the tendency to cut through any kind of noise. They were unmistakable, like the shrill cry of a baby or the screeching of brakes--they demanded attention.

His eyes were wide, one arm up and cocked, the hand groping for the rifle that had slid out of his reach. I lunged forward and he scuttled back clumsily. He yelled out again as I swung around to his back--a garbled cry of alarm, nonsensical and sharp. Then he tried to keep eyes on me as I circled behind him, turning awkwardly like a dog desperate to catch his tail.

I got behind him, pulled his rifle barrel lower on his back so there was no way he could reach the trigger or pull it up to him. Camilla came up to his front, her hands up in a fighter stance.

"Don't!" I said. "Don't hit him! It has to look like an accident."

I put him in a chokehold and tightened it. He flailed predictably, but it only takes about ten seconds to cut enough blood off from the brain to make someone pass out. Those ten seconds can feel like an eternity when you're counting them down in action, though. He went limp in my arms and I held on for several more seconds, then let his unconscious form slump to the roof.

"What do we do with him?" Camilla said.

She seemed as breathless as I was, sucking in air like she was the one who had just grappled with the man who would have killed us if he'd been more alert, or had more training, or even been wearing his gun correctly. I shook the phantom 'almosts' from my mind and came back to present.

"I have an idea, but it might be a bad one," I said after a couple moments of contemplation.

"Anything. We just need to get out of here."

"Well, how about you climb down and go start the car?" I said, fishing the distributor cap out of my pocket and handing it to her. "Someone might hear the thump when I push him off the roof."

Camilla's lips were tight, but she took the cap and complied without argument. I waited until she disappeared over the top of the ladder, then reached down and snapped the guy's neck. I could chalk this one up to collateral damage, but truth is, this guy met the criteria for my list. He was guarding human beings, preventing them from escaping their slavery. The rest of the crew would get the same treatment in due time. This guy just happened to be an unlucky first.

His heart and breathing stopped. I grimaced and unzipped his jeans, tugged his boxer briefs down a bit in front. There were only a few reasons why a guard up here would get so close to the edge, and peeing off the roof was one of them.

It seemed plausible to me. I was hoping his friends would buy the story I was telling, too. I waited until I saw the headlights of our car flicker briefly in the distance, then I drug the body to the other side of the building by the arms and rolled it off.

The landing wasn't as climactic as I'd expected--I barely heard the muffled, weighty thud, and I was listening for it. But I didn't take any chances. I ducked my head and ran with light feet to the ladder on the other side, taking the rungs two at a time in my effort to get down quickly.

The expanse of the parking lot seemed larger, the scrape of my footsteps in the gravel louder as I ran back towards the relative safety of our car. But there were no cries of alarm from behind us, no cease in the pounding of the machinery. I swung myself into the passenger seat and the car was moving before I got the door fully closed.

"Any trouble?" Camilla asked.

I shook my head, still trying to get my breath back to even. Camilla gripped the wheel, stared at the dark road unwinding before us.

"I made it look like he went to pee off the side of the building and fell off," I said. "I hope it will be believable."

"Men *do* like to pee off things," she said.

"They do." I looked out the window into the night.

Chapter 32

Back at the compound, I had Frankie send an email to Agent Wignow, telling her I had information on Alex Almeida--that *he* was the one involved in trafficking, and asking for additional details.

As expected, Hyde wasn't happy when I told him what had happened. His shoulders went back and he stood up a little taller as he listened.

"I'm glad you're ok. I don't like it when you're in danger. Then again, I'd bet this isn't close to the worst situation you've entered into on a whim."

He was right--it wasn't.

"And I won't tell you not to do something like that again," he continued, "because you are smart and capable, and were doing this kind of thing long before I was on the scene. But be careful, ok?" He yanked me and enfolded me in a hug. "I don't even want to think about you getting hurt."

"I know," I said, muffled against his chest. He smelled like cedar and eucalyptus. He smelled like home. "I'm always careful."

"Yeah. And you're good at what you do. But there are different rules in every arena we step into, Elayna. And these guys aren't the type to just shoot you. They're more the 'cut your face off and sew it to a soccer ball' type. It would just..."

He trailed off, and I looked up, meeting his eyes.

His tone was sincere, his eyes wide when he said, "It would just really bother me if a perfectly good soccer ball got ruined because you got caught."

"Hey!" I said, poking him in the ribs and pushing back from his hug.

He grinned and smooched my cheek. "You know I kid. Just be careful. I love you. Besides, I don't think you've had time to change your will since we got engaged."

I snatched a throw pillow from the bed and smacked the side of his head with it.

"So that's it, huh?" I said with a laugh, taking another swing at him with the pillow. He ducked. "You're after me for my money, huh?"

He laughed. "I told you I was broke before I came to work for you."

"You shouldn't be broke anymore," I said, lobbing the pillow at his head. He dodged the fluffy projectile with ease. "Not unless you've got some expensive habits I'm unaware of."

He was prowling towards me. I chucked another pillow

at him and used the second of distraction to get to higher ground, hopping up on the bed. I snagged another throw pillow.

"Just a little phone operator bill," he teased. "I need someone to feed my ego, you know. I call One Nine Hundred Compliments every night."

I opened my mouth in mock disgust and shock. "Dirty bird!"

"Nah," Hyde said, picking up one of the throw pillows I'd abandoned. "You don't understand. It's just a very maternal woman telling me that I can do anything I set my mind to, that my gut *isn't* getting bigger, and that people never talk bad about me behind my back...stuff like that."

I giggled and blocked Hyde's first pillow swing.

"I don't know," I said, shaking my head with faux concern. "After what you said about my money, I'm thinking we might need a prenup."

"Psh!" Hyde said, throwing his hands in the air and raising his eyebrows. "If you're getting a prenup, what's the point of getting married?"

I scrunched up my nose and threw my pillow, hitting him square in the face. He retaliated by tackling me to the mattress and tickling my ribs.

"I don't know," I said, breathless and giggling. "Love? Commitment? Forever with your best friend?"

He stopped tickling me for a moment, and appeared to be considering my words.

"Nah," he said, resuming his finger assault on my ribs and stomach. "It's all about that cold, hard cash."

A knock on the door interrupted our laughter.

"Elayna," Howard said. "Camilla is asking for you and Hyde. Caio wants to see her in the dining room."

"Coming," I called, standing and smoothing my hair.

"I am, too," Hyde grumbled. "I really don't trust that guy."

As Camilla, Hyde, and I followed Tristao down the hall, I was glad that Hyde was with us. This didn't feel right. I was tense, my head on a swivel, as we entered the dining room. I could tell that Hyde was feeling the same, just by the angle of his head. But I tried to follow his lead and keep my body relaxed, tried not to show that my gut was tight, my thoughts were swirling.

Caio greeted us with a smile that didn't meet his eyes. It felt more like a baring of teeth than a welcome, but I smiled back and stood by Camilla. Bruno, lured by our travel in the general direction of the kitchen, bumped my hand and sat next to me with a little disappointed huff. I didn't blame him--even I could smell the tempting wafts of beef from down the hall.

It didn't escape my notice that Caio had five men in the room with him. When two of those men oh-so-casually flanked Hyde, and one stepped closer to me, a frisson of fear traced my spine. I slipped my hand slowly into my pocket and pressed the button that would lock down the family wing. I hoped that they were all inside, that no one had made a late trip to the pool. Then I rested my hand on the butt of the gun at the small of my back.

"Camilla," Caio said, throwing his arms wide, his voice

sarcastic. "My darling niece. Have I not made you welcome in my home?"

Oh, so it was *his* home again, was it? I kept my face expressionless, innocent, like I didn't suspect a thing. Mentally, I was forming a plan of attack. The man next to me would have to go down first, then I could get to Caio.

"Of course, Uncle," Camilla said, her hands folded before her. "You have been very gracious."

"Then why have you betrayed me in such a way?" he hissed.

At least we weren't taking long to get to the point. He wasn't a cat who felt like toying with his prey. My heart rate increased, fueled by adrenaline. Caio obviously knew *something*, the question was--what, and how much?

"What do you mean?" Camilla cocked her head.

"You have been colluding with Alex behind my back!" he roared, spittle flying from his mouth.

All the things he could have found out, and he *still* got it wrong. It was all I could do not to laugh, I was so incredulous.

"That's not true," Camilla said, her voice even and low. "I don't know where you heard that, but it isn't true."

I glanced over at Tristao, who had sweat at his temples. He subtly moved closer to Camilla; no one else seemed to notice.

"Liar!" Caio hissed. "You met with him, spoke with him tonight!"

Camilla's brow creased in confusion. "I've only seen my

brother once, when he delivered Elayna's family to the house."

"So you admit it!" Caio said, his eyes wild. "You admit that you have been planning with him against me!"

"No," Camilla said. "I haven't. I told you that I saw him briefly. I had to convince him to leave. Where is this coming from? Who told you these things?"

It was as if he didn't, couldn't hear her.

"I am going to do what I should have done from the beginning," he snarled, his face contorted in rage. "I am going to take what has always been *mine*. And I am going to start by taking my vengeance."

A gun in his hand, and he was pointing it at me.

No--not me. Bruno.

A flash, a loud bang. And a doggy cry of pain that reached into my chest and squeezed my heart, as if in a clenched fist.

Bruno fell, and my hands were on him in an instant.

Blood. There was blood.

Roaring. I was roaring. A primal scream from the depths of my soul.

I could see mouths open, but I couldn't hear what was being said. Hyde was fighting with the men who had stood next to him a moment before. Tristao had thrust Camilla behind him, and fired his gun.

I drew my gun, but it was knocked from my hand from someone behind me. It skittered out of reach, under the table. I struck out my fist and connected with the gut of the man who had batted my gun away. He doubled over.

A weapon--I needed a weapon. The antique cutlasses on the wall, and in a second, one was secured in each hand. I didn't care if they were sharp--I hoped they were dull.

In the melee, few people were paying attention to me. The focus seemed to be on Tristao and Camilla, now taking cover behind the dining table. I hamstrung the man next to me.

I shouldn't have worried--these blades were sharp as razors. The rage was building in my head, a pressure that I felt keenly, like my head would soon burst--an ocean wave crashing in my ears. A male arm came into my field of view, and I chopped it out of my way. I was Rambo with a machete in a jungle of enemy limbs.

Sound was beginning to come back. I sliced the throat that was screaming about the hacked limb, silencing it. Only then did the face that I was honed in on turn toward me. Only then did my quarry notice me. Caio's eyebrows raised, his mouth opened--I wondered what he saw. I could feel blood sluicing from my face, down my neck--I was almost positive it had once belonged to someone else.

But all of the blood in this room was mine now. I would take it all as payment.

Caio's gun began to raise; I was too far away. I had literally brought knives to a gunfight. My rage had clouded my judgment, made me careless, and now I was going to be shot for it. Out of seemingly nowhere, Sir Darcy the cat launched himself onto Caio's head, digging the needle-sharp talons of his front paws into the man's forehead with a yowling screech.

"Aiieee!" Caio screamed, giving an involuntary shake and swiping at the cat with his gun arm. It looked as if he was wearing some sort of demented fur cap ala Davy Crockett.

It only lasted a moment--Sir Darcy bounded away with a hiss before Caio could so much as bat him away. The cat had given a two-second distraction, nothing more, but it was the time I needed to get closer.

I swung and struck Caio's hand from his wrist. A high squeal like a stuck pig, but I silenced it with a blade to the gut. Entrails followed my blade on the way out, looking like large, pale worms spilling from a bait cup.

Caio's rounded mouth and eyes told me he was shocked. His other hand came up to defend--as if he weren't already dead--but then, the human survival instinct is strong. My left blade didn't quite make it through both the bones of his forearm, but I was determined, and I yanked it back out.

I heard shouts and the sound of fighting behind me. I heard the shuddered inhale as I brought my blades up in a v, drawing them in opposite directions to slice his throat.

Blood sprayed, and he fell, but the job behind me wasn't finished. I dropped one blade, put both hands on the other, turned, and attacked.

Chapter 33

When I resurfaced from the pool of blind rage in which I had been submerged, I took stock of the room.

There was a carcass in front of me that had once been a man, but the head had rolled over to the buffet, the mouth slack and open against the polished wood.

Hyde was standing and whole, but he'd taken at least one direct hit to his face--he looked irritated about it. Camilla was still cowered behind Tristao, but appeared uninjured.

Caio and his men were all down, in various stages of death--some complete, some well on their way.

A high whine reached my ears. I scrambled over parts and bodies, slipping in a puddle of blood on my way to Bruno. He had pulled himself under the dining table to get away from the gunshots and violence, a streak of blood marking his path. He was panting, his eyes wide and glazed. I threw a chair out of my way and knelt at his side.

A sob caught in my throat. I buried my hands in the fur at his neck, where he was bleeding. The table moved, and Hyde was beside me, his hands and eyes more functional than mine. I couldn't see all that well, so I leaned back, let Hyde look.

"Ok, buddy," Hyde cooed at Bruno. "You're alright. It's ok, big boy."

"He's not," I sobbed. "He's not alright. The bastard *shot* him."

I could hear Camilla's voice in the background, but couldn't make out her words. I reached out a hand to Bruno's chest, and felt the reassuring thump of his heart, the raise and lower of his breathing. He whined again, and tears spilled down my hot and sticky face. I couldn't lose him. He was always by my side--so loyal and loving. Wherever he was felt like home. How would I recover if he died?

"Elayna," Camilla said, exasperation in her voice, as if she'd said my name more than once. "The chopper is waiting. We have to get him up. Let him go."

I pulled my bloody hands back from his soft fur. "Where are you taking him?"

"Best emergency vet in Brazil," Camilla said. "It's a ten minute flight if the pilots push it. And I told them to push it hard."

I stood, slid my palms down my jeans to wipe them off. "I'm coming. I'm coming with him."

"No," Camilla said, as Tristao and Hyde lifted Bruno. "You can't go anywhere like that."

A high whine escaped Bruno, and I flinched.

"Of course I'm going with him," I demanded.

"Elayna, I'll go," Hyde said. "You need to get cleaned up."

"What..." I said, then looked in the huge mirror above the mantel.

I looked like I was the main character of *Carrie*, right after the pig's blood scene. I was covered, head to toe. Only the tear tracks on my face were somewhat clean.

"I didn't realize," I mumbled, but they were already out the door, tracking blood behind them.

I looked around and for the first time, I *saw*. It looked like a house of horrors. There was a pile of bodies on one side of the room. Blood was splashed up the wall and was spreading across the polished wood floor, a slow-moving ocean soaking the expensive rug, lapping at the feet of the furniture.

"Let's get you out of here," Camilla said gently.

She took my hand and led me down the hall like a child. The house was surprisingly quiet. She took me to the guest wing, through an empty bedroom and into the bathroom. I wondered who would wash the bloody footprints, if there was any saving the carpets. If anyone could do it, the staff of *this* house could.

"Tell me he's going to be ok," I said.

"He is," she said, starting the shower. "Didn't you hear what Hyde was saying? He thinks the bullet went through the droopy part of his neck. There wasn't enough blood for an artery. I called ahead, and they are prepping for an emergency surgery right now. They'll have him on the table the second he gets there."

"How did you know who to call?" I said, kicking off my sticky sandals clumsily. My lip curled at the slickness of blood between my toes.

"We always had dogs growing up. That practice has always been the best."

"Are you sure they still are?" My sticky fingers clenched into fists.

"They're connected to the university--they're the best. Trust me."

"I'm sorry about your uncle," I mumbled, shucking off my sticky t-shirt and jeans.

The shower was steaming, and I suddenly wanted nothing more than to get clean.

Camilla huffed, a sound somewhere between a laugh and exasperation. "Don't be. If you hadn't done it, I would have."

"But not like that," I said, stepping beneath the spray.

"Not *quite* that colorful, no. But you know I'd choose Bruno over any of my family members, so..." She shrugged. "You going to be ok? I should really go organize a clean-up."

I grimaced. "Sorry."

"Pfft." She waved me off. "I'll get you some clean clothes so you can go be with our big guy."

"Thanks, Camilla."

.   .   .

BY THE TIME I'd showered, washing my hair twice, Hyde called and gave me the news--Bruno *was* fine. Hyde's initial assessment was correct--it was a through and through shot to the fleshy part of Bruno's neck--all that extra skin that I loved burying my hands in. It was incredibly lucky--they'd taken him in expecting surgery, and ended up giving him two neat rows of stitches instead. They were going to hold Bruno overnight for an abundance of caution, but Hyde was pretty sure it was just because the veterinary techs had all fallen in love with him.

Bruno would be on antibiotics that would make him thirsty, and pain pills that would make him sleep. There was no need for me to go down there--he'd be home in the morning, and Bruno wasn't one to suffer from separation anxiety--as long as there was someone to give him attention, he didn't quite care who it was, at least for short periods of time.

I felt better after hearing Hyde's voice, after hearing how relaxed he was. He laughed when he described all the students fawning over Bruno, how Bruno had worked them over like a pro with his emoting eyebrows and big, chocolate eyes.

"He started limping at one point, and everyone got concerned, that maybe he'd been hit twice, but he was just playing it up for the crowd. He's fine, Elayna, I promise. The only danger he's in now is from hurting his tail wagging too hard."

Which was why I was back in the dining room, wearing gloves and knee-high rubber boots, surveying the mess I'd made. Blood splattered the walls and ceiling, a gruesome abstract art installation. It had started to congeal at the edges of the puddles, though it still dripped, slow and lazy like syrup from the table. There were already two maids working in the room, removing the antique weapons from the walls. The entire room would have to be scrubbed down--the woodwork would probably make it through, but the walls would need a coat of paint.

The bodies lay where they had fallen. There was a stack of new bodybags in the corner, so I went over and unzipped one, laid it out next to the body formerly known as Caio. I figured it was my mess and I should be the one to clean it up. The maids wouldn't meet my eyes. They pretended like I wasn't there, like this wasn't really happening, and I decided to do the same.

It took some time to wrestle the torso into the bag. There's a reason why it's called 'dead weight'. There was still some room once his upper body was in there, so I added the closest limbs, even though they didn't all match, and zipped up the bag. I hadn't remembered cutting off that many arms, but I had been the only one wielding blades, so it must have been me.

It was funny--I liked people. Well, ok--not *all* of them. But I wasn't one of those killers who thought that humans were some plague upon the earth that needed to be exterminated. But once they were dead, they were just something that needed disposing of--like a huge, heavy dog turd you had to roll in plastic and throw away.

I knew some of the bodies' names--from contact or the dossiers that Frankie had handed out what seemed like forever ago--but now they were gone. All that remained were corpses, husks. I tried not to think of whether they had families, whether they had deserved this. These were the hardest kinds of deaths, for me. I hadn't targeted these men. Although some of them, probably all of them, had taken life, they were just cogs in a machine, pawns on a checkered board. They had been playing a high-risk game of follow the leader, and they had lost.

I was working on filling my fourth body bag when Camilla showed back up with two men in tow. The men wore head to toe painter's garbs, which I affectionately called body condoms.

"Oh good," Camilla said. "You got a start on things. Tristao and Javier will take them downstairs. Frankie says your family is upset that they are locked in the family wing. I'm going to wait until they have all the bodies in the basement then unlock the wing. We'll lock the main door so they can't get to the dining room."

"Sounds good."

I wanted to ask her how she was doing--how she *really* was doing. She had known some of these men well, all of them better than I had. I'd just killed her uncle. But now wasn't the time or the place to discuss her feelings. She was the boss in this situation, the boss to these people--she couldn't show weakness. She didn't have the time or the energy for a heart to heart. I tried not to think about what killing Caio meant for our plans.

I sighed, then grunted as I rolled the last corpse onto the unzipped body bag. I wouldn't need to do my leg workout today. I was pretty sure that I had done enough weighted deep squatting to last the rest of the week. Tristao and Javier worked quickly--these body bags had a long strap at each end, so they could each put a strap over their shoulder. I thought that if I'd wanted, I could probably see the extra-large body disposal tub in the basement at work today.

They already had the last body bag out of the room before I noticed that Caio's head was still there, up against the sideboard with the mouth open like he was trying to gnaw on it. I grabbed a bucket and lifted the head by the hair, dropping it in gingerly.

What happened next was a case of poor timing. I was in the hall, heading for the basement door. I had forgotten Camilla's comment about unlocking the family unit. Tristao and Javier were safely in the basement.

I, however, was not.

I heard them before I saw them.

"What happened?" Sybil was demanding.

I froze, my heart hammering a frantic tempo in my chest. For the second time that day, I thought I might die. Before I could so much as flinch, they were around the corner. They descended on me like a flock of pigeons to crumbs. Camilla was with them; her eyes went wide when she saw me.

Sybil's hands were on her hips, her head cocked to the side. "All the doors and windows were locked, and no one was answering the phone."

My eyes went wide, my mouth pinched.

Just me, my family and a head in a bucket.

My mother screamed, her hand flying up to clasp her throat, her eyes wide.

"What the hell is that?" my brother said, his forehead crinkled, leaning forward to get a better look.

My father looked stunned; Sybil looked her own, pinched version of alarmed. Jake had a perfect view from his perch in my brother's arms.

Unfortunately, Caio's head had ended up face-up in the bucket, his mouth and eyes slightly parted. His dark hair was matted with blood, and bright red was smeared across the sallow skin of his face. It was as bad as it could possibly get--the only bright spot was that he was barely recognizable. He looked like one of those wax figurines from Madame Tussaud's museum, that tourist trap in NYC.

My mouth opened and closed. I opened it again, willed the words to come, the words that would make this right, words that would explain away the fact that my family had just seen me carrying a *head* in a *bucket*. But I didn't know how to come back from this, didn't know how to verbally erase what they'd seen, what they would surmise. They'd never let me see Jake and Isabella again. They'd turn me in...

In the mental vortex, I barely heard help arriving from the most unlikely of sources--my father.

"Really, Elayna," he said, meeting my eyes and raising his eyebrows meaningfully. "How distasteful. You shouldn't be playing with props that lifelike when the children are around. They might think it's *real*. You could really frighten them."

I seized upon his words and used them like a lifeline. "We were playing with the Halloween decorations," I said, quickly. "Things may have gotten out of hand..."

"We keep trying to scare each other," Camilla added. "It's an ongoing game. But I told her this head was too grotesque. Way too much."

I wrinkled my nose at Camilla.

"You're always taking things too far," Sybil said, nodding sharply. "This is just like the T-Rex. You don't know where the line is between funny and horrifying. You need to learn what is appropriate."

I remembered what she was talking about. Last year, Jake had been heavy into dinosaurs. I'd commissioned a robotic T-rex from Wu, my robotics expert. I'd envisioned a diminutive model, about eighteen inches tall, but apparently had not conveyed that well. What Wu had come up with was a five foot monstrosity with glowing red eyes, completely controllable with a massive remote.

Wu was perplexed as to why I'd gone a different direction for Jake's birthday present. I'd stashed the monster in the closet of one of my guest rooms, and tossed the huge remote control in a junk drawer.

That was that until his birthday rolled around, and my family came over. Late that night, after several glasses of wine, I'd remembered all of Sybil's snarky comments, pulled the remote control out, and made the T-Rex stand very close to Sybil's side of the bed. I completely forgot about it until the next morning when I was awoken to a bloodcurdling scream.

"Get that thing out of here," my father said with a disgusted sniff. "And no more pranks while the children are here."

"Right," I said, turning around. "Sorry, guys."

"Wait!" Sybil said, clutching my arm before I could make my escape. "We need to talk about the security system. It malfunctioned and we were all locked in the family wing!"

Shit. I was hoping they hadn't even noticed.

"I told them that there was a malfunction," Camilla said, her tone and expression nothing but apologetic.

"But how would we get out if there was a malfunction, and then a fire broke out?" My mother said, her hand still at her neck. "Fire safety is no small matter, Elayna. We couldn't even open a window!"

"If it helps ease your worries, we *do* have a state of the art fire sprinkler system," Camilla interjected gently.

"Is it as state of the art as the security system that just locked us in our rooms for the past hour?" Sybil snapped, rolling her eyes.

"I'll make sure the issue is fixed, today," Camilla said.

"How are we supposed to feel safe," Sybil continued, ignoring Camilla, "when the very system that's meant to protect us is locking us in?"

"It's not like the family apartments are uncomfortable," I said with a smile that probably looked more like a grimace.

I couldn't help it--I was having a disturbingly normal interaction with my family while holding a gang lord's decapitated head in a bucket. I felt like I was in a fever dream, or high on some very strong drugs. Everyone else seemed to have forgotten the so-called Halloween decoration, except for my father, who kept casting dubious looks at the thing. I could feel nervous, maniacal laughter bubbling up in my gut. I fought hard to keep it down.

"That's not the point," Sybil said. "I am *claustrophobic*."

"It's like six thousand square feet in there, Sybil," Peter said. "It wasn't like you were hyperventilating into a paper bag or something."

"Oh, can't you ever just be on my side?" she snarled.

"Listen," Camilla said, her voice soothing. "I'm so sorry that this happened. It won't happen again. I have the best technicians on their way to look at it. Maybe a mouse chewed through a wire or something..."

I cringed.

"Now there's rodents?" Sybil shrieked, throwing up her hands.

"It *is* a third world nation, Sybil," my mother said from the corner of her mouth, as if that would make me and Camilla unable to hear her. "They're probably doing the best that they can."

"To make it up to you," Camilla said, not missing a

beat, "I'd like to take you all out for dinner tonight. Best restaurant in town. My treat."

"Finally, we can get out of here," Sybil said. "It's about time."

It was all I could do not to pick up Caio's head by the hair and sock her in the boob with it.

"Does nine o'clock work for everyone?" Camilla said.

"I don't mean to be rude, but will they have bottled water?" My mother asked, biting her lip. "I just don't know if I trust the tap..."

"I'm sure they do," Camilla said, graciously.

"Well, then, it will be an adventure!" she said. "Dinner in a *favela*! Exciting!"

"I have to go," I said.

Before I lose my shit, I added mentally.

"Ugh, please do," Sybil said. "Throw that awful head away."

"Will do!" I said, waving as I turned and made my escape.

"That thing was cool, Aunt 'Layna!" Jake called, as I retreated. "I wasn't scared at all!"

I took a deep breath and released it slowly. That had been far, far too close.

DINNER THAT NIGHT WAS LOVELY. It was just adults--Jake and Isabella were under the watchful eyes of the same two nannies as before. The restaurant was far from an adventure, at least not the way my mother meant it. All of us were wearing nice outfits, but we still were a little under-dressed, which made Sybil uncomfortable. I couldn't have cared less. Caio was gone, and the only people who knew it were people Camilla trusted. For one night, it seemed that we could take a deep breath.

The restaurant was open air, walled in glass, on the roof of a hotel downtown. The view was unsurpassed--we could see the dark line of the ocean and all of the glittering lights of the city below. Heat lamps were interspersed throughout the bare wooden tables, but the weather was sublime; none of them were lit. A Spanish guitarist played from the corner. It was the perfect setting for copious amounts of sangria.

They plied us with non-stop drinks and platters of seafood, bringing us fried calamari, butter-poached lobster, fragrant mussels in white wine and garlic, salad topped in chunks of crab, grilled fish, and seafood medley pasta. Sybil was at the other end of the table, and I was sitting with my favorite people. A warm breeze played through my hair and Hyde's hand rested on the back of my chair, his finger tracing a leisurely circle on my bare shoulder.

Howard kept looking at Frankie when he thought no one was paying attention. Those looks had shifted in the past weeks from anger to barely concealed longing. I could see the change coming, but it was fragile. I didn't want to crush it by trying to help it along. But I knew that all of us were holding our breath in that area, Frankie especially.

It had been a long day, and I was exhausted. It was

hard to imagine that it was only hours ago that I had been peering through a window of a factory, confirming that Alex was involved in human trafficking on a huge scale. And now Caio was gone. We'd kind of painted ourselves into a corner as far as Almeida leadership went. Camilla was the only viable option left. Tears pricked behind my eyes in the wake of the thought and I smiled at something being said to keep them at bay.

I wouldn't think about that tonight. Tonight I would think about the friends and family surrounding me, the wonderful man at my side. I would enjoy the beautiful surroundings and the delicious food and drink.

Tomorrow would be the day for overanalyzing. Not tonight.

Chapter 34

The next morning, Bruno was back with us. I couldn't stop petting and touching him--I had almost lost him forever, and the thought made me sick. Bruno was an attention sponge, and couldn't seem to get enough from all of us. He took turns leaning on our legs and shoving his massive head onto our laps with a happy, drooly grin. It didn't seem that his experience had changed him in the least--he was still happy, still relaxed, still the same great dog.

"Who's the bestest?" I crooned, holding his damp, bristly chin in my hands. "Who's the sweetest and the nicest puppo? Yes, it *is* you. It really is."

Howard snorted. "You and that dog--it's too much."

"Says the man with the psychopath of a cat."

He held up his hands with an expression of chagrin to show the fresh scratches on his hands.

I raised an eyebrow. "Need some ointment for those? A couple bandaids?"

"He got me when I let him out of his crate. I'm starting to think I should have left him in that house, blown him up with his owner," he said.

I snorted a laugh. "I don't think you mean that."

"No, not really. But I thought he would have warmed up to me by now."

I shrugged. "Don't be offended. That cat hates everyone."

We told my family that Bruno had caught his loose skin on a post in the garden, to explain the small shaved section and the bandage over the stitches on his neck. They all bought it, but ever since the head in the bucket scenario, I felt extra nervous about keeping my cover. My father kept shooting me inscrutable looks, like he was disappointed at me for playing around with such gory props.

It was raining, and I could tell that my family was getting restless.

"I wish it would stop raining so we could get out of this *house*," Sybil said, spitting out the last word like we were taking shelter in a hovel. "I'm so *bored*."

My mother's lips pursed at that comment, and I could almost hear her reply with the mantra that I'd heard a thousand times growing up--'Only boring people are bored, dear'.

It wasn't like there wasn't anything to do. There was a billiards room, board games, an entire freaking movie theater. But I could read the writing on the wall--we were going to have to get them out of the house again, and soon, lest there be bloodshed.

"Have you guys seen the atrium?" I asked, knowing they'd walked through yesterday. "Or the music room?"

Sybil rolled her eyes like I had suggested they put on galoshes and go stomp around in the mud.

"How about a manicure?" Camilla said. "Or a pedi-cure? And we can have a special menu tonight--I will ask the chef to teach us how to make pasta."

"Mmph," Sybil said, her mouth in a pout. "I don't need to know how to make that. Can we have sushi again? I thought there'd be more sushi, with us so close to the ocean."

"Of course," Camilla said, her smile not even wavering. "I'll ask that we have some tonight."

"Are you going to join us, Elayna?" My mother asked, her eyebrows raised to tell me there was only one right answer to her question. "We haven't spent much time with you. You're always off doing something."

"Probably leaving the house--shopping or whatnot," Sybil grumbled.

We all ignored her.

"Yes, I'll be there," I said. "I need a manicure and that sounds like a fun way to spend the morning."

But when the manicurists arrived, it was very clear that one of them didn't quite fit in--like one of those Sesame Street games. I could almost hear the lyrics '*One of these is not like the others, one of these does not belong*' playing in the background. Agent Wignow wore the same stark white scrub-like outfit as the other manicurists, but her red hair and pale skin set her noticeably apart.

"I'll take that one," I blurted, hurrying over to her table, which was shoved in the corner.

"Of course you grab probably the only one who speaks English," Sybil murmured.

"Sybil, you're being rude," my mother said.

Then she chose a table as far from Sybil's as possible. Sybil looked momentarily shocked--her eyes went wide, her mouth tight. I was surprised, too--I'd never heard my mother criticize Sybil--certainly not to her face. Maybe I wasn't the only one feeling the pinch of a family vacation. I shook the thoughts off and focused on Agent Wignow, who was setting up her station with surreptitious glances at what the other nail technicians were doing.

"I got your email," she said in a low voice, picking up one of my hands and filing my nails. "About Alexander Almeida being into trafficking."

"I didn't know if that would change the agency's support for him or not," I murmured.

"They don't care," she said, her voice low, her words rushed. "They've known all along that he is involved in trafficking. But they thought that he would be more amenable to their plans than Caio. We heard he's gone, by the way."

"I really don't like being lied to," I said. "And I hate being manipulated."

"I get it. But right now, they want to use the Almeida

organization. It would be a different scenario altogether if they decide that's not worth the effort."

My eyebrows drew together. "Meaning what?"

She glanced around us, made sure no one was too close. "I don't think I'm supposed to know this, but there is a contingency plan, if the Almeida leader declines to assist the agency."

"What is it?"

She shook her head. "It isn't pretty. There's two options. One-they expose the human trafficking, arrest the key players in the Almeida organization, and render it useless that way. Or they just clear the board and blame it on a rival gang. The Cobras and the Videiras would both be willing to play, for a leg up against the Almeidas."

"Of course they would." I frowned down at the nail that she was working on. She was filing aggressively, but only on one side. "Think you could pay at least a *little* attention? You've filed it into a point."

"I can't even do *my* nails well."

"Then at least file slower. I'm not going to have anything left by the time you're finished."

She slowed her motions and murmured, "I'm only supposed to be here to check in, to see if you've made contact Camilla, about the proposal."

"She's thinking about it," I said, keeping my face bland, clear of any tells. "I'll let you know when I have more information, but the fact that the agency wasn't forth-coming from the get-go makes me nervous about dealing with them at all."

Her eyes flicked upwards in annoyance--not quite an eyeroll, but close. "You know how they are. They're not going to present the full picture. Even the information I'm not supposed to have probably isn't complete. They have contingency after contingency in place."

I nodded. I knew how it was. The CIA was like a pyramid--only the people at the tippy top had the full picture. They guarded information like a dragon hoards gold. Knowledge was power, and they weren't the sharing type.

"Whatever you guys do," she said, leaning in close. "You need to make a decision soon. Even if that decision is to leave this mess behind altogether. If Alex can't lead, that only leaves Camilla. She needs to shit or get off the pot. Either seize control, or flee. The agency is losing patience. I'm not supposed to know this, but they are going to make contact with the leaders of the Cobras later this week."

She gave up filing and started slapping on purple nailpolish. I tried not to wince.

"I'll let Camilla know," I said.

"I'll try and hold them off." Wignow bit her lip. "I'm supposed to be feeling you out right now. They want to know which way Camilla is leaning."

"Tell them whatever they need to hear to give us a little more time. I'll let Camilla know we're running out. But if the agency wants her support, they need to be ready to give us support in return."

"Darby played coy at the meeting, but they'll do almost anything if it helps their goals."

"Good to know. We might need to cash that in to keep everyone happy."

I DIDN'T SEE Camilla much the rest of the day, not after I told her what Agent Wignow had told me. Her brow furrowed and she chewed her lower lip, and that was all I saw before my mother announced we were spending the rest of the day out by the pool as a family because it had finally stopped raining.

It was nicer than I expected, actually. Hyde and I played with Isabella and Jake while Peter and my father napped under a cabana. Under a neighboring umbrella, my mother read a stack of magazines that Camilla had procured, and Sybil sipped drink after drink until she fell asleep, too.

We were all walking to dinner that night when my mother said the words I'd been dreading for the past couple of weeks.

"We're thinking of heading home," she said. "Maybe tomorrow. Maybe the next day. Can Camilla make arrangements?"

But they couldn't go, not until things were resolved. Not until we weren't worried about Alex and his men jumping out from behind a tree and kidnapping my family--more effectively, this time--or just blowing them to bits to prove a point.

"Hyde and I are engaged!" I blurted.

"What?" my mother shrieked. "When?"

"Congratulations," my father said, smiling warmly and shaking Hyde's hand. "That's wonderful news."

"Anyway," I said, trying to ignore the fact that my mother had a hand at her throat and looked like she'd just seen a naked Elvis Presley running by banging a bongo drum. "We're having a party in a few days, and we were going to announce it then. I really wanted you to be there, but if you have to go..."

The mention of a party acted like smelling salts beneath my mother's nose. "An engagement party? Of course we wouldn't miss your engagement party. How wonderful!" She kissed Hyde on both cheeks. "She's so lucky to have found you," she simpered.

What am I? I thought. *A bag of banana peels?*

"Well," Sybil said, with a smile as fake as her veneers. "Where's the ring?"

"Oh," I said. "Um, they're..."

"I have them, here," Hyde said, pulling the box from the inside pocket of his jacket.

I hadn't realized that he had been carrying them around. The knowledge made my eyes sting a little. He smiled down at me, like he knew he'd just scored twenty points for Gryffindor.

"Here," he said, slipping them on my finger again.

I held my hand out for inspection, and my mother gasped. "Good heavens, are those *real*?"

"I hope so," Hyde quipped. "Otherwise, I got ripped off."

I nudged him in the ribs with my elbow, and he chuckled at his own joke.

"Gorgeous rings, but that woman really did a number on your nails," my mother said, inspecting my hand.

"Congrats, sis," Peter said, giving me a shoulder-hug.

"Yes," Sybil said, with a smile that couldn't quite erase the curl from her upper lip. "We never thought this day would come."

Sybil's barbs aside, the evening was surprisingly pleasant. My mother was in raptures over the long to-do list that a wedding naturally provoked. All evening, she'd randomly exclaim, "Invitations! We'll need to get invitations," or "Cake! What kind of cake do you like?" It was like she had developed celebration Tourette's. I didn't want to disappoint her, but my ideal wedding had no crowd at all. Just me, Hyde, our families...

Good heavens, I thought. *I've never met Hyde's family.*

I didn't want to think about that. From the way he spoke of them, they weren't close and hadn't been, ever since he'd decided to enlist. Shitballs. That would have to be fixed. We were going to have to go to Connecticut.

Under the table, Hyde reached over and squeezed my hand. He probably thought that the sudden tension in my spine was because my mother was rambling about her rabid hatred for carnations and baby's breath. Part of me wanted to insist on having nothing but, just to watch her turn a fun new color, but I resisted the urge.

Chapter 35

The next morning, my family was enjoying a horseback ride at the stables on the property. I had begged off because of allergies. I didn't know if I was miffed or glad that my mom had believed me so readily--I had never had allergies. But either way, my team was free to have a meeting that wasn't done in whispered voices.

Frankie and Howard were flanking a whiteboard in the family dining room. Frankie was trying not to smile--for the first time in weeks, there was a rosiness to her cheeks and genuine happiness tugging at her lips. Howard had a twinkle in his eye that, through experience, I had learned not to trust.

"Since Caio is out of the picture," Frankie said. "And Alex is a human trafficker, we thought it might behoove us to figure out where we stand with everyone else involved in this mess."

Howard gestured grandly at the whiteboard with an uncapped dry erase pen. "It's time to play *list our enemies*!"

Hyde chuckled. I raised an eyebrow. It was too early for these shenanigans, and my coffee hadn't kicked in yet.

Frankie flipped the whiteboard dramatically. It was covered in huge sticky notes. At the top of the board were headings.

"Vankie," Howard said. "What are the headings today?"

"Vankie?" I asked, wrinkling my nose.

"I was going to call her 'Vanna', but I wasn't sure if there would be any copyright issues," Howard said from the corner of his mouth.

"Our headings today are..." She pulled large post-it notes from the board to reveal the words beneath. "'They Want to Kill Us Because...', 'Blood Feuds', 'Deranged Despots', and 'The Great Unknown'."

"Our first contestant is..." Howard drummed his hands on the table while Frankie pulled a piece of paper out of a bowl.

"Hyde!" Frankie said. "What topic would you like?"

"I'll take 'They Want to Kill Us Because'," Hyde said, looking more interested than I expected.

"They want to kill us because we stand in the way of their gang domination of Rio de Janeiro."

"That would be As Cobras," Hyde said.

"Oh, I'm sorry. I'm going to need you to phrase that as a question," Howard said.

"But Vanna was on *Wheel of Fortune*, not *Jeopardy*," I argued.

"We make the rules, Elayna," Frankie said solemnly, shaking her head. "Don't argue."

"Who is As Cobras?" Hyde said, playing along while I made a rude noise with my mouth.

"Heh," Howard said. "Ass Cobras. It never gets old."

"You are correct! One point to Hyde," Frankie said, ignoring Howard. "Next contestant is...Camilla!"

"I'll take Blood Feuds," she said.

"She believes the Almeida family is to blame for the disappearance of her sister and now wants revenge."

"Who is Iris Montes?"

The game turned competitive, but since it was easy, Camilla, Hyde and I were all tied. It was a formidable list on the board: Caio Almeida's remaining loyal men, Alex Almeida, Iris Montes, As Cobras, General Horta. In the unknown or undecided category, Howard had listed Prosecutor General Patricia Bradley, the CIA, and Wu. They'd debated that one for a minute or two--after all, Wu was working for the CIA, so shouldn't he be included in that line item? In the end, they decided not--Wu had his own motivations that might be separate from the agency.

I sat in silence, a little stunned by the fact that my former team member was listed under potential enemies. I'd loved Wu--invited him into my home, my team. He hadn't been angry when he'd been taken by the CIA. He'd sent us a goodbye video that said as much. Apparently, he'd changed his mind over the past year. Now, we didn't know where he stood. We still didn't know if he'd sent us that address to help us discover the human trafficking network, or to serve us up to our enemies. Heck, maybe it was a little of both.

"I came into this thinking that there was an easy way out," Camilla said, staring at the board. "But there isn't."

She looked at me, and I could feel the words before she spoke them. This was the moment that I'd been dreading since before we stepped foot onto Brazilian soil. This was the moment that would break my heart.

"I think I have to stay," she said. She intertwined her fingers and studied them. "I've been thinking about this for days. I don't see a way around it, and I don't think you do, either." She was speaking to me; we all knew it. "In some ways, this is the last thing I want to do. But the last couple of weeks have shown me that maybe there is a life for me in the last place I imagined."

"Tristao," Howard muttered, his mouth turned into a grimace.

"Not just him," Camilla said, her voice strong. "There are many wrongs in this country that I have the power to right. I can start by cleaning up the mess that my brother made."

"We still don't know if you taking control is even possible," I said. "Some of Caio's men think he's out of town, but how long can we keep that ruse up? What's going to happen when Alex realizes that all that stands between him and power is you?"

"Which is why we have to act quickly," Camilla said. "I hate to do this, but the engagement party is the perfect distraction for some of what needs to be done."

I flicked my hand through the air, annoyed. "That's the least of my worries right now. I need to keep my family safe, get them out of the country. And I'm not leaving until I know that you're safe, too."

"Good," she said, a devious twinkle in her eye. "Because I've made a list."

I left the meeting with a list of action items and a deep urge to go cry in the shower. Though I knew it was coming, I hadn't wanted to believe it. But there it was. Camilla was taking over the Almeida Group. She was staying in Brazil. I tried not to imagine what life would be like now in the house that the contractor was putting finishing touches on back in California. Camilla wouldn't be returning home with me. She wouldn't cook in that gorgeous kitchen or organize the clothes in my massive custom closet, or tsk my lack of makeup on a daily basis.

Ugh, I'd have to hire someone else. I shook my head. That was a problem for another day. Right now, I had a list of people to kill--and I was in the mood for it.

Chapter 36

Heitor Pereira was Alex's second in command, the guy in charge of all the 'legal' businesses-- the ones we had discovered weren't legal at all. Alex was the head of the snake, but this guy was the beating heart of it. He was the one in charge of the human trafficking network, the money that fed Alex's power. Judging by the look of the house, his self-importance had gone to his head.

The night was dark, but I had studied the layout of this house and yard until I knew it like my own reflection. It was a four-story monstrosity--one of those places that proves money can't buy taste. The intention of the house seemed to be to put any visitor in awe--I was, but only at the paint colors. It was painted terracotta orange--which is a lovely color in small doses but ghastly when spread over eight thousand square feet.

I wasn't here as a design critic, though. I just wanted to

give the man of the house a present. Frankie, Howard, and Hyde were parked in a van down the street. If something went wrong on my end, they were supposed to cause a distraction. By the manic glint in Howard's eye when he told me he had the perfect thing in mind, I knew it involved explosives, probably a lot of them. Hopefully, we wouldn't need them.

As far as my family was concerned, I was sick. My mother wasn't the maternal sort--she wouldn't bust in trying to feed me chicken noodle soup. She was more of the 'stay over there and keep your germs away from me' type. Just to be sure, Camilla had stayed behind to smooth anything over.

I'd come over the back wall of the garden a couple hours ago when the guards changed, and laid in a very fragrant, slightly unruly groundcover until it was full dark. Hyde had checked in several times in my earpiece, telling me that Howard and Frankie were bickering about anything and everything, so at least *that* was back to normal. By the annoyance in his voice, Hyde wasn't quite as happy about it in the moment as I was.

I ducked behind an ornate vase standing in the bushes. It was seven feet tall and painted in a Grecian scene with a substance that glimmered in the low light. Gold, it looked like. This guy wasn't subtle. Several fountains burbled and splashed in the garden. I could see the outline of the two guards with my infrared glasses. They were sitting at a table towards the back, smoking cigarettes and playing cards. But I didn't think for a second they weren't danger-ous, or distracted enough to let me by easily.

The largest suite in the house was on the second story overlooking the pool. There were three possible access points on the first floor that would put me close to the inte-rior stairs, but I wasn't wild about going inside before I had to. It's really hard to explain or run when you're caught inside someone's house. Instead, I was aiming for the patio doors off the master bedroom.

I slinked from behind the enormous pot to the shelter of the bush a few feet away, my controlled breathing and sound of the burbling fountains the only noise. My foot-steps were soft in the soil. I was grateful for the gardeners who kept the area so maintained--there weren't any dead leaves or twigs to watch out for--no telltale crunch to give away my position.

My target was the pillar that supported the large balcony off the master bedroom. Because it was made of stone, the pillar had seams that I was hoping were large enough to wedge my fingers into, so I could climb it. Most importantly, it was out of sight of the guards in the yard. I kept my eyes on the guards through the infrared glasses. No change as I padded softly around the perimeter of the yard towards the pillar.

"Going up the pillar," I whispered into the mic that was taped along my throat.

Even if things got very loud on my end, the mic was sensitive enough to pick up and transmit my every word clearly to my team. There was a click in my ear that let me know they'd heard me.

I clicked my infrared glasses up as I rounded the pillar. Though I had made it through the garden, my work was only going to get more dangerous. I wouldn't feel safe until I was back in the van with my team.

I stepped back slightly and looked up at the pillar. It was about ten feet tall, with visible seams and several pockmarks that looked promising. Frankie had found a bunch of orders from when this house had been built, six years ago. Apparently, these pillars had been shipped over from somewhere in Italy. They were from some manor that had gone into ruin and been pieced out.

In the receipts, Frankie had also found records of carved doors from a British monastery, a bathtub from a French chateau, a huge fountain from Spain, and a chandelier from a now-defunct hotel in Paris. Heitor liked to surround himself with expensive conversation pieces. I figured if the pillar had survived the trip from Europe, it could probably survive me climbing it.

I quickly pulled on my gloves and planned my ascent. Then I shoved my toe into the seam closest to the ground, put my hands into a couple of pockmarks, and started the climb. It was easier than I thought it would be, and I reached the top before I broke much of a sweat. My head popped over the edge of the balcony. No one was on the stone surface--it was empty except for an outdoor sofa set that faced a fireplace.

I hoisted myself up onto the balcony. The air smelled

of rain and the wind picked up, threatening to tug my hair from my ponytail. I crouched there for a moment, waiting for a sound of alarm, or any sign that I'd been spotted. There was only the gurgle of the fountains below, the slight rustle of leaves in the breeze, and the faint murmur of the guards further in the garden.

A set of french doors was in front of me. Based on the house plans, I would find a small foyer, with doorways that led to the master bathroom and bedroom. This was the point of no return--once I went through those doors, the danger of being caught, of being killed, went up ten-fold. I eased the handle down, opening the door several inches.

I didn't hear a noise--nothing above the whir of the fan in the next room, a distant murmur of voices from somewhere in the house. I slowly opened the door, grateful for new hinges that didn't squeak, and stepped inside. I shut the door soundlessly behind me and turned to my left.

The bathroom had been trendy when it was built six years ago--vessel sinks, wall-mounted faucets, dark granite, and light wooden vanities. There was a toilet in its own little room, a huge, glass-surround shower, and massive free-standing tub underneath a window on the far side of the room. I was glad that there were two vanities--that would make it less likely that someone else would touch Heitor's things. One vanity had a silver tray holding Chanel perfume and a small dish with several sets of earrings in it. The electric toothbrush plugged in was pink.

The other vanity had male cologne, and a black electric toothbrush. I picked it up and slipped the packet from my pocket. I dispensed the thick, clear gel at the base of the bristles. It was nearly invisible to the naked eye and contained a compound that wouldn't dissolve in water, but would only release when combined with one of the active ingredients of Heitor's toothpaste. It would take about twenty minutes after he brushed for him to drop dead of a massive heart attack.

Assuming he wasn't terrible at dental hygiene, he should be dead about the time he crawled into bed tonight. Just as I was replacing his toothbrush back onto the charger, I heard it--a change in the background noise that told me a door had opened somewhere nearby, then, footsteps in the master bedroom.

My options were simple--run, or hide. Running would put me in full view of the master bedroom. The whole point of this mission was for Heitor to die from seemingly natural causes--we couldn't risk alerting Alex that we were making a move against him and his people. My options for hiding were the small toilet room or the space between the tub and the wall. The toilet room let me stay standing, but if someone came in here, they were probably headed there. I didn't love that I had to go prone to stay hidden, but I thought it was my best shot.

I ran over to the tub, sliding onto my belly on the stone floor. It was a tight fit--I was sharing the space with some pipes that came out of the floor--but I was very motivated. Then I inhaled slow and deep and exhaled soundlessly, trying to control the pounding of my heart. The footsteps rounded the corner. I heard a couple of dull thuds--most likely someone kicking off a pair of sneakers. Then the shower turned on.

Hyde's low voice sounded in my ear. "Your heart rate and blood pressure spiked. Everything ok on your end?"

I tapped the sensors on my thumb and pointer finger together twice to tell them yes.

"Received," Hyde murmured. "Any reason we should worry?"

I tapped once for no.

"Got it. We'll stand by. Click three times if you want us to blow something up."

I smiled despite the situation.

Wet-sounding clothes plopped to the ground near the shower, and a woman sighed. The shower door opened and closed again. The spray of the shower hit a body, followed by a satisfied hum. I didn't want to stay here. I didn't know if she was a brisk and efficient shower kind of woman, or if she liked to indulge in the hot water and all the body sprays that thing had.

I eased myself back, praying that the steam had fogged up the glass a little, that she'd be too distracted to look around. I was on the other side of the room, but I peeked my head up. She was facing away from me, and the numerous jets were flinging water everywhere. As I watched, she squirted shampoo into her hand and began to lather her long dark hair. Now was my chance.

I slid out of the gap even farther, then crawled towards the doorway on hands and knees. Most women closed their eyes when they shampooed, but what if she was the exception? At the doorway, I came to a crouch and looked around the corner. I couldn't hear over all the water--what if someone else had entered the room after her? But it was clear, and I slid from the bathroom and went to the french doors, exiting as soundlessly as I'd entered.

Alone on the patio once more, I let out my breath and inhaled a little noisier than I'd allowed myself to do inside. I still wasn't finished--I needed to exfiltrate the way I came in, and the only way to do that was to find a place to hide for several hours--until the guards changed over, or there was a disturbance that would let me slip away.

I glanced at the outdoor sofa, which was faced away from the french doors, and I paused. The only way someone would be able to see me on that was if they came out of the master bedroom and walked around the couch. As I had the thought, the sky opened up, and it began to rain. I smiled and made my way to the couch.

Two hours later, a thud and a scream from inside gave me the distraction I needed to make my exit over the garden wall.

Chapter 37

"You look terrible, honey," my mother said at breakfast the next morning. "Are you sure you're well enough to be out and about?"

I took another huge bite of my scrambled eggs and grumbled, "Yes."

"We really don't need the children sick on the plane ride home," Sybil said. "Maybe you should keep your distance another day."

"You know what?" I said, picking up my plate and my cup of coffee. "I think you're right. I'll see you guys tomorrow."

I finished my breakfast in blissful solitude at the table in our bedroom, feeding Bruno bits of bacon as he sat a respectful--but hopeful--distance from me. A knock on the door, and Camilla stuck her head in.

"Come in," I said.

"You need a refill?" She shut the door behind her and set a carafe of coffee on the table in front of me.

"You're the best. I'd tell you to give yourself another raise, but I don't think you work for me anymore."

It was the first time I'd said it out loud, and it hit a little harder than just thinking it in my head. I made myself smile to try and mask the pain.

"I know. But this was always coming. I mean, not *this*, exactly," she said, gesturing around her to encompass the situation. "But I am getting older. I couldn't work with you forever. Besides, you have a new life now, a different one."

I stretched out my hand, looked at the rings that still felt heavy and new on my finger. "That didn't mean you couldn't be a part of it."

"I know." She smiled. "But you know my reasons. I can do more good here than there."

"Plus, there's Tristao," I said, slyly. "So maybe you'll have a new life in that way, too."

"I'll have to teach him all the things I learned while we were apart." She winked.

A knock on the door prevented my somewhat scandalous reply.

"Come in," I called.

Howard, Frankie, and Hyde trundled in.

"It's my room, too," Hyde was saying to Howard, sounding exasperated. "I don't have to knock."

"It's only polite," Howard said. "I don't want to see anything I'm not supposed to see. 'Cause then you would probably feel obligated to take a swing, and I'd have to embarrass you with my sick ninja moves."

Hyde rolled his eyes. "We could hear Camilla in here, talking."

"Well, I don't want to see her giblets, neither," Howard said.

"Why would..." Hyde started, then sliced his hand through the air. "You know what? Nevermind."

"That's the spirit," Howard said, clapping him on the back. "You're going to need to develop the skill of letting things go. You'll be a married man, soon."

"Hey!" I started. "What does that..."

"Your skin looks radiant this morning, Elayna," Howard said.

I touched my cheek. "Thank you."

"See?" Howard stage-whispered to Hyde. "These are the kind of things you'll need to know. Women like to hear that their skin is radiant, even if it isn't true."

"Hey!" I said again.

Hyde crossed his impressive arms and cocked his head. "I'm not sure I need any advice from you in the lady department."

"You certainly don't." I narrowed my eyes. "Especially if your advice is to give insincere compliments."

"So everything went alright last night, I take it?" Camilla said.

"You mean, since I'm still alive?" I joked.

She grinned. "It was my first clue that it wasn't a total failure."

"Well, it could have been. The wife came into the bathroom while I was putting the drugs on the toothbrush." I sighed. "I don't think I'm up for another one today. Maybe after a good night's sleep."

"Why are we trying so hard to kill all these guys before the party?" Howard said, tilting his head.

Camilla frowned. "What do you mean?"

"I mean--why not let them walk in the front door? We could Red Wedding this shit."

"Speak English," Frankie said.

Howard looked around at our blank expressions and sighed. "*Game of Thrones*? Invite them in. Lull them with a false sense of security. Then stab the shit out of them."

"You want to invite a bunch of really dangerous guys to our engagement party, where my family will be, and then try to kill them?" I raised my eyebrow.

"Don't tell me you're turning into a bridezilla already," he said, crossing his arms. "If your precious party gets ruined, we'll throw you another one."

I spluttered. "It's not about..."

"How would we do that, though?" Camilla interrupted. "We'd have to keep everyone else safe. We'd have to do it quiet."

"Just think like they'd think," Howard said. "If we were trying to use a party to take over a house, what would *we* do?"

"We'd split up, try and eliminate as many guards as possible before the time came," Hyde said, thoughtfully. "We'd infiltrate, get into position."

"Right," Camilla said.

"And if one of us went missing..." I said, tapping my chin.

Hyde pointed his finger at me. "That might be the way to do it. Instead of us roaming around trying to pick them off, make them come to a central point."

"How do we do that without alerting them? Without alerting Alex?" Camilla said.

"That's going to be the tricky part," Howard said. "Cause it could go wrong right quick."

"How very astute of you," I said sarcastically.

"You know, whenever I hear the word 'astute', all I can think is 'ass toot'," Howard said.

"Can you not?" Frankie said, wrinkling her nose.

"Oh, don't lie," he said, throwing an arm over her shoulder. "You know you love the way my mind works."

Hyde, Camilla and I looked everywhere else but at Frankie's flustered blush and Howard's lopsided grin. The status of their relationship was in flux, that much was clear. None of us wanted to ruin where things were headed by pointing it out.

"In some matters, yes," Frankie said, primly, stepping out from beneath his arm. "But sometimes, I have no clue what you're thinking."

Howard frowned and opened his mouth to answer, but Hyde cleared his throat.

"I think this is a strategy worth exploring further," Hyde said. "But one of the big downsides is that we don't know how many men Alex will bring with him on that night. It could be two; it could be twenty."

"Then we'll have to set a trap big enough for all of them," Camilla said. "Now we just need to figure out how."

"Well, I'm all for killing two or more birds with one stone, so to speak," I said. "Let's make a plan."

Chapter 38

We were three days out from the engagement party. Invitations had been sent to Alex, General Horta, and Prosecutor General Patricia Bradley. They had all accepted. Camilla had made contact with the CIA. I hadn't been at the meeting--I'd been pretend shopping for antiques with my mother and Sybil, with about fifteen guards trailing after--but Camilla told me that they were set, as were Iris and her men. We had a plan, but it was very involved, and if any of the dominos didn't fall perfectly, we'd be...well, I tried not to think about that.

I'd started carrying a roll of antacids in my pocket.

Since we'd actually formulated a plan--as wild as it was--we'd trimmed our list of 'before-party' targets. But there were still a couple of people that we hadn't been able to lock down. A couple of Alex's people, Inacio Silva and

Delmo Souza, were still outstanding. The word had gotten out that Caio was no longer among the living, so a couple of his top men had gone into hiding, too.

On top of all these undercurrents was the fact that my family was still here, still needing attention and protection. My mother was in full wedding madness mode. She'd somehow scrounged up a stack of wedding magazines. There were a few from the US, but most were in Portugese, featuring dresses that were very heavily embellished, or covered in lace--sometimes both.

"What about an invitation that arrives in a box full of roses?" my mother said suddenly.

The full body jerk that accompanied this spoken thought nearly turned over her coffee cup. She blinked at me, and I realized that she was waiting for a response.

"That sounds beautiful, but a little excessive." I winced. "What about sending an evite?"

She froze, clenching her mug until her knuckles went white. After a moment, I was afraid I'd broken her some-how--that she'd had some sort of stroke.

"I'm joking," I finally said.

She gave a breathy laugh. "I know."

"But maybe we should just hire someone to take care of all this," I said, gesturing at the magazines strewn across the table. They were dog-eared, with sticky notes and pen marks.

"Like a wedding planner?" She clasped her hand to her chest. "That's a *wonderful* idea."

At last we were on the same page about something. A wedding planner would give my mother someone to chatter at, someone to talk to about all the details that I didn't give a mouse-sized crap about. And as long as I chose someone who had good taste, they could field all the questions that I'd been peppered with the last few days.

Linen or satin tablecloths?

Chiavari or bentwood chairs for the reception?

Ballroom or mountaintop? Beachfront or metropolitan? California or destination wedding? Maybe a vineyard...

I frankly did not care in general, and right now I didn't even have the available brain bandwidth to pretend.

"That's a wonderful idea," my mother repeated. "Do you know Desiree Wilton's daughter, Dawn? She was raving about her wedding planner. You remember that wedding? Well, you didn't go. But you saw the pictures."

I remembered that wedding--I was very excited to fly to Oman to knock off an arms dealer instead of attending.

"Not that lady. Too much pink," I said. "But I will find someone I like, and I'll put you in touch."

"Excellent," she said, arranging the magazines into a pile and stacking them with a solid thunk against the table. "Then it's settled."

Wanting that particular monkey off my back as soon as possible, I hunted Frankie down. I found her at the desk in her bedroom, wearing huge headphones that were plugged into her laptop. She clicked a key and pulled them down around her neck when she saw me in the doorway.

"Hey," I said. I noted the deep circles under her eyes that she had valiantly tried to cover up with concealer. "How are you?"

She shrugged. "Oh, you know. Not great. We're losing a team member again, and I'm in a weird kind of limbo with Howard."

I nodded, shut the door behind me. "Sorry, Frankie. Sometimes I get so wrapped up in my own selfish bubble that I forget I'm not the only one losing Camilla."

She laughed, but it sounded adjacent to tears. "You're not selfish. You just have a bunch of stuff going on."

I glanced down at my engagement rings and then thought of the kill list burning a hole in my proverbial pocket. "Some of it good, some of it bad."

"So what can I do for you?"

I felt guilty asking for her help when she was stressed about Howard, down about Camilla, and busy with her own work.

"Oh, stop chewing on your lip and just ask me," she teased. "Now that Elio figured out the financials, my schedule is wide open."

"Alright then. I need you to call Luis and tell him we need to hire Camilla's replacement."

Frankie quirked a sculpted eyebrow and began typing. "Do you have a list of requirements or job responsibilities?"

"You know them as well as I do."

"Alright, what else?"

"Can you find me someone to plan my wedding?" I wrinkled my nose. "Someone with really good taste, who can wrangle my mother? I really just want to have Hyde and I show up and get married and have a big, beautiful party with family and friends."

"Gosh, if you only knew someone like that," Frankie said, tapping her chin with a polished nail. "Someone with excellent taste who loved picking things out, who knew both of you... someone who could think of every detail because she knows both the bride and groom really well..."

I frowned at her, thinking.

Her eyebrows raised. "Really? No one comes to mind? No one really fabulous with impeccable taste? Who is maybe sitting right in front of you?"

I was surprised. "Frankie, do you want to plan our wedding?"

"Yes! I do." She clapped her hands.

"Then you are absolutely hired!" I said, giving her a hug. "I want white flowers, a great meal, and absolutely no open mic. Ok, thanks, bye!"

I pretended to start leaving the room, and Frankie laughed.

"But seriously," I said. "Do you think you're up for it? My mother can be difficult."

Frankie pursed her lips. "Your mom has a lot of energy. It just needs to be channeled in the right direction. I'll give her a few options, all of which you would love, and make her choose. She gets to feel like she's in control, when really she isn't. It's a win-win for everyone!"

"You're a genius. Let me know when you guys set a date and a location, and put it on my calendar." I gave a cheeky wave. "Now I'm going to sic my mother on you and go kill some bad guys."

Chapter 39

The night was stunning. The stars twinkled above us like a handful of silver glitter tossed high into the sky. A perfect breeze ruffled the palm fronds, and brushed tendrils of hair along my neck. For a moment, I wished that the party was all there was, tonight--that Hyde and I really were just going to mingle and accept congratulations, drink champagne, and dance until the wee hours of the morning.

But we had a macabre to-do list. There were many moving parts--lots of gears to our plan that had to turn just so. It was a cascade of dominos that had to knock over in precisely the right order. By the time the fireworks went off at midnight, we would know if we had won, or if we had all lost.

If it were just me, or if it were just my team, the pressure wouldn't have been as intense. But my family? They were innocent of this life, no matter how different they were from me. If tonight went well, we would save everyone. If not, we would probably not see the dawn.

So it was a little hard to care about my hair or my outfit, but Frankie insisted.

"Too many eyes will be on you," she said. "It will seem suspicious if you don't look fantastic."

I let Frankie choose my outfit, but balked when she tried to steer me towards another fitted pantsuit. I did not have time or leeway for a wardrobe malfunction tonight. Frankie settled on a long, flowing dress with a high slit. It had a floral pattern printed against a burnt red background. It wasn't my usual color palette, but it looked like I could execute a kick well without busting a seam, so that was good enough for me. Frankie had yet to dress me in something that didn't look good--it was just that she was inclined to forget that I needed to stretch and bend and hide weapons.

I sat dutifully in a chair while Frankie applied my makeup. I must have frowned or something when Frankie reached for the green eyeliner, because Frankie rolled her eyes.

"When are you going to learn to trust me?" she said, sounding exasperated.

"I didn't say a word." I held up my hands in mock defense. "Have at it."

"Hmph."

I closed my eyes and tried not to blink as she lined my lids and swept powders on.

"So," I said, finding it easier to ask this question without eye contact. "What's going on with you and Howard?"

She may have tapped the excess powder from her brush a little harder than necessary, but her voice was placid when she said, "I'm not really sure."

"Hmm," I said.

It wasn't that I didn't believe her, but I didn't think she was giving me the full dish, either.

She sighed. "Truth is, I don't think he knows what he wants. It's embarrassing, because *everyone* knows what I want. I want to get back together with him, but I'm getting sick of feeling desperate. I'm not used to waiting, but I'm trying to be patient."

I started to nod, but froze back into a mannequin when Frankie tsked me.

"He'll come around," I said. "He still gives you that look."

"I don't know," she said, sounding wistful. "I hope so, but I don't know. Now, open your eyes."

My reflection looked like me, but better. Frankie was a genius with makeup--she actually knew how to contour and blend without making me look like I had dirt on my face. Surprisingly, I actually loved the green against my eyes. Instead of clashing with my blue eyes, it accentuated them.

The party was glittering and gorgeous, and it was just getting started when I slipped into the room on Hyde's arm. Tuxedoed waiters held trays of bubbling champagne and bite-size appetizers. Profuse arrangements of parrot tulips, roses, peonies, and ranunculus were set around the room. Glamorous guests mingled near the two full-service bars. A string band played politely beautiful background music.

"Do you like it?" Frankie said, at my elbow. "I helped Camilla by choosing the flowers. I thought it would be a fun way to get a better sense of your style."

"Are you kidding?" I said. "If we didn't have so much to do, I'd say we should just get married now."

Hyde chuckled. "Your mother would have a fit if you didn't buy a wedding dress."

"As your wedding planner, I'd have to agree," Frankie said, crossing her arms. "I'll see you in a custom Monique Lhuillier or Vera Wang, or my name isn't Francine Patel."

"Fine, fine. Whatever," I said. "Just as long as there's a pocket for a forty-five."

"Deal," she said. "Maybe we could order you a custom rhinestone thigh holster."

"With all that fabric, I'd never get to it in time."

"Well, what exactly do you think is going to happen on your wedding day?" she said, sounding exasperated.

"If I'm not armed, how else do you think I'm going to get this guy down the aisle?" I jerked my head at Hyde, who chuckled.

WE MINGLED, as painful as it was. We held champagne, accepted congratulations, and smiled.

As soon as General Horta arrived, I saw Howard slip

out the door. I breathed deeply as the General approached Camilla and kissed her cheek.

"You are looking radiant this evening, Camilla," he said. "One would think it was you who was newly engaged."

I wondered how Camilla could stand it as his beady eyes took her in from head to toe--like she wasn't even there, like she was a prop, a placeholder. Though we'd already talked about it, that glance would have confirmed it--General Horta had been in contact with Alex. He was in on it, whatever was going to happen tonight. General Horta shouldn't have come; he was a bad actor. His smug, duplicitous smile would have tipped us off even if we didn't know already.

But he'll be dead in less than two hours. Hopefully.

The thought brought the hint of a genuine smile to my face, which was more appropriate than the sneer that had been brewing.

"Congratulations," he said, turning his piggy eyes to me, as if just remembering what the party was for.

"Thank you." I nodded and did my best to smile.

"We should have a toast!" he said.

As if on cue, a redheaded waitress was there with a tray of champagne flutes. General Horta selected the one closest to him. The waitress nodded, and passed around the tray. We each took one. I thanked her, and tried not to let my eyes follow Wignow as she weaved back through the crowd.

"To your happiness, for the rest of your life," General Horta said, his smile not meeting his eyes.

The words were good, on the surface. But the tone was off, and I heard the threat behind the statement. But I made myself smile and clink my glass against his, my eyes never leaving the motion in his throat as he downed the champagne. I slid my eyes from him as his head came back up. He smacked his lips; the glass of champagne now all but empty.

"Excellent vintage," he said, putting his empty glass on the tray of a passing waiter. "Well, I see some people I need to speak to. Enjoy your evening."

Even after he was gone, none of us dared say anything for several moments.

"Think it was enough?" Camilla finally breathed.

"More than," I said. "He drank the whole glass."

"That's a start, then," Camilla said with a sigh.

I understood her lack of enthusiasm. The first success had been microscopic--not nearly enough to instill confidence. I knew we all were feeling it--the pressure of what we had embarked on. We had charted a narrow, dangerous path through hostile territory. There were so many different pieces that had to come together. There were so many ways it could all go wrong--so many people that could be hurt along the way. Frankie's eyes had barely left the doorway since Howard had left.

I pressed a hand against the nerves fluttering in my stomach and tried to remember to smile. This was supposed to be a happy night, after all. Hyde put his hand on my waist and gave a little squeeze.

"Alright, Love?" he said, his voice a low murmur.

"As good as I can be."

The evening wore on. I half-heartedly ate a canape. I sipped a tonic water with a lime in it, to make it look like I was drinking. I laughed and smiled, and breathed a sigh of relief when I saw Howard return to the ballroom.

My family was having a good time--well, my mom was, at least. She was laughing and chatting with anyone in her sphere. My father was standing by her side silently scanning the room. I checked the time on my watch. Nine pm, about an hour after the General had first arrived.

I surreptitiously watched him from across the room. It took another five minutes, but he tugged his collar and beads of sweat appeared on his forehead. It was a tricky thing, this. He had to be sick enough to leave, but not sick enough to hole up in a bathroom on the compound. The General shifted, maybe trying to hold something in or work something loose, there was no way to know.

It took another ten minutes before he gave up, saying something to the men next to him. They headed for the door. Another small success, but we wouldn't know until much later if that particular endeavor had been completed. But at the very least, it was a player off this chessboard. We had plenty of them left.

It was hard to look across this glittering party and really see the undercurrent. But under the crisp tuxes beat the heart of men who would murder Camilla for Alex, or

Alex for Camilla. I had to hand it to her--Camilla had done an excellent job of cleaning house since Caio had been dispatched. The men who surrounded her were people that she trusted, but those were the ones that Alex would be looking to eliminate.

"Congratulations, Ms. Miller, Mr. Garrison," a lovely voice said near my elbow.

I turned. It was Prosecutor General Patricia Bradley.

I nodded in acknowledgement of her sentiment. "Thank you."

Her eyes briefly found Camilla's. "A lovely party, Ms. Almeida."

"Thank you," Camilla said. "So glad you could make it."

Then Prosecutor General Patricia Bradley swept off towards the bar, her security detail in tow. They looked formidable and determined. That was good. She would need them in the coming days.

Frankie was at my elbow. "The tracking worked. Alex brought fifteen men in the door with him, but there's possibly more that came separately."

Fifteen was a good amount--it meant that he was going to make a move tonight, just like we'd thought. But Frankie was right. Just because we knew how many he'd brought through the front door, didn't mean we knew how many were dispersed through the crowd. We'd lucked out--Camilla had correctly guessed that Alex and his men would come through the front door to make a statement about his ownership of the house, even though the entrance to the party had been set up around the corner.

With the help of our friends at the CIA, we'd installed misters that sprayed a tasteless, odorless isotope over anyone who came through the front door. The rest of the house had been rigged with sensors. Frankie had a tracking app on her phone, and she'd been watching our plan unfold as the men spread out, searching the house for Camilla's men.

"It's almost time," Hyde murmured.

I took a deep breath and nodded. Camilla produced a butter knife and tapped it against her champagne glass.

"Thank you all for coming," Camilla said in a clear voice. People instantly hushed to hear her. "When I decided to return to Brazil to deal with some family issues, I knew that I had to take my very good friend, Elayna. And I am so very happy she is going to marry Hyde. I couldn't imagine a couple more perfect for each other. Congratulations!"

The crowd murmured their congratulations, and a hundred glasses tinked together. We smiled and drank, and the band struck up in the corner. Couples moved to the dance floor, a fresh current of waiters moved through the crowd with appetizers and drinks, and the lights dimmed. It was time.

Hyde slipped away first, as if he was going to the restroom. He was there and then he wasn't--for a large man, he knew how to weave through a crowd. The plan was for me to go the opposite direction--out the garden doors and up the side of the building. I was smaller than Hyde, and could fit through one of the windows upstairs. That's where we had laid our trap for Alex's men. That's where our plan would be made--or broken.

I slipped out to the garden through one of the doors that was cracked open. The night air was warm, the lighting was low. I paused for a moment to listen to the murmuring insects, to let my eyes adjust to the moonlight. Behind a bougainvillea bush was a folded dark navy jumpsuit and the bottom part of a powered rope ascender. I'd used a similar one before. They were quiet, and it was a much easier way to get up the side of a building than climbing. The jumpsuit was to keep me clean--hopefully.

We weren't naive enough to think that this would be a bloodless takeover, but we were hoping it would be a quiet one. Ideally, I would return to the party in about twenty minutes, with my family and the other guests none the wiser.

I kicked off my heels and pulled on a pair of slip-on sneakers and the jumpsuit. I tugged a throat microphone over my head and into place, pulled the jumpsuit hood over my hair, and strapped a silenced pistol in a holster onto each thigh. I was stuffy nearly the moment I zipped the suit up under my chin--I hoped that the worst thing that happened tonight was me sweating off my makeup. I hooked into the harness, then pressed the button on the ascender.

The low whir of the machine faded into the background as I rode up the side of the building, leaving the sounds of music, clinking dishes, and the murmur of a hundred conversations behind me. It wasn't stylish--more like one of those stair lift chairs than something 007 would have used. But it was effective, and within three minutes, I was parallel to the fourth-story window I needed to access.

"Frankie," I whispered. "Is he still there?"

Last time I'd checked in with her, there had been a man stationed in this hallway, probably as some sort of lookout.

"Yes. There are two guys down a level. They are together. Be careful."

"Is Hyde in position?"

"Yes."

"Tell him I'm a go."

"Will do."

I peeked my head up over the windowsill. The guy in question had his back turned to me, and was about halfway down the hallway. Not far enough away that I could open this window and climb in without him hearing. But then, me getting caught was kind of the point. Our plan hinged on this moment--would this guy shoot first, or would he call for backup as we hoped?

I rapped my knuckles on the window pane, saw his body jerk in surprise. He wheeled towards the noise--I hadn't stopped tapping. In my experience, people are a lot more trusting if they know you aren't trying to hide from them. His eyes squinted. It was dark outside and bright in the hallway--not a great combination for visibility.

And then, jackpot. He brought his hand up to press

something on his chest, and murmured. I couldn't hear the words, but his lips were moving as he headed my way.

"Senhor?" I said.

My Portugese was terrible. When Camilla spoke it, it sounded like poetry, like it should be set to music. I sounded like a wheezing camel with a stutter talking around a rock in its mouth.

"Senhor?" I repeated, tapping on the window.

He stopped talking into his microphone, squinted through the window, and wrinkled his nose with confusion. Then he threw the latch, and worked the handle on the casement window, his other hand resting on the butt of his gun. I waited until the window was open wide enough for my hand.

He started to say something--to ask me what the heck I was doing, probably, but I raised my gun and put a bullet through his forehead. He fell with a loud thud, hitting his head on the way down and leaving a blood smear.

I didn't have a lot of time. He'd called for backup--he shouldn't have opened the window until they arrived. But I was a woman, and men never thought women were as threatening as men. I thrust my arm through the opening and worked the window crank as fast as possible, barking my knuckles against the windowsill in my haste. I tried to squeeze through once the window was open, but the carabiner on my harness caught, leaving me half in and half out, awkward and fumbling to push my rope out of the way.

Which is when the two men rounded the corner.

I had one down before he comprehended what he was seeing--a clean shot right between the eyes. He fell forward as the man behind him slapped his chest and yelled for reinforcements. I put him down right next to his friend, a shot through his ear as he'd turned for cover.

That was a hiccup in the plan. We had wanted to take them down silently, one by one, as they investigated why their comrades hadn't returned. But now I had more people coming my way than I could handle, at least not standing at the end of a long hallway with no cover.

"How many coming my way?" I said to Frankie.

"They're all moving," she said, her voice a hiss. "And there were some men in the crowd who seemed to be on the same channel, because at least six of them headed to the door."

"Let Hyde know. Tell him to bring up the rear, but to be stealthy about it. I've got this."

I barely heard Frankie's affirmative. I was too busy trying to come up with a plan. We had picked this spot because it was a dead-end, because there was only one direction Alex's men could come in or out. But that had only been an asset when we had the element of surprise. Now it was a definite liability.

"Use what you got," I murmured, repeating an adage that had been drilled into me in training.

I had three dead bodies and a pool of blood. I took off at a run, my sneakers splashing through the blood, and took a left. In this part of the hallway were three doors. I ran to the farthest one, a closet that held a large electrical panel, shucked my sneakers off, and backtracked, careful to avoid the bloody footprints I'd already made. Then I ducked into the next door, an HVAC closet. There was barely enough room to squeeze between the huge unit and the closed door.

Then I waited. Footsteps, murmurs. I thought there were two men who'd made it there first. I heard the suppressed cry of alarm when the bodies were found around the corner. Then I heard creeping, careful footsteps past my door. They'd found the bloody trail, were stalking their prey toward the electrical closet. Good.

Above the beating of my heart, I heard them fling open the door. I opened mine slowly, and took out the man with his back toward me with a clean headshot. He fell against the man who was facing me--which was lucky, cause he'd lifted his gun. But his shot went wide, thrown off by the dead weight of his friend. I shot him twice--a sloppy one that hit his shoulder, another one that entered through his mouth as he opened it to yell. It came out as a death gargle instead.

Now I had five men down. A lot, but not enough. One of the men was smaller than the other, I dragged him toward the HVAC closet by his foot. Before I could get him there, I saw the flash of a man peeking around the far corner-there and then gone. I dropped the foot, crouched low, and aimed at the exact spot I'd seen the man peek from.

It didn't take long--it was a rookie mistake, peeking from the same exact spot twice. He slumped forward with a fresh bullet wound to his forehead. But I didn't know if he'd been alone. I kept my eye on the spot--a 't' in the hallway, where enemies could come from the corner or straight ahead. No one else presented themselves, so I dragged the smaller guy to the HVAC closet, grunted as I lifted him, then slammed him between the door and the unit.

I went back and retrieved the other dead guy, pulling with all my might. If the other guys were taking this long to get here, they'd either run into Hyde, or they were regrouping, trying to launch a coordinated attack. I pulled the dead guy around the corner, back where the first three dead guys were. I grimaced at the smell of their emptied bladders and tried not to think about it as I stacked them like cordwood, alternating heads and feet.

It was something--not a lot, but a fall-back point at least. I peeked around the corner, and spied three men heading my direction. They were good--I hadn't heard them, and they had definitely seen me. I swung my gun around the corner and took a blind shot, aiming for where I thought one of them would be.

A pained yowl told me I'd hit *something*, but I would have preferred a heavy thunk to the ground. I retreated to my body barricade, sprawling to the floor behind it and aiming through a crack in the limbs. When the first man came around the corner, I watched his eyes widen as he saw what my barricade was made from. I took the opportunity to put a bullet through his left eye.

The second guy was the one that I'd shot. His teeth

were bared. He didn't seem to care that he wasn't hitting me--he was emptying his clip as fast as he could pull the trigger. It seemed that my bullet may have struck a nerve as well as his shoulder.

I stopped him with a bullet to the throat. Unnecessarily painful, but I couldn't get the angle I needed to get a clean shot, not with him trying to shoot me back. When his gun hand unconsciously flew to his throat, trying to stem the flow of blood, I put him out of his misery.

I could already hear more voices in the hall. I wasn't surprised. I knew that at some point, I would be met with a large contingent of men. I had only taken out seven. By my calculations, there were at least eight more headed my direction. Time to open the pockets of the jumpsuit.

I pulled the pin on a flash-bang grenade and hucked it toward the corner, then inhaled deeply, slammed my hands over my ears, and squeezed my eyes shut. Despite my precautions, I still felt it, but was up and leaping over my body barricade before there was any chance for them to recover, a gun in each hand.

There were five of them in various stages of distress. One stupidly lifted his gun and fired blindly, winging one of his cohorts; I took him out first. The others followed in rapid succession. I doubt they even saw or heard the shots that killed them.

My victory was short-lived--two more men entered the hall. Neither of them had been close enough to experience the concussion of the grenade. We all fired at the same time. I took one down before a shot to my chest knocked the wind out of me. Fire spread through my ribs where I'd taken the hit--but I'd ridden this wave of pain before. I inhaled sharply and adjusted my aim before he could adjust his--a shot to his forehead put him out of the equation.

Air hissed from between my clenched teeth--adrenaline was a help, but it didn't take all the pain away. A shot to a bullet-proof vest--or jumpsuit--still hurt like a hairy bitch. I was lucky it hadn't been a headshot, or I'd be dead. I decided to switch things up and looked around the corner. Finding that section of the hallway clear, (except for dead bodies), I ducked into the utility closet and shoved my bare feet back into my bloody sneakers.

I flicked off the light, crouched down, put fresh magazines in both of my guns, and pointed them at the door. I heard footsteps past my hiding spot. They were tentative--someone, or several someones, trying to be sneaky.

"How many in my hallway, Frankie?" I murmured.

"It's all just one blur," she whispered. "I hope most of them are bodies, but after the first few, I lost count. I'm sorry. There are five that are still moving in other parts of the house, but there's a trail of stationary ones."

I smirked. Hyde was on his way to me.

The door to the closet flung open and I was shooting--two men had been there, but only one fell dead in the doorway. The other had ducked back. I didn't like that--didn't like that he knew where I was. I slid sideways along the back wall to change my position--inches were important here. And I waited.

But his outline did not appear in the doorway again. Perhaps he had read the room--the dead bodies, the various points of contact--and decided the best course of action was to *not* put his head in range of my gun. Smart. Smarter than his friends, at least. Maybe he was waiting for reinforcements. I wouldn't have that. I wouldn't stay in this closet, cornered like a rat.

I shifted to my feet and rotated around the doorway, scanning the area as I ducked my head out to check. I jerked it back and a bullet whistled past my nose. Close. Too close. I wasn't going to luck out with a hit to my bullet-proof jumpsuit with this one. I threw myself down onto the hallway floor, aiming as I went. My first bullet went high, but the second one struck his shoulder, spinning him so that his shot flew wide--just wide enough. My second shot hit him in the side of the head as he started to turn back to me.

I was tired. I pushed myself off the floor and sat back on my heels. My ribs ached from the hit they'd taken--I would have a horrific bruise tomorrow. My face felt sticky. Frankie's makeup job was ruined. I was going to have to wash off the blood before I went downstairs. I hoped the hood had kept the blood out of my hair.

I tried not to see the bodies around me. I mean--I *saw* them, but I tried not to focus on them. At some point, each of these bodies had been someone's little boy. And probably, they were leaving people behind--wives and children, maybe. A grandma or a mother or a best friend who would miss them. These kills weren't why I'd gone into business.

I took a deep breath. When this was all over, when Brazil was in our rear-view mirror, I wanted to get back to taking true predators out.

I came to standing and as I did, I looked to my left--right into the barrel of a gun.

I couldn't help it--I flinched. Even as my arm came up, raising my gun, I knew it would be too late.

I heard the gunshot, and flinched again. But there was no pain.

I was still raising my gun when the man pitched forward, an exit wound in his forehead. Warm blood splattered across my face. The taste of iron was in my mouth. I blinked, looked up, froze.

If I'd made a list of the people I'd thought would help me in this kind of a pinch--he wouldn't have made the top fifty.

I gasped.

Chapter 40

"Dad?" I said, my mouth agape.

I felt like my mind was about to take flight and leave my body. What was happening? How was he here? I almost couldn't reconcile it--his grey hair, perfectly combed, his impeccable tuxedo and shined shoes--and a smoking gun in his elegant physician's hand.

He was breathing hard, his expression frozen somewhere between distaste and horror. I tried to see things from his perspective, then immediately stopped. This hallway full of bodies wasn't even close to the gnarliest thing I'd ever seen, but for him, it probably would haunt his dreams.

"You didn't invite us to Brazil, did you?" he said, his face grim.

Of all the questions he could have asked, I found it strange that he chose that one.

"No," I said, checking my magazines. "You think I'd

ever willingly put you guys in reach of *this*?" I gestured at the dead bodies.

"No. You wouldn't."

The certainty in his voice was a small comfort to me, somehow.

"I *knew* that head was real!" he said, suddenly.

"Look," I said, my anxiety ratcheting up every moment he was in danger. "I will meet with you, answer any questions you have. But now is not the time. There are more coming. I need you to get out of here."

"Where?'

"You went mountain climbing with Peter, right? When he was going through that phase?"

He nodded.

"Good. Down that hallway, you'll find an open window, a harness and a motorized ascender. Strap yourself in, ride down to the gardens and go back to the party and pretend this never happened."

He looked around at the carnage, and his jaw clenched, his expression grim. He nodded, once, and started picking his way down the hallway.

"And keep that gun on you," I said to his retreating back.

He didn't look back, but I saw him pause, nod again.

I braced myself for the onslaught that I was sure was coming. My heart pounded and I breathed deeply as I kept my pistols trained down the hallway. I shut off the part of brain that was nagging at me, pestering me with questions about my father, what had just happened, what it *meant*.

I needed to stay in the here and now, to keep the tension of the fact that I was still very much in battle. I needed to use that to keep me sharp, frosty.

I heard the faintest rustle around the corner, the sound no more than the wet whisper of movement. I crouched and aimed my gun at where I thought the noise might be coming from. I jerked as a low streak of red darted around the corner.

"Fucking cat," I murmured, just managing not to pull the trigger.

Sir Darcy looked like hell. He'd obviously rubbed up next to one of the bodies in the other hallway, because his entire left side was slicked with blood. As I kept watch over the corner, the cat picked its way over to one of the puddles of blood and flopped down in it, rolling like it smelled delightful.

"Gross. Get the fuck out of here," I seethed.

I swear the cat understood, cause he jumped to his feet and hissed at me, then took off running the way he'd came.

"Asshole," I murmured.

"Hey, babe," Hyde's voice called from around the far corner. "Don't shoot me, k?"

Then he was there, striding around the corner with a tired smile on his face. I lowered my gun and stood.

"We did it," he said, catching me up in a hug.

The blood on our jumpsuits stuck a little as we pulled apart, and I grimaced. Hyde chuckled at the expression on my face.

"You got the rest?" I said. "I only got…" I frowned down at the pile of bodies. "Well, I lost count."

"I got ten, I think. I checked with Frankie. She said there weren't any more that were trackable. But there might be some left that weren't tracked."

I nodded. "Still, it's the best we can do, for now."

"Yep. We better get back. I think we've been gone for about fifteen minutes." He rummaged through the pockets of his jumpsuit and came up with a pack of face wipes. "I don't think your makeup is going to survive this, sorry."

"I'm just impressed that we did. It got a little closer than I would have liked."

He looked up, sharply. "It did?"

I nodded at the freshest corpse. "That guy had the draw on me. If my dad hadn't shown up and shot him, I wouldn't be here."

Hyde tilted his head. "Your dad? Did you hit your head?" He held up two fingers. "How many?"

"Two," I said, giving his arm a playful shove. "I didn't hit my head. He was here, like five minutes ago."

He raised his eyebrows and began wiping his face. "He saw all this? He shot someone?"

"And then rapelled down the side of the building." I frowned and looked over my shoulder. "I hope. I should probably go check on that."

I took a moment and went down the hall, past the barricade of bodies, and over to the still-open window. I stuck my head out. Down below, I could just make out an empty harness abandoned in the bushes.

"Yup," I said, returning to Hyde and accepting the face wipes. "He made it down ok."

"Big night for your dad."

I shook my head. "I'll deal with that later."

"You know what this world needs more of?" Hyde said, as we shucked off our ballistic jumpsuits. "Puns."

I smiled. "Is that so? All the problems in the world, and you think we need more Dad jokes?"

"Puns are always funny." He adjusted the cuffs of his shirt and suit. "Like...you know the problem with being an assassin?"

"What's that?"

"It's a dying art."

I rolled my eyes and chuckled. I don't know how he did it, but Hyde always knew what I needed after a job. It was like Camilla, but different. After a case, Camilla treated me like a child who'd just come through a nightmare--warm cocoa, cozy blankets, warm socks, and a listening ear. Hyde made me laugh, gave me a shoulder to lean or cry on, as needed. He was my very best friend.

"Thanks for being you," I said.

"My joke was that good, huh?" He waggled his eyebrows. "I got more. What do a corpse and a t-shirt have in common?"

I laughed. "I have no idea."

"They're both casualties."

I frowned.

"Get it? Casualty, casual-tee?"

I shook my head and double-checked my hands for

blood. I had red nails, so that helped. "Be thankful you're not at an open mic night."

"Bah-dum-pish!" Hyde said.

"Exactly."

"Didn't like that one?" Hyde shrugged. "That's fine. I got another one. Why was the corpse booed off the comedy stage?"

"Why?"

"'Cause corpses aren't funny--they're dead serious."

I snickered, more at how bad the joke was than anything.

Chapter 41

We took a side stairwell and a back door into the garden. Along the way, we found evidence of Hyde's trip to meet up with me. Hyde tended to be more hands-on than me when it came to killing. Snapping a neck wasn't easy, but it was quick and quieter than a gunshot. I rarely attempted it--unless my victim was seated or was already moving their head in the correct direction, it was difficult. Or unless they kicked my dog.

Outside, I slipped my shoes back on, picked up my clutch, and presented myself for inspection. "See anything I missed?"

"Nope," Hyde said after looking me up and down. "I only see my lovely wife-to-be."

I smacked a kiss on his cheek. "Charmer."

He slid his arm around my waist and gave a small squeeze as we slipped back into the party through the garden doors. After the tension of the previous minutes and the silence of the garden, the volume and the motion of the party were disorienting. It was a wave of sound and movement, swelling and undulating. After being so attuned to the slightest motion, the minutest noise, it was hard to take in.

A woman across the room shrieked with laughter. I stiffened, and Hyde ran a soothing thumb on my waist as we approached my family, who were clustered around Camilla.

"See, Darling?" My father was saying as we approached. "I told you I'd just seen her. And here she is."

I didn't miss the relief that was thick in his voice, but I was the only one who knew why.

My mother tsked. "Absconding from your own party like a couple of teenagers. Terrible."

But her eyes twinkled. The festivities--or the champagne--had her in a good mood.

"I needed the fresh air," I said. "Too many people, you know."

"Well, they're all here to celebrate you, so maybe you should be grateful," Sybil murmured.

Peter frowned, and my mother looked heavenwards, pressing her lips together.

"I am grateful," I said. "Are you guys looking forward to getting home? I bet you'll have a patient backup, Dad. And Mom, you'll have some catching up to do, as well."

On what, I didn't really know. Lunching with her

friends and gossip, probably. She nodded in agreement, though.

"Are things all set for us to fly out tomorrow?" my father asked. "We could stay if you'd like us to."

Sybil and my mother looked at him like he'd sprouted two heads. My mother's lip even curled. They were more than ready to go to their *separate* homes. But I knew what he was really asking--whether or not it was safe for them to leave. He was the only one who knew that they hadn't been invited, at least not by me.

"Everything's arranged." I rushed to assure him. "You'll take a helicopter out in the morning, and Camilla's arranged for a special treat--one of her family's jets will be taking you home."

"Oh, swanky," my mom said. "Thank you, Camilla."

"Does it have a bathroom?" Sybil said. "My kids can't go all that way without a bathroom."

I turned away. It had been a long night already, and we had miles to go. Sybil's constant sniping chafed at my already battle-wearied psyche. I could barely grit my teeth and bear her on a good day. It was a lot more difficult when I'd just risked my life to help keep her safe.

"What is your problem?" Peter said. "Knock it off. Every time Elayna says something or does something nice, you find a reason to bitch about it."

"And that's our cue," Hyde murmured with raised eyebrows, steering me away with the hand that was around my waist. "Let's go get some champagne."

I knew what Sybil's problem was. I'd caught her in an

embarrassing situation this past year and had fixed it for her. Now, every time she saw me, she was ashamed. Add shame to a nasty, introspective-resistant person and you got avoidance at best, lashing out at worst.

The rest of the night went smoothly, even despite the fact that Peter and Sybil weren't talking. Frankie gave me several updates. The other teams had come through. There had been numerous fatalities at the factories, but none that we cared about. Slaving was a dangerous business, and rightly so--selling lives should cost you your own. I wondered how long it would take for Alex to get a call, wondered if there was anyone who'd gotten away to raise the alarm. But I kept him in my sights and I didn't see a flicker of alarm, not until a man hurried from across the room and whispered something in his ear.

Alex jerked. Then his eyes searched the crowd, narrowing on Camilla, where she was laughing with Howard and Frankie. I was glad to see Tristao to her left, grinning down at her with an adoring expression.

Still, I squeezed Hyde's hand. "Alex found something out."

"I see him."

We headed over to intercept him, reaching Camilla's side while Alex was still weaving through the crowd. In case anyone was watching us, I made a show of walking clumsily, blinking slowly, wobbling my head, and smiling inanely. After all, who could blame the guest of honor for overindulging?

"Heads up," I murmured to Camilla, my stupid smile

still in place. I slumped against Hyde a bit to add to the pretense.

She nodded, her smile not faltering. "I saw that."

"Then you are excellent at watching while pretending not to," I said, taking a sip of champagne. "My compliments."

"Dear sister," Alex said, joining the group with a smile that didn't quite reach his eyes. "Might we have a word?"

"Of course!" Camilla said. "I'm sure that you remember Frankie and Howard, and Tristao?"

Alex grabbed her elbow. "Bring them along for all I care."

He hauled her towards the doors that led toward the main living area. Tristao lifted his hand as if to stop Alex, but I snagged his eye, gave a minute shake of my head. He followed them instead, Howard and Frankie, too.

"Well I'm drunk!" I announced, as the group moved out the door, into the hallway.

The sounds of the party faded away. Hyde and I followed in Alex and Camilla's wake. I bobbed and stumbled like a drunk person does. I didn't know that anyone was paying attention, but it couldn't hurt. The opposite sides were about evenly matched. Alex had two men with him, Camilla had Tristao and us. It was time for the other part of our plan to fall into place.

We hung back once Alex entered the dining room with Camilla, nearly pulling the door off its handle and thrusting Camilla into the room. It grated on me to watch her treated so, but I trusted Tristao with her safety.

We had a plan, and we were going to stick to it. Far down the hall, we heard the door to the party open once more. I quickly poured my champagne in a puddle on the floor and bent over it, my hands on my knees as I rummaged through my clutch. Hyde picked up on my idea immediately, holding my hair back off my face with one hand and rubbing soothing circles on my back with the other. I coughed and gagged, making my whole body heave.

"Ugh," I heard one of the men say, as they passed us.

There were two of them. I recognized the sharp cheekbones and small black eyes that were too close together immediately. Inacio Silva. He was on the list. Here was the woman beating, head of Alex's fighting men...the one we hadn't been able to place. The man that Frankie couldn't lock down, the one that had been in hiding.

"I got left," I murmured, then straightened, my garrote wire already extended between my hands.

It was over Ignacio's head and around his neck before he knew what was happening. I twisted the ends together and turned my body. We were back to back, my hands on the handles of the garrote at my left collarbone. I bent over and pulled, applying leverage. Ignacio's feet were off the floor now, his hands scrabbling helplessly at the wire. He landed a donkey kick to the back of my calf--it hurt but it was weak.

Hyde had his guy in a sleeper hold. The man and Hyde were both facing me. Hyde gave a wink.

"Imagine meeting you like this," he quipped at me.

"Rude. Can't you tell I'm busy, here?"

Our victims both lost consciousness around the same time, going dead-weight and floppy. We waited ten more seconds, in case it was a clever ruse, but they were out cold.

"Closet," I said, nodding my head towards a door on the left.

We tossed them in, and I uncapped a couple syringes from my clutch, handing one to Hyde. Neither one of these guys would wake up, but it wouldn't be a painful death.

Back in the hallway, we resumed our positions--me, bent over some imaginary vomit--Hyde, the dutiful companion. We got two more of Alex's men the same way, except this time, my guy managed to get ahold of my hair when I had him strung up over my shoulder. I grunted in pain, which only encouraged him to yank harder. Not that I blamed him. Everything's fair in a life-or-death scenario.

I heard a sharp snap behind us, and then Hyde landed a hammer fist onto my guy's nose. I almost fell forward with the force of it, but he went limp instantly, and I dropped him in an undignified heap.

"Give a girl some warning next time you do that, huh?" I said, rubbing my shoulder. "You hit like a Mack truck."

"Sorry, babe."

"No, I'm just cranky," I said, shaking out my arm. "I really do appreciate it."

Hyde hefted the first guy by the shoulders and drug him to our makeshift morgue. "We really need to remember to tell someone that these guys are here. Otherwise, some poor maid is going to have a heart attack in the morning."

My nose wrinkled as I started dragging the other guy. "We have been *very* disrespectful to the storage facilities in this house."

He shrugged. "It's Camilla's house. I don't think she minds our brand of help."

"Maybe we should send her a bill." I snorted.

We took up our positions once more.

"There's some blood splatter on the wall from that guy's nose," I said. "You think the next guys will notice?

"Only if they're very observant."

"Let's hope they're more brawn than brains, then."

There were three of them in the next wave, and they seemed to be more tense than the last four. I tried my best to heave as realistically as possible, but the repeated fake puking was genuinely hurting my stomach. Then, just as they passed us, one of the men froze in mid step. He turned back, looking at the blood on the wall.

"I think he's very observant!" I hissed to Hyde.

The man opened his mouth, and I stood up and yelled the first thing that came to mind.

"Karate!" I bellowed, hitting him in the face.

Of course, this time the fight was three to two, and we didn't have the element of surprise. The man turned to hit me back, but I extended my garrote wire to deflect and redirect the blow, then grabbed his outstretched wrist, pivoted, and used his forward momentum to throw him to the ground. I was aware of Hyde engaging the other two men, but I had to focus on my opponent, who was faster than he'd first seemed.

He sprung to his feet in a fighting stance, and I didn't like what I saw. His form was perfect. In the faint recesses of my mind I remembered that Brazil had a rich tradition in street fighting and mixed martial arts. I may have grimaced. He smiled back. I waited for him to make a move. We circled each other, and he feinted. I saw it for what it was and didn't react.

Then, very purposely, I let my eyes slide past him down the hall. I raised my eyebrows and smiled, like I was surprised and delighted, letting my hands fall. The idiot bought it, swinging his head around to look for the threat behind him. The moment he did, I slung my garrote around his neck, yanked him to the floor, and wrapped my legs around his neck, applying pressure with the garrote and my legs.

We both knew I had him--it would have been nearly impossible for him to escape *without* the garrote involved. He had a matter of seconds before blacking out. But the problem is that when you're fighting, seconds can last forever. The other problem was--he knew how to fight, and there were no refs involved.

With his free hand he reached up, trying to hit my face or pull on my arm. Once he realized the futility of that, he reached up, grabbed a piece of skin with his fingers, and started to pinch the shit out of it. This would have been painful on any part of the body, but his fingers had landed just above my boob. I grunted and doubled the pressure.

His fingers slowly slid away, a tremor went through his body. I glanced down--he was a reddish purple in the face, but he'd pinched me in the boob, and I wasn't feeling generous.

"You ok over there?" Hyde said.

He was kneeling on a man's throat while the guy took weak punches at his torso.

"Fine," I grunted.

I didn't wait to get this one in the closet--I just jabbed him with a syringe right there. I administered doses to both the others, and let Hyde do the clean-up.

"I'm going to go check on Camilla," I said. "You good here?"

"Yeah." He pushed his hair back from his forehead. "Send them my way, if you want."

"You sure?" I raised my eyebrow.

"Yep. We should be getting down to the dregs, now."

"*Should* being the operative word."

Chapter 42

I slipped into the dining room and every head turned my direction. Camilla, Tristao, Howard, and Frankie sat on one side. Alex and his men sat on the other. Lynsee, the maid, uncorked a bottle of champagne at the sideboard. I stumbled and swayed, then jerked my thumb back towards the hall.

"There's like... a guy fighting another guy out there," I said, slurring my words ever so slightly.

Alex nodded toward his men, who slipped out the door.

"Sorry," I said, slumping into a chair down the table.

I rested my head on my arm and closed my eyes. Everyone promptly ignored me.

"What did you think was going to happen, Camilla?" Alex's voice was arrogant. He spoke as if he were chastizing a child who'd come home with bad grades. "Caio was delusional. I'm not mad at all that you got rid of him. But there's much more to the Almeida organization than there was when you left. We've grown--expanded. The thought of you stepping in off the street and running even a *portion* of the business is ludicrous!"

"And yet, Father left it all to me," Camilla said, her voice calm. "So it *is* mine, no matter how ludicrous you find it."

He leaned forward, a glint in his eye. He smiled, but it was predatory--all teeth.

"Well. How fortuitous that you are here, as am I. And I've drafted a document that just requires your signature to transfer everything over to me."

Camilla cocked her head. "Why would I do that? What do you possibly have to offer me?"

"Your life. The lives of your friends." He scoffed. "You just let me and my men walk right through the front door! What? Did you not think I would challenge you? Did you think I would just let you take what is rightfully mine? There was once a time where I would have gladly shared this with you, Camilla. But you left. You made it clear that you didn't want anything. And now that's exactly what you shall have."

Camilla nodded. "That's true. Well, *almost*. You see, I'm very aware of the Almeida holdings, including the factories that you run with slave labor." She glanced at the clock and folded her hands in front of her. "As of an hour ago, all of those factories have been raided. The men who held those people are either dead or in custody. The slaves have been freed."

The color leeched from Alex's face as Camilla continued. "I won't have human trafficking as an element of my
organization."

"You..." he started.

Camilla cut him off. "You must have wondered where
your men are, Alex. The ones who've been scurrying
through my house like rats. But look around. You're all
alone."

His eyes darted to the door his guards had just exited--
the door Hyde was opening and walking through.

"Felipe?" Alex called. He turned to Camilla, a snake
once more. "What have you done, you stupid bi--"

Camilla pulled a tranquilizer gun out from beneath the
table smoothly, pointed it at Alex. Before I could do more
than flinch, she pulled the trigger.

Alex was cut off in mid-sentence. A dart embedded in
his neck and he fell forward, hitting the table. Judging by
the crunch, he'd landed on his nose.

"Well, that was rude," I said, through my shock. "He
sounded like he was just getting warmed up."

Camilla didn't smile. Instead, she laid the gun flat
against the table, and expelled the breath she'd been
holding.

"Murderer!" Lynsee shrieked.

She had been standing behind Alex. All she had seen
was a gun in Camilla's hand and Alex now facedown on
the table, the gushing blood from his broken nose pooling
beneath his head. Her eyes were wild, her nostrils flared.
She was fumbling, plunging her hand down to lift her

skirt, but it was so tight she was struggling. I saw the flat thigh holster and the diminutive knife as she plucked and pulled at the material.

"Knife!" I called.

Lynsee finally extricated the blade, but there were at least four people between her and Camilla. In a flash, Lynsee changed her target. Instead of continuing her charge toward Camilla, she raised her knife above her head at Frankie. But Howard was there, and drew back and socked Lynsee hard in the face. A crunching noise and a cry, and blood spurted beneath her clasped fingers as she stumbled back.

"I knew that Alex must have people in the house," Camilla said calmly, even as Tristao secured Lynsee. "I didn't really suspect the slutty maid, though."

"You killed him!" Lynsee shrieked. "He was the son, the true and rightful heir!"

"What is this, the tenth century feudal system?" I quipped.

Everyone ignored me, which was for the best, as Lynseee was hissing and spitting like an enraged cat.

"Are you ok?" Howard said to Frankie. His hands fluttered over her person like birds that couldn't decide where to land. They settled on her shoulders, finally, and he looked into her eyes. "Are you alright?"

"I'm fine," she said.

He pulled her into a fierce hug, his arms wrapped tightly around her as far as they could go. This was not a teammate hug, or a friendship hug. It was far more. She relaxed into it with a dazed expression on her face. I couldn't hear what he was saying as he murmured into her ear, but she squeezed her eyes tight and hugged him back with a smile on her face, so they must have been words she was happy to hear.

Hyde cleared his throat. "Get her out of here," he said, nodding to Tristao, who held Lynsee.

He complied. I doubted Lynsee would see the dawn, but I couldn't muster any sympathy for her.

"You two need to get back to the party," Camilla said.

She looked tired--the lines in her forehead were pronounced. Her eyes had barely left Alex's form since she'd tranqued him. I wasn't sure if she was feeling regret, or if she was worried he'd spring up like some horror-movie villain. But it was maybe a mixture of both. It was complicated--he *was* a villain, but he was also her brother. There was a lifetime of memories there. And yes, this had to be done. Alex couldn't be at the helm of the Almeida cartel. He couldn't have that much power.

But...he was still her brother.

I gave them a backwards glance as we left the room to try and pretend to enjoy the rest of our party.

Chapter 43

The party lasted far longer than I wanted to be there. But, bit by bit, people trickled out. Until, finally, at three am, we were the last ones there. My family had thrown in the towel long before, but there had been a contingent of late-night partiers in one corner who'd stayed well after we'd turned the lights on and the caterers had started cleaning up.

Prosecutor General Patricia Bradley had returned with five SUVS and a bunch of her men to pick up Alex, as agreed. She looked so proud, so brave, that I almost hated what we were going to do next. There wasn't anyone that was going to come out of this one hundred percent happy with how things went down. But when the stakes are so high, and there's so many people involved, sometimes anger all around is the best possible outcome.

We did a walk-through with Tristao and Javier after everyone was gone, to make sure the bodies were all cleaned up. We were in the upper hall where I'd taken out most of my victims. The bodies in the hall were cleaned up, but the carpeting was ruined and there was blood splatter on the walls that might need a coat of paint.

"Oh, did you get this one?" I said, swinging open the door to the HVAC closet.

As if in answer, a corpse fell forward like a plank of wood and hit the floor.

I cocked my head. "Guess not."

Hyde raised an eyebrow. "What was *that* setup for?"

I shrugged. "I thought it might be a distraction."

"Would have worked, if someone had opened it."

"Meh. You can't win them all."

We followed the trail that Hyde took, from where he met me back to where he'd snuck up to the fourth floor. But Tristao and Javier had already cleared all those corpses. And the pile in the closet below.

In the end, it was a anticlimactic ending, the fall of Alex's loyalists. We nodded, and walked back to the family suite in silence.

And there was Frankie in the hall, her mini dress half zipped up in the back, her hair rumpled and voluminous, her sky-high heels in one hand, tip-toeing away from Howard's bedroom door.

"Frankie!" I stage-whispered. "What are you doing?"

She whirled towards us and froze, her eyes wide, her cheeks pink.

"Did you get lost?" Hyde said, his voice low with false concern. "Have you been sleep-walking?"

"That's a big problem," I said to Hyde, my voice grave. "I've seen advertisements for prescription drugs to treat that. Sure, they may cause anal leakage and pink eye, but maybe that would be preferable to getting lost and not being able to find your own bedroom in the middle of the night."

"Oh, shut up, you two!" Frankie hissed, her face flushed.

"What?" I gasped, my eyes wide. "You mean it *wasn't* sleep-walking? Then why were you in Howard's room? Wait...I know what this is about."

Hyde nodded, his face serious. "Pillow fight."

Frankie's face was twisted somewhere between horrified embarrassment and laughter. I think it was the first time I'd seen her expression less than beautiful.

"Ugh. I'm leaving you two juveniles," she said, turning away with her head high.

"Hey, we aren't the ones doing the walk of shame," I said. "Are you at least wearing your underwear?"

Frankie threw me the bird as she stomped away. Hyde and I waited until she was out of view to start laughing.

"Ah, that was mean," I said, swiping a little moisture from beneath my eye. "But totally worth it."

"I hope this means they're getting back together."

"Me too. Now, I need a shower and a greasy breakfast. Our day is not over."

"No kidding--not with a thousand ruffled feathers to smooth."

· · ·

I DID FEEL BETTER after scrubbing the makeup off my face and the blood mist out of my hair. The breakfast didn't hurt, either. By the time I padded out to the family dining room in bare feet, yoga pants, tank top and loose-knit sweater, there was a feast on the table. Belgian waffles, with warm maple syrup and fresh strawberries sat next to a platter of crispy bacon and perfectly browned sausages. Next to that was a platter of bagels, with lox, cream cheese, red onions and capers. There were fluffy scrambled eggs with chives, biscuits and gravy, and an assortment of fresh pastries drizzled in icing.

Camilla poured cups of coffee for me and Hyde, then settled back into her seat where she was already halfway through her meal.

"Good morning," she said.

"I think there should be a rule against saying that if you haven't been to bed yet," I grumbled.

"Eat something," Camilla said, smirking. "It will cheer you up."

"No need to make fun of me," I said lightly. "Although I will avail myself of this beautiful spread."

"Chef was feeling particularly motivated this morning," Camilla said, dryly. "I believe this is his version of a thank you note."

I exhaled a laugh. It didn't help the sting completely, didn't soothe the growing ache in my heart that I was desperately trying to ignore, but it was something. It helped a little to know that all of the people under the umbrella of the Almeida organization were free, even if they didn't yet know it.

There were four extra plates set at the table, and I nodded to them, frowning. "Who are those for?"

A knock at the door answered my question before Camilla could. A maid escorted Elio and Marcos in, and behind them, Iris and Ruben. It was a strange grouping-- Elio was wearing a pastel blue shorts suit, with a black and white striped shirt underneath. His lapel held a nosegay of hot pink spray roses.

Next to him, Marcos's foppish good looks seemed almost sloppy, but he wore well-fitting blue jeans and a short-sleeved, slim-fitted Hawaiian shirt with a Cuban-stlye Fedora. Iris wore black from head to toe, her expression grim, and Ruben was casual in flat-front navy shorts, a white t-shirt, and slip-on canvas shoes.

"Your guests, Ms. Camilla," the maid said, her eyes downcast.

I wondered if she'd heard about what happened to Lynsee, or if she was just uncertain about having a new boss. Either way, Camilla frowned at her demeanor.

"Thank you, Lucida," she said.

Ruben and Iris took the seats next to Hyde and I, while Marcos and Elio sat across from us.

Iris was the first to break. "This isn't what we agreed upon," she hissed, her palm flat on the table. "You said that I could kill Alex, not that he would be arrested. You said that he would die."

"He *will* die," Camilla said, calmly.

"And what if he doesn't?" Ruben said, calmly. "What if he bribes someone, or escapes?"

"He is already dead, even if he still breathes," Camilla said.

"You promised me that if we helped you, I would get to kill Alex," Iris said, her eyes flashing, her teeth bared. "I wanted to be the one."

"Yes," Camilla said dryly. "We know. Your quest for revenge, and all that."

Iris opened her mouth as if to interject, but Camilla silenced her by holding up a finger.

"But I also think that you would be the first to admit that what you fight against, the human trafficking issue... that is bigger than just you. And my brother in prison, being held and charged with his crimes...that will be a better message about the issue than his death at your hands would be. This trial will take years to come to fruition. It will splashed on the cover of every newspaper, every media outlet will cover it again, and again, and again."

"And what does this get you?" Iris hissed. "I know you didn't do this out of the goodness of your heart."

"Not solely, no," Camilla said. "I will get positive attention from the media, as the long-lost daughter returned home to clean up her family's name. Prosecutor General Patricia Bradley will get the boost she needs for her campaign, for busting such a high-profile individual. Plus, she will be in my debt in the future. Not much, but just enough."

"I knew it," Iris said, almost frothing at the mouth. "You are just like your brother. Just like your uncle. Just like your father."

"It seems you have forgotten the others," Camilla said, her tone finally less than cordial.

"What others?"

"The other victims. You have forgotten the legal reforms that will naturally come from this. There has already been an outcry--journalists are already talking about the too-lenient sentences for human traffickers. And then there are the people rescued from all those factories last night."

"*We* rescued them, not you," she said, clasping a hand to her chest.

"You rescued one factory," Camilla said, her voice hard. "My connections did the rest. You wouldn't have known where they were without us. You might never have found them. And you certainly couldn't have rescued them all at once, not without our manpower, our friends. You would have liberated one factory, the first one you found. And then they would have killed the rest. My brother may have captured your sister, but it was I who rescued her."

Camilla jerked her head at Tristao, and he nodded, opening a door behind him and saying a few words.

Marriena Montes looked just like Iris. Shorter, and older, with deeper lines in her face. But there were the same assessing eyes, the same lips. Except for the parallel scars that ran across both her cheeks, she looked the same.

"Marriena!" Iris cried, knocking over her chair in her haste.

I leaned back in my chair. Yet another thing I didn't know about, yet another facet of the plan I hadn't been privy to. Camilla was settling into her role quickly, and well.

"We found her in a textile factory," Camilla murmured. "We flew her down this morning so you could be together."

Her words were lost in the muffled crying coming from the sisters, who clung together in their mutual joy and grief.

"I cannot give you back the years my family stole from you," Camilla said, her voice gentle once more. "But I hope this is a start." She turned to Ruben. "Once they are ready, I would like to discuss turning one or more of the factories into a workplace for those you rescue. Several of the locations had worker living quarters. Obviously, there will be many who don't wish to work in a factory ever again. But for those who cannot go home, who need an option... we would offer good pay and good conditions, if that is something your organization would be interested in."

He nodded, though his eyes barely left the joy on Iris' face.

They left soon after. The fear was still obvious in Marriena's eyes. I didn't blame her. It was the Almeida family who'd bought and trafficked her, only transferring her to factory work when she'd marked herself--a fact she had proudly proclaimed. Her scars were of her own making--the only way she could control her fate. She'd done it with a ballpoint pen that fell out of a customer's pocket.

Regardless of the differences these sisters would discover, the Montes sisters had one thing in common-- they both had titanium wills.

Frankie and Howard found their way to the breakfast table soon after.

"Howard," Camilla said, wrinkling her nose. "Tristao found Sir Darcy in the gardens this morning. He was able to snag him with a fishing net and put him in one of the bedrooms in the other wing."

"Ok, thanks," he said, shoving a piece of bacon in his mouth.

"Yeah, about that," I said. "Howard, I'm so sorry, but you're going to have to give that cat a bath."

His eyes went wide and fearful. "What?"

"It rolled in the blood upstairs! It looks like an extra from *Pet Cemetery*. I can't have the kids seeing him like that."

"How am I supposed to do that without getting killed?"

"I don't know. I really don't. Hose it down, if you have to. I got lucky with the head in the bucket. If anyone sees Sir Darcy drenched in blood like that... I don't think we can explain away two gory things in one trip. Plus, we don't want him on the furniture. He stinks."

"I feel like someone should give me last rites before I go in there." He grimaced.

"You could always just... you know..." Frankie said. "Shoot it and say it got lost."

Howard's mouth dropped open; a scowl wrinkled his forehead. "It's a living creature, Frankie."

She rolled her eyes. "This coming from the guy who ate so many steaks he gave himself diarrhea."

"It's...it's different."

"Then we'll drop him off at one of those street-meat vendors in a *favela*," she said, her eyes twinkling. "Then it wouldn't be different."

"It's like I don't even know you."

Frankie laughed. "That cat hates everyone, and the feeling is mutual."

"He's just...he's... Ok, yeah. He's an asshole. But he's still my pet."

"Sounds like some serious co-dependence, enabling type of relationship to me," she said. "He abuses you and all the people in your life, and you still put up with him, defend him."

"It's not like I can get him to stop!" he said, stomping off in the direction of his room.

"The kebab guy could," Frankie murmured, after Howard was out of earshot.

I laughed.

Chapter 44

L ater, I had just finished my second mimosa, and was seriously considering a third, when Peter and Sybil found me in the living room. I topped off my mimosa based on their expressions alone. It looked like they wanted to talk.

"Uh, Elayna?" Peter said. "Sybil has something she wants to ask you."

He nudged Sybil forward and I did my best to keep a pleasant expression on my face. I wasn't a hundred percent sure I'd managed it, but it was at least civil, I hoped.

"I think that Sir Darcy would be better off with us," she said.

My eyebrows raised, and Peter cleared his throat. Sybil's eyes darted to him, and she pressed her lips together at what she saw. I didn't see his expression; I was too dumbfounded by the direction of the conversation to look.

"I really like him," she said. For once, her expression looked open, honest. Vulnerable. I didn't know if I'd ever seen that from her, before. "The kids do, too. We were wondering if we could take him home with us, since he doesn't seem to... get along with you very well."

It was the most diplomatic few sentences strung together that I'd ever heard from her. I raised my eyebrows in impressed surprise.

"Well, I'm not going to lie," I said. "I'd give that cat to you in a heartbeat, but he isn't mine to give. You'll have to ask Howard."

"Yes, yes, a thousand times, yes!" Howard yelled, sprinting in from the other room, where he'd apparently been eavesdropping.

"Really?" Sybil said, her eyes lighting up.

The happiness in her expression made her look younger, more open, almost like someone you'd want to talk to.

"Yes, please. He's already in his crate, so we won't have to catch him," Howard said hurriedly, as if Sybil was going to change her mind at any second. "You can have his toys, too. Of course, he hates them all, but...I'll go get him right now!"

I laughed.

MY FAMILY LEFT with little fuss, other than my mother's last-minute scramble to find Isabella's missing shoe, and

Sir Darcy's muted caterwauling from his crate. My father gave me a meaningful look, a hug, and told me we'd meet for coffee once I was back in California. I nodded, understanding the silent message--my father had questions, and he wanted them answered.

Camilla had the airplane land on the private strip behind the house, to eliminate the helicopter ride to the larger airport outside of town. There had been an explosion on the road last night, she explained, that had killed General Horta--the forerunner in the next election. Things were particularly unsettled right now, because the police were rounding up members of a local street gang, As Cobras, who they believed were responsible for the attack.

I couldn't help the sigh of relief that I released when my family took off safely in Camilla's jet. They were safe. I felt wrung out as a dishrag--I don't think I had fully relaxed since the moment I'd seen Jake run towards me on the front lawn. But now they were safe. I could finally lift my eyes from this problem. I could finally resurface.

Camilla had the maids pack us. We had a flight out that night. I planned on sleeping the whole way home. I was exhausted--not only physically, from the fighting and killing--but mentally and emotionally. Large parts of the plan had gone perfectly--the General was dead, the Cobras were being dismantled by the police, and Prosecutor General Patricia Bradley was the only real remaining candidate for President, as the CIA wanted. Which was payment of sorts for their men raiding the factories. Or rather, it was the start of a long and productive relationship between the CIA and the Almeida Organization.

IT WAS afternoon before I got another moment alone with Camilla. She was looking out the window. I joined her and was surprised to see Wu outside, toeing at something in the grass. He had a scowl on his face. As I watched, he kicked a shrub. Bruno ambled up to him and shoved his massive head beneath his hand.

"I bargained for him, you know," Camilla said, her eyes following Wu as he pet Bruno's ears distractedly. "I wouldn't agree to help now, or in the future, unless they let him go."

"And he's still mad?" I said, my eyebrows raised.

"Not at me," Camilla teased. "But I don't even think that mad is the word for it. It's hard not to be in control of your life. To have all your options and choices stripped away. He's not angry at you--not really. He's mad that his choices got taken away. I think in time he'll want to talk to you again, once he figures out that you aren't the one to blame. But for now, he's staying with me."

"That's good of you," I said.

She laughed. "Hardly. Don't forget I'm building a team of my own now, too."

"There's a weird thought."

"Don't I know it."

"Don't try and poach any of my people," I said, wagging my finger at her. "I won't allow it."

"Oh, I'm going to make Hyde an offer he can't refuse." She wiggled her eyebrows and did a little shimmy. "I'll show him that aged wine is sweeter."

I laughed.

"But seriously," she said. "You know you always have a safe place here. Always and no matter what. If things go bad out there, you come here."

"Thanks, but I'm not going to bring trouble to your door."

"Just remember the offer. It always stands. You are like the daughter I never had. You'll always have a place in my home. You can always count the Almeida group as friends."

Tears pricked at my eyes, and because I loved her, I let Camilla see it. "Thank you."

Elio decided to stay behind and help Camilla with the fiscal part of her new empire. There were still a lot of financial knots to untangle, a lot of legitimate opportunities to take advantage of. I didn't begrudge him the ability to stay with her, although I would be lying if I said I wasn't a bit jealous.

Camilla had been my first employee, the first member of my team. Along the way, she'd become far more than that. She'd become family. I wasn't just losing my house, gun and bookkeeper. I was losing a mother figure, a close friend.

I barely managed to hold it together as we said goodbye, as we clasped each other in that firm hug, as I breathed in her scent--a mix of sweet perfume and suntan lotion. It wasn't until I took my seat on the private jet that evening that I let the tears well over before wiping them quickly away.

Chapter 45

Marcos caught a ride home to California with us. He sprawled on a couch and propped his feet up. I got the impression he was very familiar with private jets--he had that comfort level that said that he belonged, like he'd been raised with them.

Howard and Frankie took the two seats next to him. They were holding hands.

Howard waited until the plane had taken off and then blurted, "We're back together."

Then he jutted his chin out in a belligerent manner, as if daring one of us to protest.

"About time," Hyde said with a wink.

"I wondered if you two were a thing," Marcos said with a lady-killer smile, his hands behind his head.

"Well, we are, so don't go getting any ideas," Howard nearly growled.

"I like 'em cheap and busty," Marcos said. "No offense, Frankie, but you're neither of those things."

"Hey! There will be no comments about her bust!" Howard said, his expression stern.

"Fair enough," Marcos said, holding up his hands. "I just thought you should know she isn't my type, since you bristle every time I look in her general direction."

"I do not *bristle*," Howard said, glowering.

Marcos raised his eyebrows. "If you say so."

Hyde was hiding his face behind a magazine, but I could see it shaking. Bruno seemed to sense Howard's agitation, because he lumbered over and leaned against Howard's legs, looking up at him at such an angle that his tongue flopped out the side of his mouth.

"Pet the dog, Howard," I said, dryly. "It's scientifically proven to lower your blood pressure."

"My blood pressure isn't high," he said, even as he reached out a hand and buried it in the loose fur around Bruno's neck, careful to avoid the still-healing stitches.

Bruno promptly closed his eyes in doggy raptures from the chin scruggles and increased the pressure on Howard's legs.

"Your face coloring says otherwise," I murmured with a smirk.

Frankie was the only one who seemed to hear, and she winked at me.

A half-hour into the flight, Howard put large headphones on and started humming along. Which was bearable, but only for about five minutes.

"I love you," Frankie finally said, looking at Howard. "But if you don't stop making that noise, I'm going to smother you to death with a pillow."

"Be sure to wrap the pillow in saran wrap first," Hyde said from behind his magazine.

"Yeah," I said, biting into an apple slice. "It looks suspicious if they find fibers in the lungs during the autopsy."

THE PRESS CONFERENCE began at eight o'clock sharp, just as planned. I watched on my laptop, from the comfort of the jet's leather seat. Camilla wore a light blue, silk skirted suit that hit just below the knee. The color set off her tan skin to perfection. Her hair had been smoothed back into a chignon, pearls were at her ears and throat. The effect was chic and effortless--she was the picture of elegant grief.

"Last night," she began, then stopped, cleared her throat. "Last night my brother, Alexander Almeida, was arrested and taken into custody under charges of human trafficking, unlawful imprisonment, and tax fraud."

She waited a moment for gasps to subside, although the reporters in attendance must have been given strict instructions--there was no swell of questions, no murmurs.

"My own investigators have informed me that these terrible accusations are unfortunately true. As part of his arrest, raids were performed on several locations. Numerous individuals were found to be working against their will in substandard conditions."

Camilla paused again, as if to collect herself. When she looked back at the cameras, there were tears in her eyes.

"Authorities are working tirelessly to reunite these victims with their families, or to connect them with organizations that can provide necessary services. I would also like to take this opportunity to announce that as the heir to the Almeida organization, I am donating five million Reals to support their recovery. Until recently, I was unaware of Alexander's illegal activities. When I was made aware, I cooperated fully with authorities to bring him to justice."

Camilla swallowed. "Sadly, I was informed this afternoon that my brother has died while in custody."

Here Camilla paused to wipe a tear from her eye. She took a sip of water. The entire audience of reporters leaned forward to hear more.

She faced them again, her chin lifted, her eyes blazing. "I am aware of the rumors that swirl around my family. I will not lie--the reason I left Brazil so many years ago is because I found some of them to be true. Now that I am fully in control of the Almeida organization, I plan on making sweeping changes for the betterment of the company, and the betterment of Brazil. To begin, I plan on reopening all of the factories that were raided last night. Not only will the workers be paid fair wages, the factories will be under oversight from a third-party auditor, and an anti-human trafficking organization. All profits from these factories will go to fighting human trafficking, as well as providing education and job training for survivors."

Camilla grasped the edge of the podium, her eyes blazing, her gaze trained on the reporters.

"I would like to ask that all of you help keep me accountable to my promises. I cannot change the past, but I hope to change my family's legacy into something that benefits the people of Brazil, instead of profiting from them. To that end, I would like to officially endorse Prosecutor General Patricia Bradley for the next *Presidente do Brasil*. I believe that she represents a bright future for the Brazilian people. I join her in calling for political and social reforms. I join her in calling for good education for all."

Camilla closed the press conference by calling for an investigation into the death of Alex, which was a nice touch. We both knew they would never find the true culprit. After all, the CIA was good at what they did.

"She could run for Presidente someday," Hyde said, as I clicked the laptop shut. "She would be good at it."

"She probably has more power to make change where she is right now," I said, pulling my legs up beneath me. "And it's a longer-lasting position, as long as she stays alive."

"She will," he said simply, draping an arm around my shoulders. "She's smart."

I held onto his words like a child hangs onto a security blanket. Regardless of what I wanted, Camilla wasn't mine to protect. Not anymore.

Chapter 46

It was a typical Southern California morning-- pleasant with a cool breeze, but the inevitable heat loomed, and everyone was out trying to get something done before they had to be relegated to a pool or air-conditioned space. The cafe my father had chosen was at the end of a block of houses, and the wasp buzz of lawn edgers was a backdrop to our conversation.

Of course, once we'd said hi and ordered our coffees, it had been near silent. It felt awkward and stilted--an emotional landscape I'd experienced before with my mother, but never with him. He led the way to a table under a black and white striped umbrella. It was the farthest from the other customers, and he let me have the chair with the back to the wall. None of this escaped my notice.

"So," I finally said, breaking the silence. "We're here to talk."

He nodded. The corners of his mouth were turned down.

"I'm sure you have questions," I said, tilting the end of the sentence up, so it sounded like a question.

"Not really," he said. "At least, none that you can answer. I'm sure your bosses frown on that."

I cocked my head. "I don't have any bosses, Dad."

"Sure, sure," he said, flopping his hands in the air like my words didn't matter. He didn't meet my eyes.

"I'm telling the truth," I said, raising my eyebrows.

"Did I ever tell you what my major was in college?" he asked, ignoring my statement.

I shrugged. "I don't know. Pre-med? Biology?"

"Chemistry, actually, but that's not the point." He hesitated, took a sip of his latte as if to fill the dead air. "But for a short period of time, I was an Art History major."

He met my eyes then, let his words sink in. I'd been pre-med in college, until the CIA had recruited me. As part of my cover, I'd switched to an Art History major. It was the major that all of the Stanford recruits had, in part because all of them were assigned an internship at the art museum that was a cover for a CIA office.

"And you...had an internship at the Brighton museum?" I asked, my eyebrows raised.

He nodded. "I did. It didn't last long, though. I was good at the computer work, but I didn't have the stomach for field work. Never could get the nerve up to pull the trigger. Not outside of the range, at least."

I sat back in my chair. This, I'd never expected. My dad

had been recruited by the CIA? And he'd basically flunked out?

"I've wondered a thousand times since then if it was my fault, you working for the agency," he said.

I shook my head, trying to reorder my personal and family history around this new information. I wondered now if the CIA had actually seen something special in me, or if they'd chosen me because my father had been in the program. It was like one of those families who always sent their descendants to the same Ivy League school.

I was a legacy.

"That's why you were so upset when I changed my major," I said. "You knew. Why didn't you say something?"

He frowned. "I guess...I guess I thought that you'd be like me...that you'd stop before you'd even really started. But then... I don't know. You've always been strong. And good. If there have to be people in that line of work, it should be people like you."

I blinked back a sudden moisture in my eyes. "Thanks."

"I know you can't tell me much, but do they treat you well, at least?"

It was a fork in the road--a moment when I could choose to tell my father everything--that I was an assassin for hire, that I chose my own fate--or, I could continue to hide it.

"They treat me well," I said.

It wasn't quite a lie. The CIA and I had a pleasant working relationship. Even the last case--though it hadn't worked out the way either side really wanted--we'd worked together nonetheless. I could tell my father the truth, but maybe it was better to let him believe that my schedule wasn't completely of my own making. I couldn't forsee all the potential consequences of telling my father the truth, so I decided to tell a lie of omission.

"So that was the first time you'd..." I let the sentence trail off, unfinished.

The image of that body falling had more significance now that I knew.

He shrugged again. "It was easier than I thought it would be. Especially since he had a gun pointed at my daughter."

"And the gun?" I asked, moving the conversation along. It didn't seem like he wanted to talk about it very much.

"Found it in the kitchen cupboard, in an oatmeal container, when I was looking for tea."

I pursed my lips. It had been stupid for me to leave it there.

He continued, "I didn't want Jake or Isabella to find it."

I nodded. I still didn't think that it was likely that Jake or Isabella would have climbed up to the cupboard above the oven vent, rummaged in the back for the oatmeal tub, and found a gun buried in the bottom, but my dad was right. It was beyond irresponsible to leave a loaded firearm unsecured when there were children in the house. I didn't have an argument for it that wouldn't tell my father exactly how much danger the entire family had been in the entire time.

Sorry, Dad. I was more concerned about my entire family

being slaughtered than I was in the small chance that Jake or
Isabella would find one of the guns I hid around the apartment.

But he was pursing his lips and looking down his nose at me in a way that made me feel like I was an eleven year old who'd just spilled grape juice on white carpeting, so I let it go.

"Have you...have you told Mom?" I asked.

He shook his head. "And I'm not going to. She doesn't know about my time there, and she doesn't need to know about you. That's part of why I quit, you know. I met her. I'd thought that I wanted a life of excitement and intrigue. But then, I walked into a party one night, and there she was. After that, I only wanted her." He bit his lip and looked off down the street, as if he was debating something. He took a deep breath. "I'd hoped that when you met Hyde..." He met my eyes. "Does he know what you do? Is he ok with it?"

I chose my words carefully. "Hyde knows me better than anyone."

He nodded, like that was as much of an answer as he was expecting. "Then we'll never speak of this again. Let's talk about something more fun. You may not know this, but your mother and I have been putting money aside for your wedding ever since you were born."

I snorted into my coffee. "That must be an account you doubted you'd ever use."

"You may have doubted it, but not me. I knew there had to be someone out there smart and strong enough to rope you."

Like I was some sort of runaway livestock. I smirked.

"Well, thank you for offering, but I think we are going to keep it very small. I'm sure Hyde and I can manage it."

"That's not the point," my dad said, sitting up straighter. "We want to pay for it. We want to be involved."

"Well...thank you," I said.

It wasn't my nature to accept help, especially financial help. I'd long outgrown that stage in my life. But I also understood that this event in my life wasn't just about me, or Hyde.

"You're welcome." My father nodded curtly, like everything was settled. "I do feel that I have to warn you, though. Your mother has developed some very firm opinions on wedding dresses. In her eyes, it isn't a true wedding dress unless there's lots of lace."

I laughed at the mischievous twinkle in his eye.

THE END.

Reviews are so important to indie authors like me. They are the difference between success and failure. If you liked this book, will you please take one minute to review it? A couple of lines would mean the world to me!

Thank you!

AFTERWORD

Are you curious about the five days in Miami, when Hyde was missing? Want to know exactly what went down on those cases?

Get the short novella, *Hyde and Seek*, to find out!